THE TERRIFYING ODDS AGAINST SURVIVAL . . .

'Frontier survival forms the bulk of this science fiction novel . . . but it's a frontier on an inhospitable planet, where the wildlife is telepathic, and mankind's only defence is the partnership between human riders and their nighthorses . . . There's lots of tension, and plenty of frontier-style action (bar-room confrontations, blizzards, hunting dangerous predators, and such) but it's the ever-present overlay of telepathic images, often on the edge of insanity, that keeps things tense and exciting, for a galloping good read'
Locus

Also by C. J. Cherryh
in New English Library paperback

Cyteen
Heavy Time
Hellburner
Tripoint
Rider at the Gate

About the author

C. J. Cherryh is a winner of the prestigious Hugo Award for the year's best science fiction novel. With critical acclaim, many prizes and a string of internationally bestselling novels to her credit, she holds a position as one of the most important science fiction writers of our day, an author who always proves what SF *can* be: thrilling, knife-edged human adventure, set in a complex, cohesive and constantly evolving future.

C. J. Cherryh lives in Oklahoma City, USA.

Cloud's Rider

C. J. Cherryh

NEW ENGLISH LIBRARY
Hodder and Stoughton

First published in Great Britain in 1997
by Hodder and Stoughton

First published in paperback in 1997
by Hodder and Stoughton
A division of Hodder Headline PLC

A New English Library paperback

10 9 8 7 6 5 4 3 2 1

A CIP catalogue record for this title is available from the British Library.

ISBN 0 340 68912 9

Printed and bound in Great Britain by
Cox & Wyman Ltd, Reading, Berkshire

Hodder and Stoughton
A division of Hodder Headline PLC
338 Euston Road
London NW1 3BH

CLOUD'S RIDER

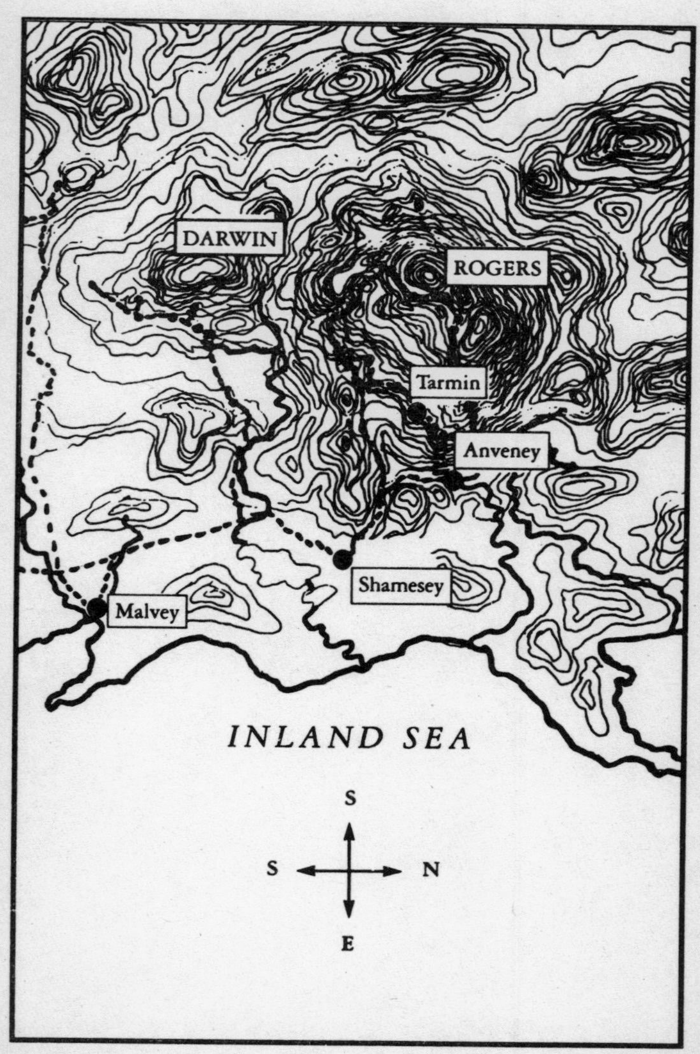

DARWIN
ROGERS
Tarmin
Anveney
Shamesey
Malvey
INLAND SEA
S
S
N
E

Chapter — I —

The sleet arrived on the wind that howled out of the Firgeberg, gray particles that abraded skin, stung eyes. Solid crystals sucked by a chance breath over the edge of the woolen scarf went down a throat already raw with altitude and exertion.

Heart hammered.

Knees ached.

To sweat into clothing that would hold moisture was to freeze. To sweat into what carried it away too efficiently was to give up vital moisture to the air—and one layered the clothing and gave up nothing, because a human in the High Wild couldn't afford to give up any resource, not the warmth in his face, not the moisture in his breath, not the day's ration of food he kept next his body, and not the nighthorse moving ahead of them on this upward road, breaking through the shallow drifts.

Especially not the horse.

You didn't rely on anything in this world of ice and sudden slips but what you carried on your own person. That was what an experienced high-country rider had told him, and it was advice Danny

Fisher now believed as an article of faith. What he'd learned and what he'd heard in a fast outpouring of detail from a senior rider in a rider shelter at the bottom of this road was going to bring him through this. It was going to get his horse through this. It was going to get the three kids behind him through this—

Or at least two of them. The hundred kilos of ironwood travois and supplies the boys were pulling up this icy road (his horse had better sense) was definitely not all resource. He personally didn't give a cold damn for the thirteen-year-old girl constituting most of that weight, lying bundled and unconscious among their supplies: but he was fighting like hell for her brothers.

And what he knew to do to get them all to safety now was to climb at a steady pace, trying to track passing time and changing conditions on this winding road hung on the edge of the sky, in a reasoned, planned progress from the shelter they'd left this morning to the shelter they'd reach sometime before dark.

But with the wind getting up and the sleet continuing to come down, when the reasoned, calculated world slowly disappeared in a veil of sleet and when the posts that told truck drivers that used this road where the edge was were only lumps of white in a boil of sleet and old snow, he relied solely on that snow-veiled darkness, that living sense of shape, life, and <cold nighthorse belly> that was moving ahead of all of them, to know where to set his feet. The most valuable asset he ordinarily had from Cloud was that inner sense of the mountain's shape—the land-sense that a nighthorse rider gained from his horse at any distance under three meters.

But all the shape he could perceive right now was the location of himself relative to Cloud and the two boys, and that stretch of sleeted rubble between him and his horse and slightly ahead of them. The wildlife from which Cloud drew his location-sense was all hidden away in burrows, as anything of common sense was dug in and asleep for the duration of the storm. It took human beings to *choose* to trek up here.

Then in the blindness of a sudden gust his horse doubted for an instant where the road was. Cloud imaged, giddily, <white> and <falling> as he shied back from what was or was not the edge.

It was enough to make a snow-blinded human who valued that horse above all human company want to sit down, grab onto the rocks and not budge for an hour.

But he was still standing. And it wasn't white emptiness beneath

Cloud's three-toed hoof—but solid, sleeted rock. Danny's heart was pounding, and that might be Cloud's heart or his own or the boys', but it was Cloud's four feet that began walking first, driven by <cold belly> and impatience to be out of this cold. The boys with the travois hadn't kept their footing through the scare: they had to pick themselves up off the ground to get moving, shaken, not wanting to be where they were any longer, that was for very damn certain.

But they couldn't stop short of that shelter, not in this wind. Don't try to camp on the high end of the Climb: more advice he took on faith from the rider who'd told him the route. It was autumn. The temperatures, bitter as they were in this gale-force wind, hadn't fallen enough to create a dry cold—and if you ever let damp form around you in the day, if you sat down where you could pick it up from the ground or the rocks, or just dressed in such a way that dampness built up, the windchill would kill you, without argument or excuse.

Tonight's stopping place, the shelter they were aiming for, could sustain them all winter if there weren't the recourse of villages and civilization in front of them, a string of five such tucked against the mountain's east face. But there was nothing in reach behind them but a small shelter that definitely couldn't sustain them, not reliably so beyond a few days, and he'd felt compelled this morning to make a calculated bet on the weather—taking them on a climb that on a good summer day and with no wind he understood from that same rider as a couple of hours' ride.

It hadn't been just a couple of hours. He was sure of that—and it was a long, weary hike. Cloud wouldn't—couldn't—carry him up this steep grade in this kind of weather. The boys had the travois to pull, and from them he felt numbness and cold right now, along with a lingering flutter of fear. Cloud's near-disaster had called up a rush of adrenaline, and the boys were using too much of their strength pulling the travois to endure many surprises like that.

Bloody hell—*he* was scared and shaky. He hadn't fallen down because he was used to horse-images in all degrees of urgency and most times reflexively walled the confusion out. The boys weren't used to a horse's sending being that close to them, and they *couldn't* sort it out or keep their feet under them in the crisis.

Or stop themselves from reliving the slip again and again. Cloud's four-footed gait had confused their balance and they wouldn't let the moment go: they'd confuse Cloud's balance if they kept it up.

"Quiet," he had to tell them out loud and in no uncertain terms. After a week together they knew he didn't mean any audible noise.

They tried to be quiet and calm down after that—as quiet as two boys could be who'd thought they were falling off a mountain.

The road they were on, by what he knew of it, followed the folds and bends of the mountain upward supposedly a kilometer and a half vertical distance from their initial start on the east face of Rogers Peak—but he'd come to appreciate how a kilometer and a half vertical translated to walking distance on a mountain. *He'd* thought it a pretty straightforward climb. They'd come from the first-stage shelter across a portion of the south face to reach the midway shelter last night, and now they were east and up toward the settlements high on the forested slopes.

But it didn't do it by logic of what would get there fastest. It did it, he'd discovered, by the logic of where the builders could hang a road and make it stay and not slide. It was a road built solely to get the logging trucks and oxcarts up and down, and the road builders had patched in rubble fill and timber shorings wherever its precarious thread crossed a gap narrow enough for them to bridge *over* a split in the mountain instead of following the contour all the way back into a recess. Places like that were wind zones. And where the builders hadn't found a bridgeable gap—he and his small party had to walk all the in and out contour of the mountain, sometimes a considerable distance, until the builders had found a place to make the road turn back the direction they actually wanted to go.

A couple of hours on a good day—hell. From the midway shelter they'd left at dawn this morning they could make solid walls again before they slept—that was what he intended: rest there a couple of days, and beyond that—

Beyond that, day after tomorrow, they'd start across the mountain toward the villages on a calm day when they could do it without struggle. There was a doctor in Evergreen, the first and largest of the five settlements. They'd get advice what to do about thirteen-year-old Brionne, ideally deliver Brionne into a doctor's hands within the village proper, which would do as much for her as ever could be done; after that the boys could find work in Evergreen or one of the other villages and start their lives over, good luck to them and God help them if their sister lived.

That would mean *he'd* done all his conscience told him he had to do, and he would have carried out a job that had set Tara Chang free to take care of a friend of his who was wintering down in that cabin *before* this road. Guil wasn't well enough to make this trip—having a hole through his side. While Tara—

Tara hadn't wanted to have them snowed in with her and Guil. Danny'd been available to run escort to the next cabin over, which meant Tara didn't have to do it. He'd saved her from that situation and gotten on her good side, in his fondest hopes, by taking the kids on—because if the kids were going to survive to reach the villages above—if the kids were going to leave that cabin for anywhere in the world—a rider had to escort them: no one, even experienced in the Wild and armed to the teeth, could get from one shelter to another *without* a rider to guard him—and village kids wouldn't be safe even *inside* a shelter and with a gun if one of the larger, cleverer hunters got the notion there was food inside.

A horse was the protection. A gun was for the mental comfort of the gun owner, so far as he'd seen.

And guns were, unfortunately, also for human quarrels, in which horses were best off if they didn't participate.

And that was the other half of the reason they were on this road in this weather: thanks to a human quarrel some days before their reaching the place, and not uninvolved with Guil and Tara, the situation at the first-stage cabin hadn't been safe—and matters had combined to say that *up the mountain* might not only be their eventual intention, but their immediate necessity.

Because at first-stage a problem had moved in on them—a horse whose rider had died, a horse attempting to attach itself to any horseless humans in its reach. It wasn't unnatural that a grief-stricken horse should do that—but the only horseless humans in reach happened to be the two boys he was escorting and, in his worst nightmares, their sister Brionne.

That had clinched his decision to move on. To hold that cabin otherwise he'd have had to shoot the horse, which wasn't an easy choice for a rider. Or he could have run the gauntlet of its presence and taken them all back to Tara and Guil for help.

But the last thing in the world he wanted was to come running back for help as soon as a problem came up with a job Tara clearly, emotionally, didn't *want* back on their doorstep. Next spring he had a rendezvous with her and Guil for a salvage job—a truck that hadn't been lucky on these same curves. Guil had as good as hired him already, there was considerable pay involved from some company down in Anveney town, and for a junior rider with no working partner, no references, and no prospects of hire this spring, that was an incredibly good offer, one which he didn't intend to foul up by destroying their confidence in him.

So with the weather seeming likely to hold fair, they'd moved for the next shelter, higher up the mountain, a barren, hard-rock place where the horse that had been haunting their vicinity would have no forage and to which it wouldn't follow them.

They'd moved again this morning—because of the weather turning foul, on a choice in which he had less confidence he was right; though thank God they'd shaken the horse off their trail somewhere between first-stage and midway. It was lost and desperate—but not *that* desperate; and it might go back to harass Guil and Tara, whose two horses would drive it off, or it might finally find the other strayed horses on the lower skirts of the mountain and find safety with them. So *that* part of the problem he'd handled.

That left getting them to the top of this road.

Truth was, this job of escorting the Goss kids, through all the complications that had so far set in, was the first job he'd ever done completely on his own, and he didn't know whether he'd ever actually told Tara so. Guil, who *knew,* hadn't been tracking too well on anything for the time they'd been there, so the matter of his prior experience hadn't actually, well, exactly come up. Tara, who knew this mountain, had been concentrating her efforts on giving him a mental map of the landmarks and problems involved.

So he didn't think he'd made the fact of his inexperience quite clear—but he damn sure wasn't going to meet two senior riders next spring to confess he'd let these kids die on the mountain. He'd do the job. He might know a great deal by now that he didn't want to know about the Goss family—but he'd do it.

Then Guil and Tara would trust him next spring and give him the responsibility that would *make* him hireable by convoys that were only a distant, hard-won hope for a rider born to a town. He'd lived through enough up here to know he *wanted* the high country and that with several good tries it hadn't killed him. He was high on his own survival, he saw a freedom for him and for Cloud he'd never known, never imagined, in town, and he saw a set of teachers he could otherwise only dream of—if he could deserve their confidence in him.

Wind *blasted* into their faces of a sudden. He'd been able to see the rocks on the right just a second ago and he felt Cloud walking ahead of them, so he wasn't disoriented; but suddenly it was just—white, with an abrading blast of sleet that made him duck his head and shut his eyes.

So had Cloud. *That* didn't help his orientation.

"God," he heard from Carlo, a voice half-drowned in the wind.

"It's getting worse!" Randy cried.

The boys had stopped walking. Cloud hadn't. "Keep going!" Danny shouted at the boys. "It's probably just this stretch! Snow coming off the height up there!"

"I think it's coming out of the sky!" Randy cried. Randy was fourteen, two years younger than Carlo, a year older than Brionne, and the kid had been gutsy and all right until now—but now <fear> was loud and clear in the ambient of emotions and images that came at them relayed from Cloud.

<Fear> was suddenly feeding on its own substance, upsetting Cloud, upsetting Randy as his own panic flooded back at him. Danny clamped down on the accelerating distress with calm images:<Still water, water flowing over stones. Snowflakes landing soft and perfect on white snowbank.>

And: "Move!" Danny yelled in a ragged voice that didn't come out of his throat half so fierce or so low as he intended. He pushed at Carlo, who was on the right-hand pole of the travois as Randy was pulling the left, and they struggled into motion—they were starting across one of those rubble-and-shorings sections, by the disorganized way the wind was coming at them.

And soon enough the wind was battering their right sides with a vengeance, pushing them toward the left, where there wasn't anything but empty air.

Cloud was <mad nighthorse.> Cloud had <cold belly.> Cloud was not pleased with humans lagging back and distracting him with their stupid arguments in a cold wind. Cloud wasn't panicked about the situation, but he was definitely struggling for footing now, sending more strongly than usual, feeling his way through the whiteout and using senses that even his rider wasn't used to having at the top of the broth of thoughts that was the ambient. Cloud was feeling <wind on his hide> and getting a vague <mountain-shape> from it somehow, Cloud was <smelling the wind,> and knowing <sky-side from rock-side> with a range of discriminations the human brain might not even have categories for. Humans being sky-fallen strangers to the world and horses being native to it, sometimes a rider just had to take the little information he could get in his own peculiar way of understanding and otherwise cast himself on his horse's sense of direction and his horse's four-footed stability.

Sink too deep into Cloud's sending and he could look out of Cloud's side-set eyes and see the tilt and pitch of his head and end up with two feet too few for the catch of balance Cloud made in the gusts. Randy slipped and fell, or lost his balance in Cloud's noisy sending, Danny didn't know. He grabbed the kid's coat and got the kid on his feet again, travois and all, still letting the brothers do the physical labor.

A nighthorse didn't wear harness or carry cargo. Neither did a rider. It was his job to know where they were—and not to be distracted by a travois bumping along and resisting. He had no possessions in the world but his guns, his emergency supplies, the life-and-death stuff like waterproof matches, knife, hatchet, pans, a little food, cord, bandages, most of which made a very compact tin-cased package, his last kit having proven unmanageable; and hell, no, he didn't trust his personal kit to their damn travois. Carlo had the shotgun and a pistol—but the ammunition, which was heavy, Danny had most of, plus the rifle.

And when this morning the boys had wanted to pile everything including his kit on the travois, they'd had sharp and angry words about it.

Oh, but they were pulling it anyway for Brionne, Carlo and Randy had protested. And it was easier to pull their supplies on it than carry them on their backs. It only made sense.

Listen to me, he'd said, and laid the law down as best he could.

They'd ignored his advice at least as regarded their personal supplies. He'd heard the maxim down in Shamesey, *Don't ever get friendly with the convoy. Don't make friends of anybody you have to guide.* And he knew why, now. He was close to friendship with Carlo, as close as a rider and a villager *could* come—and having clearly and in front of both brothers gotten his orders from Guil and Tara, he didn't seem to have the credible authority to tell Carlo no. Carlo was on a mission. Carlo was doing a Good Thing. That meant God was with them in getting up this mountain and getting away from that stray horse that wanted his sister.

That was the villager mentality. God was with them and gravity didn't count.

Maybe a lot of things else didn't count in Carlo's head either. Damn sure some of them didn't add. Danny had a good idea what was driving Carlo, and it wasn't love for his sister.

Guilt, maybe. Atonement. There *had* been a village called Tarmin at the bottom of the road. It wasn't there now. Every man, woman, child and sleeping baby in that town had died the worst death imaginable on Carlo's sister's account.

That was the news they carried toward the villages above, and the girl responsible for it all was the burden they'd lugged up this road.

For *what*? Danny asked himself—and thought as he'd thought more than once on this trek upward that Tara Chang had been right in the first place: there was nothing particularly sacred about a thirteen-year-old life that wasn't equally sacred about a person who'd proved himself a decent human being for twice that number of years.

And three human lives and a good horse were damn sure more valuable than a self-willed girl with only a remote chance of recovering—but here they were, and they tried, and they hung on.

The light had gone to that murky gray that heralded a thick spot in the clouds directly overhead. Sleet scoured off the rubble surface of the road in the windy zones and piled up in banks where the wind gave it up. Where it lay thick it afforded traction—but yesterday's sun had created melt off a previous fall that had already frozen. Worse—there'd been high humidity this morning and the temperature had fluctuated. They were dealing with patches of ice, and those patches were growing more frequent on this stretch of the road.

Then—then by the pitch of a twenty-percent grade and a sudden shift in what Cloud felt and smelled of the wind, he *knew* a picture he'd gotten from Tara, that right-angled turn in the road that led around flat before it climbed—that point where if they walked straight ahead and *didn't* bend very abruptly to the right, they'd go over the rim and into white nowhere, straight down, no barriers, no warning.

Truckers' hell, the sharp turn and the abrupt up or down grade that led to it. That was where the truck had gone off that Guil and Tara meant to salvage.That was where Guil's partner had lost her life—Tara had warned him of it, and, God, it had to be. A lot of the landmarks Tara had imaged to him he couldn't find with the sleet coming down like this, but she'd dwelt heavily on this one image, and the hell of it was—the thing that made him suddenly sick at his stomach—

He'd thought they'd passed *this* essential landmark turn a long time back.

So they weren't as far up the mountain as he'd thought they were. The whole scale of the problem shifted on him. They weren't making the time he'd thought. And that affected—

Everything. Every estimate. Every hope.

Midway was *hours* behind them. If this was in fact the infamous turn—that meant everything he'd been sure he knew the position of was completely off.

And if his reckoning where they were on the mountain was off—he wasn't sure of the elapsed time, either, and he couldn't *find* the sun: it could have passed behind the mountain into afternoon, for all he could tell. Light spread through the storm with no distinction.

He caught <scared> from the boys, who'd surely picked up his distress. He caught <white and cold.> A lot of that. He caught <cold nighthorse,> and <white> and <cold, sore feet> from up ahead, where Cloud negotiated that dreadful turn—and the damned travois, that had cost them so much time, bucked and bumped over the uneven surface beside him.

Two *hours* for this damn trek in high summer.

Dammit, he didn't know how he could be that far wrong—except if midway wasn't at all mid-way from first-stage—and, he recollected with a sinking feeling, he'd learned already that the road crews put things not where they'd like to have them but where they *could* put them. One set of expectations was skewed by processes he hadn't thought about, and other expectations could be, reason told him in this thunderstruck moment, thrown off by the same logic. He'd *assumed* by the name of midway—where he had no business to assume.

But panic didn't serve anybody. They'd make the shelter. Just—maybe—not before dark.

A little beyond that turn a fold of the mountain came between them and the worst gusts. Cloud stopped and turned his tail to the wind that did reach them, taking a breather on his own schedule and at his opportunity, which Cloud did when his needs exceeded the rests they took.

At such moments Danny and the Goss boys had generally stopped standing—but a pileup of sleet against the mountain afforded them a brake on the travois' tendency to skid downhill and afforded a chance for a rest. Danny saw it, turned his own back to the gale and stood there just breathing, with the wind battering the back brim of his hat flat up against his head, and waited as a living signpost in the haze until the two muffled figures overtook him with the travois.

Then he squatted down, and fell the last bit onto his rump, his knees beyond pain and refusing such delicate adjustments. He got up into a crouch his legs didn't want to hold, but did, as Carlo had sat down after much the same fashion—he'd taken to heart the lesson about not sitting on the ground, but Randy just collapsed helplessly downward and stayed.

Blacksmith's kids, both, and Carlo had the height and the arms Randy had yet to grow to. Carlo shoved his brother, said simply, "Squat," and Randy managed to get up off the ground and hold the position, with Carlo's strong arm around him.

After that no one had the energy to talk, just sat huddled up against the wind, the boys probably with the same sick headache, Danny thought, that increasingly pounded behind his sinuses and behind his eyes and around his skull.

It was altitude causing that. He'd felt it a little down at the cabin with the senior riders, and Guil had warned him it could get debilitating—which he couldn't afford right now. Mouth was dry. They hadn't eaten all day. He didn't think he could swallow the thawed food he carried; eating snow relieved the dryness but chilled the bones, so he just took a little mouthful, after which he shut his eyes—partly to ease the headache and partly just to warm them from the wind.

But even with his eyes shut, he saw them all <sitting in snow> from Cloud's senses, a moving sort of vision as Cloud came trudging back. <Tired horse, ice lumps in his tail, banging against his hocks.>

He had so much rather have nursed his headache and caught his breath undisturbed, but he couldn't let that annoyance go on. He bestirred himself to check over Cloud's feet for ice-cuts: the threefold hooves had a soft spot high up between the juncture of the three bones, just behind the middle and largest toe. If a horse didn't feel a buildup of ice freezing on the scant hairs of the inside, developed an ice lump and went on walking on it, so he'd had from experienced senior riders, the horse could go lame. He had to take off his glove and put a knee on the snow, and take armfuls of wet, chilled horse-foot into his embrace, one after the other, probing a bare finger into the crevice, finding no blood.

So he put his glove back on and broke the ice lumps out of Cloud's tail—three big sharp ones—by bashing them against his knee with his gloved fist and the hilt of his boot-knife. The way the weather was going they'd form again off the melt that Cloud's own body heat made, and dealing with Cloud was getting him damp, when that was what he was most trying to avoid.

Cloud paid him when he was done with a warm rough tongue across the cheek and a whuff of hot nighthorse breath in his face where his scarf had slipped. <Cloud and Danny walking free, uphill,> swam across his vision like a view of heaven. <Boys sitting under thick snow. Thicker and thicker snow.> Cloud wanted him to get up and leave the boys. Cloud thought of <village. Ham cooking.>

Cloud loved ham with all his omnivorous heart. It was so vivid he could taste it.

But so was Cloud's own case of altitude-generated dry mouth, and when Danny took his glove off to fish for a morsel in the packet he had against his ribs, Cloud couldn't more than lick it into his mouth and work his jaws about trying to find a <taste> that eluded him.

No words between Danny and his clients, nothing but breathing, a try at massaging the legs, a thump of gloved hands at one's boot-toes to be sure the feet still picked up sensation. They stayed down so long as Cloud rested, hunkered down in a knot sheltering Randy in Cloud's wind-shadow, warming the kid and slowly warming up the backs and fronts of their legs.

Couldn't do anything about the cold knees except the extra cloth they'd wrapped around—Tara had told them that trick: lots of air space and extra woolen padding. But Randy's wraps kept coming loose and gathering around his calves. Danny tugged his up again, tugged at Randy's left one and Carlo fixed the right.

Then Cloud decided it was time to walk and they lost their windbreak.

"Kid can't do it anymore." Carlo's voice was all but gone as they got up. "I need help, Danny."

"You and me," Danny said. Talking over the wind hurt his throat, and if neither of them had understood during that moment of physical closeness that his distance estimate was off, he didn't want to tell them yet the trouble they were in. Randy was light-boned and chilling faster than they were in the gale-force wind. Carlo, sixteen, Danny reckoned as stronger than *he* was at a travel-hardened year older—and maybe with the two of them really putting effort into it they could make the cabin up there not too long after dark.

So Carlo took the left-hand pole of the travois and Danny took the right one. The spot where they'd rested had had only a slight incline, which tended to be true at turns, for very sensible reasons for the truckers.

But the next stretch was a hellish steep that began on the inside curve for a downhill-bound truck, the kind of place where the builders had tended to do their worst: this turned out to be the worst grade yet, up to yet another wandering road and into the teeth of an icy damp wind.

("The mountain can surprise you." Tara Chang had even said it in words, plain as she could make it. "Don't commit to that road unless you're sure you've got several days running of clear weather. Ring around the greater moon means stay *put.* If you don't see cloud in the east—" ("She means a weather system past us," Guil Stuart had interjected at that point. And Tara had said: "The troughs from the west and over the mountains run about four days apart." And Guil: "But sometimes they lie, too.") "If you don't see clouds *in the east,"* Tara had said without looking at Guil, "and not too far east—don't budge from that shelter.")

Well, he'd seen no ring around the moon when they'd left the first-stage shelter. He'd seen clouds just past them in the east.

This morning when they'd left—hell's bells, he hadn't been able to *see* the moon, in a sleet-storm that his other source of advice, Carlo and Randy, who had spent their lives on the mountain, said could be the leading edge of a real blizzard coming down.

He'd listened most to Tara telling him how to move when the choice was move—and not enough, he realized now, to both Guil and Tara telling him he should wait for a clear, established trough between major storms—*that* was what Guil had meant, not any stupid counting. He'd known all his life that there tended to be a four-day gap between storms that reached Shamesey.

But down there you saw them coming. He'd not imagined that up here you didn't *see* the weather. They were almost *on* the continental divide—and the consequence of being on the east of the mountain ridge meant the weather came up hidden by the mountain until it broke right over your head.

The direct consequence was that a storm which hadn't even been a cloud-line on the horizon yesterday morning at first-stage had set in hard during the night of their stay at midway. They'd seen it first boiling above the distant peaks of the central massif when, coming up from that first-stage shelter at dusk last night, they'd rounded that last curve. The midway shelter had been there in front of them and, a fact with which he reproached himself now, he'd never *thought* to turn around and go back right then, when, yes, they were tired, and they'd walked all day; and, yes, there was a horse down below they didn't want to deal with—but it might have been better than this.

Last night the wind had howled about the midway cabin, literally shaking the walls of a structure poised on the edge of nothing at all. Their fire had refused to stay lit against the draft coming down the chimney. His information from Tara as well as Carlo and Randy said the road above midway and below was subject to deep, impassable drifting once winter set in. After the small stack of wood ran out in that barren, treeless steep the snow might block them from leaving, and they could freeze to death in a cabin that even with the intermittent fire last night had been colder than hell's attic.

Even knowing *that* he'd not seriously thought of turning them around and leading them back to first-stage—because he'd been unwilling to face that damned stray horse.

He'd had too much sympathy for it—since it was itself a refugee from the Tarmin disaster, lost, bereaved, more desperate than they were. Riders had died down on the lower reaches of the mountain, and horses had survived—meaning hurt horses, horses missing riders—and the one haunting the vicinity of the first-stage cabin when they'd arrived hadn't been too sane to start with, if it was the horse he most feared—a good chance it was that horse, considering where it was hanging out, where a rider had died who was, no question, crazy.

And the chance of Brionne waking up when it was prowling around the outside of their cabin—or worse, intercepting them on the trail—and having a crazy girl *and* a crazy horse on his hands—along with Cloud, who'd fight it for their protection—

He'd felt the darting, fragmented—*thing*—that *was* the rogue the night Tarmin had gone down. He'd seen and felt her half-waking in the cabin with Guil and Tara, and he had *no* desire whatever to deal with her awake and within reach of a horse that could carry her thoughts outside herself. She'd gone out cold after that brief incident the night they'd joined Guil and Tara—and nobody, not even her brothers, invited her to come to again. If it had been Tara who'd gone with the Goss kids to the first-stage shelter, he suspected now that Brionne wouldn't have lived past midnight; for the horse, Tara might have had pity. But Tara had taken him aside for a moment before he left and said, aloud and in private, that if Brionne died, he should come back.

He'd been—not horrified, but at least disturbed, and knew right then he was talking to a rider forged in a fire he'd no concept of.

But after a handful of nights at first-stage with that horse outside he'd begun to weigh what one life was really worth relative to all the others. He didn't at all have the cold-heartedness to have shot her; he didn't right now have the conviction to see that travois take a plunge down the mountain; but he'd gotten scared enough by now that the thought did come to his mind.

Sleet kept coming at them, falling from the sky, swept up off the road, blown down on them—he didn't know, but thunder above them suggested it wasn't all blowing off the heights. The light was a gray and sickly color, and he didn't like to look to the left, because there wasn't any dimension to it. They reached a place where the darkness of Cloud's tail streamed first sideways and up and around and sideways again—and when they reached it in Cloud's wake, wind literally blew him and Carlo a little sideways on the icy surface.

He found traction in patches of snow. He began counting thirty, forty steps in that struggle against the wind. It was an effort to keep his knees pulling straight. His scarf slid down. He grabbed it and stuffed it into place as best he could.

Carlo jolted down to one knee. Wind straight off the backbone of the continent had scoured the roadway here to bare, frozen, lumpy rubble, and there they were, braced, not at a good angle, on what looked and felt like ice.

"Are you all right?" Randy's thin shout came from behind, and Danny didn't want to look back for fear of losing the scarf, maybe his hat, which he had tied down as hard as he could. Carlo carefully got back to both feet.

Treacherous ground, treacherous wind. "Change hands!" Carlo yelled against the blast, and if Carlo was losing his grip on that side, Danny wasn't going to question it, no matter the difficulty of making that changeover here. He was losing feeling in his own fingers. He began, as Carlo asked, to effect the change of sides, reaching for the far pole, edging across on slick ground.

The travois bucked up under a gust, spun, half over, girl and supplies and all, and tried to sail up and out of their hands as Carlo struggled to hold it.

"Look out!" Randy cried against the deafening buffet of the wind, and Carlo desperately elbowed aside his brother's help with: "Dammit, get out of the way! I can handle it!"

Randy bid fair to get himself, Brionne, *and* Carlo blown off the roadway. The kid tried to grab the side pole, Carlo tried instead to kneel and bear the travois down to the ground with his weight; in the crossed signals, thinking to the last instant he was going to see the whole thing and both boys go spinning down the icy incline toward the cliff edge, Danny kicked Randy's leg from under him and yelled, "Sit on it, dammit!" in what voice he had left.

Randy flung himself atop Brionne and coincidentally the travois as he fell—as Danny and Carlo both fought the travois flat with their weight across him, all three of them atop.

It skidded.

Danny dug his boot-toes in and it kept going until his toe hit a lump of icy rock on the roadway.

He didn't move for a minute after that, just panted a series of deep breaths through the icy and soggy scarf, lying on Carlo, lying on Randy, lying on Brionne.

Then, waiting his time between the blasts of wind and bracing first his other toe and then the foot carefully on the surface, he got up, let Carlo up, and snarled "Stay down," at Randy.

And again, when Randy tried to get up, *"I said stay down, dammit!"*

Randy and his stubborn helpfulness was ballast. Carlo was real help. Danny took one pole, Carlo took the other, and with Randy's weight safely disposed on the travois, they struggled upslope.

There'd stopped being sky and earth and this time he couldn't tell himself they'd just walked into a gusty area. This was the wind picking up and sleet coming down so thick they breathed it.

There was one thing—one thing Tara *hadn't* known: that there'd been a horse loose that Brionne could have latched onto—and that fear of it would send them out of the safety she'd planned and into a rush up the mountain. *On* his best judgment.

Now look where he was.

What in hell were two senior riders expecting him to do with the job he'd been handed?

Not what he was doing, damn sure.

"Lousy, *lousy* weather," Guil Stuart said from the vantage of the cabin he shared with Tara Chang and two nighthorses. His horse, Burn, and Tara's Flicker (two names having *nothing* to do with each other, since Burn imaged himself as fire and dark and Flicker's name was sunlight in rapid flashes) were out cavorting in the storm, chasing some hapless creature they'd roused out of hiding—hapless since it had fallen afoul of nighthorses looking for fresh meat. Guil limped back to stand at the fireside where Tara was mending the bullet hole in his coat and, staring at the embers of a comfortable fire, he thought about a handful of kids he'd rather have counseled stay put, maybe back at Tarmin rather than first-stage.

He and Tara had disagreed on that point. But the village down the road (or what was left of it) might not have been much safer for the boys to hole up in than the first-stage shelter.

Tarmin would have been readily accessible and closer to *them,* there was that.

But Tara might have been right to insist the kids move out of their vicinity altogether. Cloud was a young male. With Burn possessive of Flicker and Cloud in the mix—there was no telling. But the fact of winter and horses in rut had been only a part of the consideration: the other part was a girl who could trigger an explosion out of all three of the horses, a girl Tara for both considered and unconsidered reasons didn't want near her.

That was the part of the reasoning that weighed on his mind.

It was remotely possible that the kids hadn't gone on to first-stage, that they'd trekked on down toward Shamesey before the snows came and were down by now and making their way across the flatlands.

And *that,* in cold clear consideration, scared hell out of him.

Tara didn't need Flicker's attention to know, not what he was thinking, but the subject he was thinking about. She frowned at him and glanced up. The next stitch pushed too hard and sent the needle through into her finger. She sucked the wound, scowling.

But she didn't ask and he didn't say anything—or intend to dwell on it in range of the horses. He wasn't usually one for recriminations. A decision was a decision was a decision, as they said down south, which was his usual range.

He didn't know as much as he wished he knew about Tara Chang *or* her mountain. But that was the way of winters. You ended up in some small cabin or in some encampment, pinned down and pent in for the season with whatever other rider, sane or not, known or not, was in the vicinity, and on many points of his present situation he couldn't complain, especially considering that otherwise he'd have been flat on his back, wounded, and alone.

Instead he was recovering tolerably quickly, situated with plenty of supplies on the forested bottom road of Tarmin Climb, with someone willing to cut firewood and shovel the door clear till he mended enough to take his turn. He'd be here, he supposed, and fairly content, till water ran downhill again.

He could have had the kids for help. That was true. But instead of that, he was holed up with a woman who'd been a good fill-in partner to him in a bad situation, a woman who'd saved his life, as happened, and the only actual fault he'd seen in her was an ironclad notion of what was sensible and what wasn't—well, that and a slight unwillingness to change her mind.

"If they stayed in that first shelter on the Climb," Tara said out of long silence, "they're *fine.*"

"I hope they did." He didn't say that Danny Fisher was a lowland kid from the biggest town in the world, and that the things Danny

Fisher didn't know not only about this mountain, but about any mountain at all, were frightening. Tara's instruction to the kids, her giving them a map of the way up, had been sensible. Charitable. Responsible.

And the foresight of riders who'd helped make the roads up here had provided ample shelters for riders, summer and winter. If you didn't use them for as long as they were designed for, and didn't use caution in leaving them, you had yourself to blame, no one else.

Problem was—they were kids. And kids didn't notoriously do well with waiting things out.

But stupidity wouldn't have carried Fisher as far as he'd gotten, and he trusted the kid's resourcefulness and common sense—as far as the kid's knowledge went.

That was a *warm* snow going on.

He decided he would sit down. With a hand on the fireplace stones he flexed his knees gingerly and did that.

The horses had just caught their prey. They'd begun a game of tag that had everything of humor and blood and wicked behavior about it, but that was Burn for you. Burn was from the borders of inhabited land. So was he. Flicker would have killed their supper. Burn played games with it.

In that, they were different. He found he had a soft heart for some things. He didn't admit to it, exactly, but Flicker's rider was a far harsher judge of humans and horses. Tara would have shot the girl—in the heat of the moment, granted, and Tara hadn't in fact shot her. But she nearly had. And the day she'd pitched those kids out the door with a map of the higher road he'd been putting up a pretense of sanity right up to their leaving. Now he couldn't entirely reconstruct what had happened or what he'd urged them to do.

"Penny for your thoughts," Tara said.

They were deaf to the ambient—or at least their share of it. They might be hearing the horses, but the horses weren't paying any attention at all to them. Which meant two humans trying to figure each other out just went by guesswork.

"Thinking Burn's a son of a bitch."

"Bushdevil." That was Tara's guess about the prey. It might be that. It was small and dark and fast in the snowy brush, and it dug fast, but a horse's tri-hooved feet dug fast, too. Even match.

There was a little silence.

"They'll have dug in," Tara said. "The kids will."

"Probably," he said. "The kid's resourceful."

Tara had bloodied her finger. Third time.

He reached out and stopped further carnage.

"Give yourself a break. Easy."

"Dammit," she said.

He really didn't do well at argument. He carried the hand to his mouth and nipped the finger himself.

"Ow!"

When maybe she'd expected tender sympathy. No luck. She jerked to get loose.

Didn't work. His hand was stronger.

"I've got the needle," she said, and held it up.

And stuck it away in the mending and rose onto her knees and gently against him as he tugged her other hand.

They'd been lovers.

They might be again, testing the extent of his healing, —except Flicker caught the bushdevil and there was the distinct taste of blood in their mouths.

Burn caught the prize then and threw it with a toss of his head.

"Ugh," Tara said.

Horse mood was contagious. Outrageous play was one thing. Carnivorous mischief was a difficult but not impossible background for lovemaking.

Next thing, the two would want to be let in from the storm.

It seemed to Carlo Goss that it had taken more than an hour for them just to make the next switchback on the road, walking mostly on ice. He couldn't always figure out whether they were turning or going straight—he couldn't see Cloud right now—couldn't see a black nighthorse, the whiteout was so total in the patch of roadway they were climbing. He couldn't see Danny next to him or even the ground under his own feet until the gray shadow of a crag on their left side hove up between them and the wind.

Then he could make out Cloud's rump, snow-spattered shadow horse, tail sprinkled with honest snowflakes, materializing slowly in front of them in a world otherwise white. He could *feel* Cloud all along. But except for Danny on the other pole of the travois and

Randy atop it, and the ends bumping heavily along the roadway, he couldn't have sworn where the ground was.

"Get off," he said to his brother, then, because the wind wouldn't catch the travois during the transaction here and his knees were growing rubbery with fighting both the slope and the constant slippage.

Randy slowly took his weight off the rig, so the load was lighter by him, at least.

"Breath," Carlo requested, then.

"Minute," Danny said.

The grade was too steep to do other than stand, but he needed the rest. His legs were shaking under him, and he tried to ease the strain on them as they stopped and stood on an icy steep where if they once entirely let go of the travois where it was, it and his sister would toboggan down a giddy stretch of rubble and ice and soar high and wide on the winds before it fell.

But in all this trek Brionne had never waked.

Never *would* wake, in his guilt-ridden thoughts and guiltier hope. His sister had *been* a rider for a brief number of days—she'd been a rider on a horse the whole district and clear down to Shamesey had known had to die—the horse Guil Stuart and others had come up here to get before it took a village out.

They hadn't been in time.

His sister had ridden a rogue horse home; *she'd* gotten it through the gates that defended Tarmin from the Wild. And in the confusion of that horse's maddened sending, sane villagers had opened doors, rushed to the aid of stricken children, dying neighbors—abandoning their only defenses in the process. In the confusion and the threat the rogue sent into the ambient, the best and the bravest impulses that humans owned had sent neighbors running, blinded by things they *thought* they saw and cries they already heard—running, some in panic, some to save others—while a swarm of vermin, coming through those opened gates and those doors no one had the sanity left to shut, gnawed them down to bone. The swarm had made the whole village prey; the virtuous, and the fools, and the innocent. Brionne had ridden through it, immune to the swarm, on the deadliest killer of all—wanting *them,* wanting revenge, wanting—God knew what—

And after the carnage, after the horse was gone, his sister had just started slipping away, not eating, not speaking, eventually not reacting to the world at all. For a few days down at first-stage, they'd been able to make her drink—but last night at midway she hadn't even done that for them. The horses down below wouldn't tolerate her. Cloud wouldn't. They imaged <rogue> whenever they had to deal with her, and it was nothing—*nothing*—a sane mind wanted to feel again.

Right now his sister didn't move, didn't think, didn't know and probably wouldn't care if she went off that edge. Not only would she not drink since last night, she wouldn't blink this morning to save her eyes from the cold. That was how fast she was sinking. They'd tied a bandage around her face to keep her eyes from freezing—Danny's idea—and a scarf around that, and then folded the skins around her with the fur side in. He could sense Danny and Randy through Cloud's sendings plain as plain, constant and alive—but his sister wasn't there. Just wasn't there.

And he didn't know whether he even grieved for her.

He *wanted* to. But maybe that was only to prove he could, after so much death.

He wanted to get her safely to Evergreen.

But he most of all wanted to get her to the doctor in Evergreen, so that if there was a scrap of a human mind left in her that could be suffering, he'd have brought her to die in a civilized and comprehensible environment, not in some bare-boards cabin on ground too frozen to bury her—where—he didn't want to think about it—the scavengers would leave of her . . . nothing more than was left in Tarmin now.

Beyond getting her to the doctor, he didn't know. God forgive him, he wished every night since they'd gotten her back that she'd just drift peacefully deeper and not wake up the next morning. Even unconscious, she'd driven them out of every refuge they had—and when that lost horse had shown up down at first-stage, the last place where they could have been safe, he'd *known* it was his sister it had come for.

He hated her—and he couldn't let her go. There was the whole story in those two facts. Danny was probably asking himself how he'd ever gotten them for his responsibility. This morning Danny had been uncertain about setting out, and *he'd* argued with him—

He didn't remember all that he'd said, but he'd bent every argument to get them on their way before that horse found them, —the way he'd wanted them to get out of first-stage, because that horse haunting the fringes of the woods down there had come up near the cabin walls that last night, calling and calling for a hapless, foolish girl who'd, please God, passed beyond answering it or any horse.

Because what in hell did they do if Brionne came to and they were in that little cabin with a horse who—Danny tried to keep the lid on that feeling, but he knew—might kill her and maybe him and Randy in spite of everything they could do to stop it? He couldn't blame Cloud for protecting his rider. And he didn't want Brionne to wake and answer that lost horse down there, either. He'd *felt* her stirring, down at first-stage, that last night.

And, God, he didn't want her near a horse.

He knew, too, he shouldn't be thinking about it. He tried to stop. He'd learned from Danny how to listen to Cloud and see not just flashes of damning illusion but clear pictures in his head.

The preacher down in Tarmin had always said if you listened to the Wild you'd be attracted to thoughts of sex and blood that came and went for no reason. And he'd *felt* them—but he wasn't even sure what the preacher feared: he couldn't have explained to anyone how *noisy* the world was when he was around Cloud—and how scarily quiet it was, even in the howling wind, when Cloud was out of range. He'd gotten to depend on that presence for safety—and it wasn't just hearing some ravening Beast, as the preachers called it—it was hearing *everything,* it was an intensity of smells he didn't smell, colors he didn't see—most of all a sense of *whereness* that he couldn't explain in words, a jumble at first that made you think you were off balance all the time, but that just—slowly turned into a sense of where things were and how far everybody was from each other and who they were and how they felt—that in this place was an assurance you were still on the mountain and not walking off it.

That was the sense you could really get hooked on, and the preachers didn't know that one—or maybe they did and weren't telling you that because it was just too attractive, the way Brionne had gone off into it and gotten herself into a place she couldn't—maybe didn't want to—get out of.

That was the other side of it—you were bound to a creature that wasn't human. And if it should die—

The world began to flatten out: Cloud had begun to pull out of range, growing more vague as the snow came between them. He knew then he'd been thinking very dangerous, scary things.

"Pull, dammit," came from out of the fog beside him.

He pulled harder, and as they came closer to Cloud the world re-expanded. That was the way it seemed.

At the same moment came a sudden *shove* in what Danny called the ambient, a flash of <water flowing over stones> and an awareness of <Danny beside him.>

Danny wanted him quiet. Danny didn't want him interfering with his horse. Danny was <upset.>

Foot skidded. Body reacted. Heart caught up late. He was too tired, too out of breath. He'd never walked this far in his life, never imagined what it did to feet and legs to walk up incline after incline with no letup.

The wind came at them from the side in a sudden gust. They couldn't *see* Cloud, but Cloud was still there, still aware of them—

Two hours on a good day, Danny had said. He *couldn't* be that wrong.

Chapter

— II —

Storm brought early twilight to a cabin that, on the east slope of a tall mountain, lost the sun in mid-afternoon, and it meant peaceful horses now that they'd run themselves silly in the gale—now that, moreover, they'd eaten something humans found entirely noxious, that left a faint aroma about them of bushdevil musk as they were let in for shelter.

It didn't stop two horses from starting a little neck-nipping and tail-lifting in the middle of their two-footed partners' supper in a very small cabin. Then there were the throaty rumbles and the explosive snorts that presaged lovemaking, which had its effect on two humans *trying* to concentrate on griddle-cakes and hash, an early supper and an early bedtime, by their intentions.

Guil hadn't been in the mood for the last several days—a hole in the side tending to discourage a man. Tara had suffered the lovemaking in the ambient in lonely resolution and was not resigned to do so tonight; he caught that impression quite clearly through the taste of hash, the smell of dead bushdevil and the musk two amorous nighthorses generated on their own. She had set her mind on making an advance just real soon now—limited to milder activity, it might be. Acknowledging he was doing well to be on his feet.

He was going to finish the hash. His horse could wait. Her horse could wait. Tara could wait. He'd all night.

Tara made valiant attempts to slow down with supper.

But the horses didn't wait, and he didn't taste the last of the hash. Neither, he thought, did she.

One thing about horses, once didn't satisfy them. They saved it most of the year for this season, though they'd not reject a little off-season recreation. But in winter, given time and opportunity and a couple of humans to care for their essential survival, they had only one thing to do besides eat and sleep. It was the force that bound herds together for the winter. It was the social impulse that shuffled the deck for pairings, that ended by spring in pregnant mares and smaller, saner groups, four or five, that hung together for the season.

And by the time two humans had wended their way through essential and polite human processes—Burn and Flicker were through the first round and far from finished for the evening.

Long winter nights. Long season.

Tara, fortunately, was taking the same precautions the mares did in bad seasons. He didn't know if she had the first time they'd made love: he hoped so. But bitterweed was something the shelters kept, right along with the tea, the salt, and the flour. Horses wouldn't touch it until there was *nothing* else left to eat: it prevented foals in years when there wasn't forage and it kept riders from getting pregnant—maybe from siring as well: he'd heard it speculated on but never proved.

He'd drunk the damn tea, too, though, out of basic courtesy, because it tasted really bad, sugar didn't half cure it, and he didn't think anybody should have to suffer it alone.

Fact was, he *liked* this woman. He hadn't said too much yet and some things the horses didn't carry in quite the human way or the human sense: nuances of emotion were real chancy. But he felt safe with her, felt as though if things went wrong he'd have solid, clear-thinking backup, and that on good days it'd be good just to know she existed in the world.

Wished she'd felt differently about the kids, that was the only thing. He was really, really disturbed about that, and hadn't, in the dose of painkiller Tara had shoved down him, had his wits thoroughly about him when she'd taken a wide decision in the matter of their own welfare for the winter. Tara didn't hesitate on a threat. Just didn't. She'd been a Darwin rider before she'd come to Tarmin, a hell of a lot rougher life than this mountain had been, and there were a lot of shadow-spots like that with her.

There would be for her with him—he *knew* he had a lot. His partner wouldn't have died if he'd had the capacity to follow blindly where she'd wanted him to be.

When the horses carried sex in the ambient, winter-long, thinking stopped in a rider shelter. *Partnership* and springtime partings were where thinking took up again—and as recent as Aby's death was, and as recent as her partners' deaths were, he thought it possible he'd ride with Tara at least for the summer to come.

Soft lips ran down his neck, gentle hands down his back.

—If there weren't the question about the kids.

—If she weren't so hard-minded.

Hands stopped. The mood crashed.

"The girl's a *killer,"* Tara said.

That was true. The girl was responsible for everything that had happened at Tarmin—for Tara's partners gnawed down to bone, still alive. That last was Tara's image, not his, because Tara didn't buckle and she didn't give the kid any slack, not for the loss or the memory of it. She was *damn* tough.

And maybe, having lost a partner himself, he needed Tara's unforgiving mind the way he needed the winter cold to come between him and what he'd lost.

She came around him, wrapped him tight, held him close.

Said, into his ear, "The mountain doesn't forgive, Guil, and I don't. I wasn't made that way." Lips brushed his, gentle and kind, belying the words that passed them. "I told Danny everything—chance to go up, chance to go down—advice to stay. But they won't *let* her die. And she should have. She *should* have, Guil. I'm not talking about justice."

The girl was still a danger, in Tara's mind. It was possible in his experience that the girl would pull out of it—but it was equally possible she wouldn't, and worse, that she'd go on living and that she'd be a problem around horses that might get worse instead of better. Tara could be entirely right.

But if they just got through the winter they could ship the girl down to Anveney—if they had to, with the first truck convoy that came up here—where there *weren't* horses, where there wasn't anything alive, including grass, for that matter. It was hell on earth for a rider. But there the girl couldn't affect anything. There she'd have no power. No means to draw another horse to its death.

He thought when the storm passed and it looked like a good day he'd ride up the road as far as the first-stage shelter and see if the kids were there, as he hoped to God they'd stayed put. The weather certainly hadn't invited them moving on.

But, God, if they had decided to move, he hoped they'd taken straight out. Most of all he hoped that they weren't up at midway when this hit.

She punched him gently with her fist.

"Dammit, Guil." She propped herself on one elbow in the furs. Her shirt was open. The firelight glowed on her skin. "Told him every damn thing I could, Guil. I swear to you. —Better than anybody ever did for me! Don't look at me like that."

"Somebody," he said, tracing the line down the middle of her chest with a gentle finger, "should have done better for you."

She stared at him. Stared as if she were really mad.

But the surface of her eyes glistened in the firelight. "My partners in Tarmin did everything they needed to do for me. I don't *need* people to do things for me."

"I know you don't," he said.

"All right, I'll ride up and check on the next shelter. I'll do it. I'll go tonight!"

"When the weather clears," he said, "*we'll* go."

"I don't need you to go. It was my doing. I'll handle it."

"When the weather clears," he said. If Tara said a thing she meant it. Tarmin's fall had done some brutal things to Tara Chang. Stripped away the veneer of camp life and cast her back to thoughts of her own growing up, in dealing with those kids. She hadn't admitted that to him.

But Darwin was a lot in her thoughts tonight when she thought about Tarmin *or* the kids.

A hard life. Growing up alone in a world of miners and loggers with no advice, no one to trust.

He'd been luckier. He'd had a partner from very, very young.

Then lost her. And almost lost himself.

Tara had pulled him back from that. But it was off the edge of one cliff and facing Tara's own drop into darkness. She was maybe a couple of years younger than Aby or than he was—but she was harder than Aby, she was colder. She both anchored him from a slide he could have taken and bid fair to take him down another of her own.

But he wasn't going to *become* Tara Chang. He wasn't going to shove Aby into the past and take on the hardened self-sufficiency that was Tara's answer to loss. He'd rather bleed. And she was scared to. That was what it came down to.

He drew her close, into his arms. He made love to her, personally, carefully, *not* the hard fast way that was Tara's own urging. She was going to *feel* before he was done, and she could do what she liked about it later, but he wouldn't be ignorable, he wouldn't be someone whose name she'd forget if she rode away. Fact was, he wouldn't forget hers, and he felt for her, and it seemed only fair.

And whether she thought so or not he was going up there to the first-stage shelter to find those kids. He'd been flat on his back on painkiller and too damned compliant when vital decisions were being made on his behalf, and her patched-together notion of going up there now to check was only to satisfy him, and protect *him* from the situation she'd protected him from knowing about when it was in the cabin with them.

That was the impression he got—though he could be wrong about her intentions. He'd see about that, too.

His own way of grieving hadn't been quiet or safe. He'd inspired a man to shoot him. Hers seemed to be ignoring the loss of her partners except for a burst of occasional anger. Seemed. That was the word.

And he didn't think so: having just been through what she was going through he didn't believe it. It wasn't easy to love him—and God knew Aby'd been patient of his faults. It might not be real damn easy to get through the barriers Tara Chang threw up.

As now he felt the panic under him. He felt the sensations she was feeling the way she felt his—and most of all she wanted haste and satisfaction he wasn't going to give her that fast or that cheaply. Not between the blankets. Not in letting her seal that shell around herself for the rest of her life.

Liar, he said to her in his mind. And she bucked and screamed and hit him hard with her fist, forgetting he was the wounded one. She was instantly sorry and didn't object to what he was doing, just—wanted him to hurry; but he didn't give her up.

He wasn't her partner. But you knew a rider by certain things: he knew the woman that had taken care of that mare of hers when her own hands were hurting so badly from the cold she'd had tears in her eyes. How she'd interrupted grieving over her own hurts to stand in as his partner when many men of good sense would have hung back or turned and run.

And by everything he'd learned about Tara Chang, he wasn't going to give her up until she could tell him—in words, at which riders including himself didn't generally excel—that she'd made up her mind to be as shut down as a rock forever.

"Damn you!" she said, for what he was doing, not what he was thinking.

Afterward she lay and shivered, and in her mind still was the firelight. And him.

Then her lost partner. And him again.

She had her hand on his arm, and could have pulled away, and didn't. Just lay there, as he did, the two of them in the firelight. His horse, Burn, helpfully came over and sniffed them over, approving.

That told him something, too. Burn didn't *like* everyone.

There was probably a glorious view from the turn next and higher, as the wind shifted into their faces again: all the peaks of the great Firgeberg Range were probably right there behind that veil of white, but all they met was wind that scoured what it hit. If they plummeted straight off the edge in their next snow-blinded steps it still wouldn't give them a view—they'd just fall and fall, Danny said to himself, in white no different from the snow that veiled the road.

From a high Shamesey window he'd dreamed boyish dreams of the far crest of the world. From the safety of Shamesey walls he'd seen Rogers Peak send out its winter banner of white and thought it the greatest beauty in the mountains—*his* mountain, *his* horizon against the evening sky.

Well, this was it. He was here. Best view he might ever have. And snow and the fading of daylight were all the view he had.

One foot in front of the other—hand was numb, arm was numb, and Cloud was getting too far ahead of them, moving into blowing sleet that didn't let up, up an increasingly sleet-gray road. Randy, walking near him, was dropping behind; Danny realized that in a distracted moment and turned his head, blinded by his scarf, to urge Randy to catch up.

"Come on," he yelled. "Keep with us." He saw their strength giving out, finally, to pull that travois. They'd dumped all the nonessential supplies. Held on to the shotgun and most of the food. Couple of blankets. And Brionne. Randy had to carry himself—but he looked to be losing his battle against the wind.

Randy might have answered his hail just now. Danny couldn't entirely hear. His ears were aching to match the duller ache racketing around the walls of his skull. But Randy didn't overtake them until Carlo stopped and beckoned and cursed and refused to go on until Randy trudged past them again.

On that steeper grade, Randy struggled to keep walking. Feet skidded on snow-packed rubble as often as they gained upward. More than once the kid slipped to his knees and got back up in what had become an exercise of raw, desperate courage. Danny's hand that held the left-side travois pole was going numb even through the gloves, and his running argument with Cloud about <bacon> and <cabin in the woods above> had degenerated to a litany of calls on God as his feet slipped and his heart jumped—supposing the preachers' Beast-hating God had a little concern to spare for a stranded and hellbound rider.

Carlo had his feet go out from under him, wrenched the travois down and almost took Danny off his feet, and that was the way it went: slow going for a long, long distance as rubble fill bridged a rift in the mountain flank. Wind blew the ends of Cloud's tail straight sideways below the point where muscle and bone had it tucked tight into Cloud's rump.

Then tail and horse alike faded into white ahead of them. Randy was momentarily a gray, ghostly figure and then gone, too.

It was like walking into a wall. Ice particles stung exposed skin. They couldn't see, and what Cloud sent made Danny sure Cloud couldn't, either. By the end of the next switchback and the change of the wind from their flank to their backs Danny couldn't feel his grip on the travois pole at all. His chest hurt, his head hurt, his lungs hurt, and the constant slipping and the scares it set into him didn't help his labored breathing or his pounding, front-of-the-skull headache.

Carlo was bearing up somehow, but Randy—

Randy by now was walking on instinct, not mentally there, Danny was increasingly afraid. He watched Randy, who'd stopped when they had, wander off to the left and to the right again, averaging their course, but not holding a steady line. The thoughts that surfaced from the boy were increasingly erratic, things about home and <Tarmin> and going somewhere Danny couldn't figure.

Cloud was struggling with the increasingly frequent idea of <shelter and shops> coming from the kid. <Cattle tails,> was Cloud's opinion of villagers walking this road—<cattle tails> describing the feature Cloud most despised on the creature Cloud most despised on the planet, adding <cattle dung> and <cattle rear ends> for villagers who confused his navigation.

Foot slipped. Randy went momentarily to all fours and got up again, amid <fear> from Carlo, who surely knew the score. They couldn't, Danny thought, afford another rest in this gale with Randy already chilled—couldn't just pile him on the travois in the open, either, if he was chilling. He kept looking for a tall rock, a snowbank, any place where he and Carlo could shelter Randy and stabilize the travois for long enough to pack Randy in the furs with his sister—if *she* wasn't frozen.

Randy lagged back by them. Danny turned his head and in the fuzzy side vision his frozen lashes and the edge of his scarf afforded him realized the boy was no longer trudging beside him and Carlo. He looked back, fighting the scarf and the wind for vision. Randy was standing still, slowly disappearing into a veil of white.

"Randy!" Carlo yelled back at him. Carlo's voice was mostly gone, too, but he yelled: "Randy, come on! *Keep up, dammit, you lily-livered stupid kid!*"

It wasn't exactly the encouragement Danny would have offered, but he guessed Carlo knew his brother, because Randy started walking, and as they went at a slower pace, caught up, <angry> and <wanting to hit Carlo.> Carlo shoved at him one-handed as he passed, cursed him and made him madder.

Couldn't have the kid quit. They were—he'd tried to reestablish a time-sense—maybe an hour from the shelter and the end of this road. It was getting toward dark.

Get the kid to a level spot, pack him on—he and Carlo could pull that weight.

Couldn't be that much longer. The shelter was supposed to be right at the crest, a broad truck pull-out, so that trucks in convoy from the High Loop could park and the drivers could sleep in them before or after that notorious steep. Villagers appreciative of the means by which their goods had moved provided soft bunks, even heated showers in the summer, Tara had said so. Tara had promised them—he could *see* the image she'd cast him.

<Hot water. Hot meals. A shelter still within the treeline> and away from this rocky face, which meant firewood available if they had to wait out a succession of storms.

He had no feeling in his left hand. With his free right, he gave a furious wipe across his eyes to free his eyelashes of the accumulating ice—and in that moment Randy slipped on a runoff trace of ice and shot past him downhill.

He dropped and grabbed the kid, and Randy's weight spun him, the travois, and Carlo all to the left and onto the ice. Carlo—he thought it was Carlo—by a miracle or a dug-in boot-toe held onto the other pole of the travois, flat on the ice, and didn't let them skid more than a body length further.

Danny lay still with a gloved fistful of Randy's sleeve and a second precarious grip on the side of the travois. For all he knew the rig might be only balanced on one pivot, ready to slide again if he moved.

He really hadn't been scared in the instant he'd grabbed Randy. Now a shudder went through him that passed to quaking shivers, a blinding acuteness of headache, and an inability to get his breath.

He couldn't let himself panic. Couldn't. He'd saved Randy. His eyelashes had mostly frozen shut and he couldn't judge where they were on the road or how close to the edge or how steep it was below them.

"Just stay put," he said to Randy, who was starting to struggle. "Catch your breath. *Don't move, dammit.*"

Cloud would realize their predicament. Cloud would give him vision if he waited. It wasn't just iced rubble where Randy's momentum had carried them. It was slick as glass. And Cloud was coming back now, worried, picking his way, fearfully imaging <dangerously slick ice, Danny in danger.>

<Cloud stopping,> he sent back, frightened for Cloud's safety more than their own at the instant; he could see <Danny and boys and travois> through Cloud's eyes, but that warning wasn't going to stop Cloud long from a rash approach if they didn't move immediately to get out of their predicament.

"What's holding us?" he asked Carlo, and Carlo managed to say,

"My foot. On the snow. On our right."

"Can you pull us?"

"No! You'll slide!"

His brain had started working. He had both hands occupied at the moment—but at very worst he had a knife in his right boot, if he could grab it and use it fast enough to hold on the ice; but he didn't want to do that if he had an alternative. He worked and found a little, little toehold for leverage. "Randy. You take hold of my arm. You crawl over me. Onto the travois. Over to Carlo."

"Can't." He could hardly understand the kid. "Can't."

"Calm down. Grab my arm. Then the rifle—the strap's solid around me. Just crawl right over my back."

The kid moved. Grabbed his arm—grabbed the rifle barrel and Danny pressed his face against the ice and hung on as the kid clambered over him. Everything shifted, slid sideways—the travois turned slowly in the shift of weight and by God knew what effort of Carlo's arms, angled him slowly toward the snowbank.

Danny got a foot onto it and let Carlo drag him and Randy both to the snow, where he could get a knee under him and get up, and they could walk.

Carlo had saved them, saved the damn travois *and* his sister—and he trudged uphill with Carlo, pulling the travois with Brionne and Randy to the snowy spot where Cloud waited for them.

"Up." Carlo hauled Randy up by one arm then and let him go. "Walk on the snow. Hear?"

Randy tried, but the scare and the cold of the ice had taken all the shaky strength Randy had left. The kid was exhausted, trying to walk, but staggering left and right, knees shaking under him. Danny got a dizzy feeling and felt pain he thought was Randy's.

"We're in real trouble," Carlo gasped. "Aren't we?"

"Shelter's going to be soon," Danny said. "It's got to be."

"Maybe it isn't, you know?" There was a wobble in Carlo's voice. "Maybe we got off the track somewhere."

"There isn't anywhere we can get off. They cut the road out of the mountain, they shore it up with logs—there aren't any side roads."

"You've never been up here!"

"I've *seen* it, trust me that I've seen it."

"I saw what you saw!"

"Don't take it for granted." A senior rider had said it to him once, when he was a week with his horse, and he hadn't believed it then, but he fell back on it now as the only authority he had. "You don't pick up the details I do. Tara told me plain enough what the road is."

"Maybe we ought to make a camp. We could find a place in the rocks—we're not going to get snowed under in a blow like this."

"There's no place to camp!" He didn't mean to attack. But he didn't have breath to argue, and if Carlo wanted to quibble and object to the only advice he had they were in real trouble. "Shelter's coming. Be patient."

"You've been saying that!"

What came through Cloud wasn't confidence. It was <spooky-feeling, bite and kick.>

<Blood on the snow> he heard then.

"Oh, my God," Carlo said.

"Easy," Danny said.

"It's behind us! *It's that horse again!*"

"Calm down. It could be the kid. Could be he's dreaming."

"It's not coming from him! *It's followed us up here! It's still behind us!*" Carlo pointed back the way they'd come with an accuracy his own direction-sense echoed plain as plain. More, *Cloud* felt it, <wanting fight.>

"No!" Danny let go the travois pole without warning to shove against Cloud's chest and sent a strong <quiet water.>

<Blood. Rifle crack ringing off the mountainside. Pain. And shock.>

"You said," Carlo insisted in rising panic, as if he hadn't heard. "You said it wouldn't come up here—"

He'd thought so. And as strongly as it had come—the <blood on snow> image vanished on them.

"It just wants *help.*" Randy was weaving in his tracks. "Maybe it could help *us.*"

"*No,*" he said, more strongly than he intended. "Toss the rest of the supplies. Everything but the shotgun and the shells and the food we're carrying. Food packets might stall it off. —Randy, you get on the travois."

"No," Randy said, but Carlo was already jerking at the ties on the supplies.

Chapter

— III —

The shutters banged and rattled and the flashing on the stovepipe on the barracks roof sang with a rising and falling note. All of Evergreen village was on the other side of the rider camp wall, and neither Ridley nor either of his two barracks mates, namely his wife and his daughter, could completely ignore that fact even in the quiet of the minds over there, a hundred meters isolated from the horses.

They lived at the very top of the world—well, at least halfway up Rogers Peak, a very respectable mountain in itself, outlier to the towering Firgeberg. And at this top of the place they called home, the horses were in their warm den, the fire was crackling in the fireplace, and Ridley had his feet up, soles to the heat, doing a piece of leather stitching, and didn't plan to budge out of the barracks tomorrow and maybe the day after that except to see to the horses.

They could be the only three people on the planet when the wind settled in to blow like this. And he didn't mind. Summer was full of hard work. Fall was long hunts and a last-minute flurry of activity stocking the winter shelters. It had been a hard autumn this year, a spooky, chancy autumn coming down to bad dreams and cold sweats in the night for no damned reason the last couple of weeks. Personally he was *glad* to see the advent of a good, hard, beginning-of-season storm.

Now it was well-earned rest. Predators and prey alike spent more time in their burrows. Some dug deep as the hunger grew and went to sleep, to wake again when the world was new with spring growth and the old year was gone. Autumn was a blood-time, a death-time, hunters' season, two-footed and otherwise. Autumn was for killing. Winter was for ease and a rider's own concerns. And for love. There was that, too, passionate in every species that wasn't numb to the rhythms of the world.

But a lonely clangor started up in the fierceness of the gusts. The ringing of a distant bell disturbed the peace and kept up in that regular and erratic way that spoke of wind, not a human hand.

The gate bell had come loose in the blow, was what had just happened, and Ridley could blame Serge, whose job, on the other side of Evergreen camp's wall, was to guard and maintain the village gate, for not tying it down better—but he couldn't quite blame Serge for not getting out and climbing after it while the wind was blowing the way it was.

So there it was, Serge's Fault, tolling a plaintive cadence in the violence of the storm, and they'd hear the damn thing all night. Pity the Santez and the Lasierre households, who lived nearest the gate, and pity the miner barracks and the logger's hostel, which were nearer still.

"The bell's loose, papa," Jennie said.

"Noticed that," he said.

"Is it going to ring all night?"

"I wouldn't doubt. But I'm not going to climb up after it. Are you?"

"No." Jennie was eight and still played. Even runaway bells skittered out of her usually skittery thoughts. She sat on the braided rug and arranged her carved horses and her carved toy trucks. She had the trucks carry blocks for crates around the patterns of the braided rags and under the table legs and back again, until they could arrive at the wood-box, where she had laid an ambush of willy-wisps. That was the knot of horse fur she'd gotten from the sheddings bag and tucked beside the box.

"So is Serge going to get it?" Thoughts had skittered back to the bell.

"I don't think so," Ridley said to his offspring. "Serge doesn't want to go climb the ladder, either, does he?"

Supper was cooking. They had a winter deal, he and his partner Callie, the mother of the Offspring: meals cooked versus trips out to break the ice on the den's water barrel—plus cleanup of said meal. He'd done the ice-breaking twice today, once at dawn before the blow had started, once before they tucked in for the evening, and Jennie had helped him with a hammer. So Callie cooked and he sat with his feet propped up.

Jennie ran her convoy into ambush and turned a truck over. "They had a door come open," Jennie announced happily. "Here's the willy-wisps. There's hundreds of 'em. Yum."

Gruesome child. Ridley kept putting the whipstitch border on what was going to be a jacket in another three weeks of spare-time work. Winter evenings were good for that, and a fancy jacket traded to a trucker come snowmelt was going to be worth, oh, maybe a tenth what that trucker was going to sell it for down in Anveney or Shamesey, and by the time it got to Carlisle, twice that. But, then, that increase in cost was the life the trucker risked going there, and the lives the riders risked getting him there in one piece, and they were all in the same business. He'd get store money for it: the village supplied their riders with very generous basics, but shirting and such, and shoes for Jennie's growing feet—they all cost. Leather from the tanner—that, he had a deal on.

"They're going to use the radio," Jennie announced. Her riders and her truckers had been shooting steadily for a noisy minute or two.

"That's really stupid," Ridley said sympathetically. "Are the riders going to tell them that's stupid?'

"No, this guy is sneaking and doing it."

"He must be new on the job."

"Here comes a spook-bear!" Jennie said. "He's going straight for that radio! Grrr."

There were snarls and pow-pow-pows.

"The bear got him," Jennie said sadly.

"Too bad," Callie said. "But they're going to have to wait. Dinner's on."

"The bear's having dinner, too."

"Oh, what a nice thought," Ridley said. "Wash."

"I'm not—"

"If there's water available, you wash, youngster. Feet go in the den. Feet go on this floor. Hands go on this floor. Hands get washed." The bell had assumed a steady cadence. A strong gust of wind caught the flashing and made it sing.

"Nasty wind," Callie said, setting down bowls.

"*We're* not in it," Ridley said, and got up and helped with the ladling-out. It was stew, good, thick bear-meat stew. They had a fair bit in the smoke-shed. They had the hides at the tannery, and that was cash, too, come spring.

There wasn't a thing wrong with the world this evening.

"I washed!" Jennie announced.

He snatched Jennie up. Hugged her tight. Growled, "I'm the bear."

Jennie shrieked and kicked with abandon.

"Supper," Callie said, unimpressed. "The bear better get the spoons."

"If I let you go," Ridley said, with his arms full of daughter, "will you get the spoons?"

"All right," Jennie said, and he let her down. She was growing. She'd landed a couple of solid kicks. The bear thought he'd have bruises.

Jennie got the spoons. The bear held the bowls while mama ladled out the stew.

Sleet had given way to snow, drifting puffs on a gentler, darker wind as light faded in what Danny knew now was storm-glow, no longer daylight. The grades where they climbed were a lot gentler. There began to be trees: that gave them encouragement that they might find the shelter. But they'd spent and struggled and spent the strength they had—and now Randy had all but run out of endurance—the kid was still walking, but from Randy now came a muddled lot of <fireside at home> and <biscuits baking> and a disturbed recollection of <mama at the table. Brionne in a red coat, coming out the door.> The kid was drifting into dreams.

Or nightmares—as he slumped down onto his knees and then

onto his face: <Brionne standing on the road, still in the red coat, with no awareness in her eyes.>

They reached him. Carlo knelt down and turned the kid and held him.

"Back on the travois," Danny said.

"Can't," Carlo said. There was panic in his voice. "He'll go to sleep. He's too tired. He's got to get up, that's all. Come on, kid. Dammit, on your feet! Hear me?"

Randy wouldn't wake up. Not even when Carlo hit him.

"He's cold," Carlo said. <Fear> was thick in the ambient. "He's gotten cold. —Can't Cloud carry him? Can't you get him to?"

"He can't," Danny said. "He can't. He's worked as hard as we have. Let the kid rest. Calm down. Loosen the ties, we'll bundle him in again."

"He'll die!"

"He'll die if you scare hell out of him—the kid's doing all he can." He jerked ties undone and opened the furs, in which Brionne was still warm, to let Carlo lift Randy, half-aware as he was, onto the travois.

Carlo wasn't saying anything now about being tired. There was just fear. Randy didn't want the cords tied down. "No!" he said—scared, Danny didn't need the ambient to understand, that the thing could finally get away from them.

"We won't let you go," he said. "It's almost flat here." He tied a couple of fumbling knots, securing the kid in the only real warmth there was, and got up.

<Blood on the snow> still came to them, a flash of white, daylight vision. It *hadn't* stopped for their supplies.

"Best we can do," Danny said as calmly as he could. "Keep going. Got to be a shelter—a door we can shut."

"I don't think it'll hurt us," Randy said from beneath muffling furs. "I could talk to it. It's lonely. I could try—"

"Forget it! We don't need a horsefight on top of everything else!" He was growing short-fused himself. And scared. Randy wanted a horse, Randy, like his sister, *wanted* a horse to such a degree that Cloud didn't like to be in closed spaces with him, and that lost horse out there wasn't in any sense one for any green villager kid to take on. When creatures in the Wild started doing the unusual they were usually sick—and for a horse to follow them up a mountain through the wintry hell they'd been through? Damn sure it wasn't behaving like a normal horse.

"It wouldn't fight Cloud," Randy said. "I *know.* If you could just bring it in—*I* could talk to it. That's what it wants, doesn't it?"

"It's not sane, if it tracked us up here, and it *will* fight Cloud."

"It won't." Fourteen-year-old logic. "If it thought I was its rider it'd come for me, wouldn't it? I can do it—"

"Shut up and listen to the rider, you hear me?" Carlo's voice cracked and broke as he stood up. "We're in trouble, we're in real serious trouble, here, kid. Don't beg trouble. Keep quiet. Think at it and I'll hit you. I mean it!"

"Let's move," Danny said, and got up. Cloud had come back and wanted <Danny walking,> ignoring the existence of boys or travois.

Worse, Cloud had his mind on the road behind them, and kept looking that way, ready for a horsefight, sending out the impression of <male horse> and <wanting mating> all over the mountainside.

It had to be the same horse that had been down at the first-stage cabin. Randy was right that if it had fastened on one of them and saw its rider among them, it would follow through hell and ice—and he was surer and surer which of a number of horses it was: a horse that had always imaged itself as a succession of horses, as something twisting and horselike and scary, and there and not-there. It was the unhealthiest image he'd ever gotten from a supposedly sane horse, and that was what, in the way of nighthorses, it called itself, no human naming it.

<Spook> was the human name he'd put to it. He'd never learned what Ancel Harper had called it before he fired on the wrong rider. Harper, the <dead man in snow,> the source of <blood on snow,> might get pity in hell. Not from him. Not after he'd ridden with the man. And if it wanted Brionne Goss—that was worse news than Harper.

<Gunfire. Rider lying in the white, blowing snow, not moving.>

"Walk," Danny said.

Carlo had found another small reserve of strength. So had he. He hadn't much left.

But thank God for the snow finally giving them consistent traction. Cloud's three-toed hooves, which shaped themselves very readily to rock, flexed enough so honest dry snow didn't pack in the clefts of those feet: Cloud was sure-footed and confident now, so were they, and they were finally making time, through trees that indicated they'd turned away from the blasted areas and gone across a natural slope of the mountain.

They *should* come to the cabin.

At any moment now.

Chapter

— IV —

Jennie was supposed to be asleep, but the wind was making a racket and she'd been bored a lot during the day. She was bored now, lying in the dark, in bed. The storm had been going on for a whole day, and she had played games and done chores and played games and she'd had a nap she didn't usually take any more. She wished there was something to do.

If she got up, mama and papa would scold. If she slipped in to sit by the fire and didn't make a sound, and just sat and watched the pictures in the coals, or maybe played with her trucks real quietly, mama and papa might not know she was up.

But the bell was still ringing out by the gate. Nobody had fixed it. The night was scary with wind and things going thump, and she began to be convinced that something spooky had waked her. She wasn't sure what: she thought it might have been a sending, and she wished she knew what that was.

Spook-bears and goblin-cats didn't ever get inside the walls. Serge Lasierre slept in the village gate house with his rifle on nights when the Wild was acting up, and bears couldn't get past Serge. Mama and papa had told her that.

But that bell was ringing and ringing. Maybe a bear had gotten Serge and *that* was why Serge hadn't fixed the bell.

Maybe out there in the wind and the dark something was really wrong.

She thought it might be Rain calling her. Rain was her horse, well, mostly her horse, though papa said she'd have to wait till Rain made up his mind, and Rain might have to leave the way Leaf had left. But she didn't think so. Rain *was* hers, and he and she were friends. And papa knew it even if he didn't approve.

Rain was, papa also said, a loud horse, because he was only two, and didn't know but one pitch to be at, —like some little girls, papa had said. And like little girls, anyway, Rain heard things older horses didn't pay attention to. Hearing everything made Rain spooky sometimes, over shadows and thumps and over things somebody remembered, so Rain's rider had to be very quiet and not think scary thoughts, even alone in bed at night, in the barracks where the horses didn't ordinarily hear them.

But in the barracks they weren't supposed to hear the horses this far, either, unless the horses were upset.

And it wasn't just Rain, she decided. Mom-horse Shimmer was nervous, too. Shimmer was pregnant again and expecting a foal in the spring, and mom-horse was getting angry, not angry at Rain, but disturbed at something Rain picked up, and that upset papa-horse.

So she *wasn't* just making-believe. Papa said don't ever make-believe near the horses, and said that that was why they built the rider-shelter so far away from the horse-den, so little girls being silly couldn't upset them.

<*Bang!*> went the boards. She knew she didn't hear it with her own ears, but the horses were carrying it to her: papa-horse Slip had kicked out and shaken the side of the den *or something*.

That was too much. She flew out of bed and grabbed her sweater. <*Bang!*> went the boards again. Rain was <upset> and <wanting fight> and thinking <shadow in the storm.>

She could tell where her door was because light from the common-room came down the hall even when the fire was banked for the night, and it hadn't been banked too long, because there was a glow in the room. She had no trouble finding her boots.

<*Bang!*> *Thump!* went the logs, one sound in her head and one in her ears. That was real for sure; and she thought about waking up mama and papa; but they were asleep and she didn't want to make a fuss and be told she was silly or dreaming, which was what mama had said the last time she'd come running to their bed, scared. She'd see first.

So she hurried and opened the door to the snow-passage that led from the barracks to the den, and took down the 'lectric light from its shelf and carried it, shining its light up and around and down the wooden walls and floor, wood planks all shiny with ice where the drips were, and icicled in places.

The dark was scary. Vermin like willy-wisps would burrow under the boards or anywhere they could when it got cold, and they got hungry and they'd make holes in the boards and try to bite your ankles; and you mustn't ever fall if they bit you, that was what mama said, because they'd swarm all over you and eat you till nothing but bones were left. Granpa when she was little had said they liked toes, especially in the wintertime and especially from little girls who didn't mind and didn't do what they were supposed to.

But granpa had gone away with grandma and not come back and now her parents didn't think they were ever coming back. Mama thought they'd fallen off a cliff. Papa thought maybe granpa's heart might have given out and grandma wouldn't leave that place. Things did happen out in the Wild.

Things happened, too, in dark passages, where the light made scary shapes on the boards around and underfoot and overhead. She wasn't supposed to be in the passage before mama and papa were awake. She might get in trouble.

But now she'd mostly done it, anyway, and she was already going to get in trouble—so she figured she might as well find out if Rain was all right, before papa and mama woke up and stopped her and she got in trouble for having done nothing at all.

So on that thought she ran, *thump-thump,* down the boards, and her light and her shadow went ahead of her.

It was awfully cold. She'd thought she'd just be a minute, and then she wouldn't need her coat, but a brisk draft was coming through, blowing her hair and chilling right through her clothes.

Then she heard another, slower thumping on the boards, one-two, three-four feet, and she knew that was <Rain in the passage> where Rain wasn't ever supposed to be. Rain showed up, his eyes shimmering beneath the bangs that mostly covered his face and his split-lipped nose working, nostrils wide, to be sure who she was in spite of the <Jennie with light> that was in his mind. She'd scared him with her giant-shadow, and he scared her with his.

"It's me," she said in a quavery voice, but it was always dependent on the rider to be the grown-up, so she talked like mama. "Silly. You can't turn around. Back up. <Back up.">

Somebody had left the door open at the den-end of the passage, she thought, and that wasn't her fault. But when Rain had backed, with her pushing at his chest, all the way back to the den, she saw the door was kicked to flinders.

Rain was scaring her.

Rain was thinking about <something outside the walls> and it hadn't any shape, or it had a lot of them, and the wind out in the dark was howling like bushdevils. She thought, There's something out there.

Or somebody out there.

But not—not someone like mama and papa. Not like the villagers. Not like anybody she knew who'd be outside.

She didn't like it. Rain didn't. And Slip left the den altogether, an angry darkness headed out into the snow from the open door. Slip couldn't get out of the camp: the outside gate was always shut. But Slip could get himself clear of every other sending but that and then in a very loud sending let it know it wasn't welcome, that was what Slip could do. Mom-horse was nervous and angry and Rain would have gone out there, too—but she hadn't brought her coat and she didn't want Rain to go out there.

Because there were things in the winter storms that could come right over the walls and get you, grandma had said so when she was little, when once she had opened the door at night. She never forgot it.

<Papa?> she thought. <Papa coming outside.> She didn't care if she got in trouble. She thought maybe being safe was better.

Something was wrong. Ridley knew it in the ambient before he was entirely awake, and came out of bed in a hurry. So did Callie, and the horses weren't reaching them sufficiently to carry what they thought to each other, but his own horse Slip was loud enough with the situation as it was. Slip was sending <females> and <male horse> and <living things in the storm> that had a vague resemblance to willy-wisps. Slip didn't trust what was running through the ambient right now, something that had to do with <Shimmer> and <Rain,> and <Jennie.>

That wasn't right. The whole center of the business was <scared Jennie.>

"Dammit," Ridley said, heart speeding with the possibilities: that his daughter was outside he had no need to guess. He struggled into his boots and slammed his foot into the heel on his way for the door. Callie was pulling on her pants. He grabbed his sweater off the chair and pulled it on as he reached the door where he kept the shotgun. "Bring the rifle!" he yelled back at Callie. If you met a vermin-rush a shotgun was the only answer. If it was a bear or a cat you'd better have a punch to take it down, because a shotgun was worthless unless it took it in the face, and in the face meant it was coming over you before it dropped. He didn't know *what* they had to contend with. The nature of it wasn't coming clear to him as he headed into the passageway to the den and met a gust of cold air the minute he opened the door.

He shut the shelter-side door—cardinal rule, not to leave a passageway end unsecured when that door might be the only barrier between you and a breakthrough of vermin.

Then he ran the wooden corridor, the ambient he was getting coming clearer and clearer, that Jennie was in distress, that Slip was upset—Slip was his horse, and Slip was giving him a rush of impressions of <snowy yard, snow falling. Night, cold wind, strange dark shapes in the ambient.> Shimmer was sending her peculiar mare-in-foal antagonism; and <bite and kick,> Rain was sending, in close company with <Jennie here.>

The door was kicked in. The horses had done that. Jennie was close by it, sending <Jennie with Rain, Jennie with pregnant Shimmer>—scared and trying not to show it.

He had the shotgun in one hand. He heard Callie coming. He hugged Jennie against him with the other arm and tried to hear Slip's notion of what it was out there, as Callie was trying to hear.

<Ridley with gun. Slip watching in the yard. Log walls standing safe in the snow-fall, in the dark.>

"I couldn't see anything," Jennie said. The kid had no coat. Ridley grabbed a blanket they used for the horses and wrapped it around her. "I heard <Rain calling,"> Jennie said. "I know I shouldn't come out. But you were <asleep.">

"You wake me up any time you think of going out, hear?" He made his grip harsh for a moment, and shook her. <Mama,> was in the ambient, and Callie came through, rifle in hand and <scared, mad> in a way that set Shimmer off in a series of <light-dark> and <hostile mare-in-foal> images.

"What are you doing out here?" Callie wanted to know, and Jennie flinched and ducked behind Ridley, holding onto him, staying close to Rain.

"There's something out there," Ridley said. "Hush." Meaning both of them. A spook in the night with the horses involved wasn't a situation for a child, but it wasn't one for a child-mother argument, either. Jennie was spooked enough, and Callie calmed herself down fast—he could feel it in the ambient and he could feel it in Jennie relaxing and being willing then to be near Callie.

"I don't want to go back inside," Jennie said in a faint voice. "I don't *want* to be by myself."

"Be still," Callie said, and calmed Shimmer down with <Callie and Shimmer, Callie and Shimmer, baby inside> with no polite regard of a man and a kid in the ambient: it was something Shimmer and Callie remembered, a physical sensation and a feeling both protective and fierce sent out into the dark and the storm. See your bet and raise you, intruder.

It was quieter after that. They stood together in the aisle of the den, where the wind could blow through from the open outside door; and Slip came inside, a shadow as fierce as Shimmer and almost as possessive of his territory. Ridley met him in the dark—they kept no lights in the den for fear of fire, and all that they could see of each other was blackness deeper than the dark of the aisle and as deep as Rain's presence.

Deeper still as Shimmer left her nook and crowded in, seeking Callie, forming a defensive bond. Get Jennie out, was the first thing that came to Ridley's mind, feeling that hostility. But Jennie wasn't a baby anymore; Jennie was a life defending itself with Rain and Rain defending himself with her: in that way they held the night around them, defining it as theirs, not provoking what was out there, but not accepting it, either.

"There's someone out there," Jennie was the first to say. *"People* out there."

Ridley felt it, too, in the same moment, and knew Callie did.

"Several someones," Callie said.

Human and horse, separated off from them in the storm and the snow.

On the other side of their wooden wall there were hundreds of human minds, deaf to the ambient.

The other side of their wall was the whole village of Evergreen, full of life that, isolated from the horses, couldn't hear the dark outside the walls, walled in for the winter, cut off from the world for the season. Snows had come before this one, and the phone lines were down for the winter. The miners had come in. The loggers had. But without a horse in the midst of the strangers out there, they couldn't have heard them that clearly—they'd have only gotten their existence from small creatures in burrows, and spotty at that. That strong a sending was a stray rider out there, maybe not alone, maybe with some lost group of miners they hadn't known about: foolish novice prospectors did come up the mountain sometimes with the truckers, and the really foolish ones were secretive, just too nervous about their finds to let riders know they were there so riders could protect them.

Or it could be some group of miners who'd planned to winter-over underground and had something serious go wrong. He knew of two such that were staying—dug in and well-stocked and betting their lives on keeping the Wild out of their burrows all winter without a rider's help.

But sometimes that wasn't a good decision, and they'd been feeling things generally spooky on the mountain for weeks. There was the ghost of that feeling in the ambient now.

The question was—where had a rider come from, and why come here and not to the rider's own village?

"I can't pin it down," Callie said finally, and Jennie said,

"I'm scared. Rain's scared, too."

"Calm him down," Ridley said, with no sympathy. "Right now. Think of <flowers."> That was what they'd always taught Jennie to do when the spooky feelings came: that was her calm-image, and

<flower> came to mind, a timid and shadowy flower, at the moment, a lost in the dark, <shivering, scared flower.>

"Callie," Ridley said, "tell the marshal what we're picking up. Better put more guards up."

"Bitter night," Callie said. "Awful time to be out."

"Sure don't envy them," Ridley said. Callie didn't argue with the need to get the marshal and didn't argue about who was staying in camp with Jennie while she went through the snow-passages to advise the marshal. Callie just traded him the shotgun for the rifle, as the thing she'd need more if somehow vermin *had* gotten into the passages, as could happen if things went catastrophic tonight. And Jennie, it turned out, had brought the hand-torch from the barracks: light flared as she turned it on and gave it to her mother.

"Clever child," Callie said. "Deserve your ears boxed, is what." Callie left at a fast pace. The light died as Callie disappeared through the shattered passage door.

Shimmer wanted to follow Callie into that passage and did, though she wouldn't get past the barrier that sealed off the village passages from the horses and would have to back out; while close in the company of Slip and Rain, Ridley put his arm around Jennie. The reprimand for taking the emergency light had slid off without a sting: worry about the situation hadn't slid off at all. They hadn't brought up a fool. Jennie knew things were serious, knew they weren't her fault, and worried because things were happening that weren't ordinary or right.

It didn't make *sense* that anyone was out there. Ice wind was what they called storms like this on Rogers Peak. If one got started, you didn't run the risk: you tucked in and kept low until the wind stopped.

This rider—these presences in the storm—hadn't done that.

And in the last of autumn the mountain *had* been carrying frequent disturbance to them, night visions of fire and blood, game on the mountain seeming to run in surges, abundant one day, gone the next, with no ordinary sense to the movements. The seniors had said things like that happened worst of all when it was setting on a bad winter. The wild things sensed the weather coming—so the seniors had said.

And there were stories how when the vermin got to moving in waves, they'd surged right over defenses and right down some miner's burrow. You stopped it fast and drove them back with shotgun blasts, or you went under for sure.

He didn't want to think about that with Jennie and Rain there: any young horse was noisy and spooky enough without encouragement—and in Rain's case, increasingly uncomfortable to have around the den. The colt would be waking the village on his own if Jennie didn't keep him quiet, and it was all but dead certain Rain was the culprit that had initially spooked Shimmer and Slip by picking up a far sending like that.

"Silly lad," he said, and patted Rain's neck, while Slip was standing close by, great fool that he was, sending <fierce nighthorse male,> and at the same time seeking shelter in the human presence.

Rain was, he decided, no small part responsible for the rolling panic that had now sent Callie over to scare hell out of the marshal and his deputies, and, remotely possible, Rain might be the entire reason the autumn had felt as spooky as it had. Rain was weaned this fall, he was coming on puberty this winter, and a young horse in that mood was all ears and all sensation. Rain kept the neighborhood disturbed, and with mating season on them, was having sensations beyond the understanding of an eight-year-old, even if she had seen Slip and Shimmer getting babies.

Slip, who'd have chased a young male out of his territory without hesitation in the Wild, was just, seniorlike in the band, increasingly out of patience with a noisy youngster. That might be all it was, and all that was out there might just be a late-season arrival with nothing really frightening about it—because they had *two* spooky minds to contend with, Jennie as well as the skittish colt. Jennie was worried about <Callie in the passages, dark villageside passages,> which Jennie didn't like, <echoey, thumping-boards, spooky dark passages. Dark, quiet dark.>

"Everything villageside is quiet," Ridley reminded her—because she was trying to listen into that dark where Callie had gone, and Jennie wasn't used to that side of the wall: Jennie had had the noise of horses and human minds around her since before she was born. The relative silence of villageside was scary to her.

"They're deaf over there," Jennie remembered. "But they hear us. Do they hear that horse out there?"

"Probably," he said. "But if they don't, you can bet your mama's going to wake them up. Your mama'll wake the marshal up, first." He felt Jennie shiver. "Cold?"

"A little."

He had her sit on the grain-bin and tuck up her legs in the blanket. Rain came and licked Jennie's face and hair. He couldn't feel the noise from outside so keenly now, maybe because Rain was distracted from it.

Or maybe not. It came and it went, maybe with the attention of a horse out there.

It wasn't a safe feeling. That was one thing he knew.

Chapter V

With the storm-light all around them, and with the snow coming down on a steady wind, the woods took on an illusory sense of peace, a wind-swept, chill peace that bid fair to swallow down the weary—the mountain proving too vast, the snowy night and the wind trying to fold them in—fatally so. What had been traction was getting to be a knee-high barrier to horse and human.

"We've missed the shelter," Carlo said.

"We'll get there."

"I think it's behind us."

"What do you want? Go back and run into that horse?"

"You said it wouldn't follow us!"

"Yeah, well, best guess."

"It can't be this far!"

"So hire another rider!"

"Don't give me an answer like that! What are we going to do?"

"If we've missed it," Danny said, struggling for calm, "—if we *have* missed it, there's another shelter."

" 'There's another!' God, it's hours on! It's getting late! The sun's gone! We could miss the shelter ahead of us, too, Danny! What are we *doing?*"

"We don't know we've missed the first one!"

"There's logging trails that spur off this road. We could be off on one of them!"

"I know. I know about them. There's three. We never bear right into the trees. That's what Tara said. All I can say. Keep walking."

"Dammit," Carlo said. "Dammit."

"Yeah," he said. He ran out of breath for talking. The shadow that was Cloud was pulling ahead of them again, nothing but a grayness in the ambient and a grayness in the softly falling snow.

They'd pull and breathe, now, pull and breathe, Randy on the travois, half-aware, neither of them who were pulling having breath to talk. But that ominous <blood on snow> sending came to them now and again and drove them to greater effort. Danny was sick at his stomach, he'd had a nosebleed, which he only realized because the blood showed up dark on his glove and <dark on the snow,> which confounded itself with the dreadful image chasing them.

We're in trouble, was all Danny could say to himself. It had assumed a rhythm along with the pulling: We're in—real bad—trouble.

"We'd better look for a spot to tuck down," he said to Carlo. "Dig in and stay. We're out of options."

It meant Brionne was going to die for certain. But they were down to Randy's life. And down to their own. There were trees. He had a hatchet.

<Snow. Blood. Gunshot.>

"Damn that thing!" Carlo cried, stumbling to a stop. "I'll shoot it!"

<Stormclouds and pain. Bite and kick.> That was Cloud answering the challenge. Cloud had swung about, also stopped in his tracks, head up, ears flat, nostrils catching the night wind, and Danny dropped the travois and grabbed Cloud by the mane, imaging <Cloud with Danny. Thin and hungry Danny. Danny lying in the snow.> He was scared Cloud was going to take out chasing that sending, and Cloud did drag him a distance through the snow, until weariness had its effect and Cloud came to his senses.

Cloud stood shivering after that. But Cloud knew his rider was beside him at that point, snorted loudly, and listened when Danny imaged <walking uphill.>

Cloud agreed, also wanting <Danny walking,> and Danny let go all but a single handful of his mane and walked past Carlo without a word, because Cloud's state of mind was as precarious as it could possibly be right now.

"Hey!" Carlo's ragged voice came from behind him. It was a moment before Carlo could overtake him, pulling the travois alone to the point where he stopped—Carlo was <mad> and <scared.>

"What are you doing?" Carlo cried. Carlo ran out of strength in that last effort and dropped to his knees.

He didn't know what he was doing. He had Cloud headed in the right direction. That was where his thoughts were. But he took one pole, Carlo hauled at the other, and they pulled in Cloud's track.

From Randy there was nothing but the image of <biscuits. Steaming biscuits piled on a plate.>

Trees were consistently on either side of them, arguing they *had* somehow missed the shelter and, almost indistinguishable from drifts, there were banks of snow-covered undergrowth that argued whatever this track was, it was used enough to keep the brush down. Trucks in this country dragged chain from their undercarriage to maintain the roads clear of brush and keep the ruts from making high centers; this was surely a road of some kind—if it wasn't theirs, if they *had* gotten diverted onto a logging trail, it might lead to a camp, deserted in this season as the miners headed for villages for the winter, or even dug-in miners, fools so crazy for digging they wouldn't leave for the winters.

But there'd be a shack strong enough to sleep in, if they could find it in the blowing snow. If they could just get a place to tuck in, even a deep place in the rocks, then they could wait it out—and hold off the horse that was stalking them.

Only if they could get Cloud into it. Only if they could keep him from challenging that horse. He might win.

He might not.

<Blood on white. Blood and a man's still shape. Gunshot echoing off the mountain. Far, far riders up the road.>

They perceived something else near them, too, something angry and curious that wasn't a horse. Wildlife was disturbed by the intrusion. Wild things were waking from storm-slumber.

Deep, deep trouble, Danny began to say to himself, and in that inattention put his foot in a hole. He went down, and made Carlo fall. For a moment they both lay there, neither with the strength to move.

Then Cloud broke the force of the wind, coming up to shove with his nose at his back, and slowly, shaking at Carlo to move him, Danny began to get up. He'd gotten snow into his cuffs. He tried to get rid of it, got his feet under him somehow.

"Need to rest," Carlo gasped.

"You got a kid freezing faster than you are. His body's thinner. Get up. Now!"

Carlo moved, and got to his knees, and got on his feet.

<Frozen trails of red. Man's glove. Man's arm. Echoes of a rifle shot dying on the mountainside.>

They struggled along what, for they knew, was indeed a logging trail. There wasn't any sense of climbing or descending, no way to tell they weren't walking to some dead-end clearing out across the broad face of Rogers Peak.

<Cloud and Danny,> the image kept coming to him: <us going up the mountain. Snow coming down on Brionne's still face, the curly blond hair. Snow making a mound. Snow in a deep, even sheet.>

<Shut up> didn't work. Cloud didn't understand anything Cloud couldn't picture and silence didn't translate when Cloud was distraught.

<Frozen Danny,> came back to him. <Frozen horse, covered with ice.> Then came: <Horse with tangled mane, sick nighthorse, horse throwing off warning, horse with staring eyes and flat ears.>

Rogue-image.

<Still water,> Danny countered desperately. <Still, warm water. Water with steam rising into the cold . . . >

But that was a trap. It was easy to get to thinking about that and just—not to come back from that image. And anything that faltered, anything that hesitated in the Wild, anything that took a wrong path and broke a leg—it died.

When Men had come down to the world in their ships, horses had been the only thing that had come snuggling up to humans, wicked as they were, being the Beasts that God had sent on the settlers—

And some of them had to take the gift and be damned to save the rest, because the rest without horses, without riders, wouldn't have made it.

You're going to hell, his father had yelled at him.

But what he was doing was *not* wicked. Trying to get these boys to safety was *not* evil.

"Slow down!" he yelled at Cloud, as Cloud began to widen the lead on them, breaking the way through the drifted snow, making a path for them.

But Cloud wouldn't stop. Cloud threatened <bite and kick> and wanted <Danny walking.>

<Bell ringing in the distance, far through the snowy woods.>

Carlo didn't say anything about what Cloud was sending—maybe he heard, maybe he didn't. But he moved as if he had heard, and pulled desperately on his pole—got up without urging when his feet stumbled on the deep snow.

It wasn't just a sending. The sound of a bell came unmistakably, now. Cloud was still breaking the path ahead of them, thinking <warm den> and <nighthorses> and <ham.>

We're going to make it, Danny began to say to himself, half in tears. We're going to make it.

But—

Rider-shelters out in the wilderness didn't have bells, —did they?

God, had he led them not past one shelter—but past *two?*

That was a village gate bell.

Had the junior rider in his blind, stupid desperation—just led them all the way to Evergreen?

The den was not only the safest place to be: it was the only place they could do anything besides stand watch in the guard-stations above the walls—which Callie reported the marshal and five men were doing, now, on the village side of the wall.

And by a stretch of awareness, once the horses caught the notion of the marshal on guard from Callie, the villageside guards were near enough to the den that the horses were vaguely aware of them as a force.

That was useful. That meant there couldn't be alarm over there villageside without them in the camp hearing it.

Better than villageside guns against the Wild, the horses were wary and watching against a sending so moiled and confused. With Slip and Shimmer on guard, nothing harmful would insinuate a sending close enough to make either the guards in the village or them in the rider camp do something stupid, which was generally how you died in the Wild—a gate opened, a latch forgotten. Haste. Confusion. Short-term memory overpowering a human's long-term thought.

Ridley didn't intend to make mistakes here. That was what they all said to each other, including Jennie, but Ridley paced and fretted, and Slip made frequent forays outside to sniff the wind and threatened, until Callie, sitting on a straw bale, said, "Quiet, for God's sake," and Shimmer's irritation came through with it.

"It could very well be miners," Ridley said finally, and leaned against the post by her. "But I don't recognize that horse. Do you?"

"Road drifted shut, maybe," Callie said after a moment—meaning some rider could be coming to them instead of back to his own village. A road drifted beyond the strength of a single horse to clear it—that was one explanation, and a rider would indeed go to the nearest village. Maybe a hunting party had gotten caught out and couldn't make it back to Mornay village, which was nearest to them down the road—the land-sense was too diffuse yet to pin the direction down.

Possible too, if somebody had been in longer-lasting trouble out there, a bad storm could be exactly when a party dug in might make their break and run for the nearest village, hoping the predators would stay put in dens. It would be a terrible risk. But he'd heard of miners taking that measure without a rider.

Except—this party had a horse.

He didn't want to think about dire possibilities in too specific images: the night was chancy enough and they had a scared and sleepy kid on their hands.

"They're coming in," Callie muttered. "It's getting stronger the last while."

"Mama?" Jennie said, and stirred awake in a frightened jerk.

"Hush." Callie stroked Jennie's hair. "Nothing's happening."

"I had a bad dream," Jennie said, and Rain came close and nosed at her. Jennie reached out and patted him, and tucked down again where it was warm.

They couldn't lie to Jennie. They couldn't hold her out of what was happening or protect her from it—eight years old, and there was so very little time in which to learn all she had to know to survive—including when it was time to be scared, or angry, or how to keep herself in check to hold onto the horses and not let them spook, because in Shimmer's and Slip's reckonings, let alone in Rain's, Jennie was all of a sudden and in this crisis a serious presence—when she wasn't drifting off asleep.

Just last fall she'd still been <baby,> and even lately Shimmer still protected her that way; but Shimmer was pushing Jennie away tonight the way Shimmer shoved Rain aside, who was her last, now-grown foal.

Young horse. No brakes on his sensing things. No self-protection. He belonged with a herd, not in a winter den with a pregnant mare, a stallion in rut, and a kid herself years from puberty in close mental contact with a horse that was in the throes of it. He *didn't* like it under ordinary circumstances.

But he could no longer blame Rain for the sending out there. It was real, and Callie was right, it was coming in: they could all feel the sense of <presence in the storm, human and horse> getting closer by the passing minute.

And it was from the direction of the Climb, not from the direction of Mornay—that was increasingly sure in the sending the nearer it came. If it was a rider from anywhere on the High Loop, they'd have had to have ridden *past* Evergreen to get to that side of the village.

"Up the Climb," Callie said faintly. "Why on earth?"

So Callie heard it the same way, and became certain of the direction at the same moment he did.

The rider with that horse had to be crazy, Ridley thought. Shimmer was <spooked.> Slip was <spooked and angry.>

And though right and justice said that once they were reasonably sure they were hearing any rider they ought by all means to beacon him in from such a storm, the skittery character of the sending still made Ridley reluctant to reach out to it.

Maybe it was just Rain's young nerves. Maybe it was the distance over which they were picking things up, impressions maybe carried by wild creatures snugged down in their dens, things of little brains and little accuracy about an image.

But knowing for certain enough that it *was* another rider: <Riders and shelter here,> he imaged out into the dark, laying himself open to whatever danger might lie in a sending coming back at them. <Camp walls,> he promised that presence. <Food and warmth.>

Callie made up her mind, too. She joined him, with, <Riders here. Fire and water boiling> and said, "I'll go tell the marshal there's strangers coming."

Plainer and plainer to human ears, the ringing of a storm-driven bell, and the delirious dream of <hot water and shelter.> Danny struggled to keep his feet and keep moving; but even believing safety was in front of them, Carlo was fast failing him, losing not the will but the strength to fight his body upright against the wind. Carlo might fall and freeze in all but sight and hail of shelter.

<Leaving Brionne behind,> Danny began to think. But that meant <leaving Randy> because neither of them could carry him, and it meant <Carlo too weak to shoot,> if he left Carlo to defend his brother and sister from vermin and went ahead for help.

He held to Cloud's mane in the deep snow, gripping the travois pole with a right hand that had lost all feeling. His feet—he didn't even know.

<Rider in the snow,> he sent for all he was worth, and drove all his efforts toward that bell that rang louder and louder—too tired himself to pull the travois alone, unable to go faster than Carlo could go.

A beautiful image began to come clearer and clearer to him: <warm den, other riders, man, woman, child shoveling the rider gate clear of snow, horse helping dig.>

There were <bunks, supper, warm mash.> They promised the preacher's Heaven after their day and night of hell, and to reach it, Danny began to believe he'd have to stand still and try to beacon help to them. Breath came raw and cold. Feet faltered repeatedly.

Then out of the bitter cold and the swirling snow—a dark barrier loomed up among the evergreens like a wall across the world, logs and snow, and <life and warmth> waiting for them behind it.

Carlo saw it, too. Cloud did, and all but pulled them through a succession of drifts by the grip Danny had on his mane.

<Randy warm by the fire,> he was picking up from Carlo. <Randy drinking hot tea, Brionne by the fire—>

There wasn't anything of <Carlo by the fire.> But there hadn't been enough of <Carlo> all up the mountain, in Danny's reckoning. It was everything for Randy. Everything for Brionne and not damn well enough of self-preservation.

"Listen to me." Danny struggled to have a voice at all as, letting Cloud go, he struggled toward paradise and the gate in that solid wall. He said it as fiercely as he could, before thoughts scattered again toward safety and comfort, and before he lost his chance, with distance, to put his own pain between them and eavesdroppers: "Listen to me. You shut it down, Carlo. You shut it down entirely—everything that happened—and you shut Randy down. They're riders. They'll kill us as soon as look at us if you go acting crazy in a winter camp. Same way Tara threw us out. So you shut up."

"We're *here,*" Carlo said, seeming bewildered. "We made it to the shelter."

"We're not in a damn *shelter*. This is the *village*, do you understand me? We haven't got any place we can put your sister but in the rider camp till the camp boss passes on us and we can't let her wake up, you understand me?"

"Yeah," Carlo said faintly. "Yeah. I do."

"You let me do the talking and you keep her as far away from the horses as you can get. You don't think about anything down the mountain. You don't *think* about it till you're over villageside. Think about <clouds.> Think about water. <Still water.> Keep Randy quiet. Got it?"

He wasn't sure Carlo understood everything Carlo said he did. He'd intended—getting to the shelter—having time to figure out a course of next action in that top-of-the-ridge cabin they'd missed. He'd had in mind a slower, more reasoned approach to the villages up here.

And they were *here.*

He kept his mind as blank of further guesses as he could manage, set the calm image in Carlo's mind, and in Randy's, in such consciousness as he felt there:<brown, smooth stones, running water, peaceful summer leaves. . . . cabin insides. Tables. Food. Fire.>

"The gate's opening!" Carlo said.

<Three horses,> Danny gathered in the ambient, information coming to him freely and abundantly now that he entered the close vicinity of other horses. <Two senior, one young male. Pregnant mare. Man and woman. Kid.>

Information was pouring at him now, as they met the muffled figures in the storm-glow, as three wary horses came out to stand by their riders. The seniors of the set were understandably protective and suspicious, wanting the kid <back,> and the horses were on guard, hearing, he knew, the spook-voice that had chased them, relayed from every creature denned-up tonight.

<"Loose horse back there,"> Danny said, first off—they must have caught their fear and desperate urgency, and that wild, troubled sending that chased them.

But he wasn't sure then at what point they'd met or when the man had gotten hold of his arm or when he'd let go the travois in favor of the woman taking it.

They were inside the rider camp, that was all that was clear to him, attached to a village that had to be Evergreen itself.

<Dead rider, horse nearby, blood on snow.> Danny didn't know whether it was his own thought or Carlo's or a sending out of the dark—and after that just saw a confusion of <branches. Snow. Road they'd traveled.>

Then Carlo was overwhelming the ambient with <dark village streets> and <Brionne and Randy in the furs> as they lugged the travois along the path between the horse-den and the camp wall. All through the ambient then, fierce and strong in the milling-about of horses, came <cold nighthorse, hungry nighthorse,> and <male horse, here> and <pregnant nighthorse,> and <fight, kick> as they came.

Danny said, being all but held on his feet, "Behave, Cloud, dammit," in the thread of a voice he had left, and managed somehow to keep the lid on trouble. He made shift to veer off toward Cloud, but he wasn't doing at all well at keeping his feet on his own. He persistently got the image of a man and a woman and a kid as the only riders there were, several fewer than he'd have expected and with every right to be skittish at them splitting up, one of them wanting the den, the other wanting the barracks. . . .

But for a giddy moment he asked himself if he'd really made it or whether he wasn't after all hallucinating, not safe inside the wooden walls of a rider haven but lying back there in the snow somewhere.

Didn't know how they'd done it. Couldn't believe yet it was Evergreen.

He didn't know how they'd come this far—except they'd been walking through trees—except, as the scale of things he'd expanded shrank again, it had been that very turn—that turn he thought he'd mistaken—

God, they must right then have been at the top of the road. They'd been right *on* the cabin they were looking for. That wasn't the turn. It was the truck park. Where the cabin had been. His estimate of time and distance *hadn't* been off.

God help a fool. He'd *been* there, and walked past shelter in the whiteout.

"You all right?" The man had his arm, helping him walk.

"Yeah."

But he kept in mind his own warning to Carlo, and on a night like this, with strangers out of a storm when no reasonable people would be out and about, he didn't want to act like a spook. He just wanted <going to den,> wanted <rub-down for Cloud, ham for Cloud> and he imaged <Brionne and Randy in bundle of furs,> in case the riders hadn't realized from Carlo's mind that there were two more lives in their company than it seemed. Cloud's welfare was absolutely foremost for him now. And he had to stay upright long enough to do that.

"I can take care of your horse," the man said. "There's mash cooked. We heard you coming. How are your feet?"

"No worse than the last hour," he said. "And my horse got me here. I'll see to him." He didn't want to think about his feet. He might be crippled for life. Bound to camp. Cattle-sentry. He couldn't think of worse he could do to Cloud, including them freezing to death. "There's a shotgun. Take it and the shells. All I can pay you. Promised ham to my horse. Got to pay him off."

"This way." The man didn't argue with him or bargain for shelter. He was aware of <male horse walking with them,> knew the horse belonged to the man, and he knew the <female horse> and another <male> were ambling off instead toward the rider barracks where Carlo was going, where the woman and the kid were going, as protective of them as the stallion was of the man.

The stillness of the air, then, the dark inside the den, the mere cessation of the wind itself were like warmth as they came inside the safe, insulated stalls. It left him breathless and blind except for Cloud's senses, lingeringly deaf from the wind, except for Cloud's hearing, mentally lost, except for Cloud's presence and Cloud's sense of <evergreen smell. Evergreen boughs.> They must, Danny thought giddily, use it like straw up here where straw didn't grow. That was a nice touch. He liked that.

And he was wandering, and staggering.

He knew when Cloud found a water pail that wasn't frozen. He knew that Cloud drank, and then they both were blinded when the rider watching over them cut on an electric torch. In that beam of light he saw details of a smallish den, snug and warm, stalls and a sheltered heap of meadow hay that had never grown on this height: had to have been trucked up here. Had to cost as much as flour. But it meant life to the villages.

And when the rider set that light in a bracket aimed at the roof and stopped blinding him, he saw a village rider muffled up in a rider's fringed leather coat and woolen scarf and broad-brimmed hat tied down against the wind. Could have been a mirror of him.

"Name's Ridley," the man said. "Callie, my partner, she's got your partners."

"Village kids," he corrected that impression. "Tarmin village." On that, he ran out of voice. He needed water. He pulled his gloves off fingers that had no feeling, dipped his hands into water that at least was above freezing, and that felt hot—and drank what Cloud had drunk, a sip or two, and a splash over his face to warm it.

But even that was too much. He thought for a moment he'd throw it up again, somewhere between the pain and the load on his stomach. He leaned on a stall post, just breathing until the waves of nausea passed.

Meanwhile the rider called Ridley had gotten warming-blankets and thrown them over Cloud, and at that he had to move, because he wouldn't have anybody else taking care of Cloud. He thanked Ridley in his shred of a voice, took up the job himself, and rubbed and rubbed Cloud's cold body and colder legs to get the blood moving.

The effort warmed both of them, set him panting and coughing, made his nose bleed and made him sick at his stomach. He'd been in such misery he hadn't felt the altitude headache in the last push toward that faint sound of a bell, but now it came back, so blindingly acute he shut his eyes as he worked. Ridley gave him salve to use, and he rubbed it down Cloud's legs and checked Cloud's feet—Ridley helped in that, which was good, because Ridley's fingers could feel the spots between the hooves and his still couldn't.

"Looks pretty good for where he's been," Ridley said after he'd inspected all four sets of hooves. "Tarmin rider, are you?"

He didn't want to talk details. Not tonight. He was sniffing back blood that otherwise dripped from his nose. "Kids are. I'm from Shamesey." He rubbed salve vigorously into Cloud's rear right pastern and down over the tri-fold hoof, which Cloud obligingly lifted and let him tuck against his knee. "Long story. Tell you inside." Working upside down made him cough, threatened him with losing all the water he'd swallowed, and the blood was drowning him.

Cloud on the other hand was faring much better. Cloud sank down after that treatment, <cold nighthorse belly on cold nighthorse legs,> seeking warmth on the evergreen boughs that were the flooring. Cloud was feeling much better and very glad to have blankets thrown over him, then. Danny swiped a salved, horsey back of his hand across his nose and made a last assault with the salve at Cloud's neck, where he could get warmth to the big artery, with the warming salve under Cloud's mane and onto Cloud's throat, which had to be as raw and dry as his.

Then from somewhere out of the dark came the girl-kid lugging a bucket too heavy for her—a heavy bucket that steamed and smelled, such as his and Cloud's altitude-ravaged sense of smell could detect, of warm mash. Cloud gave a snort, interested, as the other horses were interested, having had one supper—but, being horses, always willing to eat. Ridley took the bucket and poured a taste into the common trough before he brought the rest to Cloud, who hadn't gotten up. Ridley set the bucket in front of him.

Cloud sucked up a mouthful of warm mash, and on the strength of that, found it worthwhile to get to his feet and go head-down in the bucket—maybe not to eat much: Cloud wasn't a fool, among a canny, self-preserving kind. But certainly Cloud meant to get his promised reward.

That meant that Cloud's rider could go to the warm barracks and the fireside, and Danny started toward the door by which he'd come in, back into the snow—but the Evergreen rider pointed with the beam of the electric torch toward a second doorway, one framed by shattered boards.

Danny didn't ask. Horses were horses, and boards suffered when the night was full of alarms. He scooped up a handful of snow blown in from the outside door and pressed the icy handful against the bridge of his nose before he went back to that door, through which Ridley and the kid led him into a night-black wooden tunnel.

"Where did you come from?" the little girl wanted to know, looking back as she walked ahead of them in their little sphere of light; but Ridley said sternly, as he shone the light down the passage: "Get on to the barracks, Jennie-cub. Leave the man alone. He's got a nosebleed."

Man. *Man*, the senior rider said. People down in Shamesey certainly hadn't called him that. He'd been struggling all during the trip for Dan instead of Danny.

And a village rider saw him as a man, an equal, worth respect just for living to get up this mountain.

That was worth the hike up here.

Jennie-cub hadn't gone. She looked back this time upside down, or at least with her head tilted way back as she walked ahead of them. "I had a nosebleed once. What's your horse's name? Mine's name is Rain."

"Rain isn't your horse," Ridley said. "You wait for Shimmer's foal, miss. —Get to the barracks and open that door before I tan your backside for good and all."

Young Jennie went ahead of them. Light and shadows ran on either side of the little girl, who became a shadow as she skipped ahead of them down a course grown dizzier and dizzier. The walls seemed closer as they went and the air grew more still and dank, smelling of old wood and wet stone and earth.

Couldn't feel his feet. Couldn't see up from down in the shadows. He was passing out of Cloud's range and his sense of orientation was going.

He put out a hand along the wooden wall, seeking balance, thinking, I'm going to fall—about the time they overtook Jennie, who pulled open a door on blinding light.

Warm air met them. He dumped his handful of bloody snow and walked in blind, with Ridley behind him, caught a lungful of the heat inside, and felt himself going as his knees had just turned to jelly.

Strong arms caught him around the ribs and helped him toward the fire and the light. Carlo and Randy were sitting on the floor against the wall.

Brionne was lying there too, unbundled from the travois, but still folded in her nest of furs.

Ridley let him down. He sat against the fireside stones, that being all that was going to hold him up. He had just enough strength to take off his hat and scarf, and a moment later to struggle out of his coat and a couple of sweaters before he smothered. He told himself he wasn't going to pass out. Wasn't going to make a spectacle.

Ridley came and checked his hands in the bright lamplight.

"Not as bad as could be," Ridley pronounced his fingers. "A little burn. But not real bad." Then Ridley unlaced his boots for him and carefully pulled them off. He wasn't sure he really wanted to know; but they were his feet, he'd no choice, and it wasn't would-happen, it was already had-happened, whatever the verdict was going to be as the socks came off, one layer after another.

"Mmn," Ridley said. "Going to lose a little skin. —Feel that?"

"Yeah." It felt as if Ridley drew blood. Then Ridley stripped the other foot. He felt those toes, too. It hurt so much tears began running down his face. His ankles hurt. His knees hurt. There wasn't any part of him that didn't hurt, and Carlo and Randy didn't look any better off.

"Wasn't sure for a long time that you were human," the woman said, squatting down near him. "Lot of spookiness out there tonight. Lot of spookiness the last week or so. You know anything about it?"

"Yeah." His gut knotted up. He started thinking frantically what he could say. "But get these kids to the village first."

"You go," Ridley said (he thought) to Callie, and a second later said, "Jennie can go with you. It's all right."

The woman for her part wasn't enthusiastic about leaving Ridley alone, Danny decided, small threat that he and Carlo were. Carlo looked to be fading out, Randy was asleep, and Brionne—Brionne was a bundle of furs the other side of the fire.

They'd gotten her here.

And hadn't they done something good in that? Even heroic?

Even if he had been stupid and missed not just one shelter but both of them in the storm?

And as for himself, at the definite end of his stupid years, his do-anything, dare-anything childhood, and grown older and wiser all in one disastrous climb—he fingered his nose and his ears, wondering if they were frostbitten and whether he'd be scarred for life from this adventure, or whether he could just swear to God he'd learned and didn't need to do anything this stupid again.

The woman put on a coat and prepared to leave as Ridley pressed a warm teacup into his hands, wrapped in a cloth. That was, the pain in his hands told him, a very, very good idea.

Meanwhile the little girl—Jennie—came near, leaned over and asked, "What's your horse's name?"

"Cloud," he said, grateful for such simple, answerable questions. "My name's Dan Fisher. I'm from Shamesey."

"From Shamesey!"

He was aware her father was listening. And her mother. His voice was down to a hoarse thread. "Yeah."

"What brought you to the mountain?" Ridley asked, with clear suspicion, and the woman hesitated in leaving.

"Friend of mine needed help."

Ridley went to the cabinet and took out a bottle. It was spirits. Ridley came and poured a generous dollop into Danny's tea. And he went over and poured some for Carlo, too, who was sitting up and looking dazed, but likewise lifting up a cup.

"And what brought you all the way up here?" Ridley asked, and Carlo blurted out,

"Because there's nothing left down there. Tarmin's gone."

You didn't need the horses to feel the shock in their minds: fear, disbelief, that Tarmin, the biggest village on the mountain, their main depot for shipments going or coming . . . didn't exist anymore.

"Tarmin *is* gone," Danny said, to draw all the questions back to him and not to Carlo. He sipped the fortified tea to gain time for a breath and a second thought. The woman stood in her jacket, and Jennie, likewise dressed for the cold, came and huddled against her legs.

"What's he saying? What happened, mama?"

"So what *is* the story?" Ridley asked him, dead calm, as controlled as a rider needed to be. The horses couldn't hear them here. At least, they shouldn't be able to.

And he needn't tell even half of it. He'd given his caution, in asking that the kids leave the camp. They hadn't. He said only, "Somebody opened a gate. I don't want to give the details—don't know the range from your den—"

"Is your horse all right?" Ridley asked. The senior rider here, boss-man in this camp, had an absolute right to ask that question. He had a kid lying on his hearth stiff and gone somewhere she couldn't get back from. He had a strange horse in the den with their horses. He had a village locked in for the winter, with all its people. He had a daughter as well as a partner to protect.

And if they themselves hadn't been hallucinating, he had a horse out there in the woods whose distress had waked the wild things in their burrows and relayed its sending God knew how far, disturbing the mountain a second time in less than a month.

"We weren't there when it happened," Danny said, the horse-and-rider we, but he wouldn't elaborate more than he had to, either—didn't quite lie, just leaned very heavily on Ridley's assurance the horses in the den were beyond their ordinary range of picking up human beings.

Which could change if one horse picked up a suspicion of human distress in the rider barracks—and they had a young horse out there, an unridden horse of their own, at a stage notorious for being loud and hearing even humans unnaturally far.

So he concentrated entirely on the cup in his hands and sipped it this time not to keep his voice from cracking, but to save his mind from wobbling from the very narrow path of information he had to hold.

"I came in after the fact. These three—they're all that lived through it. They're brothers and sister. We've been trying not to think of it near the horses. Couldn't do anything for the girl down there. She's caught in it, deeper and deeper. She used to react to things. She doesn't now. I understand there's supposed to be a doctor in the village."

The woman pressed Jennie against her legs. Danny found his hands shaking so he burned himself as the tea slopped over. He didn't look at their faces. He didn't want to. A mind that wasn't right wasn't ever anything to bring near the horses.

A mind that wasn't right wasn't anything to leave within range of *anything* of the Wild. And Brionne's mind, above all else that was wrong with her, wasn't right. They were senior riders. They had to recognize the kind of shock she was in and know that she was dangerous. He'd meant to be out in a shelter tonight—come to Evergreen on a clear, quiet day with no emergency in the situation. But that *wasn't* what had happened. Things were done—choices were made around a set of facts that involved several lives, facts he didn't want to let loose just for the asking—because the truth could cause a panic that itself could get people killed.

"Was it her," Ridley asked, "making that spook-feeling out there?"

No, he thought: direction and location had been in the sending: that was what had made it so damn real. It had convinced Cloud.

"No," he said aloud. "I'm pretty sure it was behind us. A horse. Rider's died. With the sister's condition—I didn't want to stay where it was."

"Go get the marshal," Ridley said, meaning, Danny thought, get the little kid out of here and get Brionne the *hell* out of reach of the horses. The woman took the kid and went out the door to the passageway they'd used—a second and third passage had gone off from there, he remembered them in the light from the door.

Ridley went meanwhile and warmed Carlo's cup with tea from the pot. Randy was sleeping like the dead, on his stomach, his hand up near his face, head on his arm—he didn't wake for anything. Poor kid, Danny thought, and *hoped* there was better luck for the brothers. They'd earned it.

Ridley came and poured tea into his cup. And in that closeness and the quiet of the ambient Danny took the chance. "There's more to it than I've said. *We're* all right. But get the girl out of here fairly soon."

"What have you brought us?" Ridley asked sharply, and Danny ducked his head to cough—he'd been wanting to since he tipped his head back, and he didn't want to look Ridley in the eyes.

"Dammit." Ridley dropped down on his haunches to meet him eye to eye in that privacy of the fire-crackle and the wind outside; and the ambient still stayed quiet and numb as he finished his coughing fit with a swallow of tea that still had spirits in it. "What's going on down there?" Ridley asked. "What's a *Shamesey* rider doing here, for God's sake? What's the real story?"

"Rescuing a friend," Danny repeated. He heard the indignation in Ridley's voice. He knew he deserved it. "It's a long story. Get the kids safe and I'll talk." He took another sip of the spirit-laced tea, saw Carlo staring into his cup as if it held answers, and saw Randy sleeping.

Brionne didn't change. Thank God. He was all but counting the minutes until they could bring someone in and get Brionne out of the camp. And very rapidly now the very last reserve of strength was running out of him. He sipped the tea and his hands began to shake.

Feeling was coming back to his feet. They hurt. His hands did. His face did.

"The whole damn season's felt bad," Ridley said in a more moderate tone. It wasn't like a <quiet water> statement. It was a peace offering he didn't deserve, from a man he deserved worse of, in a situation he couldn't, right now, discuss. This was, Danny thought, a good-hearted and forgiving man. A man more reasonable than he deserved to have to deal with—he hadn't *wanted* to go all the way to Evergreen. But he had. And now he had to deal with the consequences.

"Yeah." Agreement seemed safest, agreement with everything the local riders said at least until he could use clear-headed judgement.

Meanwhile Carlo had edged over to try to see to his brother, lifting the blanket they'd wrapped him in to look at his feet, and that movement was a distraction for the conversation. "How is he?" he asked Carlo across the intervening space.

"I don't know." Carlo let the blanket down. Randy didn't stir through any of it, and Carlo made a fast swipe at his eyes. Carlo's hand was shaking.

Ridley got up and squatted down again to take a look at Randy's hands and feet and ears. He looked at Carlo's, too, while he was at it.

"Better than yours," Ridley said. "Work your fingers. Fist."

Carlo tried. Ridley made a doubtful expression. "Horse medicine," Ridley said, and got a small grimy pot off the shelf and squatted down and rubbed salve into Carlo's hands. "Hands and feet. You take the pot with you, son. It's cheap. We've got buckets of it for the horses. Use it. Marshal's going to find a place for you. You think you need a doctor?"

"No." Carlo shook his head fast, and Danny could read his mind without Cloud's help: Carlo didn't want to be under the same roof with his sister. Didn't want Randy there, either. "Smith," Carlo said. "Our folks—" His voice faded and came back again. "They were the smiths down in Tarmin. Need—need to find work if we can."

"Ours might take you on." Ridley maintained a tight reserve. "But those hands aren't going to be fit for smith-work for a while." He patted Carlo gently on the leg and got up to pace the floor—another not too difficult guess, that Ridley was aching for Callie to get back safely with the marshal and a means to get his problem out of the camp.

Danny drank his tea and kept his mouth shut, feeling even with the pain in his feet and hands and ears that he could pass out where he was sitting—but he held on: if something happened, he wanted to be awake. He wanted to know what disposition village authorities would make of the boys and Brionne, who came under village law.

He didn't. He was in Evergreen, looking at the authority that governed the rider camp, and what Ridley said in these walls had to be law—including the possibility that Ridley would tell him get out of the village and go somewhere else, weather or no weather. A camp boss always had that authority, and he had to respect it.

But, God, he didn't know where he or Cloud would get the strength to go on.

Chapter

— VI —

Came, in due course, a thumping in the passage leading to the back door. The door opened and Callie—still with young Jennie, which Danny didn't expect—came in ahead of a big burly man and three other village types in heavy coats.

That would be the marshal and his deputies, he supposed, the law on the other side of the wall—the dividing wall that existed here the same as it existed in substance and in fact in every town and village in the world, dividing the wicked rider camps from the godfearing and righteous townsmen—who couldn't live without them. He didn't *trust* town authorities. On principle of that wall of Theirs and Ours and on principle of his days as a bad boy of Shamesey streets—granting his father was absolutely right to have hit him harder than the deputy had—he had several misgivings about turning Carlo and Randy over to the law, and far more about answering questions.

"These the young folk?" the oldest of the men asked, as his companions shut the door and stopped the gale from the passageway. "This the young lady?" He had thick gloves on, but he didn't offer his hand, just took off his hat—he had thinning white hair—while Ridley went through the course of introductions identifying village marshal Eli Peterson, his deputies Jeff Burani and José Hartley, and, not a deputy, preacher John Quarles—the hat should have told him.

On the other side, Ridley named Carlo and Randy Goss and their sister Brionne.

Then on an apparent afterthought, as riders knew they were always afterthoughts to townsmen of any stamp, "This is the rider that got them through. Name's Dan Fisher."

"One hell of a job," the marshal said. Danny decided he liked the man. And was almost moved to get up and shake the man's hand. "Damn," the marshal said then, "you're half a kid yourself." Or maybe not, Danny thought, and stayed where he was, leaning back against the warm stones. His hand hurt too much, anyway.

"You're saying Tarmin's gone?" another man asked, him in the black hat, Reverend Quarles.

Danny nodded soberly, with a quiet in the room so deep there was just the fire-sound and the howl of the wind across the roof.

"Lord have mercy," was the preacher's reaction, that and a shake of his head.

"Don't want to talk here," Danny said. His voice had deepened with hoarseness, and he was having to force it as was. But it made him sound older. "Tomorrow. I'll come over villageside. Tell you all you want to know."

"The Lord was surely with these boys," the preacher said.

Danny remarked to himself that of course the man carefully didn't say that God could ever possibly be with a rider—just with the village-bred Goss kids. But he was a polite preacher. He'd come into a rider barracks without fuss and didn't outright insult the roof he was under.

And maybe it was true that God had gotten the Goss boys up the mountain and just had to do it with the help of a damned-to-hell rider because, thanks to original sin, that was the way God regularly did things in the world beyond town walls. Or something like that.

Truth, he'd been halfway religious before he became a rider. He was still trying to figure the ins and outs of the preachers' religion as it applied to him now that he'd heard the Beast and damned himself—because right and wrong just didn't work out with neat edges any more when you saw beyond the neighborhood you grew up in, and from what he saw on the outside looking in, it never really had. Not even *in* the old neighborhood, once you started seeing the rights and the wrongs you'd learned to ignore.

"Nothing left down there?" the second deputy asked—not able to believe the extent of the disaster down there, Danny thought, and didn't blame him.

"Just the three got out," Danny said, "them and one Tarmin rider. One border rider camped with her, in the last shelter between first-stage and Tarmin. The two of them'll come up here, come spring. I—I brought *them* up." He didn't want to go into question and answer. He wanted Brionne away from the horses, behind the solid division of a village wall. "The girl needs a doctor, pretty quick."

"We'll see to it," the marshal said. "Carlo, can you walk, son?"

Sounded like a decent man. *Sounded* kind. He approved, then.

"Yeah," Carlo said. "Randy can't."

"Might put 'em with Van," Ridley suggested. "If he'll take 'em. Under threat of God he might. They're the smith's kids, from down in Tarmin. Van *needs* competition, doesn't he?"

"We'll talk to him," the marshal said.

"We'll lay the fear of the Lord on him," the preacher added.

Carlo was meanwhile trying to pull his socks and boots back onto sore and swollen feet—his boots laced with cord, and he had a chance of making it in fairly short order. Randy didn't even wake up.

"You want a tea and a shot?" Callie asked the official delegation.

"Thank you, no," the marshal said. "Better we get these kids settled. This the girl?" The marshal turned back the furs.

There followed that small silence that Brionne's pretty, doll-like face could well engender.

"Are her eyes affected?"

"She won't shut them without the bandage," Danny muttered, tucked down in his spot. "She's been like that. Beast-struck." That was what the town preachers called it if someone went out like that and wouldn't come back. It happened, legendarily, to townfolk who either got stranded out in an area with beasts, or who, in the safety of town, had started hearing them. *He'd* never known a case but this one. Legendarily, it happened to the innocent faced with the beast-mind. Practically—it happened to truckers and such that got caught out and survived. So he'd heard. Most didn't survive.

He watched the preacher sign God's mercy over her. But they were finally leaving. With Carlo managing to lever himself up by way of the wall behind him and to carry himself; the marshal's deputies picked up Randy.

The marshal himself picked up Brionne, furs and all, like a father carrying a baby.

She was thirteen. She was blond. Blue-eyed. Even with her hair tangled and the scratches on her arms she looked like a saint in a painting.

Danny tried not to pay attention to any of it after that, just praying to God for them to get her the other side of that wall with nothing whatsoever happening while they were carrying her like that. Carlo asked for Randy's boots and socks, and Danny just shut his eyes and ducked his head, wishing them to get moving, telling himself there wasn't any good saying good-bye to Carlo and Randy—he'd be here all winter if Ridley didn't order him out into the snow, and they weren't his business now. He wasn't in their acceptable social class, and once the desperation wore off he didn't expect Carlo or Randy to have much more than a polite word for him when and if they next met.

The door shut.

So he didn't have to be responsible for them anymore. He'd meet Guil and Tara up here when the thaw came—whenever a thaw came to the High Loop, which was probably well toward summer in the lowlands. He'd do the job they'd hired him for and then he'd go down to Shamesey and let his family know he was alive.

And—give it about an hour into Sunday dinner before his father started preaching at him about hell and his horse and he wanted out of there.

In that light, maybe stuck on a mountaintop for several months wasn't so bad.

But he missed his father anyway. He thought now it wouldn't matter if his father yelled at him. He'd had guns pointed at him—which sort of put his father's well-meant yelling in perspective. He missed his younger brother Denis. He even missed his other brother, Sam, and that was how lonesome he was.

Definitely he missed his mother. He'd like one of her suppers right now.

He'd like her making tea (mama'd never, ever put spirits in it, though) and stirring up biscuits and bringing him his supper in his bed with the flowered quilt and the dingy plaster and the cracks, three of them, that had used to run across the ceiling. He could really appreciate the old apartment tonight.

The cracks were fixed now. The place didn't look like the home he always remembered when he was far absent from it.

But that was fine. His family did right well on the money a rider son gave them. As long as they didn't exactly take him back to their bosom God wouldn't damn them for dealing with him and their neighbors would go on associating with them.

He believed, well, a mishmash of things that didn't fit. But there wasn't anything he could do about being what he was, not since the night he'd started hearing Cloud in his dreams, and the day he'd gone down to the rider camp to ask the riders to do something about the wild horse that (not at all his fault, of course) he was hearing night after night while the Shamesey gate-guards were shooting at it—and not having a bit of luck: a threatened horse was real good at imaging he was where he wasn't.

A horse was good at snagging a fool, too. Helluva lot of chance he'd had. Cloud had come looking for human company and he was what answered. He'd been—

—happy. *Happy,* dammit, since that day. Most times.

All the attractive commotion was gone, now. Young Jennie was running out of energy—whining at her mother.

He thought then—he thought—he really didn't feel too energetic, himself, and that the room was getting much too hot. He was getting a little sick at his stomach, to go with the blinding headache that had never yet left him. So he thought he'd get up from where he was sitting and see if he could get an answer out of Ridley, whether he could sleep here the night—that was all he was interested in right now, a place to lie down.

He drew his bare feet up, braced a hand on the fireplace rock, got up—

Felt his center of balance off and went down backward, stupid thing to do. He knew he was going to hit his head on the fireplace.

And did. Hard.

Embarrassing move. He was blind for an instant, and then knew he'd fallen so his neck was bent forward and his legs were tucked and sort of crossed, so not only had he added to the headache, it wasn't easy to find anything with his hands to help him up again—just—

couldn't find up from down. He heard the to-do he'd made in the room as he set a hand on the hearth stones, trying to figure out the position he'd gotten into.

Strong hands pulled him away from the fire before he put his hand quite in it. That had to be Ridley, who hauled him up onto his knees and got him on his feet.

"Is he hurt?" the kid asked, all concerned, and the woman said they'd better put him to bed.

"Is he going to die?" little girl sounded worried. Or excited. But Ridley said,

"He'll be all right. Out of the way. Out of the way!"

Ridley provided balance. All he had to do was get up and sort out his right foot from his left, the way he'd done on the mountainside, just one step after another, all the way to what he hoped was a clean and empty bed.

Chapter

— VII —

Darcy Schaffer didn't know how long she'd heard the wind. The heavy storm shutters were locked tight on the windows, and didn't admit but a hint of light or dark—shutters that could keep out a blizzard or an intruder, or the world in general.

She was heating water for breakfast tea when she heard that distant kind of thump in the snow-passage that meant someone was running around at *this* hour of the morning—before dawn—and if it was those damned teenaged Durant kids again, out and annoying the neighbors before their parents were awake, she was going to call the marshal and let *him* talk to their parents.

But it was measured, heavier steps she began to discern headed for the passageway and directly for her door, and more than one of them. Her heart unwillingly picked up the sense of panic she felt when, first, she was sure someone was going to call at her door, and second, that someone had come with a cogent need for her to deal with them. She didn't *want* to deal with the outside. She dealt with it only on emergencies—and that was when they came to her, someone with a pain or a hurt that sweet oil from the grocer wouldn't cure. She *was* Evergreen's only doctor.

Well, dammit, she thought, wiped her hands and left the kettle on to boil as she walked down the three steps from the kitchen that led to the snow-door. She reached the door from her side exactly at the moment the visitors knocked on it and the preacher's voice called out, "Darcy, it's John, open up!"

John Quarles and at least one other set of footsteps in a hurry. Definitely an emergency—and John didn't usually come unless it was serious. She lifted the bar, shot the bolt back and opened the door wide.

She was, being the village doctor, prepared for blood and disaster of every kind. John's involvement usually meant somebody was dying or damned close to it—and she saw marshal Peterson and deputy Jeff Burani further back in the dark passage, the marshal carrying a fur-wrapped body.

John was saying, "Darcy, there's a case—"

But she wasn't just seeing the marshal. She was seeing her daughter Faye in the marshal's arms, wrapped in those furs. It was Then. It was That Day, the preacher was at the door, and Eli Peterson and his deputy were coming toward her down the passage, bringing Faye, who was dead; and soon then Mark was . . .

. . . dead.

But they were both in the mountain, where the village buried its dead. That Day was sealed away and she couldn't relive it, couldn't say, to Faye, No, you can't go. . . .

"Darcy." The preacher had her arm, trying to move her back from the door and its cold draft. The teakettle on the stove reached a boil and screamed a steady, maddening note.

Distracted, she gave ground and let them in: marshal Peterson, Jeff Burani, preacher John Quarles, and a hurt kid—whose kid, she wasn't sure, and her thoughts went flying distractedly down a list of kids that size and that weight. Above all else she didn't like treating kids or dealing with anxious parents. But there was no one else for the hard cases and the broken bones and the appendectomies and such.

"Sorry, Darcy, sorry to bring this in on you—" Marshal Peterson turned the body to pass her and the preacher in the threshold. His heavy boots clumped loudly on the hollow wood and the kettle was still screaming fit to drive a body mad. The first thing she did when she reached the level of the kitchen was to go and lift the kettle off the fire.

The scream went on in her head. She hadn't screamed aloud, Then. She'd shut in, shut down. She didn't panic, now. She put on a professional face and calmed her heart, listening without giving a damn to what they were saying about a rider coming in, which didn't make any sense with a storm raging out there, and that rider bringing three kids up the road from Tarmin, which made much less sense.

"We took the boys on to Van Mackey's," John said. "Figured it was asking enough for you to take on the girl, Darcy, but the Lord has set a particular task on you. The Lord has had His hand on this child of His in a special way, and maybe in His good providence He's given you this precious charge. She's been in the passage of the Beast. Her mind's gone to sleep."

John said other things. She didn't believe in his God but she believed in John. They were partners in life and death, John doing the breaking of news and dealing with the next of kin, and that was a very useful thing to her. The marshal she had far less to do with and didn't give a damn for most of the cases he brought her—miners and loggers who'd gotten drunk and bashed each other senseless or tried to shoot up the barracks.

But then they folded back the furs and showed her the girl, and it was Faye. It was Faye's blond curls, it was Faye's pale face, just that age.

Her eyes were open. Faye's hadn't been. Hadn't ever been again. Faye's eyes in this child looked through her, blue as the sky in summer.

"What's your name, sweetheart?" Darcy asked, and brushed her hand across the girl's forehead. But the girl didn't blink.

"They're reporting Tarmin's entirely wiped out," the marshal said.

She listened to it. It wouldn't come into focus. Tarmin—gone?

"The girl didn't come out so well as the brothers," the marshal said. "They were swarmed. Kids holed up. She's the youngest. Her mind's affected. They say she's getting steadily worse, don't know how many days."

Not my field, Darcy would have said. She'd dealt with a couple of shock cases—miners, generally, who in their profession had to get along without riders to do more than check on their camps now and again, and just made do with guns and dugouts. The miners were tough. One had come around. The other hadn't.

"Her brothers and one rider got her up here, storm and all. They've been through hell. I know it's cruel, Darcy, but I honestly didn't know who else to take her to. Mackey's going to take the two boys in or I'll break his neck. I just don't know what else to do with the girl. I know you got one guy over this. If you could just take a look at her—"

"Take her upstairs," she said. Downstairs was the clinic. Upstairs was where *she* lived. "Warmer up there, most-times."

"All right," Peterson said, and furs and all, carried the girl out of her kitchen, around the corner to the stairs. Darcy followed with the lamp and got in front for the ascent. Peterson carried the girl up, and the preacher came behind her, with the deputy clumping after them, up, up where there was a small landing and a choice of rooms.

The whole upstairs wasn't warm yet: the kitchen stove was only just getting going. Their breath almost frosted, and the storm had torn something loose outside that banged and thumped. But Mark had planned for stormy days. Mark had set prism glasses in the steeps of the windward side of the roof where snow didn't stick when the wind blew. The light came down four mirrored tubes, and it didn't need kerosene to keep the upstairs lit even when the shutters were closed.

Faye's room had one. She opened the door. Dawn must be starting, because there was a faint glow coming in above the lamplight. She hadn't noticed how much dust there had gotten to be. But the sheets were clean under the coverlet, and she had the marshal lay the girl down there.

"You sure you're all right?" the marshal asked her then, and she knew damned well what he was thinking *and* asking of her.

"Fine." She wasn't angry, just ready for them to get out of her way and let her find out what the girl's chances were. She wasn't sentimental about Faye's things. She could use this room when it was practical. And it was practical now, a matter of light that didn't risk fire or cost money.

Such a pale, cold face. She couldn't keep her hand from the blond curls. She knew it wasn't Faye, but it was something to deceive her eyes and her hands and, at least for a while, the blank spot in her heart. "Oh, honey, can you blink for me? Can you do that?"

"Let us pray," John said, and launched into something about the Lord and lost sheep.

"Yeah," she said, instead of amen—she said things like that habitually and John kept his mouth shut and winced: John could *have* the souls on their way to the next world, but she wanted this one alive.

So she herded the three men downstairs, as of no use, and had no time to spare for tea or cordialities: she shoved them out the door, with them promising to check this afternoon, and John Quarles promising to bring groceries if she needed them.

"I have everything I need," she said, maybe foolishly, because it wasn't the truth, and she shut the door on them, then shot the bolt and dropped the bar.

Faye, all done up in furs and softness. It was a beautiful dead child the marshal had brought her, That Day, and she began to cry.

But old thoughts came to her and prompted her to stop sniveling and get something done. She found the dusty warming bricks in the downstairs closet and set them on the kitchen stove top, and stoked it up with another few sticks of wood.

She took the hot kettle upstairs, moving faster than she had moved about her business in long, long months. She *knew* it wasn't her daughter—she *knew* better; but she didn't choose to know: that was the real difference between sane and crazy.

In the thoughts she chose to think, Faye was home, the marshal had brought her, and she had a chance this time to fight death, hands on and by *her* effort—slim, but at least this time, a chance.

The smith, Mackey, hadn't been exactly hospitable.

But Carlo thought now, sitting in a warm nook in Van Mackey's forge, with the faint glow of embers for light as well as heat, that he was very willing to put up with pain in his fingers and feet. He was grateful that Danny Fisher hadn't let them quit—even if Danny had missed the shelters in the whiteout.

He could say now that they'd made it. And he'd have wished to talk to Danny before he left, but Danny'd had his head down, ducking things that they'd agreed not to talk about, he guessed, or what he might have to be grateful *for,* which seemed all there was left to talk about.

Thanks, he'd have said, at least, if he'd had his wits about him, and if that duck of Danny's head hadn't stopped him cold. When the rider woman had said he and Randy probably wouldn't lose toes he'd been so grateful for Danny Fisher's persistence and bullying toward the last that he'd sat there and sniveled like a five-year-old.

His eyes burned. He wanted just to sleep, and it was so still, so quiet in this place. The whiteout—

He suffered a mental slip, chin on his chest, thinking <himself back on the mountainside with horse-sendings shivering down the nape of his neck and running through his brain.>

At next blink it was <Danny in the rider camp.> And <passage-ways.>

No, they were in the forge shed. He and Randy. The preacher and the marshal had said they had a place for Brionne, and he and Randy should go on where the deputy took them, warmest place in Evergreen, someone had said.

And it was. From the branching of the dizzying wooden passages they'd parted with the marshal, taken a separate lantern which he lit and carried for the deputy who carried Randy, and they'd gone far down another spur to a side tunnel where it seemed even the earth was warmer.

Knock on the door, the deputy had said, having his hands full with Randy, and he'd knocked. They'd waited. He'd hammered with his fist, though it hurt like hell, figuring people were asleep, and the deputy had carried Randy all the way from the rider camp.

It had taken three such assaults before he heard steps inside, and finally the door opened on a sleepy, burly man in his underwear, who'd gazed blearily past the lantern he carried while they stood in the dark of the tunnel.

"These kids hiked up from Tarmin," the deputy had said. The deputy had gone on to say they were the smith's kids from down there, and that the marshal wanted them to have a job, at which Mackey acted as if he'd slam the door in the deputy's face.

But the deputy had gotten his hand against the door, and without saying anything about why they'd walked up from Tarmin, said something about the tavern and the miners and young boys not being safe in there. Details blurred. The passage doorway had. Carlo had been thinking he hadn't the strength to go through another round of where to lodge them.

But Mackey had said then that they weren't firing up the forge in this blizzard anyway and they could stay there till he could talk to the marshal in person. After which Mackey slammed the door.

They hadn't mentioned the details about Tarmin. The marshal had said not to tell Mackey anything but the absolute least they could say. They didn't want that public yet, because, the deputy had said, the village had so much stake in Tarmin, and there were people who might take advantage of the situation.

The deputy had brought them through the side door over there, into the forge, this vast shed with stone walls, a blackened timber roof, a stone floor that looked like a solid piece of the mountain itself. The forge was banked and almost dark, but even so the warmth in the air here was considerable.

His greatest desire in the whole universe had been to sit down and peel out of his coat and sweaters and the knee-wraps and all of it, and he'd done the same service for Randy, then covered Randy in his coat, thinking he might need it. At some point—he didn't even remember—the deputy had left. With the lantern. He'd thanked him. He thought. His thinking wasn't clear at all.

Randy made a sudden sound in his sleep and flailed an arm from under the coat Carlo had settled over him. His eyes came wide open. "Where are we?" Randy asked in panic. "Where are we?"

"Warmest place there is," Carlo said. "It's all right. Nothing to do but sleep." He didn't know even whether it was day or night. He thought it might be daylight, but he hadn't been able to tell in the passages. Mackey might have been asleep, or sleeping late—but if people had come in after risking their necks on that road he thought the man could have been civil about a knock on his door. "Storm's still blowing," he said to Randy. "Hear it?" He sat down as close to Randy as he could, while the wind kept on howling like devils outside and thumping at the flue.

"We aren't *home*, are we?"

"We're in Evergreen," he assured Randy, and chafed Randy's shoulder. It did look like home, mostly. The place was put together a lot the same, except the forge faced differently. It smelled the same. Cindery heat. Hot metal. Fire. The stone walls and floor of the place accepted and gave up heat slowly and it wouldn't chill too much despite the uninsulated roof above soot-blackened timbers. There was a metal tank that sat elevated on a masonry wall, probably taking rainfall and snow-melt from the roof. He got up, hobbled over and got a forge-warmed drink of water for Randy in a cup he'd found sitting near the tap.

Then he threw on a couple of logs he didn't think the smith would miss, less for the heat than to have brighter light until Randy could get his wits about him and know for sure where they were.

But Randy quickly faded out again, exhausted. And, so tired himself he could fall on his face, and completely unable to sleep, Carlo paced. Then drew off water in a quenching bucket and set it beside the fire to get warmer.

Pain brought tears to his eyes even yet when he dipped his hands in that lukewarm water; he pulled his boots off and endured the heat in the stone pavings just off the hearth of the forge. He waked Randy again and put him through the same routine, warm water and warm stones, though Randy broke down and cried and complained.

Randy was due that. He'd been hard on Randy on their way up the mountain. He'd done what their father would have done and said the words their father would have said because those were the things Randy was used to. It took that, to get Randy's attention and put the fear of God into him.

His father would tell him, the same way *he'd* told Randy: *The weak die, kid.*

They hadn't died. Their father was dead.

And they were where they'd stay—maybe for the rest of their lives, if things worked out to get them a job in this forge. Riders came and riders went when they decided to leave, and he knew Danny would go with the spring breezes. But not the blacksmiths' kids. They were the kind to put down roots. They'd never looked to leave Tarmin. And here—was a staying place. They had to think that. They had to work to get on Mackey's better side and make their lives better than they'd been.

The wind found a plaintive note, on a loose shingle, maybe. It was a lonely sound. He didn't hear the bell that had called them in, and hadn't in a long while. He guessed someone must finally have secured it so it didn't ring.

He'd never hear it after this without remembering that thin, wonderful sound that had given them the strength and the direction to keep trying.

Now there were walls, the world was ordered again, and they were back inside a zone of safety the riders with their horses, in their camp, maintained for a village that sustained them—

Only now he knew how fragile that zone was. He knew now that the riders' protection could be broken, and he didn't know if he could ever feel quite so safe here as he'd been before in his ignorance of the Wild.

He'd *heard* the sendings as the rogue prowled the darkened street, looking for mama, looking for papa—and the whole town died, house by house, swarmed over by vermin and larger predators that had held the village for hours. He and Randy had clung to each other, tried not to hear, tried not to think—

It hadn't gotten in. It had tried the door. But it couldn't get in.

And they couldn't get out. *That* was what had saved them.

<Gunshot. Blood on the snow.>

His heart jumped.

It was there again, that vision, that one, time-stopped moment. That overwhelming confusion. It had *nothing* to do with Tarmin. The horse belonged to a dead man—but Danny said horses didn't understand death when it came too suddenly and too isolated from other minds. It was *looking*, was what. Looking for its rider. Looking for *a* rider. It was hard to say.

What if the smithy was up against the village wall? He had no sense of location, having come here through the tunnels. He didn't know. He didn't have his orientation to the village, he couldn't even imagine what it looked like, and in a handful of days with Danny Fisher, he'd gotten used to *seeing* things and *hearing* things, even to finding it a shortcut to speech when he and Danny and Randy couldn't, in that hellish wind, make themselves heard.

<Lonely. Snow and branches.>

<High in the branches, looking down.>

He pressed his fingers against his eyes. But that didn't work. It wasn't *in* your eyes. It was in your brain, inside, where you couldn't run, couldn't ignore it.

<Fear.>

Go away, he wished it. Go away, you can't get in here.

Randy stirred in his sleep. But went on sleeping. And the world got quiet again.

The preachers said once you started listening to the Beast you couldn't ever really stop, and if you came near horses or anything native to the world, they'd talk to you and you'd have to hear—they'd haunt you, and you'd dream wicked, godless, animal dreams.

Was it really out there, that horse? Or was it his remembering it? Sendings were *like* memories, some vivid enough to wash right over your vision and make you see and smell and hear something else. And horses thought. Horses reasoned. Danny said horses didn't hold a purpose long and they forgot what they were about unless a human being was there to remember for them. Danny said when humans had come to the world horses had come to them because they were curious, and they carried riders now because they were outright addicted to human minds.

A horse could remember things so long as he had a rider.

That was why the rogue had been so deadly dangerous—because it had had Brionne on its back.

<Horse running, running through the woods. Fear and anger.>

He pressed his fingers against his eyes until he saw red flashes.

The preachers said the Wild separated man from God and led you into bestialities. Sex, and blood-lust, and just not hearing God anymore when God talked to you.

He actually wasn't sure God had ever talked to him. But he knew beyond a doubt that Cloud talked to him in his head. He knew that Danny Fisher had. Randy had. Randy, who'd been saying things about dealing with that spook-horse. About *wanting* to be a rider.

So had Brionne.

So had Brionne.

He wanted to go to church and smell the candles and the evergreen boughs.

He wanted to hear about God's mercy and have his mind and his thoughts his own again, and his dreams safe from horse-sendings.

Danny had said you didn't hear the horses if you weren't near them. That people might send a little—they must—but they were deaf as stumps without a horse to send to *them*. You didn't hear other humans without a horse or something in the bushes—and if you did it was bad, because *little* creatures didn't have the brain to intrude real easily. Sending *sight* was their real defense and their hunting tactic. If you got something strong coming at you—it was *big,* and big regarding anything in the Wild meant predator.

He just wanted peace from all of it.

<Dead riders. Lost horses. Dead streets. Fire reflecting on glass windows.>

He began to shiver. He thought that was a good sign, maybe a sign he could be horrified again, and not just accept images as they came. But the shivering made his travel-bruised joints hurt and it might disturb Randy. In the warmth and the smells of the forge, he could blink and think he was in his father's forge in Tarmin and that nothing he remembered had ever happened—but that was dangerous, too: it *wasn't* that forge, and Tarmin didn't exist anymore. Nothing could ever bring Tarmin back the way it was. It was lost.

Nothing could bring their beliefs back, or their innocence . . . certainly not his. Maybe Randy's. He hoped Randy had a chance to forget.

And for him—he'd find a niche for himself. A smith could always find work—he and Randy had nothing but what they stood in, but they had no debts, either. They could work slave wages if they didn't fit in here, just stay until they had a stake, then move on with a truck convoy in the summer to wherever some settlement needed a fair-to-middling smith. A whole village could grow up around a couple of enterprising craftsmen, where miners and loggers could know they could get equipment fixed, and some cook set up shop, and they put up walls to protect the facilities—and then—then miners and loggers came to do their drinking and their rest-ups because it was a safe place. That was the way a lot of villages had begun.

And the two of them would do all right. Randy was at that gawky, all-elbows-and-thumbs stage that didn't in any sense look the part of a smith, but Randy would put on muscle given another year, the same as he had, by working the bellows. You did that, you did the rough work, get the job going—the master smith would step in to finish it. Damn right, you put on muscle fast.

Hands weren't in good shape. If Mackey who owned this place gave him a chance he'd rest up. But if not, if not—he'd take what he could get. He was fighting for survival in this place just as surely as he had been on the road that brought them here. The house, the forge, the money and the respectability so Randy could have a wife and kids and a normal life, getting as far as possible from what had happened down there. That was what he'd fight for.

Everything right this time. He'd see to it.

* * *

Danny set himself on the edge of the bed, and Ridley tipped him back into it while Callie watched from the open doorway.

"Made it to the mattress this time," Ridley said, and flung at least five kilos of blankets atop him.

"Yeah," he said. They'd had warming bricks on the mattress. He felt apt to pass out from the heat.

But he'd done that already and had a sore spot on his head to prove it. His eyes wanted to shut, heat or not, and he wished they'd just go away.

But they didn't. They hadn't. They'd gotten him up after they'd determined he might be concussed, they'd kept him awake sitting in the chair in the common room, talking about the camp, talking about local custom—anything *but* Tarmin and the trip up—being sure, they said, that he didn't have a skull fracture.

He'd heard that staying awake after a crack on the head was a fairly good idea. But Cloud had dumped him harder than that and his skull had survived. He was just godawful tired. But if his fingers and toes all made it through the event, and they seemed to be going to, he was happy.

And they hadn't thrown him out into the snow. And they let him go back to bed.

"Pretty good job you did," Ridley said, lingering at his bedside—which made him wonder if they were going to continue the sleepless treatment. It was morning outside. He was relatively sure it was bright morning. And he so wanted to go to sleep.

"Yeah," he said. Yeah covered most everything. And he'd already forgotten the question.

Callie's voice: "Damn good for your first time in the mountains."

"I had a fair map," he said. You didn't *ever*, as a junior, attempt to take credit for what a senior had done—or pretend to have done what you hadn't. "And good advice." Which he wished he'd understood at the start rather than the end of the trek. But he'd lived to learn.

So had the kids.

"Who gave you the advice?"

"Tarmin rider." His heart rate kicked up a notch. He'd wondered when they'd start asking on the matter of Tarmin, and here it came. The ambient was quiet, the horses were snug in their den, the dark-eyed little girl with the lively curiosity was safely in her room. They might be about to go after answers on the subject they'd danced all around for at least an hour.

And if they didn't like what they heard—they could still throw him out.

"Who?" Ridley asked. "Who survived?"

"Tara Chang." He thought by their expressions it was a name they knew. "The others—didn't make it. Friend of mine—Stuart—he's down there. With Tara. Near Tarmin." He wasn't tracking well. The mind was trying to sink into deep, deep wool. He tried to sort out what they must assume. What he'd said and not said.

"How did she survive? What *happened* down there?"

"Dead." His tongue was getting thick. He was thinking about <snow> and <cabin,> but there wasn't any horse to carry the ill-assorted baggage of his mind and he was both protected by and held to words that wouldn't contain half his thoughts. The kid was in bed, but if a horse got curious, even asleep she might pick something up. He hadn't remotely counted on a kid in the camp—even if he'd come in to consult in advance what to do with Brionne, there'd have been the kid—

Which, with what he remembered, didn't make him comfortable winter company. Maybe he should hit the road.

But he hadn't told them—

"Fisher."

"Don't want to think now. Tomorrow."

Ridley sat down on the bedside and Ridley's hand closed hard on his shoulder. "Hate to be inhospitable, Fisher, but we have a village missing. The horses are out of range. So just tell us the rest of it."

You couldn't swear when a horse was listening. You could just swear to when it was sending. He was scared of being pushed, scared of spilling just enough to make them want more and more and more, until they got more than they wanted to hear, far more than he wanted to give. He was scared of spilling stuff that was his, and stuff that was the Goss kids' business, and Tara's and Guil's as well.

But he was in real sorry shape to survive now if the Evergreen riders told him go on, get away from their village—just another day, he'd be all right—

Something had stalked them here—he thought it had. But he

couldn't swear to it. It was so, so dangerous, imagination. A rider kept it in his pocket and only took it out on sunny days with no shadows.

Ridley's hand insisted and hurt his shoulder, shaking at him gently. "I want answers now, Fisher. Hear me?"

"Yeah." He didn't even remember exactly what information of all he held that Ridley had actually asked. "What was the question?"

"To what happened down at Tarmin." Ridley's mild voice grew angrier. "To who you are, where you came from, how the *hell* you got up here in the first place, and how safe is your horse?"

That was the most dangerous accusation. Cloud's safety. That question scared him. He shook his head, and even the pillow hurt the back of his skull. "Horse is fine. No problem with us."

"Ask him what brought him up from the flatlands?" Callie asked, coming close to his bed. "What cause to be here in the first place? Was there a convoy down there?"

"Friend's partner died up here. He came for her. I came—came for him. He was pretty shaken up."

"Names," Ridley said. "His. Hers."

"Guil Stuart. Aby Dale."

"Oh, damn," Callie said with what seemed real sadness, and Ridley's hand let up its vise grip on his arm. "Not Aby," Callie said. "We just *saw* her."

"Last convoy down. She was in the way. Just—" He didn't want to go into all of it. Most of all he didn't want to think about Tarmin tonight. There was too much white in his mind, and winter was such a dangerous time. Dreams turned real when the wind was howling like that outside, and the horses carried the worst imaginings. "Just—she died. They said—they said a rogue horse spooked the convoy. And Guil came up here to get it."

"But it got Tarmin?"

"Up at the gates—just—people opened doors. I was in the woods looking for Guil, and I heard it go—and—I don't want to tell this around the kid."

"She's asleep," Ridley said. "Keep going. Horses aren't hearing you. You just happened into Tarmin when a rogue *happened* on the mountain. And where's this other guy and why isn't *he* up here?"

Rogue horse—was rare as legends and campfire stories. And they *shouldn't* believe a pile of coincidences. But he couldn't begin to tell them the connecting strings without giving them leads to other things. He just strung it together as best he could.

"Gunshot. This guy—Harper—not from this mountain—he thought—thought, I guess, I mean, he'd seen a rogue once before, or he thought he had, and he wasn't real right in his head. He really, really hated Stuart. The rogue wasn't him, you know, it wasn't Stuart, but everything just got tangled up in his head. I knew this guy was on his track, and Harper—Harper just—just went crazy. Tried to kill Guil."

"Before the rogue got Tarmin," Ridley said. "Is Guil this rogue? Is Harper?"

"Horse. Rogue horse." Danny forgot and shook his head. "Harper's dead. It's dead. Shot it. Guil shot it."

"You're sure of that."

"Yeah."

There was a little easing of tension.

"You came in with a damn spooky feeling," Ridley said.

"Yeah."

"So what *was* it?"

"Horse—followed us. Maybe five, six horses loose down there."

"Followed you up the mountain. Through that?"

"Kids with me—nobody alive down there. None without horses. Can't go down the mountain, snows down there . . . avalanches . . ."

"And?" Ridley asked. "Fisher? You're not going to sleep until you talk. What happened with the rogue? What happened to that girl?"

"It was just—" <Fire on the window-glass. Horse walking the streets at night, in the falling snow. Tides of vermin rolling from under Cloud's hooves.> He didn't *want* to lie. He didn't dare tell the truth. "Just—when Tarmin went down—kids hid out. I rode in. Searched for survivors. Babies. Old people. There wasn't anything. —I *felt* it go, understand me? I *felt* it go, I don't want to remember it in this camp, I don't want to remember it near the horses."

"Damn," Callie said.

"I'm all right. My horse is all right."

"And those kids?"

He let his eyes shut, closing out the questions. They could hit him. They could toss him into the snow. He had to keep the lid on things until he could get his story straight. He didn't need to pretend to drift toward sleep. His mind kept going out on him—and he didn't trust them—didn't trust them not to call a horse close to him—outside the wall.

"What about the rogue horse?" Callie came to stand over him. "How bad is this kid, Fisher? *What happened?"*

"Just—" He had ultimately to tell them all the truth. But not tonight. Not tonight. The girl was beyond the wall. The gates were shut. It was daylight. "Just—the kid was affected. Keep her *in* the village. Don't bring her near the horses. Had a hell of a time on the road. My horse is all right. Didn't ever come near the rogue. Couldn't think about Tarmin, though, I didn't want to think about it all the way up. And the kids kept remembering it, spooking my horse. Didn't help. Didn't help at all."

They had no more questions for a moment. He didn't open his eyes to see, but he thought he'd answered everything.

"Jennie's *eight*," Callie said, nothing else, but he understood what she meant. As if a whole village on her hands wasn't reason enough in itself to worry about him *or* Cloud in the camp.

"I'll leave if you like. Give me a day or so."

"Not saying that," Ridley said.

Decent, *good* people. He'd had all the way up here to imagine the godawful situations a lone junior could get into, including finding himself in some shelter alone with a bunch of guys older and rougher and maybe far crazier. Winter came down and bunched people up in shelters at the same time the horses were in rut, and memories and sex flew thick as falling leaves through present time.

You didn't want to get in with a rough crowd, damn, you didn't, and he hadn't wanted to scare Carlo and Randy about that possibility. He'd held his own nerves together and was so, so relieved to find himself with a solid, sensible lot of people with an ordinary little girl—

But he'd never . . . never thought about a little kid exposed to the outspillings of his mind . . . he just . . . wasn't safe . . .

<Blood on the snow. Rifle shot. Man lying dead.>

<Tara and Guil and Brionne on the road, coming down the hill toward them. Brionne with nothing behind her eyes.>

"Here." Callie came near, but it was Ridley's voice, and a smell of vodka. He'd been out, or almost out. They'd had time to go and come back again, and Ridley nudged his hand with a glass. "Drink it."

They'd done it to him before, and he'd hit his head on the fireplace. "Drunk won't help."

"Panic won't either. Just calm down. An eight-year-old in the next room—we're a little protective. You understand? There's yellowflower in it. Drink it."

Understood Ridley'd shoot him before they let him spook the camp, or hurt the kid or Callie.

They'd shoot him before they let him go off the mental edge, the way Spook's rider had gone. Harper should have had somebody a long number of years ago, someone who'd hand him a glass of yellow and figuratively hold a gun to his head and say straighten out or I'll blow your brains out.

Might have saved a lot of people.

Might have saved Harper himself.

He drank it. At least three fast mouthfuls.

"You think that horse followed you all the way?" Ridley asked. "Or where did you lose it?"

"Don't think it came near the village. But it could be on the road."

"Must have a real strong notion what it wants."

"Yeah," he said, and felt a rush of fear—what it wanted.

"I'd hate to have to shoot it. But I will if it comes around."

"Yeah," Danny said. "I know. Five, six, loose, though." He had no idea. Predators could have gotten some, but it could be more than six.

"Bachelors are the fools. Mares with the lot?"

"Mare down with Tara." He recalled Stuart, and the cabin, and Tara's mare, and the vodka and yellow began to hit him like a weight. "Yeah. Tara's mare. But there's a stallion with her." <Beast-feeling in the dark. The whole mountain alive with it.> He wanted it quiet, quiet, just barricade it out of his mind. He'd held his sanity this far—but he felt himself not able to hold onto the vodka glass, and it burned his raw throat when he took another sip. "You better take it. I'm going to spill it."

Ridley took the glass back. Danny couldn't even coordinate his fingers to turn it over to him. His head spun, and his temples pounded, and that and the cough went with the altitude.

He hadn't slept in a bed since Shamesey.

Couple with a kid wouldn't put on him or rob him.

Nice little girl. Cute kid. He missed Denis—he really missed Denis. Last time he'd met Denis he'd hit him. He'd ridden out of Shamesey without a word to his family. He really wished—wished he hadn't done that.

Dark, then. He thought they'd blown out the light.

The morning—it *was* mid-morning now, though the sun hadn't even been a faint suspicion in the sky when the party had come in—settled down finally to quiet, except for the wind and the snow still going on outside. Ridley made a late, late breakfast for himself and Callie. Jennie was still sleeping like the dead after her unprecedented night wide awake in the den.

Young Fisher was asleep, too, and might not get out of bed for three or four days, by the look of him. He was anxious to get Fisher over to Peterson and see what else he knew.

Fear had come up the mountain with those kids. Fear had lent them the strength to do what only a couple of young men could do, in making (Ridley didn't question that part of the story) the whole trek from midway in one day and most of a night, up that iced slant. It was the kind of thing young folk could do, maybe once in their lives—and that some didn't survive. And the trouble they brought wasn't going to bed as quickly or as easily as Dan Fisher had.

But the kids—including the problem the girl posed—were disposed of to the village side of the wall, out of the reach of their horses, Fisher wouldn't stir for thunder, and that was enough to let him and Callie at least draw breath and have their breakfast and a following cup of tea in quiet, mental and otherwise.

All the same Callie had to go look in on Jennie—just checking.

And that, from Callie's partner, required at least a look up when Callie came back. He generally disapproved Callie's hovering over the kid. Today there was reason.

Callie—who was used to reading his mind, literally so when Slip and Shimmer were in question—didn't tell him Jennie was all right when she came back into the main room. Callie didn't give him a bit of information, meaning he'd have to go look in for himself or he'd have to ask her, dammit.

"She all right?"

"She's fine." Callie went to the fireside and poured herself a cup of tea.

It was their hardest argument, how much exposure to the realities of life, sex, and death was too much too soon for their daughter, and when they shouldn't baby her. It was certain as sundown and sunrise that Jennie would take off on a horse and go long before either of her parents thought she was ready. Kids always did. Young horses didn't *know* their young riders were too young, or that two horse years and eight human years didn't exactly make a mature decision.

They'd been worrying about Rain. But with this arrival in the camp they knew there could be much worse going on. He'd *heard* of rogues, and in the tales that ran among riders, if you got one in a district you could have others.

And dammit, Fisher offered to trek out of here, but the kids he'd escorted were here. There was no way in good conscience to pass that mess on to Mornay village, which was smaller than Evergreen and less equipped than they were to handle the kids.

Especially the girl.

Tarmin gone?

There'd been five riders down there. *Five* riders hadn't been enough, against what had come down on Tarmin.

And these kids survived?

"It's quiet out there," Callie said as she joined him by the fire. "I'd think the horses would have been out and about."

If there were any intrusion into their hearing, that was what Callie meant, specifically—if that loose horse Fisher had talked about had come in. There'd been a disturbance before they'd put Fisher to bed, a little queasiness in the ambient—but it might have been a bushdevil, something stirred out of a burrow nearby. They hadn't heard anything they could be certain of.

"Just hope the quiet lasts," he said as Callie warmed her cup with a dollop from the pot. He truly *didn't* want to have to kill a horse—but, dammit, he was defending a daughter. "If that stray comes in—I don't know. The horses down the mountain may attract it back down. I hope so."

"It could have been us, you know that?" Callie had been upset since he'd brought Fisher into the barracks. He'd seen it in every line of her body. *She'd* been dealing with the village kids—including the girl. "What got Tarmin could have come to Evergreen instead."

"Well, the last rider in Tarmin must have done something right. It's dead. He swears they did get it, Callie."

"*If* we've heard the truth," Callie said. "We're leaning an awful lot on Fisher's word."

"He's got no motive to lie."

"The hell he hasn't! He brought that girl up here, in her condition—what kind of judgment is that?"

He had to think of Jennie. "I'm not sure I could have let her die. And she was getting worse."

"And they've got a horse after them. We have his *word* the rogue is gone. We don't know that's not what chased him up the mountain! He had walls down there, shelters near Tarmin—and why did he leave there? Because the girl would have died? Or because something was chasing him?"

"We have his *word* it ever existed in the first place, Callie. If he was a thoroughgoing liar, why would he have to tell us anything?"

"In case the phone lines *aren't* down for the winter here. In case we'd already got a message from Tarmin! In case we listened to him and caught how damn scared he is! In case we asked why he didn't go down the mountain if that's where he's from? Look at the *girl,* for God's sake! He said—when she came out of it—she shouldn't be near the horses. What did he mean by that, except that she's not safe here, she was spooking him and his horse, and *I* don't think she's safe even in the village!"

He didn't have an answer for that—not one Callie couldn't knock down. Callie wasn't a trusting woman. And she'd formed conclusions it was well to listen to.

"The lines going down early this year," she said. "Maybe it wasn't just the ice on the lines, you know? As crazy as things have felt for weeks, the way things *felt* out there when he was coming in with those kids—oh, I believe him when he says there was trouble at Tarmin. I don't believe him when he says the rogue situation's done with. And he's under this roof and that girl's just the other side of the camp wall!"

"Are you saying we should put him out? The little I did catch from him while we were in the den—I believe he's honest; I also think he's young, he's skittish, he's holding stuff in, but I don't think he's actually lying to us. I think he's told us what he feels safe telling and I don't blame him for not letting all he remembers loose on a night like that."

"I wish I thought he wasn't lying."

"Wish I had an answer for you," Ridley said. But he didn't.

And by now he'd had time to realize that not only did they have a winter problem, they were facing a spring and summer and years down the road problem, and the very scary prospect of not just Evergreen but all the villages on the mountain going into next autumn without supplies.

Much of their supply source for equipment and half their trade with the lowlands was a company down in Anveney town that might—who knew the minds of townfolk?—be very reluctant to send even the usual number of trucks up here without some hard dealing. The main source they had for food was Shamesey. Oil and gas came from the south. One truck lost, when Aby Dale had died—that happened. But Tarmin gone?

That was the staging area for all trucks going up to the High Loop and it was the depot for supplies, the warehouses for trade goods that were just too heavy to ship *up*: warehouses for everything coming down off the mountain and everything that had to be sent up—some items by oxcart, as things moved when the villagers were paying the freight; and some by truck, when the trucks hauling company loads had space and the item wasn't too heavy.

Food for the High Loop villages stayed in warehouses in Tarmin before it moved up the Climb by oxcart. They were going to be eating a lot of bushdevil and willy-wisp if they couldn't get lowland beef and pork. Flour already cost twice what it did in Tarmin, which was already three times its cost in the lowlands.

Gasoline and freight costs could easily quadruple for Evergreen.

And the oxen that made those runs—the only transportation for goods that didn't run at Anveney's cost for fuel—he didn't need to ask young Fisher what their fate had been once those gates were open. They were gone. The *men* that drove those teams were gone along with everything else edible that wasn't cased in steel or locked behind it.

Tarmin gone meant *no* local goods moving until they replaced the oxen and the drivers. And oxen with experienced drivers didn't exist except over on Darwin Peak—a far journey—or down in Shamesey district, which had a long-running feud with Anveney, which *had* no oxen. Anveney was Rogers Peak's primary contractor—and the best source of people with the nerve to leave the big towns and venture into the High Wild.

"I tell you," he said, "we'd better spend less time sitting in camp this winter, do a little extra hunting, store whatever we can. It's going to be a long year."

Callie shot him a look that said he'd caught her attention. "Think Cassivey will deal hard?"

That was the company in Anveney.

"Will snow fall this winter?" was his counter. "He's a townsman. I tell you, if we don't get some ox-teams up here it's going to be a cold, damn expensive next winter, or we're going to make a lot of trips with wheelbarrows up and down that road."

"Shamesey's going to know we're in trouble. And *they'll* jack the price. It's not going to be easy this summer."

"They'll rebuild Tarmin," he said, and as he said it a thought came to him, the glimmering of an idea that, yes, Tarmin *had* to exist: Anveney and Shamesey were as dependent on Rogers Peak as Rogers Peak settlements were on them, and even if they had help from Anveney's most desperate—it wasn't townsmen from the flatlands that were going to be able to bring it back to life.

Chapter VIII

Hearing Randy stirring, Carlo stretched the kinks out of his back; he'd been sleeping fitfully, coatless and in his stocking feet, leaning against the stones of the low furnace wall. The stretch stopped in a dry-air cough.

"You all right?" Randy asked.

"Yeah." Carlo took a drink from the metal cup and then took a stale, crumbling biscuit off the fireside wall and offered it to him. "You want a biscuit? Saved it from the rider camp. There's no tea, but there's hot water. Tastes awful but it feels pretty good on the throat."

Randy didn't look enthusiastic—less so when Carlo got up and poured him a cup of hot water from the pot he'd set on the coals.

"Isn't anybody going to feed us?" Randy asked. "Where *is* everybody?"

"This is what we've got." Carlo kept his temper down, kept his voice calm and reasoning. The kid had a temper of his own and he didn't want to provoke it. "The guy they waked up to put us in here wasn't real happy. He's the blacksmith. And I get the impression he'd just as soon we weren't here, but the marshal put us here, and that's that, I guess, till they straighten things out."

"Well, *ask* him where we can get something."

"Kid, —we don't have any money. Tarmin credit isn't worth anything because there isn't a Tarmin anymore. We won't have any money to live on if we don't get a job here, and right here in this place with this guy who doesn't want us here is about the best job I'm going to be able to get, and the best *you're* going to be able to get. So eat the damn biscuit. I saved it for you and *I'm* hungry. There's the ham you carried up the Climb."

Randy took the biscuit, got into his coat pocket, took out the greasy packet of thawed ham and opened it. "Maybe we should have gone to Shamesey."

"We don't *know* towns. We don't know anything about the flatlands."

"Danny would be there."

"Danny wouldn't be there. He's not a town rider. He travels. And maybe he's done all for us he wants to do." He remembered that duck of Danny's head. But going down to Shamesey and asking Danny's help to do it wasn't an idea he wouldn't consider—if all else failed.

"But—" Randy said.

"Are you ready for another hike through the snow? Next village? Maybe the next after that?"

"No." A quiet, dejected no.

"If it happens—" Carlo said. "If it happens this place doesn't have room for us, we'll move. *Then* we'll think about it. —If we have to."

Randy took a bite out of the stale biscuit sandwich and washed it down with hot water. The kid looked on the verge of tears. Carlo's throat was sore, his ears hurt and he was so stiff he could hardly move.

"I did knock quietly a while back—" Carlo nodded toward the door that didn't lead outside, but to the smiths' house, unlike their arrangement down in Tarmin. "The house is catty-angled to that door. In a passageway. And they're not answering. It's daylight, but they're not stirring around much." Carlo took a look to the side where the outside door showed light in the cracks. "But they weren't going to fire up today because of the storm. Maybe tomorrow."

"On a lousy *biscuit?*"

"*Best we can do,* all right?" He shouldn't have raised his voice. "I'd say go back to sleep. Your stomach won't feel hungry that way. If we can't raise the house and work something out by tomorrow, I'll go out and see if Danny can slip us something and then we'll see where we *can* go or how we deal with these people. All right?"

Randy considered the half biscuit he had left, much more forgivingly. "You want part of it?"

"Had mine."

"The stuff on the sled was ours."

"We threw everything off the sled. Remember?"

Maybe Randy didn't remember. The kid looked entirely dejected. "Yeah, but—"

"Best we can do, I'm telling you."

Fact was, they'd only had the ham in their pockets because Danny had argued them into it, in case they got separated. He'd just never imagined it might be in Evergreen that they'd need it.

"I should have asked the riders," he said to soften the tone. "I should have thought of it when we left the camp, but we had enough carrying you, and I didn't know where we were going. Didn't know they'd be so hard-ass and not feed us, to tell the truth. —And right now I don't want to be gone from here in case the owner comes in to talk to us. It was hard enough getting in here in the first place."

"Where's Brionne?"

"With the doctor. A widow. Has a big house. She's all right. Well, —as all right as she's likely to be."

"She doesn't deserve it."

"She's off our conscience. We did what we could do. *We* don't have to worry about her, all right?"

"Maybe we should go to the camp and ask Danny for our stuff."

"I want to be here, hear me? Danny's there if we absolutely need him—but we don't know *how* the rider camp and the village get along. Let's just not muddy up *this* deal till we know what we're doing here."

"We're going to starve."

"We won't starve. I opened the outside door a while ago. The storm's winding down. I figure they'll fire the forge tomorrow morning. Then I'll talk to them."

Randy didn't look happy.

"Nice house she's in?"

"What I hear. Yeah."

Randy didn't say anything else, just tucked up, arms across his chest, and shut his eyes.

"However this works out," Carlo said, trying to comfort the kid, "we'll get some kind of work in this place, and if we don't like it here, we can stash some money and move on. We'll be all right. There's got to be jobs for us somewhere. There's villages up here, there's camps on Darwin—"

"Not much on Darwin," Randy muttered.

"We'll manage," Carlo said.

So it wasn't home, so they were hungry for a day. They'd found a place to sleep. They were out of the storm. They didn't have Brionne to take care of. And if they had to go somewhere else, Danny might help them. Danny might not really want to—but somehow they could make it.

He sat down next to the furnace wall. His head ached and his body ached, and he just wanted to shut his eyes. The stones were warm. He didn't need the blanket. He'd gotten used to the cold.

Randy waked him once with a coughing fit, had a drink of warm water without complaining and went back to sleep again.

But, left awake, finding the light had gone entirely from the cracks that had admitted it earlier, Carlo found himself sitting by the forge looking at hands that had taken about all they could bear, and thinking, and growing more and more worried about the situation. *He'd* argued for going up. Danny had agreed with it, but mostly he'd pushed it—being scared to death of that horse, and Randy's stupid notions, and his sister's chance of waking. They could still be down there, fairly comfortable.

Now they'd gotten into a place where the local smith wasn't happy to see another smith in town—and might *not* be willing to take on help.

Randy looked to him for a way out. Randy slept now, expecting his older brother to do something to get them breakfast next morning.

But going back to the rider camp wasn't the answer. The riders couldn't take them. And close relationship with the village riders wouldn't give them respectability at all, when their only source of help might end up being the church.

Maybe, he thought, maybe if he showed the smith he knew what he was doing—firing up without leave would be impertinent, but there was a lot of other work that wanted doing, right in front of him. The smith might in fact be shorthanded, considering the fact that the floor wasn't swept and that the stock was lying and hanging in no particular order—there was just a lot out of order in this place.

He was awake, it was night. There was a broom leaning against a support post.

So he used it.

There was a slovenly stack of wood and he put it in order without making too much noise. Randy snored, oblivious to the movement around him.

There were leather aprons and such thrown about and he hung them up on pegs where they logically belonged.

He located the rag-bin and, ignoring the pain of his frost-burned hands and the stiffness that had set into his fingers, began the kind of cleanup his mother and father had insisted on, wiping up along the edges of the furnace, around the vent. If the forge was ever cooled down, you scrubbed everything you couldn't get to when it was fired up, that was his father's and his mother's cardinal rule. You kept things in order. You set the tools out by kind and by size. If you didn't know you had it you couldn't use it, his mother was in the habit of saying. If you didn't know you had it, you couldn't sell it. If you didn't know you didn't have it you couldn't make a likely item during your downtime so you could sell it next time somebody wanted it in a hurry.

The surly man in charge might *think* he didn't need a couple of assistants, but he at least wasn't going to turn them down in the mistaken idea they didn't know how to work or that they didn't know up from down in the trade or in his shop.

He'd done all that and sat down to catch his breath and salve his aching hands by the time he heard the opening and shutting of doors somewhere nearby. Inside the house, he thought, which meant—he cast a look at the cracks in the door, confirming the guess—it was daylight again. There was just a smidge of ham left. Randy had eaten all of his, so he saved half for Randy and had enough breakfast at least to take the wobbles out of his legs and the complete hollow out of his stomach, on half the remaining ham and a cup of hot water.

He heard footsteps coming and going next door. The day was definitely starting, and he was ready to make as good an impression as he could or know he couldn't have done more than he'd done.

The door opened—the man they'd dealt with when they'd arrived came in, big man, wide of waist as well as chest, big jaw set in what seemed habitual glumness.

"You're still here." It sounded like a complaint.

"Yes, sir. Name's Carlo Goss. That's my brother Randy. Thank you for the place to stay."

"So what in hell are you doing up here? *Tarmin,* is it?"

What did he say? Protect the marshal's information and say there was trouble down in Tarmin, but not say what? And that they'd run from it? What was the man to think?

"Tarmin's wiped out," he said. "We're the only survivors."

"Damn-all," Mackey said. "That the truth?"

"Yes, sir. It is. Gates came open." He didn't say how. He tried to obey the marshal's instruction by not saying enough. Making it sound like mischance. "Snow was coming down. The whole town was overrun with vermin. We were smiths down there."

"Huh." The man shook his head, scratched his chest and walked over and picked up a piece of wood. *Threw* it on the fire, scattering ash over the freshly swept stones. Tossed another on, carelessly, scattering more soot. "Sad story. Not my business."

Not *his* business. Tarmin was dead, everybody he knew was dead, and it wasn't Van Mackey's business?

Carlo drew even deep breaths, asking himself whether the whole truth could have shaken the man, but he'd never know. Randy was waking up and he went over to take hold of his brother's arm and drag him up to his feet where he had the ability to jerk him hard, in the chance Randy had heard the exchange or might hear something else to inspire an outburst of indignation.

Meanwhile the man was poking up the fire, opening the main flue, starting up for the day, as it seemed.

"Randy," Carlo said, "this is the man who owns the place. This is the man who's put us up for a day or so. Say good morning to Mr. Mackey."

"Morning," Randy mumbled.

The man didn't say anything. Didn't even look at him.

"What's the matter with him?" Randy asked, aside.

"Quiet," Carlo said. "Don't say a thing."

"So what's he say? Are we staying here?"

He gave Randy's arm a hard squeeze and Randy took the cue and shut up. Mackey went on poking about the fire. Somebody else came in, a young man maybe Danny's age, maybe older than that, with the same large-gutted figure as Van Mackey, not quite as far advanced, and the same sullen jaw—brown hair cut way short, so you could see the scalp through it, and it stood up on end. The guy stood there with his hands in his pockets until Van Mackey gave a sharp order for him to work the bellows. Then he ambled over and gave the bellows a couple of shoves, waking up the fire.

"You actually work in the forge?" Van Mackey asked.

"Yes, sir. Pretty good, myself."

"Lot of work in Tarmin?"

"Not now," fell out of his mouth. He wished it hadn't. But the man didn't react to that, either. Bad joke. Bad mood, dealing with this glum son of a bitch who clearly didn't like the sight of them.

"Mend a wheel?" Mackey asked.

"Truck or cart. *Make* a wheel, or a barrel. Minor mechanics. Some welding on the trucks."

"Welding takes equipment."

"We had it."

"What's the kid do? Eat and sleep?"

Randy sucked in a breath to answer. Carlo squeezed his arm hard. "Fix-ups. Scrub. Inventory. Small chain, kitchen stuff."

"Skinny kid."

"Stronger than he looks," Carlo said, thin-lipped. Randy was about to explode. "I'm sorry we got dumped on you without warning, Mr. Mackey, but we *can* work."

"Got help."

If he meant the other guy it didn't look prosperous.

"I'm good. Food and a room. That's all we ask."

"Food and you eat and sleep in the forge."

A grim-looking woman had meanwhile come through the door and stood staring from the doorway. "And you cook it," the woman said. "And do your own damn laundry. No dishes from the house."

"Take it or leave it," the man said.

"That stinks!" Randy exclaimed, and Carlo jerked the arm hard enough to hurt, with, "Shut up," and "Yes, sir, but we need at least a small cash wage."

"No wage."

"Thirty a week or I look elsewhere."

"You won't find elsewhere. You're lucky you're not outside in the snow, kid."

"Twenty-five. The two of us."

"Fifteen," the woman said.

"Twenty."

"That's ten for you and five for the kid and first time either of you's drunk on the job you're fired. That's the deal."

"Can you *get* drunk on that?"

"We don't need 'im." That from the younger one. "Tell 'em go to hell."

"I'm competition," Carlo said, arms folded. "*Somebody* might set me up."

The man might have glowered. You couldn't tell past the usual expression. He walked over and took out a rod from the sorting he'd done. Let it fall back. "This ain't Tarmin. Wages are lower here. Fifteen, and you eat and drink down the street. Buy your own food and don't let me catch you drunk in here or leaving food lie about or I'll lay you out cold. Hear me?"

"Yes, sir." Fact was he didn't drink, or hadn't until Tarmin went down and he'd met Danny Fisher.

"All right. Done deal. You fire up. Going to make up some logging chain, heaviest gauge. Any problem?"

"Easy." The son of a bitch never had acknowledged the cleanup he'd done. He couldn't resist walking over, confidently laying hands on a bar the right size, which *he'd* set in order out of the jumble of bars, and carrying it back to the forge.

"Huh," the man said, and he and his wife left.

The other one stayed, the young guy, who sauntered over to the forge.

"You better get it straight," the young guy said. "There's *one* job here. You just do what you're told, collect your pay and don't give him or me any backtalk or you're out in the cold. Hear?"

Carlo faced him. The guy poked him hard in the chest.

"You hear me?"

"Yeah. I hear you."

"You want a fight?"

"Not actually, no."

"Hit him," Randy said.

He didn't *want* a fight. "Name's Carlo Goss," he said. "This is Randy. You're . . . ?"

"Mackey. Rick Mackey. This is *my* place. Long as you keep that clear. That's my old man. And you're *not* staying."

"Fine. Come spring, we'll likely be out of here—if we make enough. Not staying where we're not welcome. Meanwhile I compete with you or I work *for* you. Your father's smart to hire us."

"Fancy talk. 'Compete,' hell! You learn those words down the mountain, fancy-boy?"

"Sure didn't learn 'em here." Maybe that ill-considered retort went right over Rick's head. At least it wasn't a remark Rick could answer without thinking about it, maybe over several hours; and he *truly* didn't want an argument. "Look," he said, and dropped down to a grammar his mother would have boxed his ears for. But Rick probably wouldn't catch that change of gears, either. "I got work to do. Which I'm getting paid for." He went on to the woodpile and started gathering up wood, trusting Randy to keep his mouth shut and restrain himself from provoking the situation.

Rick wasn't excessively enterprising, he picked that up, Rick wasn't inclined to move or think at high speed, and Van Mackey couldn't get him to work; Rick was probably the reason the place looked like a sty before he'd cleaned it up, though for all he could tell, nobody who lived and worked here might even see the difference.

"Your brother a coward?" he heard behind his back.

"He can beat hell out of you," Randy said.

Both fools. If he warned Rick not to hit his brother that meant that Rick was of course, being Randy's mental age, immediately going to have to hit Randy. Then he was going to have to hit Rick. So he said nothing and trusted Randy to dodge if the ox upped the ante.

"The kid says you can beat me," Rick said to him, and nudged him in the shoulder as he walked to the furnace.

"Maybe. Maybe not. Fight doesn't prove anything. Waste of time."

"You're a coward."

"Yeah, fine." He had his arms full of potential weapons, and he didn't want to put himself in position for Rick to badger, but Rick stepped between him and the forge.

So he dumped the load. Rick skipped back as logs bounced everywhere about his shins and his feet, and Rick stumbled back against the furnace, in danger of bad burns. Carlo reached out and grabbed him forward, got swung on for his pains and let him go.

"You all right?" he asked with all due concern—which wasn't much.

"Go to hell."

He didn't even answer. Rick grabbed his shoulder and tried to swing him around, and he broke the hold, a move which popped a button on his shirt and gave Rick a straight-on stare, which evidently exceeded Rick's plan of action.

"You better not steal nothing," Rick said, and left, sucking on the side of a burned hand.

The door slammed shut.

"You should have fought him!" Randy cried.

He grabbed a fistful of Randy's shirt and jerked him hard. "You acted the fool, kid. What do you want? What'll satisfy you? We need this job!"

"He called you a coward!"

"Yeah. So what?"

"So you could beat him!"

"I know that. He doesn't. Pretty clearly I matter to him. He doesn't matter to me." He let Randy go and started picking up wood. "He shouldn't matter to you. Be useful. Feed the fire."

"He's going to make trouble for you."

"Kid, you know how close you came to him hitting you to provoke *me?* Did you figure that out or do I have to say it in smaller words?"

"I'm not scared of him. I'd have ducked."

"Yeah, sure. You listen to me. You'd *better* be scared of him. That guy is *stupid.* You should be afraid of stupid people. You don't know what they'll do. Don't get into fights with stupid people."

"You could beat him!"

"Yeah, and you tell me where our food and board's coming from."

"There's that horse out there in the woods. I could—"

"No."

"I could be a rider and I'd make a lot of money."

He was disgusted—he was sick at his stomach only thinking of Randy going out looking for that horse. "Did you learn from your sister, or didn't you?"

"I'm not stupid."

"Yeah, well, don't talk like it." He grabbed up scattered logs and took them to the fire, not willing to argue, not with feet that hurt, hands that hurt, ears that hurt and knees that said a biscuit and a piece of ham yesterday wasn't enough to keep a guy going stoking furnaces.

"You're scared of him."

"Yeah. Sure. Grow up."

"Don't talk to me like that!"

"I mean it. Grow up. This is serious."

"You could still beat him up."

"That'd be real useful, wouldn't it? We're in no damn position to start trouble, we've no place to live, it's the middle of the winter, we've no tools, nothing to our names—figure it out, kid. He *wants* me to fight him. Doesn't that give him everything he wants?"

"You could still beat him!"

"Then what?"

Randy sat and scowled and hugged his stomach.

"So what's the matter?"

"I'm still hungry," Randy said.

"So stoke the fire. I'll go next door and talk to the man about cash and where we get some kind of breakfast. —Which we don't get by bashing his son. Got it?"

Randy didn't answer him. His answer wasn't the way Randy wanted the world to be. Randy was going to sulk about it because Randy's belly hurt. Sometimes he wanted to bash Randy hard until Randy used the brains he had.

But that *wasn't* the answer, either. Getting the fire started and getting an ember bed going was ahead of breakfast, at least if he was going to ask for an advance on their earnings.

Wouldn't hit Randy. No matter what. He'd hit Randy to keep him alive on the way up. But he wouldn't do it here. Randy had seen too much of hitting. A whole lot too much.

And finally Randy quit sulking and got up and brought a few logs for the fire.

Chapter

— IX —

"No, sir," Danny said to the question from the marshal, "there *was* a rogue horse and it's dead. I *know* it's dead. That's all I can say."

"And it got inside," the preacher said.

"Reverend, it did, but it wasn't all that did. It was just vermin everywhere. I don't claim to know much. I'm a junior rider, only two years out, but the things they say about the vermin going in waves when there's a big kill, I saw it. There was blood all over—" You didn't talk about the ambient with religious townfolk or villagers, and, he guessed, least of all with a preacher. "All over. Willy-wisps were running from under my horse's feet, there was a lorrie-lie going over a wall getting away from us, bodies, bones—it was a real mess. I was out on the mountain when—when my horse started getting upset. When I rode into Tarmin gates, it was night, the gates were wide open. The kids were the last ones alive. They'd held out behind a locked door, and that's all I know. A lot of other people just—lost their good sense and went outside when—" Sometimes you just couldn't explain it any other way. "—when they heard the goings-on. Sometimes—sometimes you'll paint your own image on things.

You'll hear neighbors, people you know. That's true. It was pretty scary when I rode in."

There were dismayed shakes of heads. The preacher gave a sad sort of sigh and mouthed something that looked like *merciful God.* And they didn't have anything to say right off.

He'd taken the excuse of his feet to avoid a walk out to the den—or over to the marshal's office—and it was partially, but not insurmountably, true that he was lame. At least he was still limping and sore as hell, and neither Ridley nor Callie had pushed him to do anything for the last number of days but eat, sleep, and sit by the fire and tell stories and play kid-games with Jennie.

He'd dreaded this meeting fit to give him nightmares.

But he was embarrassed to go on claiming that feet that had gotten him up the Climb couldn't quite get him over to the marshal's office, or that the small crack on the head was still affecting him that badly. On the day he'd for good and all agreed to walk over to the village side of the wall, a howling cold had set in, and he'd really, really hoped they might cancel the meeting at the last minute, but Evergreen, having its snow-passages, didn't let a little thing like that stop them. Ridley had brought him through the dank, timber-smelling dark of the tunnels and so over to the village side—so that to this hour, having avoided the horses who might have carried him some sort of mental map from Ridley, he was quite helplessly disoriented and still had no idea at all what the village looked like.

The marshal's office where he sat was just a desk, some pigeon-holes stuffed with various papers, a board hung with keys, and a door that could lead to the marshal's house, or the village jail, or even the courtroom. The mayor was there. The preacher, who seemed to be a particular friend of the marshal, had shown up to ask questions. So had one deputy—Burani was his name, he remembered that—and a couple of other people, one man, one woman, both gray-haired, whose position and reason for being here Danny couldn't figure, so he didn't know entirely what they wanted, whether they were people who had relatives down in Tarmin or what.

On that ground, he didn't want to say anything indelicate—that was his mother's word—about the dead down there, or paint the situation too vividly. He just wanted to let them know what the kids had been through without saying too much.

Those were two of the anxious points he was skirting around. And he kept having to remind himself, as he'd never had to remind himself down in Shamesey, that he *could* lie comfortably, that as closely as he'd lived with other minds in all the wide open space of the mountains, and as small and claustrophobic as the villages felt to a Shamesey rider, both things were illusion. Cloud and the rest of the horses were far enough away when he was in the barracks, let alone on this side of the wall, that he was as safe from Cloud carrying unintended images as he had been in Shamesey town before he ever met Cloud.

That kind of privacy wasn't always true in Shamesey's huge camp, where a thousand horses wandering around among the barracks meant anything you thought could travel. But here, without Cloud near him, he could lie with all a townsman's skill at it—and if he could get his mind onto other tracks and calm down, once this meeting was past, he could afford to go near the horses again in Ridley's company—he was sure Ridley had been wondering why he wouldn't go out to the horses, and why he'd get uneasy when Cloud or one of the other horses came up near the windows of the barracks, as they'd done. He'd fed Cloud treats from the porch.

He'd tried to keep his thoughts on very mundane things—and didn't know how successful he was.

Until, dammit, he was absolutely ashamed to face Cloud, who couldn't know *why* he wasn't out there when the food buckets came out. Cloud was stiff and sore and being put upon by the other horses, particularly by Slip, who was boss horse in the camp. Cloud didn't understand being left alone in the den or cared for by Slip's rider while his own rider was lying about the barracks.

Meetings on the porch weren't enough any longer. Not as of today. His feet that had walked him over to the marshal's office could support him while he worked in the den. The headaches had stopped, and even young Jennie had to have picked that up out of the ambient. He just didn't have any more excuses.

Not that for any guilt of his own he didn't want to tell the village the truth; but there were details he was still convinced he had to be as careful of as a loaded gun. What he'd seen in Tarmin was nothing to show Jennie, for one major consideration: he was carrying a lot of memories he didn't want to relive, and least of all to give a little girl nightmares winter-long.

There were also matters of Carlo's and Randy's business he didn't want to bring up—things that didn't help Tarmin and couldn't help the dead.

Fact was, he knew he was badly shaken in his ability to keep his thoughts private—and *knowing* Cloud would spill everything in his mind to the local riders made it likely that was exactly what would happen, early and fast, with the worst possible implications.

And if things went wrong, it could conceivably touch off a panic in the village or in the camp, and possibly get Cloud hurt by the other horses. Carlo and Randy, under constant threat of the unknown, that horse, their memories—they'd been throwing off high voltage emotional upset nonstop, so intensely so that it had *been* the ambient, with Cloud's spookiness in the mix in the hour they'd come in, Cloud being upset as hell about Brionne being near him, about the weather, about the horse nosing about, about the general spookiness in wild things all over the area—which he guessed had traveled up here before they did: Callie had said they'd felt it—and if he started trying to explain all that—he didn't know where it would lead. Callie and Ridley had been forgiving, had been hospitable to him, had made no threats of making him move on, and had treated him very well, give or take Callie hadn't quite entirely decided he was reliable: not that Callie was *mad* at him, because Callie didn't seem the sort, but that Callie thought he was unreliable, possibly not too bright, and maybe lying.

Mad would have been easier to deal with. Callie's conclusions about him were going to take some long, consistent work to counter, and what he had yet to tell them wasn't going to make Callie happier with him.

Trouble was, there wasn't, to this hour, any neat, sure answer to what he'd brought up here except the essential piece of comfort he'd given them: his sure knowledge that the rogue was dead.

But if he let rumor get loose about Brionne or let people go flaring off on suppositions, Carlo and Randy weren't safe—let alone their sister. And disturbing Brionne, and threatening her, and maybe rousing her to a pitch of fright at which she *could* reach a horse's attention—

God only knew what could happen if she came to and panicked, and some of it got to the horses. Gates *could* come open. People could spook and take up weapons or bolt for imagined safety, or take actions he just couldn't foresee. He hadn't talked yet to Ridley or Callie on that score, and while Callie was watching *him,* he was watching *her*, and telling himself that while Ridley seemed a calm and reasoning man, a woman who judged that fast and who condemned that quickly might not be the woman he'd trust with a handful of kids who needed forgiveness.

Well, hell, he didn't anticipate *needing* to trust her, unless something went wrong.

So he and Callie were at a standoff and it was likely to last a while.

And he sat on a hard chair in the marshal's office, with Ridley sitting near him, and he answered question after question from the marshal that trod near the center of his concerns: "Does Shamesey know what happened? What did they report down there?"—all the while he was hoping to God none of these people thought to question the locked door story about how Carlo and Randy had survived, never asked whether Brionne was with them, or asked why other locked doors in town hadn't worked to keep out the vermin.

So far he was lying with a skill his father would be ashamed of.

But, God, if he could just figure out what to tell and what not to—what they needed to know in order to protect themselves and what they didn't—

He'd warned them, hadn't he?

He'd told them not to let Brionne near a horse. He'd told them about the one that had followed them.

He'd handled everything his seniors had trusted him to handle. Hadn't he?

And getting this business out of the way would make him calmer. A lot calmer. So he could deal with Cloud and act normal. And maybe he could think more clearly what to do next.

Except—

Except every night they drank a glass of vodka and he wouldn't swear his wasn't tampered with. He slept soundly. He didn't remember his dreams. Maybe he was just that tired. Maybe they just didn't want him walking about or going out to the den at night.

"Do you happen to know prices on fuel oil down in the flat?"

"Don't know that," he said. "I know it's gone up a little." The authorities of Evergreen village, deprived of the warehouses down in Tarmin, were worried about their supply and what kind of base cost they were facing: he knew that from overhearing Ridley and Callie on the same topic. "But I do know that it was a good wheat crop this year. Oats, too."

There was a slight relief in tense, worried faces. He could give them good news in a lot of regards, because the bitter Anveney-Shamesey quarrel had taken a quieter course. The hoarding that had been going on in Shamesey during the spring and even into the summer was cooling down—he knew: his parents had been laying in supplies, and then weren't. Probably it was the same story on both sides of the long-standing argument, Anveney with its metals and Shamesey with its grain sometimes downwind of Anveney's smokestacks.

"I think," he said to their further questions, "that that's got to bring prices down. I don't know that much," he added, "but my father's a mechanic in Shamesey, and I do kind of know what he pays for supplies, and what wire's running per foot, and so on."

The woman was interested, not alone in the price of wire.

"You're out of the town itself."

"I was born in town. Grew up there. Mostly."

Evidently not all the information he'd given had gotten passed on—or they hadn't understood. There were all kinds of riders. Most were born to the life. A few, like him, weren't. And a man could say he was a Shamesey rider without saying he had ties actually inside the town itself—which he did truly have.

But after they knew that, the cautious atmosphere warmed considerably. He'd become a human being in their eyes, he guessed, though he wasn't exactly flattered by it. With town connections, he became nearly as respectable as—well, at least as respectable as their own riders were, which didn't seem to be too bad a relationship. He wasn't, like Stuart, a borderer, a rider of the far Wild, half wild himself and unobservant of town manners. He was, instead of a foreboding arrival out of the storm, a rider of some background, even understandable to them.

He didn't, however, react to their reaction: he might have, a few weeks ago—before he'd been really on his own, before he'd dealt with the things he had to deal with. Now a distance had come between him and towns and villages of every stripe, a kind of uncaring deadness where it came to town sensibilities and an increasing unwillingness to give a damn where it came to a village accounting him righteous.

So he didn't come across with a sudden burst of truth for them—he *still* didn't want to damn Carlo and Randy. Horse business was rider business. Townfolk didn't understand, wouldn't understand, couldn't judge *why* anyone down below had done anything—and the conspiracy of silence among riders he'd gotten accustomed to down in Shamesey evidently held here, because Ridley hadn't said a word about a loose horse, either.

And they didn't ask about Tarmin anymore. They diverted themselves into meticulous questions about the prices and the market down in Shamesey, which he could answer, his father's shop's prosperity or lack of it being tied to prevailing costs.

In the past couple of days, he said to himself, among things Ridley hadn't told them—Spook-horse *hadn't* shown up. That was a benefit. Spook-horse hadn't come into range or made itself a trouble to the village and, by the lack of questions this morning, apparently nobody had heard it.

That could mean the horse had gone down the mountain again, or in feckless grief slipped off a cliff and broken its neck, or that, with the only humans it wanted out of reach, it had just given up and frozen to death in the storm. He was more sorry for it than scared now that he had the solidity of village walls between Cloud and a horse that wanted company enough to fight for it.

And even to this moment he wasn't entirely sure they'd not all imagined it, on the strength of Randy's desires and his and Carlo's fears—all hallucinating the creature, including the riders in Evergreen. Real and not-real had gotten very disconnected during the last of their hard journey, enough so that they'd missed not one but two shelters, and he could well believe they'd imagined its presence and scared each other into some very stupid and fortunately survivable choices. Ridley and Callie declared they'd heard something exceedingly faint that had disturbed the morning they'd arrived, but *he'd* been nursing a headache and couldn't figure whether he heard it or whether his apprehensions were contagious, maybe from young Jennie's apprehensions of <bad horse> that she'd caught from her parents or from him. And then he'd drunk the vodka and gone out.

Well, if Ridley hadn't told them, he wouldn't mention it, not until that horse did pose a danger. Which it hadn't.

And until and unless Brionne Goss came to, nothing from down in Tarmin meant anything but hurtful gossip to anyone in Evergreen. That might be a very high and wide decision for a junior rider to take on his own advisement, but, dammit, the two boys he'd guided up here had been through hell enough, they *weren't* bad on the scale of bad he'd met in his short experience; and if he could make their acceptance by this village more likely just by keeping his mouth shut on the details of Tarmin's fall and watching the situation, yes, he'd take that option. He was wintering here in Evergreen and the truth was always available from him to the village on a moment's notice if it became critical for them to know before he left.

He'd tell Ridley and Callie—soon—about Brionne. Maybe. Or maybe they'd never need to know. If she died—they wouldn't need to know. He guessed, in the absence of anyone available to ask, being a man meant not spreading the worry about for something two more worriers couldn't fix.

So it was his to hold. On his own. If spooky stuff once started to spread where horses and an eight-year-old kid were involved, it could turn scary for sure. And no one would ever figure out who had contributed what to the pot.

So he answered the villagers' questions, at a safe remove from Tarmin *or* the intruder on the mountain slopes, and the Evergreen marshal's office provided hot tea and the preacher provided cookies until they seemed to have run out of questions.

He was free and clear.

"We'd like," the marshal said then, "for you to come back tomorrow."

If there'd been a horse near at that moment of distress it would have told everything in the district he'd just panicked.

"I told you all I know," he said.

"We'd like you to tell the council," the marshal said. "Won't take too long. General meeting."

There wasn't a way to say no. It wasn't as if he had a tight schedule.

And the weather today had certainly proved a storm didn't stop Evergreen officials and their meetings.

"Yes, sir," he said. "No trouble." He collected his hat, his scarf, his gloves, and a couple of cookies for Cloud, for a peace-making.

Ridley nipped a few for, he was sure, deserving horses who would expect the same of someone who came remembering <cookies,> and the same for Jennie and Callie, too.

"Oh, we provided," the preacher said, and came up with a whole sackful, which Ridley took with a grin and a thank-you.

So they went out into the passages with the bag of cookies, and trekked back through the echoing boards toward the camp.

"What do you suppose they want?" he ventured to ask Ridley, and Ridley shrugged.

"Got to tell it firsthand," Ridley said. "The village wants to know. And the miners and loggers, they have their rights to know. It's just the way they do things. It's their rules with the miners association."

"Huh," he said, and tried instead, in preparation for coming into camp, to think about cookies—good cookies. And he let himself think how his feet hurt, and he let himself limp and think about his sore knees, which didn't take any pretending at all.

They walked back through the passage and past the post-and-jog that was the horse-barrier, after which they were in the rider camp, and through the door that let them out into the yard.

Jennie ambushed them out of the snowstorm, having been listening to the horses. So did Cloud, who was lurking near the den and not pushing too much against the horses that owned the place. Cloud came trotting over, black turned gray in the driving snow, and when Danny thought of the taste of <sugar cookies> Cloud switched his ears forward and Cloud's nostrils dilated.

Then Cloud caught the notion of <cookies> in Ridley's possession. So had Jennie, who danced about Ridley, trying for the bag, as Slip and Shimmer moved in to assert their claim.

"Pig," Danny said laughing, when the ambient went to <bag of cookies in Ridley's hand> as opposed to cookies his rider had. <Cookies,> Danny sent, and held them out, which seduced Cloud right back before heels started flying around Jennie's short and unpredictably located self.

Jennie got cookies along with a scolding from her father about antics around hungry horses, and one of Jennie's went to Rain, so Jennie naturally had to have another; Slip made off with one, and well, Rain and Slip had had one apiece from her, so she had to have one to give Shimmer and one for Cloud.

Callie came out into the yard before the bag was gone, and got one, at least, before Shimmer persuaded Callie fairness dictated she was due the other one.

Danny took his chance and left for the porch while it was all happiness and horses high on sugar. He limped up the steps and went to sit by the fire, figuring Jennie would distract Cloud at least long enough—Jennie was good at scratching chins and had not a troubling image in her young head: Cloud seemed to like her, and that hadn't been the case with his own brother Denis.

His feet *did* hurt. He hadn't lied so much in that.

But, God, he wished there weren't tomorrow to deal with. He'd thought he was free and clear: he'd thought he could go back to camp and dismiss Tarmin from his mind for good and all—at least until spring, when he could get out of here. Dirty trick on their part.

Very dirty trick. So in a concentrated effort to empty his head of everything he didn't want broadcast, he just stared at the stones and the fire and thought about Shamesey, where things were safe, and about Carlo, whose company he missed, and about—but there were reasons he couldn't go and talk to Carlo.

The marshal and the village would imagine their questions going to Carlo's ears, for one thing; they might trust a young rider who was under the orders of a camp-boss they knew, but they'd have no way to know Carlo's self-restraint, or lack of it.

He wondered if Carlo would be at the meeting tomorrow. Maybe he'd see him there and have a chance to know how he was getting along.

But he didn't want to betray an interest in the question, no more than he wanted to talk about other things he knew.

Chapter

X

The weather had settled down after yesterday's snow—as generally the weather had been more moderate than the storm of the night they arrived.

It proved, Danny thought as he and Ridley set out down the barracks steps, that it would have been smarter to sit it out in the cabin at midway. Yesterday had been bitter wind, but nothing still like the storm and the ice they'd climbed in, and the weather today was bright blue sky and only a little white bannered overhead from the heights.

Fool again, he thought. He should have stayed put.

Maybe.

But then—that came of flatlanders climbing mountains in the winter. He'd lived through it. He learned from it.

He asked Ridley what he thought of the weather-chances for the next while and Ridley said, Oh, should clear for at least two days. When he asked how Ridley knew that, Ridley looked puzzled and didn't answer at once.

Ridley just knew, that was the real answer. It was complicated, the system Ridley had for knowing, or at least rendering good guesses. And no flatlander was going to be sure of it on a single telling.

Assuredly, though, it was a day too good and too sunny to take the passages, and they walked through the camp gate into the village on the surface, past a head-high snow-blown drift along the rider camp wall, and matching ones along the sides of two gray, unpainted board buildings. There were deep piles of snow on either side, but that had been shoveled. The village had cleared the short street from the camp and as they came past those two buildings, which Ridley pointed out as warehouses (not surprising: no villager wanted to *live* in close proximity to the horses), they came out into the village proper, where industrious and, Danny was sure, constant work against the days of bad weather had shoveled all the street clear, making rumpled piles of snow head-high along the way and a truly huge pile on which children were sliding and playing.

The village as a whole was one street, no more, and the buildings were of unpainted boards, with incredibly steep roofs, a village made quaint and beautiful with a deep, deep coating of snow, and snow-coated trees, of all things, trees right in town, the evergreens that gave the village its name, thick-coated with white where they stood out of the range of children. He was delighted by the trees. And by the fact the snow-piles were white, not brown with mud.

And maybe the village wouldn't look so pretty when the rains came and the mud took over, but under its coating of pristine snow it was the prettiest human-built place he'd ever seen, including Shamesey's middle square where rich folk lived.

They went toward the mountain—up the street—and Danny began to build a map in his head out of the general one he'd been drawing slowly from Ridley's chance thoughts and plans. In the cluster of the village's fanciest houses, toward which they were walking, was a long, bright yellow building—one of a very few with paint—which he guessed might be the village offices.

"Meeting in the church," Ridley said, as they walked. "Right down there."

"In the church." He was mildly surprised. And alarmed. *They let us in there?* he almost asked. But that might be rude.

"Middle building, there. Church is the biggest place in town. Except the tavern down at the other end. So the village council meets here, the court does, any what they call *sober* meeting. We were over in the left-hand row, endmost, yesterday."

The church he'd have definitely taken for offices. In Shamesey they wouldn't for any reason be asking a couple of riders under the hallowed roof. Practicality of using the space made a logical sense that wouldn't have mattered to the hellfire and brimstone religious down in the flatlands.

But he figured level ground in a village tucked tight against a mountain had to be too valuable to leave sitting idle.

It was an impressive building when they came up on its wide-roofed porch, and they went in through a foyer with religious pictures over a painted blackboard with a notice that the Wagstaffs had had a girl and that they needed volunteers to patch a leak in the church roof.

He took off his hat. Ridley did, and they walked on through.

The inside of the church was painted bright blue, with a huge mural, not too badly rendered, of God letting down the Landing Ship in His hands, and of green and gold fields, and white villages all over. And mountains with villages above the encircling clouds.

It was certainly a lot more cheerful then the murals in his parents' church, where an angry God sent lightning down and black beasts slunk along the edges with fangs and claws and glowing red eyes that gave sinful children a lot of bad dreams.

In Evergreen, God had a smile on His face, and nighthorses stood on the edge of the green land, looking curiously up at the vision of God with an attitude real horses took.

He let go a sigh without thinking about it, and wasn't so scared of this church and this preacher, who maybe wasn't going to threaten him with Hell; he found the courage to go and meet the cluster of villagers who were enjoying the tea and cookies at the rear of the hall. Ridley walked in the lead, in search of cookies, Danny suspected, but first came a round of introductions and hand-shaking, and to his absolute embarrassment, villager admiration for a young rider who, an older woman said, holding his hand and shaking it an uncomfortably long time, was a real brave boy.

"There's the ones that came with me," he said, constrained, if somebody was about to hand out benefits and good will, to remember those that needed it worse and far more permanently than he did. "I'm fine. The Goss boys lost pretty well everything." He didn't see them in the meeting. He thought he should at least speak for them.

"Lord bless," the woman said, and introduced him to the district judge, Wilima Mason-Hodges, a gray-haired woman who couldn't shake his hand: hers were full of teacup and cookies, but she nodded in a friendly way and introduced him to a Mr. William Hodges Dawson, attorney and proprietor of something about or near the tavern.

At that moment the marshal and his deputy wanted the mayor and Wilima Hodges, and Danny was left to mumble through an uneasy conversation with the lawyer, who wanted to know what the status was of the Anveney-Shamesey quarrel and whether the negotiations were making any progress.

He said what he knew. If the blacksmith Carlo was staying with was part of this meeting, nobody mentioned the fact to him—and he didn't think that by the less-than-good things he'd heard about the Mackeys that anybody had bothered to invite them—though he would think the blacksmith ought to be a fairly substantial businessman.

Meanwhile Ridley was discussing Jennie's homework with a man that might be the village teacher: Jennie *was* getting lessons and did know how to read, over Jennie's loud protests, from what Danny had picked up, and if there was one odd small thing in which he'd won Callie's approval, it was the demonstration about the second evening that *he* could read, and telling how he'd read since before he was her age, and how useful it was, disposing of Jennie's contention that it was just her parents' heartless decision to restrict her freedom.

Dawson the lawyer asked about his connections in Shamesey. "Mechanic shop," he said. "My father's a mechanic."

Then the marshal called out that everybody should take their seats, and Danny took refuge at Ridley's side with the thought that Ridley would know what was proper.

The proper thing seemed to be to stand there, and the assembly turned out to fill the front four rows of the seats. Reverend Quarles got up and offered a quiet, thankfully brief prayer respecting the dead down in Tarmin and the survivors that had gotten up to Evergreen.

After that the mayor got up and straightway said, "Rider Fisher, if you'd come and tell us what you witnessed down in Tarmin."

"Yes, sir," he said, and walked up to the front of the meeting, hat in hand, to stand and talk while others sat down, but he'd talked in meeting in the riders' camp down in Shamesey, so it wasn't his first time to talk to so many people—and these weren't drunk, crazy, or armed.

And he figured he should at least cover all the details he had given the marshal in his office, how the Wild had gotten over the walls one night down at Tarmin, that only one Tarmin rider had survived from the camp, and that the Goss kids had lived till he rescued them.

But he began to sweat, then, hoping he hadn't opened a question on that matter.

He didn't mention this time either how there'd been a fight between riders down the mountain, didn't mention riders dying or Spook or other horses being loose; but neither had Ridley brought that matter up yet, even to him back at the camp, after he'd heard his account at the marshal's office. He didn't know why they'd called him and not the Goss boys to question—though maybe they had talked to Carlo and Randy.

He reckoned himself the least involved of anyone, not even being from Rogers Peak, and probably the most impartial witness, and he figured if Ridley at this hour wanted any question raised about rider business whatever, Ridley was the boss in the rider camp, and that meant they should ask Ridley.

Which was exactly what he meant to say if they asked him anything of that sort: he'd resolved that matter early on.

But before he'd received any signal that they were finished with questions, one gray-haired man asked Judge Hodges about the legalities of inheritance, and Dawson stood up in the audience and said there were rights like for any salvage.

Then a woman who seemed to be *another* lawyer in the village said that, no, the Goss kids could have rights to the whole town.

Then the lawyer who seemed to be the judge's relative, Dawson, said maybe to the smiths' shop, but not to anything else.

Danny drew in a breath and sidled from the conspicuous center to the aisle and then near the door, really wishing to be away from here, and just listened while people who didn't even have relatives in Tarmin argued bitterly about rights to it, and then—

Then the notion dawned on him that Carlo and Randy could be rich.

That was a good thing, he supposed, if they survived the honor, counting some of these people, the miners and loggers, he supposed, looked real rough. But he didn't think Carlo and Randy wanted ever to go back to Tarmin to live.

But not just Carlo and Randy had a right. The preacher stood up, called Brionne Goss "that poor child," and "that pure soul," and said how "there must have been a state of grace on the Goss family to have those brave children survive, as proof of His infinite mercy."

Being by now used to being damned, Danny stood with his hat respectfully in his hands and waited to be bypassed if the preacher was polite, and he thought this one with the pretty blue church was far nicer than preachers down on the plains.

The preacher added, "And God chose this brave young rider to guide them."

That meant God had somehow ended up guiding a rider into the bargain—past two perfectly good shelters and on to Evergreen, half-killing them in the process.

No, that was sacrilegious. Maybe they wouldn't have made it at all if they'd stayed in those shelters. Maybe something terrible would have happened to them or that horse would have caught up to Cloud and Cloud would have gotten killed. Then they'd have been stuck there helpless. He could easily construct sufficient disaster in his mind to explain why God would have had them bypass the shelters. There was a scared small spot in him that was still devout in his mother's and his father's religion, mortally scared of his own lately-come-by irreverence.

But after that Dawson and the other lawyer and the judge were out of their seats and a couple of other people began arguing.

He was glad, then, not to be named too directly. He wished he dared go back after another drink of hot tea back on that table. His throat was still sore when he talked for any length of time and the lawyers had started dicing things in terms of village law and inheritance law, over what, while he stood there on sore feet, really began to sound like some sort of compromise where Carlo and Randy—and Brionne if she ever waked up—were entitled either to money or to their parents' property, but not to the whole town and all the salvage in it.

That was still a lot of inheritance. And by all they said he didn't think they had ever talked to Carlo and Randy.

One person stood up and said technically there couldn't be salvage since there hadn't been a wreck.

But, the judge argued, there couldn't be next of kin to consider, either, since with the exception of the Goss kids all the next of kin of Tarmin folk had died right there. Nobody in Tarmin had married outside the village that anybody in Evergreen knew about, and it was first come first claimed, so the one faction maintained.

God, it was a gold rush. Except the prize was buildings. Stores. Houses. Personal goods. Equipment, all lying intact down there—because the vermin wouldn't have destroyed that. The people in this church were talking about inheritances because they were priming themselves to go down the mountain as soon as they could and lay claim to vacant stores and houses in Tarmin—

But what would they do with their own? Danny asked himself. What about their *own* houses, their *own* jobs and their lives up here?

And what about the other villages, that they dismissed with a reckoning that Tarmin villagers hadn't any relatives up here or anywhere, and there was no legal need to notify anybody else?

So Evergreen was going to get it all?

Damn, he thought. *That* was why the marshal had wanted him to come and tell what he knew to this gathering of the important, the powerful, the *rich* people in the village.

They were going to organize an expedition come spring, faster than any other village knew anything was wrong in Tarmin except the normal downing of the phone lines in winter storms. They would go down there, not just to loot the place of what was portable, though a lot of that might happen, too, but abandoning their stores and houses, or leaving them, he guessed, to relatives, or maybe just flinging them to the first comer along with all the winter privations of the High Loop, to gain what he understood was the easier weather further down the mountain, where *they* could be the shippers and run the mills and do the other things that siphoned off profit before it filtered up to the High Loop.

Did the vermin get everything? he'd been asked yesterday.

And he'd said, the truth: No, not but what was alive or stored food. And the hides in storage they'd probably get—because the winter hunger was that fierce, and vermin usually gnawed up the hides of whatever fell in the High Wild. What went down anywhere in the Wild was gone before the sunrise, down to the bare bones and few of those. But Tarmin—Tarmin had been so rich and so full of food even the swarm that had occupied it hadn't scattered the bones. Hadn't gnawed through all the doors by morning.

Had by now, he was sure. And what did Tarmin get now? A swarm of humans to follow the vermin?

Nobody yet seemed to have talked to Carlo about these rights everybody was arguing about.

Then someone who identified himself as the representative from the miners' barracks stood up, a thin, bearded man who hooked his thumbs in his belt and said lawyers were all fine and good, but that any miner who staked a claim first was the title-holder.

"This isn't a mine!" the mayor said, and the judge said.

"When value's added by human hands, it's not a find."

"Beg to differ," the other lawyer said.

"Words," the miner rep drawled. "If we get down there first we stake the claims and then you lawyers can come down there and try to talk us out of 'em."

Applause followed that, from a handful, boos from others.

That kind of wrangling was going to go on for days and months, Danny thought. He wished he could find an occasion to go back to the table, or better yet all the way back to the rider camp. He was more than glad when Ridley, perhaps in the same frame of mind, walked forward from the back rows and said to the assembly and the marshal that they'd go back now and stand available for further questions if the village needed them.

"That's fine. That's real fine. Appreciate your help," the marshal, Peterson, said, and shook Ridley's hand. Their departure stopped the debate, and various townfolk and several of the disputants came and expressed their appreciation for the report. "Glad to have you the winter," one said, which was a lot better than riders got out of Shamesey folk. Then Reverend Quarles came and said, "I know I can't convince Ridley there, but we'd be happy to see you in Sunday services, son."

"Thank you," Danny said. He was astounded by the offer. "I might," he said, and found occupation for his hands in keeping the brim of his hat uncrimped. "I might do that."

"Any time you, you know, want to talk, I'm just the other side of the wall."

"I won't forget that, thank you, sir."

But by then he was sure the preacher's invitation simply hoped to separate him from Cloud and thereby save his soul, and his partnership with Cloud wasn't even remotely negotiable. John Quarles and his heaven-blue church was certainly a kinder-spoken and more forgiving preacher than the fire-and-brimstone peddlers down in Shamesey town. In Shamesey as a whole a rider's leathers and fringed jacket weren't welcome, not in the town streets and least of all in respectable places. This village as a whole seemed a *lot* better.

But he didn't linger to quibble. He had his escape, and took his leave with Ridley, out the front door through the foyer and down the porch steps.

It was done, then. He'd told what mattered.

"Wasn't too bad," he said to Ridley. "But what are they going to do? Wait till spring or what?"

"They're going to be down that mountain like willy-wisps," Ridley said, "some maybe if the weather holds good, hoping to get a jump on the others, and if they leave down the road, I'm damn sure not guiding them, and if they go overland I'm not rescuing them. They've lost their damn minds."

Village riders were very different from town riders, he'd begun to figure that. Ridley cared about Evergreen. Shamesey riders, who hadn't any sense of personal attachment, just drew pay for guarding herds and fields, or they got hire as he had with the convoys that took commerce back and forth between the towns. But if people Ridley knew were fools, Ridley might still go after them—that was how he understood the man, and Callie as well.

Jennie complicated things. Immensely.

And walking back from the meeting in which neither he nor Ridley had told all the truth—for what he suspected were very different reasons—he said to himself he had to talk to Carlo very soon and *tell* him what the thinking was in the village, in case no one got around to explain to Carlo what his rights were, because Carlo, being an outsider like himself, didn't have anybody but him to do that. But he couldn't run from here to there or people would draw fast connections.

A rider visiting a villager was going to occasion talk. No way not. But he could at least be smarter about it than that.

He watched the village kids throwing snowballs up and down the street. There were shrieks and name-calling, and no harm done.

Sleds plied the street further down, children amusing themselves on a white surface—while in Shamesey, snow meant muddied and dirty piles along the sidewalks. Here there were such snow-hills, but they were clean and clearly fair game for sledders.

On the way to the meeting he'd seen what was beautiful in Evergreen; in there, in that church, he'd seen what wasn't.

But maybe they weren't to blame for what they were doing. Ridley was mad and Ridley didn't like the talk in there, but, he realized suddenly, the villagers in that church were proposing things that were going to hurt the village and draw off people the village needed, that had to be Ridley's view of things.

And what was the truth? The notion in these people's minds must have started small—just the notion that the staging area for everything they relied on was gone—and they were legitimately scared for their lives and safety up here.

So he couldn't blame them too much at all for their plans, and he doubted Ridley did. When he thought about it—why *shouldn't* they take what was down there? They were overexcited and maybe a little quick to protect their own interests above others, but he didn't think they were bad people.

He didn't know what it would be to be a kid in this sparkling and white wintertime world that riders who went with the trucks would never see. Maybe a little more innocent—maybe less. He didn't figure their minds. He'd be leaving come spring and probably wouldn't spend another such winter—he'd be on his way and guiding the trucks and earning his living.

"Where's the smith's place?" Danny asked as they walked this street imperilled by snow-battles in which two riders enjoyed a curious immunity.

Ridley pointed a gloved hand toward the end of the village. "Near the gate, third building back."

It wasn't the building he'd guessed it was. It was much less conspicuous. "What are the big ones?" he asked.

"Miner barracks. Tavern."

Of course. If miners and loggers came in for the winter, they had to have somewhere to stay. In Shamesey there were several hotels for the truckers who didn't rent space in private homes.

For good and certain they didn't stay near the horses in the rider camp.

"This house here, now," Ridley said, and indicated a painted, prosperous-looking house on their way: the owner evidently didn't believe, unlike most everyone else up and down the street, that a little space of sun was the signal to unshutter and enjoy the light. "This is the doctor's. This is where they took the girl."

"Huh," he said, but nothing else. He didn't want anything to do with the matter. And didn't want to discuss Brionne in any detail. But Ridley said further, as they walked toward the rider-gate, that narrow portal that led into the camp:

"She lost her daughter."

"The doctor did?"

"And her husband, right after. He was a good man. A real good man. All the kids were going skating—they do, when the weather's been socked in for weeks: special outing. You know kids. Bouncing off the walls by then. Callie and I, every month or so we take 'em out to the pond just up the road, and sometimes you'll see kids from Mornay join us. And there were some then. Faye, that was the kid's name—she was fourteen the week before—Faye got to talking to a boy from Mornay, and she was kind of at that age, you know, skated off from the rest, she and the boy, just kid stuff, just flirting. It was about this time last year. The ice wasn't solid in the west end—the waterbabies keep it churned up there by their burrow, where the falls comes out, and it wasn't at all safe. I spotted the kids. I yelled—"

Ridley shook his head. Clearly it was a bad memory. And Danny didn't know what to say. Maybe Ridley just wanted to talk about it, or wanted him to know something essential about the girl he'd shepherded in and what her situation was. He didn't look at Ridley, just walked beside him.

"They skated off the other way from where I was," Ridley said. "Playing games. She hit the thin ice. I yelled at her to go flat, and she maybe started to, but the ice split, and the fool boy tried to grab her—which put twice the weight on it. They both went under. He climbed out. She didn't come up. Her father went in looking for her, without a rope, and he nearly drowned. The marshal and his deputy got her out, sucked into the waterbaby den, right where the water flows out. Just too late. Wasn't anything to do. Sometimes the drowned ones will come around. But this one didn't." Ridley shook his head. "Her father went along quiet till spring and the ice started melting, just made his call on an old man who'd died, and then he went home and locked the office door and blew his brains out."

"Damn."

"Yeah," Ridley said. "Darcy Schaffer, that's his wife, she's the surgeon for us and all the miners, only doctor we've got since her husband died, but she just isn't opening her doors. I don't know how the marshal talked her into it. I know what they were thinking when they took the girl there. But—"

"Hard on her, then, if the girl dies."

"Yeah," Ridley said. "Real hard. I'll tell you, she was in the house when her husband killed himself. Middle of a storm, the windows were shuttered—she never unshuttered them after, just stayed like that since last spring. If you get a cut that's not near your heart, you go to the druggist, that's all. The Sumners—they own the pharmacy—they've gotten real good at first aid. And," Ridley said with a sigh, "single women and doctors both being scarce here on the peak, God knows there's been a lot of men on her doorstep this year—one guy, a real nice fellow, everybody thought sure she'd take to—and one night this last summer three drunk loggers carved each other up on her porch, trying to get clear space to talk to her on the subject. Didn't impress her in the least. She'll see to a birthing or go over to Irma Quarles' place—the preacher's mother. She's got a chronic lung condition, and Darcy'll come out and see her, but that's about the limit."

"Doesn't sound as if the woman needs more grief," Danny said, thinking to himself that he wouldn't give a spit in hell's furnace for the chance Brionne Goss would wake up and answer to the doctor rather than to her own brothers.

And God help the doctor if she did. God hope she never did.

But that was an ugly thought, an ugly wish, and he didn't want to think it, because they were reaching the gate that led into the rider camp, where the horses might pick it up.

He buried his thoughts real fast in the meeting, and the argument, and the lawyers, none of which Cloud would understand, as Ridley pulled the chain that lifted the latch on the gate—a simple affair, a gate with a free-standing post that a human could walk around and a horse couldn't—same arrangement as in the board and earth tunnel that ran as a snow-covered mound and windbreak beside them, like a little hill, the only structure that went right through the camp wall—or that the camp wall humped over. They went through into the rider camp, to home, at least for the next several months, into that warm bath of the horse-carried ambient, with <we're here,> and <we're here,> on either hand, human and horse.

That caused a nighthorse excursion out into the cold, Cloud and Ridley's Slip immediately, and Rain, who seemed to have his inquisitive nose into every event. More leisurely out of the dim light and close warmth came pregnant Shimmer, and then with a thump of a wide-flung barracks door, came the human offspring, half into her coat and trailing a scarf, onto the porch and down the steps, to be caught by her father and swung aloft.

"Getting too big," Ridley complained, setting her down; and Jennie said, "I bet *Danny* can lift me."

"Not on your life," Danny said, far from willing to provoke jealous competitions with father and daughter. "I'm not as big as he is. I'm a *junior* rider."

"I'm a junior rider, too," Jennie said.

"Yeah," Ridley said. "When you get a horse, miss, and you *don't* count Rain."

"I *love* Rain," Jennie cried, "and Rain loves me!"

And before that could flare into an argument Callie came out with her coat wrapped around her, asked if they'd break the ice on the barrel.

"I can!" Jennie declared, and was off with Rain kicking up his heels across the yard.

So he and Ridley followed and took a heavy log and broke up the ice as Callie went back inside.

Came a heavy thump behind their backs and a burst of nighthorse hooves on the frozen snow. As Ridley looked up and Danny turned Jennie was on the ground flat on her back beside the porch and Rain was still dancing off with his tail in the air. Ridley ran, he ran, but Jennie was already getting up, brushing herself off.

"Have you lost your mind?" Ridley asked. "Stay *off* him!"

The pieces of the situation were all there to figure: the porch, the skittish and indignant colt—who'd probably been willing to have Jennie on his back until it *felt* weird. She'd used the porch edge for a mounting-block, the corner post of the porch for a handhold, and Rain had shied right out from under her—luckily she hadn't hurt her back—or her head; it was crusted snow below and a thick coat and a heavy knitted cap. She'd just had the breath knocked out of her, minor crisis, a lot of gasping and trying, red-faced, not to cry.

"See?" Ridley said, angry; Ridley already had not had a good morning, in the meeting, and Jennie cried and stormed and went running off to Rain.

To Rain, not to her mother who was working indoors. Danny marked that fact.

So, he thought, did Ridley.

"Damn!" Ridley stormed off toward the den, to his daughter and to Rain, with Slip trailing after. The ambient was full of <Jennie and Rain> and <unhappy male human and unhappy Jennie.> Rain was thinking <mating,> Shimmer was thinking <bite,> and Slip and Cloud were understandably on edge.

But it was peace-making Ridley was after, and Danny saw him standing in the doorway of the den, leaning against the post, talking to his daughter.

Maybe Ridley believed he could stop nature and growing up from taking its course. Danny didn't know. Maybe Ridley was trying to explain the facts of life to an eight-year-old.

They'd talked about maybe taking Rain to another camp next spring. Maybe Rain leaving of his own accord when the foal was born—a colt horse often did take out on his own at that point. But to say so to Jennie . . . that well could be the frown, the downcast look, the refusal to look at her father.

He felt sorry for the kid. And the colt.

And while he was thinking it, Cloud nudged him in the side. Cloud thought if human hands were otherwise unoccupied they could be <scratching itchy chin and itchy ears.>

He did. Cloud rewarded his charity by licking his ear.

He was ever so glad to have the interview in town behind him. Now he had absolutely nothing in front of him but a winter in this camp, with the reserved but congenial company of Ridley and Callie, and he didn't need to worry. Down in Shamesey his family might worry about him—and figure he was staying out the winter because of the fight they'd had in parting. They might even guess he'd gone off into the hills and gotten snowed in—

Fornicating all winter in some village was what his father would think.

Less chance than Rain had, was the fact.

And his own family would miss him. The money he'd brought would have run out come spring. They'd be back on what profit his father and mother earned from their own business, but they'd survive very handily till he got back; they had before. And then maybe he'd come back with enough in his pockets to set his father up with the kind of tools the shop needed.

Most of all he'd finally paid off his promise to Cloud, who'd wanted this winter in the High Wild, from the beginning of their partnership, two years ago, when a crazy young horse had played tag with gunmen atop Shamesey walls getting the rider he wanted, which for some reason happened to be Danny Fisher. Cloud had surely been foaled in the mountains, the camp-boss had told him that, and he thought it might have been on Rogers Peak itself, in the wild herd—he had no images of villages out of Cloud and never had had any. Cloud had wanted his winter in the High Wild, and, Cloud having brought him up this mountain, well, here they were: their duty was done to the village folk, Ridley said he could work for his keep and even said he'd talk to the marshal, meaning he'd go on the village tab.

That was generous, very generous. He'd help Ridley for his room and board; he'd cut leather, he'd mend roofs, he'd ride guard on villagers who had to go out, and most of all he'd hunt and gather hides and meat for the village.

He couldn't imagine a happier situation than he'd found for himself. He'd had his doubts when he was coming up the mountain, half-frozen; he'd had his doubts in that meeting in there and even walking back from it—but this wasn't at all a bad place for a young rider to stay for a summer—help Guil out, for that matter, and *let* his family worry.

Or not, if they got the phone lines spliced again and if he could get a phone call through to Shamesey. He thought maybe they'd let him do that. Maybe—he had to factor that unpleasantness into the picture, too—he'd be available to guide a number of people down to Tarmin around spring melt. He might well get that job—having been there recently, and not being senior, and Ridley and Callie being burdened down with Jennie.

He *didn't* at all want the job. He'd accepted the one with Guil and Tara. He'd plead that and the villagers could wait.

Meanwhile Ridley and Jennie had made peace. The ambient was quieter. <Jennie and Rain> was the sense of things as Ridley came walking across the yard toward him.

"I don't want that," Ridley said to him. "Girl-kid and a colt horse. What in *hell* is she going to do?"

"There were pairs *like* that in Shamesey. I don't know—" He didn't want to discuss sex and an eight-year-old with the eight-year-old's father. "I don't know exactly how all of them got along. But I know two mismatches that paired up and they seemed happy."

Ridley didn't discuss it. "Worries us," was all he said. And about that time <Jennie!> went through the ambient like a scream and Ridley and Danny ran as Rain first bolted out of the den in a spray of snow and then came back, <upset> and upsetting Cloud and the other horses.

Jennie was on the ground again with the breath knocked out of her. This time she didn't get up so quickly—hardly moved until Ridley picked her up and set her on her feet.

About that time Callie came running, and a guest and a stranger in the rider barracks could only stand and keep his mouth shut.

The little girl wanted that horse *so* bad, and was anxious to *be* with that horse, for reasons a rider who wanted to understand could well figure out and could feel not just in his heart, but in his gut. Equally, Rain wanted *her*: he was also very upset about <hurt Jennie> and wanted to defend her—it wasn't Rain's fault he'd dumped Jennie twice in ten minutes and didn't quite put it together in his horsey brain that *he* was the cause of Jennie falling.

It wasn't really Jennie's fault, either. She loved that horse. And Rain loved her, in his adolescent way. Rain, male, in mating season, didn't know what to do about something light landing on his back, boy-horses being especially skittish in that regard, and young ones more skittish than they'd ever be in the rest of their lives.

And what did you tell an eight-year-old about her horse's reasons for dumping her? How much did the kid know and what did her parents want her to know?

The truth, if they were smart.

But he damn sure wasn't going to argue that point with Jennie's parents. He just hoped Jennie's skull held out.

Chapter XI

It was blue sky and scattered clouds overhead, snow blowing off the trees and sunmelt glistening on the surface of the crags. <Horses,> was Burn's occasional impression, and Flicker's; but nothing close or threatening, nothing that would, Guil thought, make Burn jog, which he truly didn't want this morning, considering the aches in his side.

The woman beside him was much more cheerful than she had been when they'd set out. Tara had begun to mope and to lose appetite yesterday—maybe understandable if she had never been anything except a village rider, and unaccustomed to lying snowbound all winter in an isolated cabin.

But she wasn't; she'd been a free rider over on Darwin, and the ambient told him it wasn't the closeness of the cabin that was bothering her. It was an occasional, uneasy, and angry despair that he didn't want to invade with his advice or even his good will. Right now it felt like approaching storm.

He didn't want to acknowledge it. She had a gun, an indispensable part of their job. He'd seen a crash coming—he knew it was inevitable, and when it came, it helped that they both had a place to go and something yet to do. It was a dangerous search, a perilous venture for a woman whose method of dealing with her loss had been to shut down and shut in for a while. He'd wanted to go up here from the hour they'd agreed they were going and she'd placed all sorts of interpretations on that haste, from his disapproval of her actions with the kids to a need to prove something to her on *her* mountain.

The latter had switched about to her need to prove something to *him*, and come down to an hours'-long fight, their first real partner-style disagreement.

But increasingly since their agreement to come up here *she'd* started thinking about those kids, and about Tarmin, and *she* was riding on a mission, not just tagging him. *He* could stay back in the cabin and she'd undertake this to prove something to herself, was what it sounded like to him.

Angry. She was that. It was an anger flying about and trying to find a place to nest. She blamed the Goss family, not the boys, by the rags and tags he picked out of the ambient. She was mad and she had no place to turn it.

And if there was one place that anger could still fasten it was the girl who'd opened the gates, whose selfish whim had ridden the streets of Tarmin, looking for satisfaction. That wasn't just his guess. It was what they'd both gotten out of the ambient while the boys were there, it was what had roused Tara's outrage even before the girl had waked, and that outrage had almost pulled the trigger in the instant when sensible fear had drawn the gun—and Danny Fisher had intervened to the hazard of his own life.

She'd put the brake on the temper—and lost her forward motion. Lost the moral justification to do what in her mind wanted doing.

Lost her way, in a world suddenly lacking everyone she'd known.

Well, and there was him, out of his head with painkillers.

And there was this chance, today, to try again to deal with those kids.

The blue sky and the cold air, though, could lighten anyone's mood. He was too sore to have Burn frisking about like a fool and too sore to think about climbing up and down—but on a day like this Burn found it very hard to behave, and jolted him now and again. Tara's Flicker had her mind divided between Tara's purpose and the skittish self-awareness of a mare in heat—which just didn't raise the common sense to any high level.

Hell of a set they were, as they trekked up the road.

"I'm *fine,"* Tara said shortly, so he knew she'd picked up—not the literal thoughts—but the mood and the images flitting about his brain.

"Good," he said.

She didn't say anything for a long, long space. Then: "Real quiet for a sunny day."

"Might be the horses scaring them," he said, because the little creatures that ordinarily filled the ambient with their flittery images, the minds that gave a sense of shape to the land, would shut down and lie quiet if a horse was hungry and hunting—or they'd all project being elsewhere, which could turn a whole section of the mountain queasy and treacherous.

But a while later he caught a number of strange, deliberate images he'd seen before, which at first he thought *were* wild creatures, and then he realized it was Tara right beside him, trying to call the lost horses out there, naming their names in the ambient, names not all of which he knew.

Flicker had a chancy, there-and-not-there kind of presence in the first place, light flashing through leaves, and Tara's presence when she rode Flicker's senses . . .

Hard sometimes to say what was due to the horse and what was the rider's own difficult-to-corner nature. It wasn't unusual for a horse and a rider to grow alike. It wasn't unusual for two of the same disposition to pair up. And that was certainly what he had beside him.

While Burn, male, whose essence was <dark, pain, and fire,> with a <fine nighthorse mare> in mating season, was no stable presence in the ambient himself. Guil thumped him occasionally in the ribs to keep his attention to what was going on in the visible world, not wishing <Burn falling in hole> and the consequent <pain in Guil's side.> It was sharp enough as was.

But the curve on that part of the road that faced the rest of the Firgeberg Range was a cure for any glum mood, a glorious sight which he was seeing for the first time—Aby would like it, Guil thought, just as natural as breathing: the snow-covered peaks, the blue sky, and snow-brightened forest as far as the eye could see.

But the fact came down on him then like a hammer blow, that Aby'd known it very well. She'd died here, and sights like this were the last she'd looked on.

"Damn," Tara said.

"What?" He thought she'd seen something and he cast about with his vision and his hearing, not horse-sense.

"Just damn," Tara said, and he knew he'd been far too loud with that realization of his and tried to shut down.

"Listen," Tara said. "You won't let *me* alone. I won't let *you* alone. Want to go back? Want to avoid this?"

"No." He didn't like the exposure of his thoughts—not when he was thinking how Aby had begged him to come up on this route with her. And he hadn't.

"Yeah," Tara said. "*You* can be standoffish and you're fine."

"Sorry," he said. "Pretty view."

"Just letting you know."

"Had it coming."

"Pretty day," Tara said.

"Yeah." The ambient was still quieter than it ought to be.

Maybe, they'd said to each other, the swarming that had taken Tarmin had dislodged wildlife from their territories and driven them further down the mountain.

Or onto the north face of the mountain, where the road wasn't so well maintained—where the road wasn't maintained at all, in fact: he'd come up that way, and he knew its deteriorating condition.

Burn took a moment to bump against Flicker and take a nip at her neck. Flicker gave a little kick. <Quiet water,> Guil imaged, and Tara: <sun through branches,> to calm it down.

They gave their horses' legs a rest after the next turn of the road—slid down and sat down on the rocks, instead of walking as they usually would: he still wasn't feeling up to a hike. The horses sniffed around the rocks and raked at a burrow where there might be vermin, and caused a minor rockfall onto the snow.

But there wasn't any reaction in the ambient. There was nothing there. It was as lonely as it had been.

He needed a hand up when they were ready to move again. Tara made a stirrup of her gloved hands for him, and got up herself, rifle and all, with a skip on the snowy ground and a hand on Flicker's back. Which was pretty to watch—but an annoyance to a man who was in the habit of doing that and knew any such move would have him lying flat on his back.

They rode sedately, words now and again, long silences, as the road climbed, as the sun passed overhead and finally began to sink behind the mountains.

The day lasted longer in this pass than it did where their cabin sat surrounded by tall trees. The gold of the departing sun crept up the snow, up tops of the rocks and the tips of the evergreens, and vanished altogether as all the world turned to blue shadows, snowy rocks, snow-blanketed evergreens and the untracked expanse of the road that had received a layer of honest snow.

And before the light was gone—they'd set their pace quite slow for his sake—a turning of the road brought them to the first-stage cabin, nestled against the mountain shoulder, set in among such trees, with snow blocking the door.

The ambient was utterly quiet as they rode up on it.

The kids weren't there.

"Well," Tara said, and the sigh went out into the world as a breath of steam and in the ambient as <pain.> "They're down or they're up from here."

He'd personally bet on up, and that they'd used the cabin. He was <worried> and Burn was <worried,> too, picking up a scent of <male horse> that blurred on the wind.

But at this hour they'd no choice but dig their way inside, unless they personally planned to spend the night in the open—and, borderer though he was, and accustomed to open-air camps, he really wasn't averse to a warm fire and a decent supper and a warm, soft bed.

Burn and Flicker did a lot of the digging of that drift at the door. Tara had to do the last part with the shovel that was racked just under the eaves.

"You stay put," she said when he thought he could take a turn. "God. Fool."

The woman had a way with words.

And truth was, he couldn't do much but sit there, with his side warning him he'd pushed the limit in the riding he'd done.

But when she'd gotten through the snow enough to get the door open, he got up. She used her boot heel to get the last of the ice away from the door edge—ice that indicated that door had been shoveled clear once—and pulled the latch-cord.

He wasn't used to having partners do all the work. He walked in behind Flicker and ahead of Burn, who had their own right to look things over, and who would be in with them all night.

But not now. Burn and Flicker made one circuit of the place, sniffed it over as <Cloud and boys and sickness here recently,> smelling nothing that was there now as a rival to what was most important on Burn's mind, which was Flicker.

And out they went again, right past him with a scrape and thump of hooves and a thump and bang of the door they knocked into on their way out to their own winter antics.

He dodged. Even before he thought about fire or comfort or food or rest, he was interested in the rider board, the square of smoothed wood that sat atop the stone mantel. Tara had gone straight to it.

And sure enough, he saw a wealth of information. He'd had Danny Fisher tell him what he used for his own sign was a letter that started his name—the only letter he'd learned to read in his life, in identifying Danny's mark—and it was there, that letter in the middle of what he could agree was a cloud. There was the sign that said Danny was convoying three people, and nothing that said anything about a death in their number, so he guessed the girl had lasted to get this far.

There was a sign that said village, there was some writing—unusual on a rider board—and the slash that meant dead: the kid was giving warning in case no other message got to some of the villagers who might come down this road expecting to get help at Tarmin.

The kids could have gone on down the mountain without wasting time here—and that would have taken them on to Shamesey and the help of senior riders who in no way would allow that girl near the camp. They'd take her deep inside the town, where sendings didn't happen. But he'd never been easy with that notion. Shamesey was just too unstable.

And sure enough that wasn't the way they'd gone. The directional sign said they were going up the road, not down.

There was one more sign: *danger* coupled with *bad horse.*

"One of the horses came in here," he said. "Damn."

He didn't know what Tara thought about it. They were getting a lot of horsey loveplay and chasing at the moment: the ambient was muddy with it and they weren't hearing each other except with words.

But Tara just sank down by the fireplace as if the wind had gone out of her, and ducked her head against the heels of her hands.

It wasn't a time to push. He knew clearly what he wanted. But he didn't say it. He could at least lift the kindling from the stack. He brought that over and knelt and got a fire going, one match, with the tinder the shelter offered in a hanging box by the fire.

Light began to glow in the hearth. She'd turned her head and the light showed a dry and composed face.

"Kid's got a horse giving him trouble," she said in a level voice. "He's taken his party out of here, he's gone up in the theory it won't follow him up, but it might follow him down. He *wouldn't* come back to us." She had a dry stick in her hands, broke it and tossed the ends into the fire.

It cost him to get up or down. He didn't want to get up and move away if he was going to need to sit down to talk to her. Trying to solve things without the horses to carry feeling and memory was like dealing blindfolded and half mute.

And he knew what he'd make up his mind to do in a second if he were in one piece. And he asked himself whether he had a chance in hell of making it on his own.

With her help—he could. But he was in a position of asking for the help of someone he knew wasn't happy about the situation she'd created and who was very likely going to take it as a criticism from someone who'd twice intervened to stop her from shooting Brionne Goss, for reasons about which he now felt very queasy.

"Kids could be in trouble," was his opening bid. "They pushed it getting out of here. No question they've been caught in the storm."

"In which case they froze or they made it."

"Danny's pretty levelheaded."

She ducked his opinions for a moment by ducking her head down, knees drawn up, elbows on knees. She was sorting things out. He knew. He waited.

And the head came up. She shook her hair back and set her jaw. "You're saying go up there."

He didn't answer for his own long moment. The fire beside them grew. Tinder went red and dropped down as ashes.

"We didn't figure on one of the horses coming *this* way," he said then. "That's forced them out of here. That's put them on the road."

"Danny understood," Tara said slowly, "that the real chance was in his waiting here. And that eventually—as kindly as possible—she'd die. But if a horse called—if she woke up—"

"A healthy horse won't come near her. One that isn't—"

"They've gone up. To Evergreen."

There was a truck off the mountain, where Aby had died. There was a box of gold in that truck, that a company down in Anveney wanted really bad—a company that had hired him to recover it and to get it on to Anveney. But he'd stopped caring about it. He'd revised a lot of things in his head when Aby'd died, and when he'd found out what had happened up here.

A lot of death—around him and Tara both.

Meanwhile Tara had become important to him, just a constant amazement to him to see her, to look at another living being in all this isolation and see the firelight on her hands, on her face, to discover, day by day, another set of living thoughts in the void where Aby'd been—and to know that if she rode off from him—he'd feel he'd lost—hell, he didn't know.

He thought Aby would approve of her.

And he knew he was being stupid and too cautious. He'd not felt nearly so anxious about Aby's risks as he did about risk to Tara—Aby having been there, left hand to his right, a fact of the world since they both were kids, and capable of taking care of herself. God, yes, he'd loved her—there'd always be a hole in his world the shape and size and duration of Aby. But the matter with Tara was here and urgent, because the woman was apt to do any damn thing—and he wanted her safe, and didn't want her to have done things she'd be sorry for, and meanwhile he had things *he* needed to do and she'd be up here by herself rather than see him go—it had a very Aby-like feel, her stubbornness did. And he wanted to protect her from that—

The way he hadn't done with Aby.

His thinking was in a real mess, was what it was.

Horseplay outside had come near the cabin. Attention had turned to them, and they were aware of each other like a light switch going on.

"Dammit!" he said to Burn, caught, and knew it was going to be <mad Tara.>

A hand came to rest on his knee, took on weight, patted it hard. And the ambient said that Tara wasn't mad.

"You aren't going up there," she said. "*I* will."

"No. *I'll* go."

"I *said* I'd do it. Go by yourself, hell. This is my mountain. You sit here."

"No." They were back to *that* argument.

"There's a short way up there. But it's a lot of walking, a lot of climbing, and rough ground. You can't make it."

"The kids are on the long way. If I can't make it, I'll know it. I'll stop. I can camp and stay warm."

"Listen to me." The hand on his knee shook at him. "You hear anything?"

"You and two horses."

"And nothing else. *Nothing* else."

He took the point. Soberly.

"The mountain isn't over with what happened," Tara said. "It's not safe out there. For someone who maybe gets sick, *can't* move—"

"Or just as well somebody that travels alone. With you or behind you, woman. Take your pick."

"Your life. Over those kids. They can damn well take care of themselves or they've got no business up here."

"The kids didn't have much damn choice about being out of the village," Guil said. "And can the village up there take care of itself? They could need help. We sent *our* problem up there."

"Where there's a lot more resources than we've got."

"And a mountain that's still in an upheaval. What do *they* know about it? I want to know where that horse went that drove them out of here."

"Damn you, Guil."

"Yeah, well."

He sat there beside her at the fireside, and then—then the horses outside were mating, and they sat there bundled in their thick clothes, receiving that.

"Doesn't help the thinking," he said on a heavy breath.

"Not damn much," she said.

But the horses wanted in, at that point. Having had their fling they wanted to get warm and muddy up the floor.

He made supper for the two of them plus horse-treats. He figured he could do that: she'd done everything in the day including putting him on his horse.

"They'd have gotten caught by weather at the midway shelter," he said during supper. "They could be holed be there. Suppose we ought to try the road?"

"Windchill on those high turns is too fierce. Uphill's easier. Longer. But easier. *They* can come back down a lot easier than they can go up. *Surely* they've got that sense, if they're stuck there."

"No sign of it yet," he said.

"Maybe they made it up before the weather. Just pushed on."

Maybe they didn't make it. He had to think that, too.

In that case he'd be sorrier than he could say. And he and Tara would be wintering in Evergreen.

But they had to go there anyway.

There was nothing right now in the ambient but themselves. There was that silence all around them, a mountain swept clean of life. Or life gone underground, gone into hibernation, as happened in deep, foodless winter.

But there'd been more food on Tarmin Height, grisly thought, than anywhere he'd ever heard of.

"You suppose," he said, "everything's eaten so much they've all gone to burrows?"

"Possible," she said. "Possible, too, they remember the rogue, and they're scaring each other, one to the next. Or possibly—that horse is out there. I don't think it belonged to my partners. I'd know."

"Harper's horse," Guil said.

"Yeah," she said. "No question in my mind."

And long, long after they'd settled down to sleep, tucked down by the fire, in all the blankets they'd brought and found, came a strange, spooky sending that drew an alarm from the horses.

Ghosty thing, just a shiver over the nerves. Guil lay still, but Tara sat up, and got up, and he stirred onto the side that didn't hurt and sat up, too.

The horses were upset.

"Something's wrong," Tara said, with her hands on Flicker's neck.

Burn came over and stood right over him, <hearing trouble. Nasty shapeless thing. Lot of things.>

Burn was going to defend him, that was clear. A shiver ran up Burn's leg and over his hide and Burn snorted and hissed at an unseen enemy.

"Can you make it out?" Tara asked. "It's not a swarm."

"Don't think so." He made an effort to get up and did, leaning on Burn's shoulder. From Burn there was another snort and a violent shake of his mane.

Not good, whatever it was.

Tara was <upset. Haze of snow, night, terror, horses running> came from her and from Flicker, he couldn't mistake that.

They were armed. They had supplies. But there was that notice on the board that Danny Fisher had written, that <bad horse> warning.

The kid hadn't been a rider that long. The kid hadn't ever been into the High Wild. And if he'd heard something real damn confusing—he might not know what he heard. But *two* experienced riders and their horses—

—didn't know, either.

It was a moral question to Danny—whether his responsibility for Carlo and Randy continued or ought to continue; and it was still a common-sense kind of question whether he could get Carlo in some kind of trouble by running over there to inform Carlo on what lawyers were doing, and including Carlo into matters that obviously involved the rich and powerful people in the village. Such people weren't as rich and powerful as they might be down in Shamesey, granted, but seeing Carlo was accidentally between these people and a lot of money, he'd spent some extensive worry on the matter, at some times concluding he shouldn't go, then thinking that while some were for protecting Carlo's rights, some weren't. And then again thinking—if Carlo was seen *not* to know, Carlo had a certain amount of protection, in that ignorance—if ignorance was ever protection, and his own experience said it wasn't as much as the ignorant thought it was.

Most of all he didn't know at what point of their own morality these people from the pretty blue-muraled church would conclude they were doing wrong. He was scared of lawyers. He was scared of courts.

Most of all he didn't want to mess up Carlo's future by making a decision that he didn't have the information to make, and he'd held off till this morning hoping he'd hear some kind of wisdom out of Ridley or Callie during their evening talks.

"You suppose they're going to treat the Goss boys all right?" he'd asked finally in desperation. "Are the lawyers honest?"

"They're fools," was all he'd been able to get out of Ridley last night. Ridley was mad about the situation, and that was what Ridley had on his mind: losing people from his village. And to the question of the lawyers being honest— "At poker," Callie said, which didn't tell him much about Carlo's chances with them.

"You suppose I ought to *tell* Carlo?" he'd asked Ridley then, deciding on the direct approach.

"Don't know what he could do about it," was Ridley's answer.

That put him in mind of what his father had always said about the law, which seemed the only wisdom that applied—just don't sign anything.

He'd slept with it, and waked with it, and worried over it.

His first trip this morning had to be out to the den, and he left the breakfast table, dressed for the cold—a light snow was falling—and took Cloud a biscuit from breakfast. The other horses, crowding him as he came into the den from the open-air approach, were obliged to wait: Ridley encouraged him to do that, saying that waiting their turn was good for them: they'd gotten out of their summer manners, meaning when they regularly had strange horses in the den, and they could learn they hadn't a right to every biscuit that came into their sight.

So while Ridley was helping Callie clear the dishes, he fed Cloud his treat and rubbed him down from head to tail and oiled his feet, quiet in his mind for the first time since he'd come to Evergreen.

Cloud was satisfied, making that curious contentment sound, enjoying the importance of the first and only biscuit of the day. Cloud ducked his head around while he was working and licked the inside of his ear, which Cloud *knew* he hated.

Both of them were moving a little more freely now, on feet less tender and joints less sore, and, able to go to Cloud and do such basic, ordinary things, Danny felt a great knot of tension that had been in him unravel. Conclusions hard to come to in the guarded ambient in the barracks were far clearer to him when he'd gotten out here to ordinary work.

The truly difficult things were over and done with, the emergencies were all settled, and there was almost nothing to do but brush Cloud's tail and feed Cloud and bring him biscuits.

Cloud liked that idea. If there'd been females available, the winter would be absolutely perfect. But, next best thing to please his horse, Danny thought about <hunting,> and expected Cloud to approve that idea.

Cloud wasn't as enthusiastic about it as he might have been. Cloud lifted his head and looked toward the walls and shivered.

Danny found that very odd. He stopped the brushing with his fist still full of Cloud's tail, and he looked in that direction without even thinking he'd done it.

He'd never been wintered-in anywhere before. Shamesey didn't have weather to require it, although a lot of riders arrived there to winter-over and the trade died down: Shamesey never felt isolated.

But Evergreen village suddenly seemed very small and very fragile against the mountain shoulder. It dawned on him then for the first time that there just wasn't any human civilization in the world farther out on the edge than Evergreen and the little string of villages down its lonely road. Over on the other side of the mountain—there was just the Wild, where humans who'd dropped down from the sky had never visited, not on their farthest rides. No villages, no trails, no camps, no riders. Civilization just stopped—maybe just around the shoulder of the rock outcrops on the road they'd ridden. Civilization stopped in the mountains he'd not been able to see from his whited-out vantage on that high turn. Nobody had been out there. Ever.

Cloud's skin twitched. Cloud snorted and the other horses acted bothered, but the ambient was otherwise quiet, and Cloud settled to being brushed again, rocking gently to the strong strokes Danny put into it.

A rider just shouldn't think about spooky things, he told himself, not up here, not when the wind had started to blow out of the unsettled Wild.

The snow was coming down thick and hard when he walked out of the den with the notion increasingly sure that in this edge-of-the-world place friends were hard come by.

The end of winter might not see him better settled in the barracks than the beginning had: he had every legitimate *right* to be in the rider camp for the winter, but he still found himself in an awkward position as an intrusion in the common room of the barracks—which turned out to be a family's living room: not that it was *supposed* to be that, but there just wasn't another child Jennie could play with—even as easy as the rider camp's relationship with the village seemed, *that* line was one people wouldn't send their children across—and the barracks that in some places was a very rough and careless environment, was unquestionably a family living arrangement in Evergreen, an arrangement in which a teenaged visitor of outside origins was undeniably suspect in motives and personal habits. He didn't think even Callie thought he'd do something so awful as have designs on Jennie; but clearly Callie didn't leave him alone with Jennie, He wasn't *friends* with Callie. He never would be, he strongly suspected. He probably would never be friends with Ridley, on Callie's account.

He didn't know what his relationship was with Carlo, and why he hesitated so long and resisted so much going over there, whether he didn't want to get the rebuff he'd had from some of his old townside friends, or whether he was beginning to believe Callie that he was a fool in the path of rational people, and he was scared to give Carlo advice on something he really didn't understand any more than Carlo did.

He was spooked about the law, was one thing. *His* early association with it hadn't been that of an honest and upright citizen

And *he* held too damn many secrets to sleep sound at night—Callie not even trusting him to keep to his bed. He'd tried turning down the vodka last evening.

Funny thing, Callie had said her feelings would be hurt if he didn't drink it. So he had drunk it, all but certain now his very deep sleep and morning lethargy had something to do with it. People who'd do *that* to you—maybe they didn't want you wandering across the line between camp and village. That was the other matter that had him spooked—but at least this morning he knew for sure what he'd suspected about his nights there.

And *they* were the source of all the advice he had.

Maybe they had their own set of problems. He had his.

So he found no need to tell them he was going.

He cast a look toward the barracks veiled in blowing snow, and no one was stirring—he'd given the excuse of going out to the den—he didn't have to give them excuses, and there was no reason he couldn't go over villageside on his own, absolutely no reason. Ridley was camp-boss, and could forbid him, but then he'd be out that gate and elsewhere.

They'd say later, Where did you go and what did you do? not as if they had a right to ask.

And he supposed, as he walked toward the camp gate and toward the village, that if he told Carlo what he knew, things were going to get out that could speed up the gold-rush mentality that was working among the rich. And that could rouse a little of the anger he knew was stored up and waiting for him when he finally *did* let loose what he knew about the Goss kids.

It wasn't a happy situation he'd landed in. In some measure he'd like to walk up to the barracks, fling open the door and lay out in two minutes everything he had to say.

But once you let a matter out of the proverbial bottle, it was out.

And panic wasn't at all a thing to let loose in a place like this, with all the High Wild around them—at least that was the only wisdom on a situation like this he'd ever gotten from anyone. Panic in the ambient was like blood-smell on the wind.

There were two other people who knew everything he knew. And Carlo began to be not only somebody he owed the truth to—Carlo began to be the only human being in Evergreen that he'd rely on.

So never mind what the village marshal wanted, or what Ridley expected. With a quiet walk through thick snow-fall over to the gate of the camp and past the restraining post into the village side, he was gone, on his first foray into the village alone, into the quiet of the villageside ambient, this time without Ridley's voice to fill the silence.

He found it spooky to walk among utter strangers. He felt cut off, deaf in a very important sense. Passersby became a threat to him in a way merchants and chance encounters in his own neighborhood in Shamesey town had never been. He didn't know these people. For the first time in his life he was in a place where he didn't know people either by long experience or by the thoughts they shed.

Which was stupid. He *wasn't* in danger and neither was Cloud.

But he'd sure felt safer when Ridley were with him.

Right now—he'd feel safer with eight-year-old Jennie for a guide, which told him how entirely silly he was being: the street was mostly deserted, and while a rider in his leather breeches and fringed jacket was as conspicuous as a horse walking down the street, he was in a mostly deserted neighborhood in heavy snow, and it wasn't exactly as if he was walking among hostile crowds.

The few venturers outside their passage system did stare. One man even said hello. A couple of girls—he thought they were girls—walking along bundled into shapeless coats talked behind their hands while they approached and giggled as they came close. "Hello," he said, defiantly taking the offensive in the deadness of the ambient; "hello," one said, and then they went into a spasm of teenaged giggles and raced off down the street.

Very young, he said to himself in all the maturity he'd assumed. Too silly. He wasn't interested. Much.

He passed the public tavern Ridley had mentioned—Ridley hadn't said whether in so small a camp he and Callie ever crossed over for an evening of what his father called ale and riot—or whether it was going to be a dry winter. It looked like a comfortable sort of building, with lights glowing behind glass windows, with tracks on the snow going up onto the porch and inside.

Then, next to a rusting and untidy stack of iron scrap and old truck parts mostly buried under snow, was a huge evergreen tree, and the smiths' shop.

The double doors were shut, as came as no surprise. But he took the handle and turned it and pushed, testing whether the place was open, and as it proved to be, walked from the snowy outside white into the shadowy, smoky heat of a large, low forge-shed.

"Yeah?" said a burly young piece of trouble who turned up standing right beside him.

In the same moment, across a low stone wall, he'd seen the ones he was after. Carlo and Randy were working at the forge, Randy with his hand on the bellows lever and Carlo with a set of tongs in his gloved hand—which, if Carlo's fingers felt like his, Carlo wouldn't find comfortable.

"Looking for the Goss boys," he said. "Hello," he said cheerfully, walking past the surly, close-clipped kid, him with his hair growing long and a knife in his boot. "How's it going, guys?"

The burly kid said, from behind him, "You the new rider, huh?"

He stopped so as to include the guy in his field of view—not inclined to ignore a provocation behind him, not in Shamesey alleys and not here. "Yeah," he said. The guy was big, but there was soft fat over the memory of muscle. The gut argued for more acquaintance with the bar than the bellows. "Wintering over, at least." He didn't like the tone. At all. And Carlo hadn't answered his hail—

Carlo hadn't given him a clue what the situation was except to say something low and fast to Randy. But he was getting bored with the threat, and walked on.

"So what do you want?" the big kid asked, not satisfied with one look back.

"Friendly call," he said, just about hoping the guy would pick up one of those iron bars and come at him. He'd *not* been a thoroughly good kid back in Shamesey streets. He'd been very good since. He'd learned to be smart. But God should give him some satisfaction for his reformation.

Carlo came to meet him, and Randy stayed. Quiet, real quiet, for Randy.

"How's it going for you?" Carlo took his gloves off and offered a handshake.

"Fine. Want to talk to you. Private. Got a minute?"

"Sure."

"Place to talk?"

"I'll get my coat. —Randy, you just keep the heat on. Be back in a minute."

"Wait a minute!" Randy began.

"Back in a minute, hear me?" Carlo tossed the gloves at him and Randy caught them, still not happy.

"You better get your ass back here," the other kid said. "Pretty quick. You don't get paid for talking."

"Yeah," Carlo said. "—Come on." He nodded toward the door and shot a look at Randy before he picked up his coat off a peg near the door, grabbed his hat, and the two of them went out into the milky white of a snowy morning, near the big evergreen. Carlo led the way over beside it and stopped.

"Just a real pleasant fellow in there," Danny said. "Is that the owner's kid?"

"Yeah," Carlo said. "Son of a bitch." And more cheerfully: "How are you doing?"

"Oh, I'm doing fine. Nice family folk I'm with. Nice kid. Pleasant place. —Is that guy somebody who stays around? You have any trouble with him?"

There was a small silence. Carlo ducked his head, arms tucked, then looked up with his jaw tight. "I tell you I'm getting out of here come spring. Me and Randy, we want to go with you when you leave downland, upland, I don't care. Anywhere we can get work. I'll have a little by then to pay you with—or owe you. Whatever it takes. I never hired a rider. I don't know—"

"Save it. I won't take your money, long as you don't want to go off the road I'd take—which is down by east or down by west. Anything else, you'd fall off the mountain."

"I swear—" Carlo began.

"No big favor. I'm going anyway. Might as well have good company."

Carlo let go a huge breath. "This guy," Carlo said. "It's not just *me,* understand. I've tried."

"This Mackey guy—the senior—I don't gather he's got a good reputation in town, clear out to the rider camp. Ridley sure doesn't think much of him."

"I tell you," Carlo said, thin-lipped, "I'd like to pound his head in. But he'll take it out on Randy. So will the old man. We wouldn't have a roof over our heads. And *I* could end up in jail."

"I think people in the village know—"

"I'm the stranger here. This guy has property. Listen—I want to ask you. If it ever got real bad—I mean *real* bad—or if something happens to me, could Randy come over to the camp? And you take care of him?"

"If it gets bad—*both* of you come over. There'll be breaks in the weather. I can get you on to Mornay or somewhere no matter the weather. Winter's bad. But it doesn't mean a horse can't move."

Carlo drew several slow breaths. "That's real generous."

"I'd take you this week if the weather clears. But—" He suddenly remembered the whole reason he'd come—and it dawned on him the import of what he knew and the village's ambitions, and maybe that it wasn't a real safe thing for Carlo and Randy to try to *leave* the village with their news. Respectable people could do some damn dirty things—for less money than was involved—and while there might be some who'd take a chance to see there *weren't* any heirs to Tarmin property but themselves—there might also be those who'd kill to be sure no other village heard about it.

Carlo could be living with one of the chief suspects in *either* eventuality, to judge by Mackey's blowhard son and the fact Carlo was talking about refuge.

But the plain fact was, riders weren't in great abundance up here. All of Evergreen had better reckon they couldn't get ten meters through the Wild without a rider to guide them, and that came down to him, and Ridley and Callie—with an eight-year-old they didn't want in rough circumstances. Things came crystal clear to him of a sudden, just being over here in this environment, that if he made it real clear to the village at large that he and Carlo were close friends, it might be the best protection for Carlo and Randy he could arrange. *Nobody* had better piss off the only rider-for-hire there was up here.

"Has the marshal talked with you yet?" he asked Carlo in his new sense of immunity. "About your rights to property?"

Carlo squinted at him through the blowing snow and went very, very sober. "No."

"There's lawyers involved," Danny said. "There's lawyers talking about how you've got inheritance rights down in Tarmin. That you own the smith's shop and the house and all. And there's a lot of people talking about going down there, families here just sort of homesteading all those vacant buildings."

"You're serious. They're going to do it."

"No joke." He felt keenly the lack of the ambient that would have made him aware what Carlo was thinking. "And it might work out all right. There'd be plenty of neighbors. Plenty of work fixing up. If you could stand to go back and live there—you'd *own* your papa's forge, the shop and the house and maybe more than that. Anything you'd legitimately inherit. Anything your papa's or your mama's relatives had. You could be the richest guy in Tarmin."

Carlo looked disturbed. He raked a hand through his hair, which had been damp with sweat and which was developing ice crystals in the snowy cold. "Mama's property. *And* the forge. And the house."

"You could be real comfortable—if you can be comfortable down there. This village *has* to have Tarmin operating. Only place they can really warehouse goods. You know that better than I do. And until they can get oxen, or trucks and fuel to haul whatever they normally get from Tarmin, they're probably going to have to port supplies up the Climb on hand-carts. That means it's going to be a real lean spring up here. Prices are going to go sky-high. Just immediately as soon as the snow melts this village or somebody on the High Loop has got to get somebody down to Shamesey and buy oxen, hire drivers *and* get some truckloads of hay up here to the top of the treeline, or the Anveney truckers are going to gouge them for everything they've got. Not saying what Shamesey will charge—if they get wind of it before they've made a deal. They're not going to wait around. These people have to move fast before word gets out."

"Where'd you hear this?"

"There was a meeting. Actually a couple of meetings. I—should have come sooner—but—" He was embarrassed in the face of Carlo's questioning look. "I wasn't sure. Wasn't sure who'd be watching. I get the feeling they haven't come here to tell you you've got rights. I'll expect they're going to talk to you. They *better* talk to you."

"They haven't. I figured—I figured they'd do *something* about getting the warehouses down there going. But—"

"I get the idea a *lot* of people are thinking about claims down there. And you have rights. So's Randy." He hesitated. "—How's your sister?"

"Don't know." Carlo's whole body said he didn't want to think about it.

"You could take care of her. And Randy. This Mackey guy is the *only* one that would be interested in the forge down there. He might try to buy you out, trade you here for what's down there."

"That wouldn't be a bad deal—"

"No. Don't take it. That's what I'm hearing: there's a chance—a real chance—that this village could go under—if the important people, all the people who know how to *do* anything, head downhill at the first thaw. It'd leave just miners and loggers up here—unless, I guess, people from the next village over decided to come over here and the next claims them—it's going to be a scramble, is what."

Carlo bit his lip. "I could go back down there. I *would*. Dammit, I would. I could set us up proper. *Hell* if I couldn't. Damn Mackey!"

"If they come to you don't sign anything. There's lawyers involved."

"Yeah. I hear you plain." Carlo looked then as if he'd just been stung. "I got to get back to the forge."

"Sure. I didn't tell Ridley I was coming over here and Callie thinks I'm the devil on her doorstep. I didn't tell 'em I was going."

"I owe you a drink. At least. Several, in fact."

"No difficulty. Anytime. You can come to the rider camp. No reason not. You get some time off—I can come across. I guess I can.

Nobody seemed shocked I was here. —Suppose they'd serve riders in the tavern there?"

Carlo looked embarrassed. "I don't know. I'll ask."

"Hey." It dawned on him that was one of a set of things more that he could do. They *needed* him. The village might have yet to figure it. But they needed him. The Evergreen *riders* needed him—or it was going to be an ugly scene, people wanting escort and Ridley and Callie with a kid they wouldn't want involved. He suddenly resolved he wasn't as down-and-under the local situation as he'd assumed—and that his situation was in some respects like Carlo's. "Who'd guide anyone anywhere but me? And there's horses painted in the church. This *isn't* too bad a place. We should *have* a drink."

"I'm supposed to get paid the rest of my wages. He *better* pay me."

Cash money was a problem he hadn't solved—having not a penny to his name. Villageside, it mattered.

"Sure," he said. He had a time to do something. He had somewhere to go. Amazing how that pinned the world down. "Sundown?"

"We'll be there."

He went with Carlo back to the door, and when it opened the heat inside was stifling and the inside was obscured with shadows and fire.

The heavyset kid was standing real near that outside door. Randy was still keeping the bellows going, looking their way the while. "See you," Carlo said, tight and careful. And shut the door between them.

Danny turned and walked back up the street, through the veiling snow.

Pretty town, all the evergreens, shadows in the white. Pointed roofs. Nice place.

He was still a little worried about Carlo. He didn't know what he personally could do until the day Carlo and Randy showed up and said Get us out of here.

Well, he did. He could go in there, let a fight start, and beat hell out of Mackey's offspring. He could tell the whole village to swallow it or choke, so long as they wanted his help. He'd *not* been a good kid, in town. He had what his father called real bad tendencies when somebody shoved him.

But—pushing back too hard and trying to deal his own hand in this apart from Ridley could make *him* a target for those who didn't for one reason or another want a rush down to Tarmin. That included Ridley, it included Callie, and probably the marshal and the judge and maybe even people who'd like to go but who didn't want certain other people to go.

It could get just real complicated.

One thing was sure: with gold, furs, and timber and all, Tarmin village wasn't going to die. Tarmin was going to rise from a bloody grave. He hoped—*hoped* Carlo and the kid could benefit, and that they wouldn't get robbed. Or hurt.

And he hoped Carlo kept the lid on Randy. When the news got out, and it was, he was sure, all over town—except near Carlo and Randy, which he found troubling—it was going to be just real uncomfortable in the Mackey household.

Because if the rest of the town was going to benefit from claiming free property in Tarmin, the smith couldn't. Not while Carlo and Randy and Brionne were alive.

But Carlo wasn't a fool. Carlo was *far* from a fool. Carlo had understood everything from the first hint of what was going on.

And Carlo, who'd swung a hammer for his living, wasn't defenseless, either. That surly guy crowding him was running a real risk.

Chapter

— XII —

Van Mackey had been at the tavern all afternoon. Van Mackey had drunk quite a damn lot, as fairly well seemed his habit in the afternoon, and was a fire hazard around the forge when he came down to have a look around and criticize what those who *had* worked during the day had done.

Fact was, Carlo said to himself, watching this inspection, and with Danny's warning racketing all day in his consciousness, there wasn't any fault to find. He'd worked hard and he'd stayed later than he was agreed to stay, and *he* was ready to go out to the tavern to catch a cheap bite of supper with his brother, when Van Mackey came in showing the effects of having been there for some time. He'd worked till his shoulders ached and his hands hurt like very hell. He'd hammered and shaped and finished the whole pending job for Mackey's inspection, a job for which Mackey would get paid a lot more than *he'd* see. He'd done a day's work in anybody's book out of a great deal of pain, and if after he was through and after Randy had cleaned up the place, Van Mackey was going to find any fault or mess up what he'd done, he was going to—

He was going to have to sit on his temper and not say a thing, that was what, figuring that any other course was going to get them bounced out of the shop and put on Danny's tab. He'd been building up a real head of resentment where it regarded the Mackeys—and he held it under an especially tight lid, watching the man poke into this and that.

But after looking it all over, Van Mackey came over to him and said, cheerfully, "Come inside. Have a drink."

He really didn't want to. In two ticks of his heart he knew for dead certain what the deal was, but he didn't see a way to duck it.

"My brother, too," he said. "I don't want him knocking around the street alone. It's our suppertime."

"All right," Mackey said, and the way he didn't object also said a lot.

So they all went inside the house like good friends, Rick clumping after them, clearly out of sorts and maybe, at least Carlo thought so, puzzled.

The wife met them in the hallway, a narrow wooden hall with torn and sooty rugs, and they all went into the sitting room, where the rugs were new and not cheap but only slightly cleaner. The wife had a bottle of spirits on the table, and she set out five glasses and started pouring.

"Not for my brother," Carlo said, "thank you." A glass of that and Randy would be flat on the rug. Randy knew it, and didn't more than sulk.

"There's tea," the wife said, and waved a hand at Rick, who hulked on the fringes. "Tea."

Wouldn't trust him not to spit in it, Carlo thought: he kept an eye on the process through the open door to the kitchen adjacent, and in the midst of a short course of small talk, watched Rick Mackey carry the ready teapot and a cup to the sitting room and the wife pour it. Rick went and slouched in the doorway, a picture of grace, with his hands in his pockets below a sagging belt.

"I have to tell you," Van Mackey said for openers as he and his wife sat down with them, "it's fine work you're doing. Just gave you a couple of days to prove it and, I tell you boys, I'm real happy with what I'm seeing. Fine work, real fine eye."

For damn sure the Mackeys knew what had come out of that meeting. And steam was all but coming out Rick Mackey's ears, but he was keeping quiet under threat of his father's hand, Carlo would lay odds on it.

Mackey poured the drinks, and the wife offered spiced crackers. "Hey," Randy said, surprised at the change in things. "First-rate stuff."

And after that, for half an hour at least, Van Mackey and his wife sat and chattered idly and in detail about shop business, neighbors, the mayor, the marshal, the whole situation down on the Ridge, and orders they expected and who they dealt with.

As if they were going into partnership—which, Carlo began to think queasily, just might be the game the Mackey household had in mind, a third possibility that Danny *hadn't* named.

The Mackeys downed two rounds of drinks and poured his glass full the instant it emptied, and considering he hadn't eaten, Carlo downed crackers at an equally rapid rate. If he and Randy had remotely dreamed of a warm and cordial reception in the village, right down to the crocheted doilies and the tea, the polite asking after their sister and the sympathy the wife—Mary was her first name and the last name turned out to be Hardesty—offered for the demise of their village, they couldn't have concocted anything as extravagant.

Right down to the offer of an inside bedroom, as soon as they could refit the pantry and install beds.

"We're pretty comfortable out there," he said, and Randy, with his mouth full of cracker and another in his hand, looked at him in indignation. He went on regardless: "Might rig a couple of cots out there, though. The floor's warm, but—"

"I don't know why we should," Rick said, which clearly said he *didn't* know exactly what was going on, or was stupid enough to ignore it.

"Shut up." Van Mackey said to his son, and to them, in a different tone of voice, "You can't go sleeping on the floor, good God, boy. I tell you, I was just real suspicious Peterson had fallen for some story, until I saw the work you do. And you're just real fine. Real fine, praise the Lord and His mercy you boys made it in."

"Yeah, I could see your position. I could really see that." Carlo controlled his temper and his bellyful of alcohol and crackers real well, in his own opinion. He didn't walk out, or even come close.

"I mean," Mackey said, "a village goes under, you just don't know."

"Yeah," Carlo said. "You couldn't."

Mackey might have spread the news around to the neighbors about Tarmin's going. He wished he hadn't had to tell the man anything; and it might be why they'd been left out of the information Danny had gotten, that the marshal knew he'd talked to someone and had decided they couldn't be trusted.

Mackey for an ally wasn't an attractive prospect.

Meanwhile Randy was darting glances at him—mindful of his strict order to shut up and *not* to talk back to the Mackeys ever, and not to talk to the Mackeys most especially if *he* was talking to them. Randy was doing all right so far, and held his silence on a mouthful of crackers while the wife said,

"We'd still be pleased if you boys would move inside while we fix up the place,"

And he said,

"Oh, no. We're just real comfortable out there, a lot of room, all of that."

"You boys have got to have some more blankets," sweet wife Mary insisted, while Rick burned and Randy stuffed his mouth and his pockets with crackers. "Would you like the rest of the crackers, son?"

"Sure," Randy said.

And on that, it seeming they'd gone about far enough, Carlo set his glass down and pocketed a fistful of crackers himself.

"Join us for Sunday dinner," Van Mackey said.

"No, no," Carlo said. "We don't want to disturb you. You have your lives. We're not here to intrude on your house. We're grateful enough for a place to stay." Then he decided to push it, about the time they stood up, taking their leave. "Could use a little extra cash for meals at the tavern, though. Growing kid there. —If we're worth it. Sure be nice to have the seconds."

"Hell," Rick said from the doorway.

But Van Mackey said, "You just put meals on our tab over at the tavern. We'll work it out."

"That's real kind. That's real kind, sir." He meant to make it fair-sized tabs and hide away things like crackers and other stuff that did all right on the trail—supplies were mobility, and mobility for him and Randy might be real necessary on short notice. Feed up real well on Sundays, when they had a real good table—

And maybe take the actual cash he got and put it with Danny Fisher, who wouldn't rob him.

Rick would turn his bunk inside out looking for it. He'd lay odds on it. And if Rick was a real fool—might try outright strong-arm robbery. Rick was bigger than any guy he'd seen in Evergreen, including the loggers. Rick was used to having his way—he'd seen Rick elbow his way in the tavern. And he saw the look Rick had now.

"You sure you won't come to dinner," wife Mary said.

"No," Carlo said, thinking he'd as soon snuggle up to a nest of lorrie-lies. "We're fine. Our papa always said, Don't get personal on a business deal."

If he was right it was only going to make them twice as determined, and sure enough, they took no offense at all. He could have tossed his glass onto the floor and they'd have smiled. Except Rick.

"Well, we understand," the wife said. "We appreciate your attitude. But you boys won't mind if I bring out some roast tomorrow."

"That'd be real kind," Carlo said, and with Van and Mary in close attendance all the way down the sooty, worn rug of the hall, got Randy out the door before he exploded.

"What's that for?" Randy asked when they were in the forge and far enough from the shut door of the house.

"Hush," he said, and got himself and Randy across the forge to collect their coats and go out to supper.

"Why in hell'd you turn them down?" Randy said, getting his coat on. "You crazy?"

"Tell you later," he said. "Let's go to supper, all right?" He buttoned his own coat and took his brother out into the snow, by the outside door, not by the passages.

There he could be relatively sure nobody was eavesdropping. And then he told Randy—while they were walking toward the tavern, in the trampled snow of a lot of traffic headed the same direction—as much as he was sure Randy was apt to hear, meaning the whole thing.

"People are going down to Tarmin come spring," he said, "and redo the whole village. We own the forge down there, and the house, and grandma's house and maybe aunt Libby's shop and *her* house, do you get it? They just figured out who we are. People from Evergreen are going to claim the houses and everything there's nobody to speak for. And we're all that's left. We're *rich*, kid, and we can kick 'em in the ankles and they'll grit their teeth and smile at us."

"That's why they're being nice."

"First prize. The only way they're going to get anything is if we make a deal with 'em, and I'm not ready. So you watch it. *You* keep your mouth shut and let me handle it." He wished he hadn't said that about kicking them in the ankles. "First thing, kid, we could end up *dead*. This is real serious."

Randy got a strange look. "You think they'd poison us?"

He hadn't thought of that. And wished he had. But it was one more reason not to take Sunday dinners at the Mackey table. "It'd be pretty obvious to everybody. But they might do about anything else. Like an accident in the forge. Like something happening to you. Or threats to you. So *you* stay out of dark places and stay where I know where you are. That's an order. Hear?"

Randy's eyes were big as saucers as he stopped at the tavern steps and looked up at him. "Yeah," Randy said.

"I think we're going to hear some deal out of them about the property down in Tarmin. Real soon."

"Danny say so?" Randy asked.

"Yeah. He heard it in a meeting. He came over to tell us."

"You know what I think? The Mackeys are scum."

"I'd say so. But *you* don't. Just don't say anything. Especially anywhere the Mackeys can hear you."

"You should *get* him. Rick can't beat you."

He didn't think. He grabbed Randy's arm and then knew he'd grabbed too hard and hurt the kid. He let go.

"You don't talk like that. —Kid, I'm sorry. But you be careful what you say."

Randy looked scared. And rubbed his arm.

"This is a public place," Carlo said. "And you behave. You behave, brother. Or I'll knock you in the head when I get you home. I mean it."

"*This* isn't our home!"

"Yeah, well, that's fine. This is what we've got, kid. Quiet. Quiet! Hear me?"

"Yeah."

He clapped Randy on the shoulder then and they went the rest of the way up the steps, opened the door—there was a glass pane with *The Evergreen* painted on it and a white tree below it, with light coming from inside, lamps and a couple of fires.

You weren't ever cold in The Evergreen. Overheated, maybe. The food was good.

Real good, if you'd gone hungry.

They walked in with not near the silence and the stares there'd been the first night they'd come. But the ducked heads and hushed comments from the gathering there did notice them—again and in a different way. *News* had gotten around; and now people were re-interested, in a way that warned there was something in the undercurrents, and that there were people here who'd really like a chance at exactly what the Mackeys would.

But hell if he'd spook, or let Randy spook. The kid was picking it up, not knowing what to do with it and on the verge of showing out like a fool.

"They're looking at us," Randy said, being at that age: but the fact was, everybody *was* looking at them.

"Yeah," Carlo said. "You wanted to be famous, right?"

"Shut up! They're staring."

"Fine."

By now they knew where things were and how they were. There was a set-fee buffet. What they'd been spending gave you one serving. But if you laid down double it was all you could eat up to three bowls, which was more than fair: the bowls were large. He and Randy went to the line, which was none by this time, found a table and sat down to stew and, at the bar help's order, a short beer for him, a cup of tea for Randy.

Then a shadow fell across their table, and a big miner or logger (devil a way to tell when both were in their tavern best) loomed across the light and sat down at the table with them.

"Hear you're the Tarmin kids."

"Yeah," Carlo said, and nudged Randy with his foot under the table, a signal for Randy to keep his mouth shut.

"Hear you saw what happened down there."

"Yeah." He refused to let the guy ruin his supper. He and Randy had *had* supper in the middle of the carnage, in the store which was the only safe place with food, and he didn't intend to be spooked. "I was there. It was a mess. Lost my whole family."

"Hear so," the guy said. "Real sorry. Stand you a drink?"

"Yeah, suppose so."

The guy—he turned out to be the head of the miner's union—seemed bound to talk. And after a little chatter about the oddness of the winter so far, and how spooky the Wild had been—asked the lay of the village, the size of the buildings in a jump so fast Carlo didn't even see it coming.

He answered, having no reason not to.

Then other miners began to gather round. Pretty soon a good many of them were asking questions, or repeating information they'd heard, and a couple of men said they'd been there years ago but they didn't know the place now.

"Not many would," Carlo said without thinking, and didn't intend to let emotion color his statement. But it did, and he saw Randy twitch to it and he saw a shifting-back among the crowd.

At that moment he saw Danny Fisher coming through the crowd—long fringes on his coat, gun on his hip: rider and no question of it, from the cut of the boots to the battered hat with the braided cording around the crown.

"Dan," he said, half-rising—Dan or Danny had gotten confused in his head down in Guil and Tara's cabin. But either way it was, he offered Danny a seat at the table as the one this time in his element, as Danny had been elsewhere.

There was a mild fuss made, and a beer gotten—Carlo wasn't even sure who'd ordered it. But Danny was mildly famous, folk immediately drawing the conclusion that this was the rider who'd come up with them.

And folk *wanted* to buy Danny drinks.

"On me," Carlo said, and with a wicked thought, got up and ordered at the bar: "What the rider drinks is on the tab."

By the time he got back through the crowd to the table, there was a dish of the stew, a mug of beer, and a cluster of miners and loggers.

"You taking hire?" one was asking.

"Not yet," Danny said. "Lord, I just got up here."

"Fool," someone said to the asker, and shoved his way in to introduce himself as Frank Remere, and head of a small mine.

Which could be real small.

"Excuse me," Carlo said, and Danny pulled the chair back for him one-handed, so he could get past the guy trying to sit down. "Let the man have his supper, all right?"

"What about the Tarmin riders?" someone asked. "Why didn't *they* stop it?"

"Because somebody ignored the rules," Danny said. "Somebody was an exception. 'Scuse me. I came to have supper with my friends. *Excuse me.*"

"Move away," someone said, "move away, let the man be."

"So what *did* happen?" a logger asked.

"Shut *up!*" another man said, and there was nearly a fight among the crowd drawing off.

But Danny was quite calm about it, and began talking, between bites, about how he'd figured there'd be a to-do, and how he'd told Ridley, who was camp-boss, where he was going and Ridley said there wasn't anything against his coming here.

"Different than Shamesey," Danny said.

"Everybody wants to talk to you," Randy said, clearly impressed.

"Yeah, well, I'd just as soon not." Danny met his eyes past the kid and had a much more sober expression. "Just kind of got worried about you guys."

"Doing all right," Carlo said, and picked skin off a peeling hand.

"No trouble from the jerk."

"Not as much as he'd like," Carlo said. And caught sight of Rick Mackey over by the door. "He's here, actually."

"He's a pig," Randy said.

"Yeah, well, don't say it too loud."

"Pig," Randy said.

Danny might have kicked the kid under the table. Danny moved and Randy jerked and looked sober.

"Be smart," Danny said.

Amazing, Carlo thought. There was actually sobriety from the kid. And hero-worship.

He didn't have that on his side.

But they made a kind of pie for dessert, and he thought if the Mackeys were buying, it might do real well for finishers. "Pie," he said to Randy. And while Randy was gone on that errand, he filled Danny in on the essentials.

"No offer yet, but, funny thing, Mackey wanted to be real nice to us today."

"I'll bet."

"Danny, watch your back. Just watch your own back."

"I'm not worried," Danny said. "But I do. I will. Do you like their offer?"

"They haven't made one. But they'd sure like me to be in debt."

"They'd sure like to have my help," Danny said. "That's why I came. I was going to say earlier—watch *your* back. Watch the kid."

"I tell you—"

Said kid came back with the pie, three helpings, with his thumb in one.

"Thanks," Carlo said, and, "Did you wash that thumb?"

Randy made a face, sucked the thumb clean and sat down. "Carlo thinks he's smart."

"Generally he is," Danny said.

"So do you *like* it over there?"

"In the camp? It's all right." Danny didn't sound enthusiastic. "Nice people. Not too much to do. But we've been talking about going hunting. If the game weren't so spooky."

"How—spooky?"

"Just not out there. There's been some village hunters clamoring to go. But nothing's there. Horses know. And there isn't. So we sit. Wait for the weather to get better. Everything's likely in burrows."

"*We* could go hunting," Randy said.

"I don't think so," Carlo said.

"Meanwhile," Danny said, "we're bored."

"Could do with a little boredom," Carlo said.

"Yeah," Danny agreed.

"So what are they like over there?" Still, things weren't quite right—Carlo felt so, anyway. And Danny took a swig of beer and sighed.

"Real tight, together, you know. Nice folk."

That might, Carlo thought, be the complaint. He wasn't sure. But Danny had himself a second beer, and they sat and talked about Danny's family down in Shamesey, and where he'd met Guil Stuart, and about Danny's first trip on the road. Just idle stuff. Danny was circumspect, and didn't drink more than the two beers.

He had his dinner, declared he should get back because his horse didn't like his long absence—and stuffed some of the biscuits in his pockets, to make amends, he said: Cloud wasn't as fond of yeast bread as of biscuits.

After that—Danny left.

And the curious closed in, the miner who'd bought him a drink, among others. "So what was *that* about?" the fellow wanted to know, little that it was his business.

"Friend of mine," Carlo said, seeing exactly what all that idle talk had been about. "*Friend* of ours, got us up the mountain—"

"Yeah, but what did he want?"

"Just passing the time of day," Carlo said. "Talking. Promised each other a drink when we got through."

"Amen," said one. "That's due."

"After which," Carlo said, "I'd better get home."

"No, no," the guy said. "Have a drink. You got it coming. The kid, too."

"My name's *Randy,*" Randy said.

"He drinks tea," Carlo said. And beers arrived. "*Tea,*" Carlo insisted, and that was what Randy got.

Himself, he'd just the one more. And talked to the miners and loggers about Tarmin until that ran to the bottom. Then he got up, took Randy, and said that he had to get back to the forge.

"Give old Van Mackey hell," one said. "The lazy clod." Ordinarily talk like that was a joke. But he picked up that Danny was right and the Mackeys weren't favored in the least. Rick had been there during the time Danny was; Rick had left after a quick supper, and hadn't waited around to make a case of anything with Danny. Off to tell the household, Carlo would bet, that he'd had someone else on the tab, and to tell them *who* he'd had on the tab.

He didn't personally give a damn, not for gossip in the Mackey household and not for gossip at his back in the tavern, of which there was considerable. He didn't have to give a damn, he said to himself.

And he made it most of the way to the door before a drunken miner grabbed his arm, introduced himself as Earnest something-or-another Riggs and said he'd be glad to look out for—his words—"two nice kids like you" and keep away the "bad lot, real bad lot," that would otherwise move in.

"That's real kind," Carlo said, and maneuvered himself and Randy out the door minus the offered escort.

"Damn!" Randy said. "They're crazy!"

"Wait till spring," Carlo muttered as they went down the porch steps from the tavern. The Riggs encounter had persuaded him they weren't as safe as he'd hoped. That there'd be numerous offers of that ilk, and it wasn't going to be easy to figure out other interests. He halfway expected another offer to follow him, after the rest saw Riggs' move.

But no one accosted them. Snow was coming down thick, haloed in the lanterns they'd hung on poles to keep patrons from breaking their necks. It looked peaceful. He wanted to think of it that way.

"So what are they going to do?" Randy asked as they walked home. "Those guys—they'll strip the place for nails. That's our stuff down there! I mean, I didn't think we'd go back for it and it's pretty godawful, but I don't want those guys carrying off my stuff and getting into mama's stuff—"

"You know how the phone lines go down every winter?"

"Yeah."

"No way any other village up here can find out about what happened down there until somebody hikes there from here or Tarmin doesn't come on-line in the spring. Evergreen, all by themselves, is going to swarm down there at first thaw, bet on it. *That's* what Danny's here for. He's making a point—showing he's *our* friend. Because otherwise we're in real sincere danger ourselves. You hear me?"

"Why? Of what?"

"Because there's folks here poor as poor, there's miners don't own anything but a no-pay claim and owe the suppliers their shirts and the nails in their boots. It's the chance of their lifetimes. These are rough people, kid. And that guy who stopped us on the way out—"

"Mis-ter Earnest Riggs?"

"Listen, you. Take it seriously. We're in their way. We're *owners,* you figure it? And more than the Mackeys might want us for partners."

"Why?"

"Kid, figure it. We're the only way that the Mackeys or somebody else could have a real, legitimate claim to the forge and the house and everything down there. If we sold it to them or if we partnered with them somehow—"

"Not with the Mackeys!"

"I'm not going to sell and I'm not partners with them. Just let me handle it. Danny said don't sign anything. And that's real good advice, because, to tell you the truth, right now I'm not sure where we're better off. There's no guarantee there'll even *be* an Evergreen if half the village moves down the mountain and there's nothing here but miners."

"You think they would?"

"Maybe." They'd almost reached the forge-shed. He stopped Randy where he and Danny had talked, by the scrap-heap and the big tree. "Listen," he said. "If they're up to anything they'll be eavesdropping on us, especially Rick. So if for some reason you have to talk to me about something Rick shouldn't hear, you say, 'I think I'll go outside.' Just exactly those words. Hear?"

" 'I think I'll go outside.' That's *stupid."*

"It's smarter than 'I want to talk secrets'!"

"Maybe we could go over to the rider camp. Maybe they'd let us live there till spring. I mean, *we're* not afraid of the horses, are we?"

"Forget it."

"If I was a rider we'd have money. And you could be."

"I'm a blacksmith. That's what I want to be. That's what I want to do. And forget this stupid notion. We've got *rights* to a hell of a lot of property down in Tarmin."

"We could sell it and go to Shamesey."

"What'd we sell it *for?* Smiths here have got everything tied up in their property. What's this business about Shamesey all of a sudden? What's wrong with here on the mountain?"

"Rick's a pig."

"Yeah, well, and if we don't go to Tarmin and take our stuff back pig Rick is going to get our house and live there till he dies of stupidity. I don't want them to be rummaging through our stuff, either. I don't want them living in our house. You want that?"

"No."

"Then don't talk stupid. You only go to the rider camp if something happens to me—"

"Nothing'll happen to you."

"Oh, 'nothing will happen.' 'Nothing will happen.' God! Did we look for anything to happen down in Tarmin?"

"I'm not stupid! Don't talk to me like I'm stupid."

"Then don't talk like it! You're a minor! You're fourteen! If something happened to me, the Mackeys could get custody of you *and* the property down there, you understand? I don't want that!"

Randy ducked his head. "Nothing's going to happen to you," he muttered, not because he was stupid, Carlo thought, but because Randy had lost enough, that was what he was trying to say; he didn't want to go down to Tarmin where everybody was dead; and Carlo hugged him hard.

"Not if I can help it, no. I'll take care of you."

Randy cried. Randy wasn't in the habit. And he couldn't go into the shop like that: Rick would make capital on it, for sure, if Rick happened to be lurking about inside.

So they stood out in the snow with no one around them until Randy got himself in order.

It was a chancy evening. Maybe it was the spookiness of a strange place. Maybe it was just suddenly realizing the person he was trying to do everything for was justifiably upset with the choices he was being handed. He pushed the latch up and went with Randy into the warmth and the firelight, out of the wind and the cold—but not clear of the leaden upset in his stomach and the feeling that shivered along his nerves.

He needed Danny, not just for his professional services, but—because he needed *someone* who wasn't his kid brother. Foolish that it was, he'd been vastly surprised Danny had really come across to warn him in the first place.

And that Danny had crossed all the lines to come tonight.

He still felt warmed by that gesture, in ways no fire could touch. He looked forward to getting together with Danny maybe next Saturday—and he'd gladly have gone over to the rider camp himself this evening—if he didn't have Randy and his silly notions in tow.

But Randy—Randy just didn't have anybody else. Fourteen was a hell of an age. Everybody was looking at you (as if they had the time), you were obsessed with your own stupidity and you were just so damn knowledgeable about what other people were thinking—fact was, nobody was interested in your opinions and it was a hell of a time to lose every friend you owned. Randy was going through his own grief, and it hurt, too.

Randy sat down and sulked on the stone wall where the heat was, and he could just walk over and hit the kid. That was what he felt like. God, he hated that expression.

"I could be a rider," Randy muttered.

It was the one thing that just sent whiteout over his reasoning. "No," he said for the hundredth time. "No. You can't."

"You won't even talk about it!"

"I just told you not to talk in here!"

"It's not about that. It's about what I want to do!"

"Well, you're not going to."

"Who made *you* my papa?"

He crossed the intervening space in two strides and grabbed the kid by the shirt.

And didn't—didn't hit the kid. Their father had done far too much of that. For a lifetime.

Randy stared at him, surly, full of his own notions, full of confidence he could go out there and tame a horse that might be a killer like the last one.

"Damn fool is all," he said, and walked off and got a rag and wiped soot off the water barrel. There was always soot in this place. The chimney didn't draw as well as theirs down in Tarmin. They breathed it. It got on their clothes, on everything they touched.

"You're always so damn right!" Randy said. "You aren't, you know? Somebody else knows something besides you."

He didn't say a thing, even an advisement to shut up. He didn't go back and hit the kid. That was what Randy was following him, begging for—so *he'd* be in the right.

That was the kind of argument Randy had grown up understanding.

Now *he* was the villain. He didn't know what to do about that.

He truly didn't know what to do.

Danny sat by the fire and braided leather coil for Ridley's leatherwork—which was really very good. He'd mastered round-braiding now, himself, though he still counted and got confused if Jennie interrupted him.

Jennie thought she'd learn, and after a while of his instruction, turned out to have more fingers than she thought.

Jennie was growing discouraged, and short-tempered, about the time Callie decided to send the kid to bed.

"I want to stay up," the refrain began. Which didn't work.

"To bed," Callie said. "Or you don't go outside tomorrow."

Jennie got up, put away her leatherwork and solemnly kissed Ridley, and Callie, and then, new idea, came over and put a big kiss on Danny's cheek.

"Good night," he said calmly, aware that Callie was vastly upset at that inclusion. "Pleasant dreams."

"Night," Jennie said, and flitted off with Callie hot on her track.

Ridley didn't say a thing. And Callie might have, to Jennie, but when the door shut and Callie came back, things were quiet—give or take horses out at the wall, bickering with something in the dark. Wasn't unusual, Ridley had said on an earlier night. It kept the horses from being bored.

"Might do some hunting tomorrow," Ridley commented. "Feels more normal out there tonight."

"Normal's come and gone all season," Callie said. "Everything on the mountain still feels upset." Callie was pouring vodka, two glasses, and a third one ready.

"None for me, thanks," Danny said. "Had my limit tonight over at the tavern."

Callie frowned a little, and didn't pour the third. She and Ridley had theirs.

So Callie couldn't doubt, now, that he knew very well why he'd gone out so thoroughly the moment he went to bed every night. But he tried to act oblivious to any hard feelings over it. He didn't look in Callie's direction.

"So how are the boys doing?" Ridley asked cheerfully—Ridley was very much the peace-maker in the house, and if he'd headed at the matter of the yellowflower in the drink every night he was sure Ridley would have a perfectly cheerful way of putting it that they'd feared he might slip around the barracks at night and threaten sleeping children.

"Mackey's found out there's money to be had," Danny said, and added with not quite double meaning regarding his own situation in *their* company, with drugs dropped nightly—but politely—in his drink: "and Mackey's being real nice to them."

"Man's not to trust," Ridley said, as if there wasn't a double meaning in the village, and as if they trusted him implicitly. "Between you and us."

They talked a while, mostly about hunting. And Callie was quiet.

Callie certainly wasn't happy he hadn't drunk the vodka, Callie wasn't happy about him being included in Jennie's good night. He didn't know what to do about it, except to make sure he didn't have wicked dreams strayed horses could carry and that whatever Callie's fears he didn't walk in his sleep and shoot up the barracks tonight.

He wished Callie trusted him. It was very hard to keep Ridley's kind of cheerfulness when he knew all the while Callie was probably planning to know right where her gun was from her side of the bed tonight.

And maybe a little of his thinking leaked out, the horses being stirred up. He wasn't sure. But Callie frowned the darker and Ridley talked on about last year and the hunting.

It was the craziest kind of conversation he'd ever tried to navigate.

Go at Callie's distrust head-on? Say, —Callie, I swear to you, I won't murder people in their beds?

Not if he didn't want a confrontation. And he didn't.

That got around to serious wondering—like—what had he missed while he was out cold, and *had* that horse been hanging around, and was there a solid reason for Callie to hate him and Ridley to be nice to him?

"Going to bed," he said. "Ridley, if you want to go hunting, I'd sure like to exercise Cloud, before he takes to digging under the wall."

"Hope it stays quiet out there," Ridley said. "Yeah, hunting would be a relief."

"Yeah." On the thought that there was still more being said while things were being said than any sane person could track, Danny got up and quietly left for his own barracks room, shut the door and started undressing in the dark by the light that came down the hall and under the door.

He'd *liked* dealing with Carlo. He'd liked being where he was appreciated. Didn't any human being?

He was getting out of his shirt when he heard <dark. And fire.>

A cold sweat came over him. He reached after his gun—he'd disposed his pistol on the bench beside the head of the bed when he came back from the yard, as he usually did, and he caught it up the instant he'd gotten his shirt back on. His rifle was over in the corner next the shelves—and he knew at the same time his brain was handling those locations that Cloud was <by the fence,> that it was a sending <from outside> and that it *wasn't* one of their horses.

"Mama? Papa?"

Scared kid, in another room. He didn't blame her. He heard a door opened and bare feet running down the passage—Jennie was ahead of him as, mostly into his shirt and carrying his gunbelt in one hand and his rifle in the crook of the same arm, he opened the door onto the hall and followed the kid to the main room.

"It's not Cloud," he said as he found Ridley and Callie putting on coats.

"That damn horse is back!" Callie picked up the shotgun. "It didn't go downhill! I told you it never went downhill!"

"Let me see if I can deal with it," Danny said. "Maybe I can get its attention."

"Don't you dare open that gate!" Callie said.

He didn't say, I'm not a total fool. Or, What do you think? I won't risk my horse.

He just went for his sweaters and his coat, against the cold out there.

"Funny damn thing," he heard Callie say to Ridley, "that it shows up the night *he's* wide awake."

He was stunned. He tried to cover it, but he knew he'd stopped moving for a heartbeat.

Then he flung open the main door and went out onto the porch, beset with a <blood on snow> image.

His waking wasn't the question on his mind: Brionne's was.

Carlo sat in the glow of a banked fire, blanket hugged about him. His teeth were chattering and he couldn't find the presence of mind to get back under the covers.

It might have been a particularly vivid nightmare—except it was still going on.

<Blood on the snow.>

As if it was its *name*, for God's sake. As if that was what it called itself. The way Cloud was storms, or summer puffs of white. <Shot echoing off the high rocks. Snow and a man lying dead.>

As if in the reaches of a shocked and grieved mind, it had been born anew there, in that place, at that moment.

<Snowy woods. Snowy woods with the glow of winter nights. All the mountain.>

<Something in the shadows, among the trees.

<Wariness. Movement behind walls.>

The world wasn't flat anymore. He could *see* and *hear*—the way he had on the Climb, and he sat there and shook—

Then it was gone. Just gone.

And the world flattened out again—crashed into flatness and dullness that left his heart beating hard. He sat there thinking of the journey up the mountain, thinking how that *sense* had been their guide in such desperate, blind moments—recalling how Cloud had beaconed them up that road and they'd known there was mortal danger every time that sense went out.

Danger of losing their way.

Danger of freezing to death.

He found himself with a lump in his throat, vision blurred in tears that just—spilled over and ran down his face. He wiped at them with a hand shaking so he almost couldn't find his face.

Randy hadn't wakened at that sending. Thank God. But he wasn't sure—wasn't at *all* sure about Brionne.

He'd thought he'd been able to hear Danny and Cloud, and maybe others they were near. It was that loud. It went that far. Danny said there was a limit and you couldn't hear that far, but if it reached him it might reach Brionne.

God! he didn't want that.

Spook-horse was gone, Danny was all but sure—headed away from the village before he and Ridley ever got out to the walls. The horses were all out in the yard, upset, lifting their heads with nostrils flared, sending <challenge> into the night.

Meanwhile nobody at the village gate had fired a shot. Danny had his rifle. Ridley had his. But they'd had no target. Danny knew he had to shoot it if he couldn't get it to come to hand and become part of the herd—and he had a sense, with Rain as much disturbance as he already was, that it wasn't going to be practical to do that.

Cloud and Slip and Rain came near them, <wanting fight,>and pregnant Shimmer kept sending <blood> until the nerves shivered with it.

"Too late," Ridley said in distress.

"Listen," Danny said. "Callie's right: I don't want to open this gate—Cloud would take after him for sure. I'm going to go over to the village, the little door—there *is* a little gate, isn't there?"

"Yes. But you'd be a fool to go out there on foot."

"Been one before this. My horse will back me up from inside the camp, with a wall between us so *he* can't get out—and he'll keep my head clear. Damn if I'll shoot that horse without a try to bring him in—if it's the horse I think it is, he knows me. I might have a chance to get him to come to me—"

Ridley caught his arm. "No." And when he made an effort to break that hold: "Don't take what Callie says as against you. She's worried about Jennie, understand?"

Ridley was worried about Jennie. Ridley, like Callie, would rather not have had Brionne Goss over in the village, which Danny knew was his fault—and he didn't want to discuss it, now of all times.

"Just let me go. I *know* what I'm doing! I know that horse, I *knew* his rider. He may just be coming to Cloud, to a horse he knows—or to me. I don't want that horse shot if there's a chance otherwise—"

"Neither do I!" Ridley yelled at him, but he let go his hold, and Danny took the chance and ran, with the notion of <upset and frustrated Ridley> in his wake.

A wall of darkness darted in front of him, came up on hind legs and plunged aside with <stormclouds and lightning.> Cloud was beyond upset, and more so when he dodged and ran from Cloud's intervention. Cloud chased him clear to the rider gate, close enough to breathe on him as he ducked through where Cloud couldn't go, and Cloud let out an indignant squeal and hit the post.

<Cloud beside the wall at the rider gate. Danny outside. Ridley with gun.>

He didn't know if Cloud understood that he wanted Cloud to go toward the rider camp's outside gate—he heard a nighthorse squall of outright rage and a sending that burned out into the dark full of <threat> and <fight> against any horse that harmed his rider.

Danny ran for the village main street, rifle in hand—pulled a sharp right by a big pile of shoveled snow and ran down a deserted snow-veiled street toward the village main gates.

"Here!" the gate-guard exclaimed, running down the wooden steps from the watch-tower. And maybe the guard had expected Ridley. He seemed momentarily confounded.

"Need outside!" Danny gasped. "Loose horse—outside! Little gate! Watch my back—just—don't shoot—don't fire a gun!"

The guard didn't look wholly convinced—but he maintained a defensive position against any unexpected inrush of vermin as, fully sure vermin weren't there, Danny flung up the weighted bar of the little gate, inward opening, wide enough only for a single human being, no more. It was for crews to go out to clear the outward-opening main gates. A horse might make it. Barely.

But there was no horse.

No vermin, either, just a gate-sheered wall of waist-deep snow blocking his path. He had to hold his rifle up and fight his way through it to get out, half climbing, half kneeling, until in calf-deep snow he could go along the outside wall toward the rider camp's outer gate.

The snow beyond, the forest, the road that had brought him—all of that was at his left and in front of him, deep in night and falling snow. He could see the deep snow disturbed on an approach and retreat that the horse had used. It went off into the trees and it wasn't a place to go afoot. He had to trust the guard for his back and proceed with no time to attend to self-defense, aware of Cloud's loud sending now, aware of Cloud's outrage at the camp wall separating two who weren't *made* to be separated.

But Cloud's sending was what he relied on for safety as he took a stance facing the woods and called out <Spook-horse!> in his mind, letting Cloud carry it—

"Spook!" he yelled aloud, hoping it was still in range. He never had known its real name. Harper had never said.

It was a lonely voice, going out over all of a mountainside on the very edge of human habitation, and searching into a deep evergreen woods.

"Spook!" he called—telling himself if a sane horse did answer him Cloud would know *where* it was with a nighthorse sense that wasn't as easily confused as a human mind.

And he *wanted* it to come to him. He had the rifle against everything else that might answer a hail into the snowy dark, but he wanted that lost, lonely horse to know he was a rider from the low plains, that it was Danny Fisher, Cloud's rider—calling him, another rider, who wasn't the enemy. He wouldn't harm Spook. Spookhorse might remember they'd traveled together, might come to him quietly, peaceably, for food, for human help. He'd escort it to the next village or wherever someone might want it as much, as desperately, as this horse wanted human help.

He'd see it fed, warmed, treated if it was hurt—he'd make a place for it outside the camp, and bring hay and biscuits—

<Bite and kick> was Cloud's indignant sending. <Male horse. Strong male horse here, defending rider.>

That aspect of his plan wouldn't help attract a stray male, and if he went further away from the wall to entice it to trust him, Cloud would go absolutely frantic to reach him—with good cause. Wade around out here with no protection but a rifle and put a foot down into some burrow, and a nest of willy-wisps would eat his foot off to the knee before Ridley's help could reach him.

Bang! Cloud hit the gate, wanting *out*.

"Get back in here!" That was a human voice. Ridley's. Urgent and angry. "You've done enough! It's not going to listen to you! Get in here!"

"Fisher!" Another one, higher-pitched, which could only be Callie. "Dammit! You don't have to prove anything! Get back inside!"

"It's no problem," he began to say—and stepped into a hole.

Damn near jumped out of it, scrambled on hands and knees—the gate-guard was witness, and Callie and Ridley and Jennie were, because of Cloud, who hit the wall again in outright panic.

"I'm all right," he yelled back. "I'm all right—it's only a hole! *Don't open the gate! I'm all right.*"

He turned toward the track he'd floundered and waded across, finding it the course of least resistance back to the village gate, and not at all wanting Ridley to open the camp gate, for fear Cloud would be out it in an instant.

Then anything could happen if that horse was here, lurking, and cannily quiet.

He reached the gates, out of breath and having worked up a sweat despite the cold, and in the little time it took the guard inside to get down the steps from his rifle-slot and to open the gate—for that moment he could feel how all the snowbound wilderness and darkness at his back waited for an outcome.

The latch didn't open fast enough. He really, badly wanted *in. Now.*

There were hunters in the Wild that could image not being there. Or make a foolish human think that safety was right toward its jaws.

The gate opened.

"Figure it's long gone," the gate-guard said.

"Figure so, too," he said, trying to be calm—the guard likely couldn't figure all that was in the sendings. But he was embarrassed to be shaking as he was. "Thanks," he managed to say and, after his moment of panic, set out down the street, slowly, feeling the long run he'd made getting over here in sore feet, aching joints.

He passed the smith's place, the tavern, the miners' barracks. Everything there was dark and still. It was possible no one had noticed—but down the street he saw some few lights.

The doctor's house wasn't one.

Horses were disturbed. Burn sent a feeling of <disturbance> and Flicker got on her feet with a sudden thump of hooves on boards that would have wakened the sleeping dead.

The just plain sleeping were an easier scare, and Guil reached instinctively for the gun he always kept to his right.

Right now there was Tara, who was suddenly up on one elbow, a feat of flexibility Guil didn't quite manage. He lay still to do his listening. So did Burn, for some few moments, while Flicker was up on her feet, a living shadow against the wall.

"Damn!"

For himself, Guil couldn't swear to what was ordinary or not in a given area. The lay of the land and the mix of creatures that lived there made a lot of differences from one mountain to the next and down to various zones of the plains. He'd been in a lot of them, at one time and another.

He'd never heard this particular flux of panic—except when a piece of a mountain snowbank dissolved and creatures died in a boil of snow and air, giving off their I'm-not-here and I'm-over-there that was their ordinary defense of their burrows.

There was death up there.

"You have a slide zone up there?"

"No," Tara said. "Feels like it, doesn't it?"

She got down in the blankets, cold from the air, and he put his arms around her. She shivered, then.

"Second thoughts," she said.

She might well have them. But he thought about <kids and avalanche,> and <kids and spook-bear,> that being all the image that would come to his mind for what they'd felt.

"You're crazy," Tara said. But she was thinking something far worse. She was thinking about her <escape from Tarmin,> in total white, with the whole world in flux.

That was the closest to what they'd felt. And from Flicker came an answering <white-white-white> that was Flicker's camouflage in direst straits. She'd spooked her horse—he hoped that was all it was.

"I wish you'd stay here," she said. "Something's real wrong up there."

He hadn't looked for that, for her to be thinking in the midst of this to be going alone.

So did he, except for knowing he'd be a total fool. Tara didn't have a hole in her side. Tara didn't have any debt to the kids.

Or maybe she did. She thought of <boys playing in the snow.> And right along with it was <Carlo and Randy in the rider-shelter. With Danny.>

She was thinking about <Tarmin streets. Bakery shop. Old woman, offering her a muffin from a sack, on the walk outside.> She was thinking about <group of people in the village, all holding lights, walking together through the snow.> He didn't know what that was. He thought it might be something to do with the church, but <happiness> had gone with it.

"You don't know, do you," Tara asked him, "what I'm remembering."

"No."

"Don't recognize it?"

He didn't. But for some reason that was an impetus to hold him close and kiss him on the cheek. It wasn't sex she meant. Just—friendliness. Just—something kind. He wasn't sure. He held her, she held him, Burn got up in a fair racket, and Flicker lay down again with a noisy exhalation.

Burn lay down.

The place was quiet, then.

"Wind's fallen," he said finally. "Snow might stop soon."

"Good traction," she said. "Anything but ice."

At which point she burrowed close, and he shut his eyes, never having figured what she was talking about, but he knew she was bent on going up there, and that somewhere in her battered sense of loyalties and obligations, she'd remembered her village and a couple of boys she'd known for years before the disaster.

She'd remembered a closeness with the village he'd never felt for anything made of boards and nails and involving roofs over his head.

But then—the things she remembered weren't just buildings, either.

Chapter XIII

There was a presence in the passage, early in the morning, and Cloud knew it—Cloud was aware of <men underground> and disturbed about it, following along the ridge as the <burrowing men> walked under the wall, and picking up <frightened men, angry men> all the way.

Danny wanted <still water. Quiet clouds in the sky> and decided it was time to get up, urgently so. He flung clothes on, hearing a stir in the barracks from <Ridley and Slip> and <Callie and Shimmer> and lastly and not least from <Rain> and from <sleepy Jennie,> who instantly rolled out of bed and tumbled onto the floor.

Danny was no slower into his clothes than Ridley and Callie, and into the hall at the same time.

Ridley knew the <burrowing men> and wanted <quiet clouds,> too. Callie was <on edge> and Danny sent out a strong <behave!> to Cloud, who was <digging at burrow.>

A knock came at the passage door about then, and Ridley opened it without hesitation, letting in three men, one with a shotgun, all with a weathered, outsider look about them, leather breeches, leather coats with the fur turned in—no fringes such as a rider wore, but never having seen high-country hunters as a group, Danny still had an idea what they were, and by that, guessed what they wanted—and also that they weren't used to being harassed by a rider's horse.

"Sorry," Danny felt obliged to say, even before introductions, as the men wiped their feet on the mat and Ridley and Callie offered tea. He had an <upset horse> and had to duck outside, coatless, onto the porch, about the time young Jennie was arriving in the barracks' main room behind him.

Cloud was out there in the dim first light of dawn, perplexed about the <burrowing men> and not sure what he should do about it, but Danny came down off the porch under a still black-as-pitch morning sky, hugged Cloud about the neck and reassured him with pats and his presence and showing him the men in his mind, perfectly ordinary men, <frozen Danny going back inside.>

Cloud was only mildly reassured, but he'd at least settled on the image of <men in coats, men inside by fireplace> and had the notion of <Cloud coming inside to fireside.>

But <flimsy boards> on the steps dissuaded that with a strong argument, leaving a mildly <upset nighthorse> behind, with Slip and Shimmer, who didn't find anything unusual in the <men inside.>

Danny went back into the barracks, shivering and very glad to go to the fireside and meet the three men. Harris was the senior of them, with gray in an impressive beard. And there was Golden, younger but not much, and Brunnart, who might be related to Golden, but Danny wasn't sure. Tea water was on to heat, and the talk was, excluding the matter of anxious horses, about the horse in the neighborhood and the game moving off.

They were the hunters Ridley had been going to take outside this morning—hunters responsible for seeing the village provisioned with meat that *didn't* come up the mountain dried, canned, and expensive—their supplement to low-country beef and pork, as well as hides and furs other businesses depended on.

And the hunters heard from Ridley and Callie what Danny also felt as the state of the mountain this morning, that there wasn't anything stirring out there.

"Spooky quiet," Jennie put it, sitting on the stones and with her hair uncombed and her feet still bare and her shirttail out.

"Quiet," her mother said, meaning a too-talkative child, not the ambient.

"This commotion last night," Harris said. "This business down by the gate—didn't see anything of the horse?"

Harris was questioning *him,* and Ridley didn't object. "No, sir," Danny said. "It was pretty well out of the area before I got out there."

"The horse came up from Tarmin," Ridley said, and went on to say what Ridley hadn't said to the marshal: "Male, lost his rider, followed Fisher here up the mountain."

It wasn't his place to talk to outsiders to the camp when the camp-boss was there to talk for him. That was the rule down in Shamesey, and it had never made so much sense—but it left him nothing to do but sit and feel guilty as hell that his—maybe manageable—problem down at first-stage had now become these men's problem, and the village's problem.

"Got to be dealt with," Harris concluded. Danny figured Harris must be senior among the hunters, and probably stating the position for a lot of unhappy people including the grocer and the ordinary village folk. "We're offering help."

"It's a dangerous kind of business," Ridley said, and in the passage of a horse near the walls—probably Slip—there leaked a little bit of <Jennie> and worry into the ambient. "Jennie-cub, you have to understand, a bad horse is worse than a bear or anything. It's dangerous. Nobody *wants* to shoot it. But sometimes that's our business to do."

"I don't want you to," Jennie said.

"You hush," Callie said, "you sit still, and you learn. Questions later."

"Yes, 'm." Jennie said faintly, and stared at her hands.

"Fisher," Ridley said, "you and I better go out today."

"Yes, sir," Danny said. "No question." They'd made their try at luring it in. They couldn't let it start stalking the village. He didn't like to think about shooting it. But he could think of worse things, including having that horse waylay a rider or a hunter.

"We're offering backup," Harris said. "Three of us."

"I think," Ridley said slowly, "that none of us have ever had to hunt a horse, and a man on foot is just too vulnerable. I'm not turning you down. I'm saying let us see whether there's any chance at all of us getting it without taking that risk."

"You don't—" Harris cleared his throat. "I don't want to talk in front of the young miss, but—is there any chance—it's here for somebody inside?"

"Not for our daughter," Callie said in no uncertain terms.

"It's possible," Ridley said.

Danny sat burning with what he ought to say, and with what *he* knew, and things he didn't want to say. But the water was hot and tea-making and hospitality after a cold and spooky walk for these men was at the top of the agenda.

He thought—I have to say something.

But what in hell could his information do? If the horse was trying to link up with Brionne—it was in serious trouble. A healthy horse wouldn't do it. He was sure of that. And *that* chance was what made him sure they couldn't take half measures in getting rid of it. Sometimes—sometimes you had to protect the non-riders who were relying on you, and sometimes you had to protect yourself and your horse, or the camp you were in. And if it meant doing something he'd ordinarily not choose—well, he saw less and less choice about it.

Sleep didn't cure the confusion *or* the anger. Carlo waked in the morning and lay in the blankets thinking that maybe, it being a new day, he would feel better and not lose his temper and maybe Randy would be his cheerful self.

But the more he tested his feelings the more he raked over thoughts he didn't want to lie in bed with, and didn't want to be idle with.

Fire on the glass. The rogue had sent that while it prowled Tarmin streets, while it drew people out their doors and the vermin had swarmed in.

People hadn't died quick deaths. Maybe there were some large predators like goblin-cats or lorrie-lies with jaws that could make a quick end of someone, but mostly—mostly the end wasn't quick.

Their mother had died that way.

Their father—

Explosion in his hands. A shock that shook the world.

Papa stopping in midstep and mama—mama's mouth open, and maybe a sound coming out—he didn't know.

Faces below the village hall porch. People with lamps and electric torches. Angry faces. Mouths open there, too, but he didn't hear. He just kept hearing that sound. That explosion. Feeling that shock in his hand. Brionne was lost and their father was blaming them for every fault, every failure of ambition or expectations—

It *wasn't* his fault Brionne had gone outside the walls. Their father had believed they were murderers—that out of jealousy they'd shoved her outside and locked the gates.

Give me back my girl! That was what he'd been yelling. *You did it, you were the one!*

And he'd fired. He'd fired when their father headed at him with the intent to take the gun away from him, and after that to beat him and Randy for God knew what. He never knew why their father hated them, and why Brionne was perfect. All their lives, he never knew: that was the hell of it—until this time, their father—

For the first time in his whole scared life, *he'd* held the threat, he'd *told* his father to stop. But his father wouldn't—constitutionally couldn't—hadn't.

He didn't remember firing.

There'd been the explosion.

The faces below the porch, all looking at him. Tara Chang speaking up for him. His mother damning him for a liar and a murderer—*I want my Brionne,* his mother had yelled.

And the jail. Himself and Randy—the bars.

All of Tarmin had heard the rogue in their streets, had opened their doors and gone out to help their neighbors.

But the marshal's wife had taken up a shotgun and spattered herself all over the office so as not to open that door. He and Randy had sat blank with horror while the rogue and its rider had gone up and down the street, calling aloud and in the ambient—all Brionne's anger, looking for mama, looking for papa, looking for them.

They'd sat locked in—listening—and Brionne had found them. Had screamed at them to open the door—but they couldn't.

And she couldn't. She'd tried. She'd tried and kicked and battered at the door in a tantrum. She'd called them names. And *things* had come through the ambient, things swarming over each other, snapping jaws, biting and feeding and tearing each other in their frenzy, and people screaming and people dying and screaming and screaming—

And when Brionne gave up and went away, the swarm had come against that door and gnawed and scratched at the wood for hours after the light went out.

They'd sat in the dark. He and Randy. For hours. Knowing that while their cell had bars to keep out the big predators it wouldn't stop the little ones. The vermin had been working at that door just now and again, but they hadn't been out of food yet and the jail hadn't been the only source—yet.

Then Danny had come.

In the dark, after all those hours, they'd *heard* Danny calling for survivors. He'd led them out without a question of where he'd found them and guided them down a darkened street littered with the scraps of flesh that had been their mother, their neighbors, every living creature in Tarmin.

<Daylight. Storm on the mountain. Blood on the snow.>

He didn't want to stay still with thoughts like that. He flung the blankets off, got up and got himself ready for the day before he went over to Randy, who was sleeping like a lump, and nudged him with his foot.

"Time to get up," he said, and Randy just snarled and hauled the covers over his head.

He'd had himself calm and forgiving until Randy did that. He knew the kid was sulking. He knew the way Randy would react if he wasn't sulking, and it was without question a sulk.

"Come on," he said.

"Leave me alone."

"I said get up."

"Go to hell."

He was mad. Mad enough to think of pulling Randy out of those blankets and bouncing him off the wall.

But it was those same thoughts running through his mind this morning. He didn't know what he'd dreamed about. It was those same feelings, those same memories of rage—Brionne's, his—his father's and his mother's—it was all there again. He didn't *want* to be angry, he didn't *want* to raise his voice to the kid. He never wanted to have another blank spot in his life like the one that night when the anger had come over him and come over their father and he knew his father couldn't back down, and neither could he. *Don't,* he thought he'd said. *Don't grab it.* Just before the gun had gone off and he'd waked up, just standing there with the smell of gunpowder in his nostrils and the shock quivering in his hands, in his arms, in his gut—

Came a door slam, and a great deal of clumping about in the passageway—*not* there, but here, in Mackey's forge, which probably meant early customers, and he had to get control of himself. He didn't like the Mackeys. They could provoke him and he didn't want to be provoked to lose his temper—it was too close to the surface right now. He knew what he could do. He *knew* what he was capable of and they didn't, and today he just wasn't doing damn well at holding himself together.

But the visitor wasn't somebody coming to the shop. It seemed to be more than one person applying themselves at the Mackeys' door.

So deciding the business didn't concern them and was some private visit to the house, he went to the forge to fire up and incidentally make as much racket near Randy as possible, to get him up in advance of the Mackeys coming in without having to argue with him.

But too late. He'd just taken the first push on the bellows when Mary Hardesty came through the door from the passageway and the house to say there were visitors and they should come along, and, she added coyly, that there was breakfast and hot tea ready.

"Thank you, ma'am." His stomach was upset. He *didn't* want to eat breakfast with the Mackeys, but it was sure something was up, and it didn't take many guesses to know it was something to do with money or their rights or something that interested the Mackeys. She shut the door, and he went and nudged Randy solidly but restrainedly with his foot.

"Breakfast with the house, little brother, and something's up. Put on a good face and behave yourself or stay out here if you want to sleep and I'll bring you some biscuits when I come back. This is real damn serious."

There was a moment's quiet from the lump of blankets. Then a slight stir. Finally a tousled head and an arm appeared and Randy crawled out muttering damnation on the whole world.

But bet on it first that Randy had good sense where it came to dealing *outside* the family, and second, that Randy's curiosity would kill him if he wasn't there to know what was going on.

"Wash first." Carlo went over to the washbasin that he'd set on the hearth to warm last night. He didn't shave much yet. He rubbed his upper lip and decided the job he'd done yesterday was good enough for any visitors the Mackeys had. And he waited for his brother to wash. He could guess it was the authorities that had shown up.

Maybe the lawyers.

Randy toweled his face off and was still in the sleepy sulks as the two of them went out the short exchange of passages that led from the smithy to the main passages and to the house back door. Carlo knocked and opened it himself, and he and Randy were already inside by the time the wife showed up to escort them down the soot-matted rug to the sitting room.

There were two men and a woman there besides Van Mackey, one he recognized as the preacher who'd met them at first in the rider's barracks, and the woman in sober clothing he took maybe for a church deacon. He was going to be vastly disappointed if this turned out to be a church visit: he'd had his attack of religion while he was afraid of dying. He wasn't, now, he hated being conspicuously prayed and preached over, and there were aspects of his situation he didn't care to meditate or confess.

But the third man was the marshal, Eli Peterson, and maybe that made this official, unless the marshal was a deacon or something in the church.

"This is Connie Simms," the marshal said, after he'd shaken his hand, and the woman he'd taken for a deacon stuck out her hand. "She's a lawyer."

Oh, God, he thought, having dismissed that idea and now having to get his wits a second time oriented in that direction, as he smiled a wooden smile and said how glad he was to meet Connie Simms.

"Sit down, sit down, won't you?" Mary Hardesty said, which he felt as a rescue in that instant, and Van Mackey pulled out chairs for the group at the table. Rick sulked in the doorway, on the periphery, and finally slouched his way to a seat between the marshal and his father and across from the preacher.

There was grace said: "Oh, Lord," it went, "bless this house, bless this food, bless these strayed children of Yours which have come through Your storm to the bright sunny clouds of Your blessing." And so on. It was long. It was a drain on the emotions of someone who'd hiked through that storm—or it pitched over the edge into maudlin. Carlo, having swung from one pole to the other, hoped Randy kept his head down and didn't smirk or fidget, and was glad when after three close passes the preacher reached amen. The lawyer chimed in an amen, too, and so, of course, did Van Mackey and Mary the tightfisted.

But they'd not stinted on the meal. There was ham and potatoes, there was bread and jelly and ham-drippings and cooked cereal and hot tea. Randy ate so much he was likely to be sick. Carlo kept nodding dutifully at the platitudes and observations of the preacher, and putting away the high protein stuff that was hard come by.

"The Lord be blessed," the preacher said at one point, "your sister is making slow improvement."

Damn. He should have asked. That didn't make a very good impression of him or Randy.

"I guess," he said quietly, feeling guilty as he said it, "I guess I was afraid to ask. I didn't hold out much hope."

"She's still feeble, but she's taking food and water."

Carlo tried to find something reasonable to say and couldn't, except, "I'll go see her, if it's all right with the doctor."

"I know it'd be a healing on that afflicted child. Bless you, young man, for carrying her up here."

The man couldn't talk without blessing this or that. He was worse than Denton Wales down in Tarmin.

But preacher Wales had been something's supper, and he shouldn't think ill of the dead, even if he had one more preacher sitting at table and snuggling up close to two more substantial citizens who mouthed amen and cheated at any chance they got. He just said, "I will, then," and had another helping of bread and ham-drippings gravy.

Rick meanwhile had put away enough for a road crew and two of their oxen.

Then lawyer Simms said, "We've come here, actually, in the interests of *your* legal rights."

"Yes, ma'am?"

"You're the sons and daughter of Andy Goss and of Mindy Wallace, his wife, who were the smiths in Tarmin, owning the premises and the house."

"Yes, ma'am." It was going exactly where Danny had said, and from having lost everything they owned, they suddenly had a lawyer saying,

"If there are no other surviving heirs, you're the sole heirs of that property and inheritance, and of your mother's property and inheritance. For the court records—easier if you might have identification on you—"

"We didn't come away with any."

"Too much to ask, I'm sure. Is there anyone besides rider Fisher who can identify you?"

"Tara Chang knows me. She's a Tarmin rider—but she can make an identification, can't she, legally? She knows me. She's down at a shelter with a border rider."

That came as a shock to certain faces: Van Mackey and his wife. They might have planned a fast one, Carlo thought. But the lawyer only nodded.

"The High Loop district has *no* difficulty with her profession. Is rider Chang coming up here?"

"I understand she is—come spring."

"Would she go *back* to Tarmin?" the marshal asked—meaning as a guide, as a village rider, maybe—he wasn't sure, but the marshal had pounced on that with some speed.

"I don't know. I think she'd go there. I don't know if she'd stay." Guil Stuart was a borderer, and there was no pinning *him* down to a village, he was well sure of that. But he wasn't here to answer for Stuart.

"The Lord bless her," the preacher said fervently. "Blessed are the faithful."

There was a lot more talk, the same kind as they'd met in the tavern, asking what buildings were where, and the sort of knowledge of the layout of Tarmin and the extent of properties he didn't think Danny could have possibly told them. The questions were in such detail they taxed his memory and his understanding of the village he'd been born to—and called up too much he'd dreamed about.

There was question about who'd lived where, and how many people there'd been in Tarmin—Simms was actually taking notes—and he didn't know what they wanted with the numbers. He was sure the real question was how many houses there were to take over.

But reverend Quarles said then that he'd like to hold a memorial service for the dead of Tarmin.

"Yes, sir," Carlo said. It was the only thing anyone had said yet that had brought a lump to his throat. The notion made it hard for him to think for a moment, but nobody jumped on the chance it offered them. Rick just sneered and didn't say anything.

Then Van said, well, they'd talk about plans for the future. "Maybe we can help these lads," Van said.

Rick kept sneering, maybe hoping looks could kill, and shoved half another biscuit in his mouth.

"They're good boys," Mackey said. "Real skilled. We'd give 'em a stake. Or talk a deal. Wouldn't we?"

"Sure would," Mary said.

There it came. And Van and Mary started saying how they'd offer money and want a share for staking them to food and supplies and transport.

"I don't know," Carlo said to that proposal. "We'd have to think about it. There's other possibilities."

"What?" Van asked, startled into bluntness and clearly not happy.

"I don't actually know," he admitted. He wasn't going to offer them a trade of facilities. And he didn't *need* their finance. He could get down there. Danny would take him for free. He owned the equipment down there. And the premises. "I'll have to think about it."

"Don't think too long."

"I'm just, you know, getting over this."

"Of course," reverend Quarles said. "Of course. If you need any counseling, either of you, you come to me, hear? Any hour of the night. It doesn't matter."

"You should come to *me,*" Van Mackey said. "Got to lay plans. Don't be listening to anybody else."

"The boy's *thinking,*" Mary said, and swatted Van on the arm.

Van didn't say anything. The breakfast was over and the visitors got up to go in a general shoving back of chairs from the table.

Only the marshal and the lawyer had a paper they wanted him to sign.

"No," he said.

"It's only acknowledgment that we've advised you of the situation," the marshal said.

"I know it's on the up and up, but I don't read much, sir, and I'd like to think on it some and maybe get some advice from several people before I sign anything."

Randy gave him a look. He ignored it. And the marshal and the lawyer both said he was smart to be cautious, and they'd make a copy he could take to anybody he liked to be sure what it said.

"I do appreciate it," he said, thinking that he'd take it to Danny, who not only read, but read better than anyone he'd ever heard.

And after that he and Randy and the three visitors thanked and apologized and chatted their way out into the hall and into their coats, in the visitors' case, and out into the passages.

He was for going to the forge and getting to work, but Van and his wife were in the hall and in his path.

"That's a real serious offer, staking you kids," Van said. "You're a big, healthy guy. You can do it. But it's a lot of hard work down there. What *you* got to have is a stake and some help, and all hell's going to break loose when these other villages get onto what's happened. They'll try to do you out of what's yours. God, some of these miners—they'll cut your throat for a tin cup, let alone real money. You take it from me, Carlo, it's a lot of real rough guys going to be going down there. You *need* some muscle. Maybe cash to pay some guns of your own."

"I don't doubt that," Carlo said quietly. "But I guess that's all in the future and I'd better get to work, or I can't afford my place here."

"A good worker like you," Van Mackey said, "we don't have to worry about. I tell you, I'd have *no* trouble backing you and your brother."

"And our sister," Randy piped up, having said nothing troublesome all morning. It was to make Van Mackey give and give, every step he could, and Carlo knew it.

"And your sister," Van Mackey added.

"I've got to go visit her," Carlo said—wanting just to get it over with. Wanting—just to know how she was or wasn't doing, and not to go back there soon. The whole world seemed in flux. What was past kept coming up in his face. And he wanted to convince himself that Brionne wasn't the bad dream she'd become to him last night.

"Anytime you think is good. Take extra time."

"Thanks. —*We'd* better get to work." He wanted to get Randy out of the house before Randy said something just too far, and he wanted time, himself, to think what to do. He did his serious thinking here in Evergreen as he'd done at home, in the forge with the bellows hissing and the fire and the wind roaring and the hammer setting up its kind of rhythm. That was his privacy, his sanity, nobody being able to get through the racket except by shouting, and work always being an escape and an excuse from somebody trying to push him.

So he worked his way out the Mackeys back door, smiling until his teeth ached.

"You," he said to Randy, "fire up." And he went to get his apron and his gloves.

But as he came back to the forge and was pulling on his gloves, shouting and thumping broke out inside the house.

Randy stopped work and stared in that direction. There seemed to be one hell of a fight going on inside, Van shouting and his son Rick shouting, and then wife Mary shouting.

"Remember what I said about stupid people being dangerous enemies?" he remarked to Randy while the shouting ascended to a crash of something breakable. "You don't know what they'll do. It won't be smart, but it'll be something he thinks will hurt us."

"The old man?"

"Rick."

"Because he's jealous?"

"You could say so."

"Well, his papa isn't too smart, either."

"He thinks he is. —And don't *talk* here! I told you."

"You're doing it."

"Yeah. You're right. I shouldn't."

"They can't hear us. They're all shouting."

"It's a bad habit. Mistakes come from bad habits."

"Are you really going to see Brionne?"

"I think I better." But he couldn't face it straight from *that* going on inside the house. It wasn't a day for family visits. "Tomorrow. We'll go tomorrow."

Randy's face assumed a sulk. "I don't want to."

"You go this time and you keep your mouth shut. Just when we go, walk in, look sorry, say how nice she looks. Say something decent and we'll leave. We won't stay ten minutes. I won't make you go again."

"I don't want to go this time!"

"It'll look bad! Just shut up and be polite. Hear me? Or I'll bash your head. We'll go Sunday. After church."

"Church!"

"We have to look decent!" It wasn't clothes he meant. He was ashamed of what he'd blurted out. "We'll go Sunday, when we're cleaned up already. Be done with it."

Breakfast wasn't sitting well. It was probably the ham-dripping gravy.

Probably it wasn't sitting well on Rick Mackey's stomach, either. He heard the house door slam. He heard the door to the main passage slam. He didn't need to ask Rick what he thought of the business, when Rick's parents were suddenly showering good will on two strangers who were a real threat. Rick had never had competition in his life, and now Rick had a couple of strangers move in who were probably better smiths than he was—if they'd ever seen Rick Mackey do any work—who were more polite than he was, brighter than he was, and worst of all, rich enough to buy what Rick Mackey had sort of hoped to slide into ass-backwards and without lifting a hand.

Bad news for Rick. His papa didn't need him anymore.

Bad news for two strangers that turned their backs on Rick Mackey, Carlo said to himself. Randy could gloat over Rick's discomfort. *He* couldn't. Randy to this day didn't understand about stupidity and danger.

He did. Much too well.

The hunters stayed for breakfast, no second thoughts there—Ridley and Callie had served up a healthy portion of biscuits and a small portion of ham, which was, in the light of what he understood about the economy of the villages, a generous act, and an increasingly expensive gesture. The village could reliably freeze meat for the winter. It just took what the barracks had: a strong unheated shed, in the village's case vermin-proof, in the case of the barracks—horse-proof. But if there was nothing to freeze—that was that.

And if there wasn't game in reach of the village, Ridley was going to have to take the hunters out on a much farther hike than they were accustomed to.

There was talk, during breakfast, that the horse's presence and the game having migrated elsewhere could be related in another way, that the horse might have gotten confused as the game moved and swarmed. *Swarm* was a bad and a dangerous word—one that couldn't give comfort to men whose business was going where they couldn't retreat as fast as riders could and without the kind of protection riders could get during a retreat by staying physically against their horses.

A real bad situation, Danny said to himself; and when after breakfast the men agreed that they should leave the hunt for the horse to riders, and left, Danny didn't even question that he and Ridley were going out today.

Ridley went back into his and Callie's room, advising him without any discussion of the matter to put on his cold weather gear. Nothing Callie had heard this morning had made her happier, Jennie was very much in a down mood and angry, for reasons young Jennie probably couldn't even figure out—

But, Danny thought, if Jennie had asked him whether he was angry, he would have had to say that he was—both angry and sad. But nasty business that it was, it was *his* business, it had come up the mountain with him, and he had finally to see to it as he should have done back down at first-stage.

So he went to his room and put on everything he owned, everything he'd worn up the Climb, and came out lacking only the sweaters he'd kept hanging on a peg in the main room as something he needed when he went out to the den.

He put those on, catching the ambient from horses who'd perceived <men burrowing back under the wall> and who'd hung about the cabin, aware of <hunting.> Jennie was still <upset> and Callie was holding her feelings to a very low level, cleaning up after breakfast.

He had a foolhardy streak. But not enough to go over there right now, when a woman was probably thinking that if she didn't like him sleeping under the same roof she sure didn't fancy staying here and sending her partner out with him.

He very quietly put on his outdoor gear.

"You shouldn't shoot it," Jennie said.

"You mind your business," Callie said sternly, and for just a moment that veil lifted on a worried, angry woman.

"I won't be a fool," Danny ventured very softly, "remembering *he's* got a kid to come back to."

He didn't wait for Callie's answer. He took up the rifle and ducked out the door and out to the porch and down, to give Cloud and the rest of the horses a light before-dawn breakfast. Cloud understood <going hunting,> which Cloud was greatly in favor of—but <hunting male horse> was a lot chancier feeling, involving Shimmer and foals and his rider's worry.

He'd ducked this, Danny thought, just too long. But he hadn't villager kids in his care now, and he and Cloud wouldn't be alone trying to deal with Spook-horse.

Ridley came out after a delay Danny suspected had nothing to do with dressing or putting his coat on, and everything to do with partners and daughters. Ridley was not in a cheerful mood when he came into the den, and Danny volunteered to go shovel the gate clear.

The sun was well up, casting full daylight barred with evergreen shadow on snow lying white and untracked along the road. In the stillness of the morning they were the only presence—and even a town-born rider could feel the vacancy about them.

The mountain was *gone,* as far as the ambient was concerned. Or at least wrapped in a silence like some vast fog in which the mountain might be there—but no one could see it, no one could hear it, and all the life that ought to be there didn't talk to them.

A normal horse, a wild one or a horse that had known a rider, ought to have made its territory clear to them. And it didn't challenge them, either.

"I knew the man that rode this horse," Danny said quietly as he rode. "He wasn't too reasonable. Once he took a notion into his head—he could get real stubborn. This horse coming back again makes sense in that regard."

"Not a Tarmin rider."

"Not Shamesey, either. Out of the south. That's all I know."

"Fisher, —"

Ridley was <not happy with him.> It was down to the moment Danny had dreaded. He'd called their bluff in showing he knew about the <yellowflower in his drink.> He knew that was dangerous. But <last night going after Spook-horse> he'd done the most he could <protecting the camp—> to show he meant to do just that. Just—

Cloud went light-footed, <scared,> and Danny didn't see what of, except that there was something in Ridley's mind he couldn't penetrate. Ridley *was* a senior, and *did* things in the ambient Danny didn't always expect. All of a sudden, out in the woods alone with the man, Danny's horse was picking up some uneasiness between them, after some unspoken dissatisfaction on Ridley's part. He feared, considering the matter, that he'd assumed all along that his enemy was <Callie> and that the surface of Ridley's intentions was the whole truth. Good humor didn't answer everything—and he never had thought that Ridley believed everything he heard.

Slip likewise wasn't easy to figure—Slip's image was a *lot* like Spook's, just went sideways on you when you were most trying to get a fix on that horse, there and there and there and there, until you didn't know *where* Slip was within a few feet of distance, and then—

Then Slip stopped and Cloud stopped and swung around and Ridley very deliberately lowered the rifle he'd been holding aimed generally skyward for safety.

The barrel came down toward *him.*

"Need some answers," Ridley said. "Fisher. Just you and me."

"Yeah," Danny said, and Cloud wanted <fight,> but he didn't, and kept sending <still water,> like a poor silly kid—because with somebody he didn't want to shoot, he wasn't much better armed than that. He was truly, deeply embarrassed to be so outright helpless, and so taken in by the man.

"You're pretty sharp," Danny said, while Cloud's withers rippled in a shiver of fight-flight stymied by <confusion> about the danger.

"I'm asking again," Ridley said with all his ordinary calm. "Fisher."

"I don't know exactly what you want to know."

"Yes, you do."

Danny heaved a sigh. "Can you put that thing down?"

"No," Ridley said plainly and simply. "I've got a village and a partner and a kid. You *know* what I've got to protect."

"Yes, sir, I do know that."

"On the other hand, you don't seem to me to have a lot of responsibilities to be protecting. Which leaves me and my partner wondering sort of what you *are* protecting, do you follow me?"

"Yes, sir. I truly do. And I'm not good at lying."

"Oh, you've done all right at that."

"No, sir, if I were as good at being quiet as you are, I wouldn't have spilled anything. And I've probably sounded worse than I am. I've *wanted* to talk to you."

"You're not sounding too trustworthy."

"I lied, all right? I lied to the marshal. I think." He'd been through so many ins and outs of the story he wasn't sure where he'd told the truth and where not. And he'd faced a gun before. More than once. He'd never added up how much had happened to him in a very few weeks. "I'd like your advice, sir. I'd have *come* to you for advice before I came in the gates, except my friend down there was hurt and I was all there was to take the kids and try to get them here—which I was going to do. But I didn't plan to do it without talking to you."

"Do what?"

<Brionne> hit his thoughts. And he knew he'd better come across with the whole Brionne business while he had any credibility with Ridley, and while his chances of riding home with Ridley were at least even.

"Fact is, sir, the <rogue>—" He wasn't managing his thoughts real well. They were far too colorful with <fire and death in the street> and the horses, neither one, liked the memory. Slip jostled Ridley sharply. But Danny stayed still.

"The girl we brought," Danny said, "she rode it. She got it into Tarmin. When it died—she became—like she is. And I've been scared to death, sir, —" His teeth started chattering. Fool, he said to himself. He *would* sound like a liar. "I didn't intend to come all the way to Evergreen. I didn't *intend* to have a loose horse follow us all the way to the top of the Climb, and I'm afraid it's after her—"

"Damn you," Ridley said. "You didn't *intend.*"

"I didn't."

"How much else isn't the truth? Chang surviving? Your friend? Aby Dale?"

"I didn't lie about that. I just—didn't know what to do about the girl. Tara Chang wanted to shoot her. My friend, Stuart, he said no. She's been out cold ever since, *I* think she's dying—I just—didn't expect the horse. And if you want me to leave, right now, and not come back till I've shot it—I'll do that. I figure—maybe—that's what I ought to do. I've put the village at risk."

The ambient was full of <anger.> But <doubt> figured there, too. And the gun stayed level in a long moment of silence, while Danny only hoped to God, whatever else happened, Cloud wouldn't be a target.

"How old are you?" Ridley asked, absolute confirmation he'd acted the junior and the fool.

"Seventeen," he confessed, scared as hell to turn the situation into that, senior and junior, knowledgeable rider and one whose decisions all along had been wrong. He *owed* Carlo and Randy to stay responsible for them and not to plead off on being a fool. "Going on eighteen. This winter."

"From Shamesey."

"Yes, sir."

"Who in *hell* put you in charge?"

"There just wasn't anybody else, sir." The tremor got away from him. "It wasn't Tara's fault. She was in Tarmin when it went, and she wasn't in good shape. And Guil sure wasn't. This guy shot him in the craziness down there. The same guy that rode the horse that's loose—I think. —And I didn't exactly tell Tara I was going to go up the mountain. She told me the route, but I don't think she ever thought the girl was going to make it and she didn't know there was a horse going to close in on us. —So we had to get out of there. And I never planned to go all the way up from midway in one day—so I couldn't ask you about the girl. But I had to leave there—the weather was closing in, and I didn't know how to judge how bad it was going to get. I just—left the shelter and it got worse and we kept going because I didn't know where I was on the mountain."

"Bloody hell," Ridley said, and slowly set the rifle back on his hip so it aimed at the sky. Danny let go a breath. Cloud liked it a *lot* better and was on the edge of <mad horse.>

Danny thumped him with a heel, patted his neck, wanting <quiet water.> For a moment the ambient was completely charged, completely volatile.

Then Danny ventured: "I'm sorry, sir. All I can say. I should have trusted you when I came in."

Ridley's face was absolutely grim.

"I'll go after that horse," Danny said.

"Let's just use a little better sense than we've had around here," Ridley said sternly. "*All* of us."

"Yes, sir." Meekness was called for. Ridley had met him with a great deal of restraint—well short of shooting him, which Ridley could have done with no village marshal calling him to account for it. "Another thing, sir."

<Scene in the barracks that first night, Brionne by the wall, Carlo sitting against the wall, Randy asleep. Himself—sitting against the fireside.> He didn't want to tell things he knew but he thought Ridley, if he trusted him now, might be an ally and if otherwise—he didn't know what he might have brought on the interests he was trying to protect.

"Carlo Goss," he said, feeling as if he had something stuck in his throat. "Carlo said he shot his father. The whole town was going crazy. The rogue was coming down on them—it was his *sister.* And there was a family fight. I don't say it was even Carlo's idea to shoot. I can't say it wasn't. I don't know what the reason was. I just know he's no killer. He survived the swarm in the jail. He and the kid—that's where they were, and Randy's only fourteen. I figured—figured with what they'd been through—I didn't need to bring that up. Let him start over again. Let him take care of the kid and the sister. That's what I thought."

Ridley drew a slow, deep breath and let it go, a cloud in the frosty morning.

"Any *more* cards you want to lay on the table?"

"No, sir. That's all."

"I think," Ridley said, "that you did pretty damn well under the circumstances."

Danny asked himself if he felt that about himself, and he thought not.

And as Ridley imaged them <going on through the woods,> he thought it might be well to keep the ambient very quiet, very subdued while he and Ridley went side by side, and until he was certain what Ridley was thinking.

He didn't look forward to going back to the barracks until Ridley had gotten his mind made up what to do. Callie might vote for shooting him.

And he didn't ever want to see an accusing look in Jennie's eyes, Jennie who had as much reason as Callie not to trust him anymore.

"We're after <a horse,"> Ridley said.

"Yes, sir." He tried to call <Spook-horse,> then, but he couldn't put the conviction of harmlessness into his own image that he needed to.

"I don't like this any better than you do," Ridley said shortly. "None of us like this."

"Yes, sir." He was completely rattled. He felt like a traitor to a decent man on the one hand and a thoroughgoing traitor to an unlucky horse on the other—a horse who'd never actually threatened, who'd tagged on to them but never done them harm, who just for God's sake wanted the only humans in reach to do something to straighten out the mess it had fallen into. Its sending was *lonely,* most of all, just terribly *lonely.*

"We all feel sorry!" Ridley snapped at him.

"Yes, sir," he said in real contrition, and for a while there was quiet.

Then Ridley said, "Let's go back and pretend we shot at it."

He thought Ridley was making a bad joke. But Ridley wanted Slip <turning toward home,> and Cloud followed Slip into a turn.

"Do we say that, sir?" he ventured to ask. He still wasn't sure what was going through Ridley's mind.

And after a moment of quiet, Ridley said,

"We've got to tell the village something, don't we?" Ridley fired his rifle off without a blink in warning and Cloud jumped and Slip jumped.

"That might scare it off," Ridley said.

It might draw it in, too. It was hard to know, with a horse. And he didn't think even yet he could get into Ridley's thoughts.

He didn't think, for one thing, that Ridley had made up his mind what to do—or that the principal reason Ridley had come out today with him was to hunt horses. He didn't know—maybe Ridley had caught sympathy for it from him, or maybe Ridley wasn't so sure now that he wanted to be alone with him so far from camp and wanted simply to set him off his guard.

Maybe *he'd* been Ridley's real quarry, today. He began to think so.

He didn't know even yet if he trusted Ridley. He had a far better idea where Callie was.

Outright dislike was a lot easier to map.

Saturday night, and the talk in the village was the horse haunting the vicinity—far too high on the mountain, far too late in the year, and far too coincidental to the arrival of strangers to be chance.

Carlo heard it from Rick, who lounged, thumbs in belt, near the forge. "I hear you brought us a gift. I'd say somebody who'd done that ought to be shot. What do you think?"

"What gift?" he'd said, as if he couldn't mostly guess—he'd been in such a state he'd let Rick back him against one of the walls in the forge and try to intimidate him.

"Outside of that pretty little sister of yours, who's cold as yesterday's fish? A *horse,* mister. A *horse* come around the walls last night and there's a lot of people asking why."

"Not my problem," Carlo said.

"I'll bet," Rick said. Rick's attempts to make trouble were always tedious and full of bluster.

And it took maybe a quarter of an hour and Rick heading off to the tavern before they were rid of him.

"Was there a horse?" Randy asked. "I *dreamed* about a horse. I dreamed that horse was following us."

"Yeah," Carlo said, "well, I guess it did. And don't talk here."

"Pig Rick's gone."

"Just don't start finding excuses," Carlo said. "This isn't a *game,* have you got that figured? This isn't a *game* we're playing with *rules* and *exceptions* and *time-outs.* You do what I tell you."

"I don't see the reason—"

He laid a very careful hand on Randy's shoulder. "Little brother. Let's be done. Let's have a beer."

"You don't let me drink."

"I'll let you drink tonight. One beer. All right?"

"All right."

He let go of Randy's shoulder. He'd had only one thought in that, that it was just best if Randy slept soundly tonight. And if he had to carry the kid home that was the way it would be.

So they went and closed up shop.

"Can we talk?" Randy said when they'd got outside. "About the horse, I mean. I mean, people are going to ask us."

"You keep quiet. You don't mention it."

"Do you think Danny's going to come?"

"I don't know. How am I supposed to know?" He didn't mean to be sour with the kid, but Randy was being fourteen. Or thirteen. Or whatever. He was tired. His eyes watered with the smoke that water didn't take away, his arms hurt, his shoulders hurt, and his hands hurt, and most of all his gut hurt from the desire never to have to deal with Rick Mackey, who was bound to be inside.

They walked up onto the porch, stamped the snow off on the mat and walked in.

"There's the ones that brought the horse!"

"Pig!" Randy yelled at Rick.

Carlo jerked him sideways and Randy yowled in protest—which didn't get the public fight Rick was spoiling to create. Carlo just went toward the back of the tavern, found a table on the borderland of miner's territory and headed Randy at the chair.

"Hold the table."

"I don't think—"

"*Hold* the damn table," Carlo said, and maybe he looked mad. Randy shut up and sat down and held the table while he went over and put two meals on the Mackey account.

"Watch those," he said, set the bowls on the table and went after the beers.

He kept an eye out all the same, to make sure the kid stayed seated and people stayed away from the kid.

"So what about the horse?" the bartender asked.

"What *I* hear," Carlo said in all sobriety, on an instant's impulse, and very conscious what he was saying, "is it belonged to a rider down at Tarmin who crossed a friend of Danny Fisher. It's looking for another rider. Drove the last one crazy. Just stark staring crazy."

"God bless," the bartender said. "Don't need none of that."

"I'd lock the doors at night," he said. He was being a fool. He didn't have any business pushing the matter. It had just gotten on his nerves, and now he knew the whole story would be all over town by morning—tell the *bartender,* for God's sake. And mention *crazy* after what had happened down at Tarmin. He'd meant to get the matter of the horse off him and Randy. And what he'd just done hadn't been at all bright.

He thought—he thought he'd like to go to church tomorrow.

He brought the beers back. Meanwhile Randy was trying to ignore a miner who'd sat down in the other seat and was asking questions.

"My seat," Carlo said. "My supper. My brother. 'Scuse me." He quietly got possession of the seat, glared at the departing miner, and shoved a beer at Randy.

"There."

Randy picked up the mug and took a gulp.

"Go easy on that. I'm not carrying you."

"You should have bashed Rick."

"Yeah, well, I'm not thirteen."

"I'm fourteen."

"Then act like it."

"Listen. You—"

Another commotion started near the door, but it wasn't Rick, it was Van Mackey, who was tolerably drunk, telling his son go home.

Rick didn't want to go.

There was pushing and shoving.

Carlo sipped his beer and had a spoonful of stew. The Mackey family argument was headed for the porch when the door opened and Danny Fisher came in.

Danny paused for a look at the argument going out the door past him, and walked through the murmur of people who'd moved in with questions for a rider to answer.

Like what about the horse, he was sure. Danny meanwhile spotted them, came to the bar and gathered up a beer, probably telling enough in the process to make him look like a fool with the bartender. He *wished* he had had sense enough to keep his mouth shut. God! he was a fool.

Then Danny came toward them. Randy scrambled up and got an unused chair from another table, and Danny joined them, the object of every eye in the tavern, at least it felt that way.

Danny had certainly said something to the bartender. Gossip had started there, heads together with the bartender, a buzz of conversation just out of range of hearing, the nearer tables preferring to stare and hunch down over their beers.

"I heard—" Carlo began, "—about last night."

"We went out today," Danny said, "with no better luck."

"I *dreamed* about the horse," Randy said. "I heard it. I keep saying, if you'd just let me go—"

"No," Carlo said. "He's still got a notion about being a rider."

Danny shook his head. "No. Not that horse. Take it from me, not that horse."

"I *hear* it."

"Him. If you *heard* him you'd know it's him. He's confused, he's lost. And if you were going to be a rider—you wouldn't want that horse. Believe me."

"I'm telling you—"

"Listen to him," Carlo said.

"I don't *want* to listen. I want somebody to listen to *me*."

"Randy," Danny said, "when I was not too much older, I took up with Cloud. And we were fools together, down in the warm flatlands, in a good season. We managed not to break our necks—close as it was. We managed not to get shot. I'm telling you—plain as I can say it—this horse is likely to get shot."

"You *can't!*"

"I've been trying not to. So's Ridley. But there's a limit to what he'll let go on near this village. We can't put this village in danger."

Randy was shaking. Literally shaking. He looked as if he'd cry. He had a gulp of beer instead.

Danny reached out and put his hand on Randy's shoulder. "Believe me. Randy. I'd do anything but shoot that horse. We're up *here* because I didn't want to shoot him. But that's not saying anybody belongs with him. This horse isn't for a kid. No way. A senior rider might be able to pull him out of his confusion, if he could get close enough, but I'm scared of him—I'll tell you *I'm* scared of him, as far as putting Cloud at risk. I went out hunting him today, but I went with the camp-boss and *his* horse, and he wouldn't show. We did some shooting. Might have scared him off."

"You said you can't hear a horse over ten meters," Carlo said. "That sure wasn't the case on the road."

"Yeah, well. Most times. This is the exception."

"This horse? Or this *time?*"

"Don't want to talk here," Danny said.

"Yeah," Carlo agreed. Randy had taken down too much of the beer and too little supper. "Eat, kid. Remember when you went hungry."

Randy began to pick at his food.

"Eat it while you've got it," Danny said. "There's *no* game out there. Biggest damn vacancy you ever heard. Meat's going to get real scarce and the flour's going to rise come midwinter, what I hear."

"I want to live in the rider camp," Randy said.

"Randy," Carlo said. He never called his brother by his given name. It got the kid's attention. "Twelve. Hear me?"

"Shit."

Carlo got up, went to the bar and got another round of beers. Brought them back and set them down.

Danny gave him an odd look and didn't say a thing. Randy, heart set on being a fool, didn't say, No, I've had too many. Randy finished off the one when the second arrived.

Carlo tried to hold himself back, because tonight he'd rather the beer than the stew, himself.

"Buy you supper?" Carlo asked.

"I'm having supper in the camp," Danny said. "Maybe next week."

"Sure. But the beers are on the Mackeys."

"Thank 'em for me," Danny said.

"Sure," Carlo said. He spooned down his stew and the part of Randy's Randy didn't eat. Had two pieces of bread. And by that time Randy was sotted.

"You ought to beat Rick up," Randy said, out of nowhere.

"Yeah. Sure. Someday. *Don't* push it. You're not cute when you're drunk and you're getting there real fast."

"Am not."

"Yeah." Carlo watched, and finished his beer, and had the notion with Danny never saying a thing that Danny wanted to talk to him in private before he left.

And in not too long Carlo shoved back his chair, gathered up Randy by an arm and had Danny's help on the other side. They got his coat and his hat on. And theirs.

There might be a village rule against drunk kids. Nobody said anything and they walked Randy out into the chill air.

Randy didn't come around to sobriety. They walked him down the steps and across the intervening yard toward the junk pile and the tree.

There Carlo stopped. "Let the kid sit," he said, and he and Danny let Randy down to sit in the snow.

"So what couldn't you say inside?" Carlo asked.

Danny drew a long breath. "That I had to tell Ridley about your sister."

"Damn!"

"I think," Danny said, "he's all right. I think he's all right about it. He knows we didn't have much choice. Rider business and village business don't cross from one side to the other. He's worried—he's worried about the horse coming for your sister. That's the main thing. *Have* you seen her? Do you have any idea—whether there's been any change?"

"I can find out," Carlo said. He didn't *want* to know. He was supposed to go there tomorrow. After church. And he didn't want to. Not after finding out the riders knew. He didn't know if he could keep himself calm around her. "What's he going to do about it?"

"I don't know yet. I think he understands we were out of choices. —Carlo, I—had to tell him the rest of it. About where you were. And why."

Supper went to ice on his stomach.

"He won't tell the marshal," Danny said. "It's just—if I'm going to ask Ridley's help, I have to tell him the whole thing."

"Yeah," Carlo said bitterly.

"No one will know."

"The rider camp is *no one?* I don't believe it. I've got a brother—"

"Nothing will happen to him."

"Dammit. *Dammit. I trusted you!*"

Danny was quiet for a moment. "He won't go to the marshal with it. I don't think he will."

"You don't think. Danny—"

"Or I'll get you *out* of here. I promise you. I *promise* you."

He couldn't organize his thoughts. He didn't know what he thought, and two beers didn't help. He wanted to sit down where he was. He wanted not to think about it.

"Yeah," he said. He'd learned—adults didn't take things for granted. Adults didn't trust blindly. Adults didn't expect other adults to keep extravagant promises.

Danny walked away.

Carlo gathered Randy up by an arm and got him moving. Maybe Randy'd heard enough of it for a thought or two to penetrate his brain. Maybe he hadn't.

He didn't know himself what he'd just heard. He was mad. But he wished he had the sense not to be walking away from Danny. He wished he could go back and say, because he *had* no other friend, Let's talk about this.

But when he looked back, from the door to the forge, with Randy's weight on his arm, Danny hadn't hung around. Danny was a distant figure down the snowy street.

Chapter — XIV—

There were evergreen boughs on the altar, there were lamps burning with sweet-smelling oil, and after the social announcements from the various families, the preacher preached a sermon on the righteousness of God and His Mercy, and turned it into a kind of memorial for Tarmin.

Carlo liked the smells and the sights, and the church murals weren't so fine as those in Tarmin, but they were amazing to his eyes—portraying creatures of the New World, which wouldn't have pleased preacher Wales down in Tarmin, not by a long way.

And the preacher really got to him when he started talking about the kids down in Tarmin. He had a lump in his throat and noted people in the seats down the row were using handkerchiefs. The preacher proceeded to the old business of how nobody ever knew the hour or the day they'd die, which was predictably grim, and then segued into an exhortation to enjoy the world—which was so sharp a left turn from the expected path of doom and gloom that Carlo tried to reconstruct in his mind exactly how the preacher had gotten where he had from the point where preacher Wales had always concluded the world was the source of evil.

Enjoy life? He could get along with this preacher.

Randy fidgeted. He always had fidgeted in church. Carlo nudged his ankle and Randy slouched. Randy always would do that, too. Neither of them had ever favored church—but it was a comfortable and comforting thing this morning, after so much was out of joint, to be sitting in the smells of winter Sundays and hearing a sermon just like every week. Reverend Quarles went on, in his quiet manner, talking about right actions and not cheating your neighbor—and *redeeming* the damned world with good living and right dealing. That was a new twist, and it ought to have made the Mackeys squirm, but probably not, Carlo thought. Most everybody could feel comfortable with Reverend Quarles. Even *he* could. He thought if things worked out, he could very easily get along with this church.

The sermon didn't conclude in hellfire. It meandered off into how there was a horse out there, but they had it on good information it wasn't mad, or even particularly dangerous. Reverend Quarles praised the riders for going out to deal with it, praised the Lord that the world worked and the seasons happened on schedule, and segued somehow to the choir's next social. There was, the preacher announced, a sign-up sheet for various projects in the foyer, and there followed more talk about a social and dinner the deacons were putting together in honor of some elder member's seventieth birthday.

Then the preacher got up again. "Carlo and Randy Goss," he said. "Would you come up to the front, please? Praise the Lord for that loose bell that night. Praise the Lord He guided you through the dark of the storm, lost sheep brought to His blessed fold."

Carlo thought to himself that he'd just as soon the Lord had lightened the dark of the storm instead of guiding them through it, or at least dropped the wind a little or let them see that rider-shelter, but there were a lot of reasons, too, the Lord shouldn't be too happy with him and didn't owe him many favors. He stood up, taking Randy with him, and had a lot rather not stand up in front of the congregation, but he didn't see any way out of it.

Randy was no happier than he was. But they stood in front of the altar while (the most embarrassing moment of his life) the preacher laid hands on them, prayed over them, and then invited the whole village to come by and welcome them to the congregation and introduce themselves.

"I don't want to do this," Randy said in anguish.

Their clothes weren't church clothes. They didn't own any church clothes. They only had one change, and something was always sooty and something was always drying in the heat of the forge. What they had on was what was clean.

And he wasn't *used* to going to church dressed in work clothes. He was embarrassed. He thought Randy was going to die of embarrassment or bolt for the door—at that age when the whole world was looking at him constantly, anyway. But two old women were first in line, who called them heroic boys, and Randy shook hands and smiled—

Kid ought to run for office, Carlo thought, dealing with the same elderly women. Once Randy got into the swing of handshaking and being congratulated, he seemed to have discovered he *liked* being a hero, and positively blossomed under that much attention—so did the Mackeys, who were over in the aisle being congratulated right along with them, Carlo caught that fact out of the corner of his eye. Van Mackey and Mary Hardesty had maneuvered up to the front seats right where the outflow of congregation was going to pass them, and there they were, shaking hands, grinning and just enjoying the moment.

Sons of bitches, Carlo thought. For all the preacher's talk about redeeming the world, he didn't see Danny Fisher invited into the congregation. He didn't see Danny Fisher being offered several new outfits by the owner of the general store, as had just happened, and he didn't see Danny Fisher being told by the preacher that he was God's chosen model of His mercy.

But then, Danny didn't expect to be, either, by what he guessed.

He *hoped* Danny was still speaking to him.

They had to stay through absolutely everybody coming by and shaking their hands, including some of the girls—the boys on their own weren't so inclined. The younger girls—there were three—giggled. Two older ones showed better sense.

After that, they could escape, except a last handshaking with preacher Quarles and an actually friendly embrace, out to the foyer to get their hats and coats.

Then it was out to the street where the Mackeys were lying in wait. Mary Hardesty immediately took Carlo's arm and beamed and prattled on and on how they were their own personal miracles.

Amazing, Carlo thought, wishing he knew how to break that hold with some kind of grace. Truly amazing, the depth of godly enthusiasm the Mackeys found when the neighbors were watching.

Totally oblivious, apparently, to the shading of lips with gloved hands, as certain village folk spotted the show and talked about it, Carlo could just imagine—the Mackeys not being universally believed as saints.

But neighbors were neighbors. Two hundred permanent neighbors in a village, and you couldn't afford open feuds with anybody. Even if you'd like to shoot them. You shook hands and you smiled.

God, they could put off going to see Brionne until tomorrow. Today was full enough, public enough. People were paying *attention* to what they did, the whole village was paying attention to what they did, and he kept walking. They passed the doctor's house and Randy kept walking beside him, not, thank God, reminding him in front of the Mackeys.

They walked back to the end of town in the company they had to keep, sanctified, prayed over, written down in the church rolls, and gossiped about all the way, till the most of the traffic left in the general outflow from the church was miners and loggers on their way to The Evergreen for a pint of philosophy.

Behind them, the church bell rang. Sometimes down in Tarmin after a snow-fall, when there were few sounds on the mountain but nature and when the wind was just exactly right, you could hear bells in the winter air. The bells of heaven, he'd thought when he was a little boy.

He'd never known that sound had come from here.

The year past was a bad dream, but this morning with the church bells ringing out through the village and echoing off the mountain, Darcy had put on one of her prettiest winter outfits—Mark had brought her the blue wool sweater from the store before she'd ever seen the shipment up from Tarmin that summer, that happy summer before Faye's accident, and she'd hired Angie Wheeler to sew up a pair of gray wool slacks out of a book of patterns.

She hadn't had occasion to wear them until now. She scarcely went out except for groceries.

Still, it was the sort of day to think about the condition of things. She wiped the year's accumulation of dust off the bureau and swept the carpet. And it wasn't as if she hadn't been aware of the dust piling up and the passage of a spring and a summer and a fall—because she wasn't crazy. She knew how much time had passed that the sweater had lain in a drawer. She knew Mark was dead. She knew Faye hadn't waked from her drowned, chilled sleep. She'd cleaned the office herself of Mark's blood and she hadn't greatly blamed him for deserting her. Faye had just cost him too much, and she with the relationship they'd had, all revolving around Faye, couldn't make that loss up.

The dust just hadn't mattered after that.

But today she found herself thinking that the dust had gotten too thick on the downstairs table and remembering that it had had a nice sheen and a pretty grain.

And once she'd done that, she saw the curtains, how dingy the white had become.

She started around the office polishing the tables and Mark's bookshelves.

But straightened bookshelves had made her notice the rugs there needed sweeping.

Then she took out Faye's pretty things from the chest and bathed the girl and arranged her golden curls—they were so like Faye's—and changed the sheets and dressed her in Faye's fine lace-collared gown.

Clean sheets meant putting on a washing, of course, which meant heating up the kitchen, and firing up the boiler for the washing machine, which she only did on Sunday afternoons, but there hadn't been the volume of washing in the house in, oh, a long time.

And those curtains were due a laundering.

That took a good deal of time, and when the sun had gotten to the window in Faye's room she made hot soup and arranged a napkin to protect Faye's pretty gown, and ever so carefully fed the girl. The sun came through, bright and blinding, and made the white sheets into snowbanks and the girl's hair into golden glass. Darcy fed her young patient, and the girl ate as she would eat if she was coaxed.

But at the second sip the girl blinked, and blinked again and passed a glance around the room.

"Where is this?" she asked then.

"Evergreen, honey. You're all right."

"How did I get here?" she asked. She was porcelain and gold, wind-blushed and delicate despite the signs of exposure. Darcy scarcely dared breathe, feared to say something that might drive her back into that silent world and shatter this tenuous contact.

"Honey, your brothers brought you. They carried you up the mountain."

"Who are *you*?"

"My name's Darcy. This is my house. I'm the village doctor."

"Are you?" The eyes drifted shut again. And opened, and wandered across the details of the room. "Can I stay here?"

"Honey, you can stay here as long as you want to. Would you like some cereal?"

A thin, pale hand explored the crocheted white roses. "It's a pretty room."

"It was my daughter's room. Now it's yours."

"Did your daughter grow up?"

"No. She died. So you see—" Darcy set the bowl and the spoon down on the table. And the girl didn't slip away. She touched the white coverlets and explored a ribbon in an eyelet cutaway. Darcy couldn't resist the curls. And Darcy found she could say the hard truth about Faye without a lump in her throat now. She wound a curl around her finger and made it perfect. "There's no one to use the room now. I'd like you to stay, sweet. I would."

"I want my mama," the girl said. "I want my mama." But white-gowned arms reached for her and hugged her, the way no one had since Faye died. Not even Mark. And the girl was so thin, so weak. "I want to go home,"' the girl said.

Not Faye. Brionne Goss. From Tarmin. Which didn't exist anymore.

"Honey, I don't think you *can* go home. This is Evergreen. I'm afraid nobody's left in Tarmin. That's what they say. So you can stay here as long as you like."

"Where's my mama?"

"I think she must be dead, honey, like my daughter. Like my husband. —Like your papa."

"Not my papa!" It was an angry voice. Terribly angry, weak as it was. "*Not* like my papa!"

"I think everybody's gone, honey, except your brothers. They brought you here."

Darcy watched tears start. She sat down on the edge of the bed and brushed the windblushed cheek with a gentle finger and let the tears run for a moment before she gathered the frail body against her and let the child cry her eyes dry.

Then she mopped the child's wet lashes and gave her a handkerchief from Faye's bureau and let her blow her nose.

"I could make you a bowl of cereal," she said, "if you don't want soup."

The blond head turned away.

"A sandwich."

"No." A frail fist wiped at a tear.

"Do you want me to bring your brothers?"

"No!"

"There might be cookies. I might have some."

The girl turned her head toward her. Sniffed.

"Would you like some cookies, sweet?"

A nod.

"All right. I think I could do that, sweet. I certainly could. It'll take me a bit. But you'll have cookies."

She hadn't the makings of cookies. It meant a trip outside and asking the shopkeepers on a Sunday afternoon, at which time some were open and some weren't. But she was willing. She put on her coat and her scarf and went out to the bakers' house and roused Alice Raigur out and bought cookies, as the fastest course to produce them. She went and called on the grocer's house and bought dried beef, ferociously expensive, and pasta and sugar-sweets, which the grocer just happened to have. She went back with her arms full of groceries and to her own surprise found herself nodding and being pleasant to one of her less-liked neighbors in the passage coming back.

The child was asleep when she got back. When Brionne waked to her urging she seemed listless as before and didn't remember her name, but all the same Darcy kept her word and served Brionne the cookies with hot tea—Brionne ate half of a cookie.

Danny couldn't say exactly there was peace in the barracks, or that the business with the horse was settled. It hadn't come around last night. Maybe it had been scared off by the shot Ridley had fired. <Gunfire> was part of its personal nightmare; and maybe with guns going off it just hadn't wanted to stay.

But Ridley hadn't proposed going out on a Sunday, maybe village custom: Danny didn't ask. He spent a lot of time out in the den, taking the occasion to do some clean-up around the place, raking and turning the bedding, doing a lot of things that weren't needful, exactly, but they'd have to be done later, if he didn't do them sooner, and he really wanted to make Ridley and Callie happier with him than he'd merited.

He didn't know what Ridley might have said to Callie. His spending time out at the den at least gave Ridley and Callie a chance to talk matters over without him hearing it in any sense, and he figured if he'd moderately won Ridley's better opinion, he couldn't have a better lawyer with Callie.

He hadn't heard any explosions.

Cloud followed him about, getting him to <scratch Cloud's chin> and finally to <brush Cloud,> of which Cloud never, ever tired.

Jennie came outside to tend to Rain, and brushed Rain—well, as high as Jennie could reach.

"Was that girl *bad?"* Jennie wanted to know, and the ambient carried thoughts of <girl on floor in furs> and <mama and papa talking and yelling.>

"That girl didn't mind the way she was supposed to," Danny said. Having a kid brother, he knew the tracks an eight-year-old mind wandered, and knew not to make it too complicated—or too lacking in detail. "A rider who knew told her to stay inside the gate and she went out anyway. And that's what happened."

"I wouldn't go out the gate," Jennie said.

"You're smart." Compliments never hurt. In his experience. Once you were praised as good for one thing, you didn't so readily do the opposite. "That horse out there is dangerous. If a gate got open Rain might go out to fight him."

"Why?"

"Because boy horses do that. And if Rain got in a fight, that's a big mean horse, and he might hurt Rain real bad. So we have to be real careful that one of the boy horses doesn't get out the gate."

"What about Shimmer?"

"Shimmer, too. The horse out there might try to come inside where Shimmer's den is, and she'd fight him, and she might lose the baby."

"I'd get the hoe. I'd hit him."

"If that horse ever gets in here, *you* get into the barracks and you bolt the door and you let the horses handle it. Our three boy horses together can put a strange horse out of the yard. And they would. But Shimmer could still get hurt. That's why your papa and I want that horse to leave."

"Would you *shoot* him?"

Delicate question. "Wouldn't you shoot him," he asked, "if he was going to kill Rain?"

"Yeah." A reluctant and unhappy yeah, that was, but Jennie did agree to the premise.

"Your papa would never shoot anything if he didn't have to. He's real smart. So if he ever did, you'd know he did the right thing."

"Yeah." Not enthusiastically.

He applied himself to a vigorous brushing of Cloud's far side in hopes Jennie and her questions would go inside the barracks again.

But in the same moment Slip went outside, and from there Jennie caught an impression of <Ridley going to the rider gate> and <Slip wandering along after him.>

"Where's your papa going?" Danny wondered.

"To the hunters," Jennie said.

"To go out?"

"To the village," Jennie said. "To talk to the hunters."

Ridley hadn't asked him to go along. Which said something, he supposed. He hoped that it didn't say Ridley was filling the hunters in on his and Carlo's problems.

He applied his frustration to the tangles that crept into Cloud's mane. He kept quiet in the ambient and was aware of Ridley leaving it, the other side of the wall.

Jennie flitted off. And he eventually ran out of tangles.

He thought—maybe he should go to the barracks and try to talk to Callie, personally, reasonably. Nothing worse could happen to him than what had happened yesterday with Ridley.

Well . . . on the other hand, *she* might pull the trigger.

Cloud wasn't enthusiastic. He didn't want <Callie shooting.>

"It's all right, silly." Danny gave Cloud a pat on the shoulder, put away the brushes and went out into the yard.

But Callie had come out onto the porch, dressed for a stay in the cold, and had called Shimmer to her.

Callie spotted him, then, and the ambient went—tense, if not foreboding. Callie, he was sure, didn't want the meeting with him; but there he was, and Callie knew he was there and knew he was looking to deal with her, he was also reasonably sure. Shimmer, maybe because she was pregnant or maybe because she was protective of Callie with Slip upset, was touchy and standoffish. Slip was occupied trotting up and down along a track beside the village wall, listening for what he could hear out of that strange full-of-people place Ridley went that a horse couldn't. Slip was frustrated and anxious. But Shimmer was wary in particular of <Danny.>

So was Callie.

Danny walked toward the barracks, necessarily on a course to intercept Callie and Shimmer.

"I'd like to talk," he said. "Mind?"

"About what?"

"About my being here. About my not telling the truth first off."

"What about it?"

"That I'm sorry. You knew I was holding back. And I knew I was in trouble, but fact was—"

Jennie came running up. "I finished my problems," she said. "I'm going to brush Rain."

"That's fine," Callie said.

"Can I go over to the grocery and get some candy?"

"No."

"Just one piece?"

"It's Sunday and the grocery's closed."

"But papa went to the village!"

"That's fine. Papa's talking to some people. I'm talking to Dan. All right? Run away."

"Papa's talking about shooting that horse. Isn't he?"

"Jennie, do you have lessons to do?"

"I don't want him to shoot that horse!"

"Jennie—"

"I don't want him to!"

"I'll bet I can find you something to do inside if you've nothing better to do."

"I'll brush Rain."

"Good. Go do that," Callie said, frowning, and Jennie ran off to the den.

"I," Danny said carefully, "just wanted to explain. I don't know how much Ridley told you about what I said. But I did offer to go out and deal with the horse. I know I shouldn't have brought the girl here. I knew it then and I didn't plan to go all the way to the village until I was in a position to talk to the riders here and find *out* what I didn't know. I made a mistake. A lot of mistakes. I don't know that does anything—"

"You're full of dark spots, aren't you?"

"I don't intend to be. I know you'd have been within your rights to have tossed me out. I just—"

"Just kind of miscalculated."

"More than once. But—"

He could *see* Jennie making another try at Rain, off in the doorway of the den. Jennie was using the manger wall to stand on and the support post to hold on to in case Rain moved out from under her.

But this time Rain didn't move.

This time Jennie slid on, and got a fistful of mane, and sat there. Cloud, out in the yard, turned his head. The ambient went full of <Jennie on Rain> and Danny held his breath between fear that Rain would pitch her off on her head and fear that Callie, catching the scene first from the ambient and from him and then from <Jennie and Rain,> was going to explode in a shouting fit that wouldn't help junior nerves at all.

Callie didn't. Callie was very quiet. He caught intense <unhappiness> and <fear,> enough to upset the neighborhood if it broke loose, but she remained very, very quiet. So did Shimmer.

"Look!" Jennie crowed, and out she rode into the yard, no great burst of speed at all, just an easy amble across the well-tracked snow.

Cloud (Danny remembered those first wild dashes across the hills near Shamesey) had dumped *him* from a flying run twice the first night he'd met him. The memory made his bones ache and made Cloud dance and throw his head.

But Rain had certainly dumped Jennie the requisite number of times during the last several days, and now the young fool of a nighthorse seemed to have figured out that his own wild moves were dumping the youngster off and hurting Jennie—which was a difficult thought for a nighthorse. Trying to get <threatened Jennie> and <strange-feeling thing on nighthorse back> all sorted out taxed a nighthorse concept of location to the limit.

Rain moved sedately, now, skittish at the same time, and Callie stood there—upset that this was happening at all, Danny was well sure, and upset that something so important was happening while Ridley wasn't there, and upset with all that going with a colt horse meant to young Jennie's future.

Shimmer gave out a challenge call that was part <excitement> and part <dismay> mirroring Callie's restrained distress, and at that, her offspring Rain set into a jog trot, not a nighthorse's best gait, but comfortable—until the horse in question had forty kilos of human bouncing unskillfully on his back.

But Jennie stayed on. Jennie even wanted <going faster,> while other humans could only hold their breath and hope Jennie stayed undamaged. Rain obliged, running a circle around the den while Jennie clung like a burr.

Danny let go a breath. He didn't know if his opinion was welcome to Callie, but he *knew* the hellish quandary Ridley and Callie were in in the matter of that colt and Jennie: he couldn't live that closely with them and the kid for this number of days without picking up parental worry and their resolution *not* to have this pairing—and an initial year which they couldn't conveniently supervise, if Rain did the ordinary young male nighthorse foray out and away from the local group—out the gate next spring and off in a giddy exploration of the whole mountain, nosing into everything. Spring—spring called to a new pair like them in a way that was just one sensation after another.

He *knew.* Every rider had to have known, at some point in his life, that first sense-ridden spring—the smells, the colors, the *life* that was breaking on both horse and rider after the long white days of ice and enclosure. And coupled with a winter pairing—when there were so many, many new sensations to get used to—

"Mama! Dan! See me?"

Oh, he <saw.> A rider could drown all his good sense in it. He found gooseflesh on his arms that had nothing to do with the cold; he felt Callie <struggling for breath and scared—so scared—>

But <Jennie and Rain> wasn't just a visual picture. Not any longer. It was an accomplishment. It was a new creature. It had to be dealt with as rider and horse—even a fool junior could understand there was no redoing or undoing it, not now.

"We see you!" Callie called back. "Try not to break your neck!"

Callie was crying. There were tears on her face. But Callie was holding the ambient very quiet, and he gave her all the help he could in that.

"Slow it down," Callie shouted to her besotted offspring. "You're going to take a spill!"

But about that moment <happy> washed through the ambient with all the noisy force of a pair of youngsters—God, it *deafened.* It had to reach Ridley. It had to reach Guil and Tara at the bottom of the mountain. And Danny laughed. He couldn't help it. Cloud kicked up his heels, and pregnant Shimmer gave a little hop—there was nothing in the whole world like that happiness, and he couldn't but remember <himself and Cloud,> the way <Callie and Shimmer> came to him—and <Ridley and Slip> from clear across the wall.

Ridley knew. Ridley had heard—God, who in all creation hadn't? Danny had trouble breathing. And an unexpected attack of tears. Jennie and Rain had just that instant gotten—there weren't words for it—but it was a coming together that made total sense of each other—or at least as far as which body had four feet and which one had two, which one was jogging about the yard and which one was sitting where Jennie had known for weeks she belonged and where Rain wanted her to be. He saw Callie take a surreptitious wipe at her eyes.

"She's still a baby," Callie complained aloud, he guessed to him. "So's the damn horse."

"A *good* horse. He'll take care of her."

"A damn colt!"

"A smart one."

Then—came a *feeling* from somewhere outside the walls that was <horse> and <lonely> and <wanting, so, so badly.>

There was <someone>—Danny couldn't pin it down. Couldn't figure it, though it—it wasn't Ridley.

Which said to him that was the comparison he'd instinctively made.

Another rider.

Another horse.

And *not* one that was supposed to *be* here.

Rain had stopped still, head lifted, nostrils flared. Shimmer looked toward the wall. Cloud did.

<Blood on snow. Lonely.>

"Damn!" Callie cried, fists clenched. <"Get *out* of here! *Damn you! Go away!*">

Rain was protecting Jennie: <nighthorse with rider> was clear from that quarter, a horse that would fight—no doubt of it, not by Rain's action or Cloud's or Shimmer's. Slip was <wanting Ridley> with all his considerable force. There was no way, no way, Danny thought suddenly, that Jennie could be tempted by the stray, now.

But Brionne could, and Danny started toward the village gate to know whether the ambient was as threatening there as here.

But before he could get there, Ridley was coming back, at a dead run if he could judge. Slip was <at the rider gate to meet him,> and Danny stopped, figuring that whatever there was to hear on that side of the wall and near that house where Brionne lodged Ridley would have heard and would tell them.

<Jennie getting down. Helping papa with gate.> Jennie slid down as Rain came near the gate and Ridley came through.

"Are you all right?" was Ridley's first question to his daughter.

"I rode Rain, I rode Rain and he let me!"

Ridley picked his daughter up and hugged her tight.

Rain was throwing out the same <horse with rider> that would underlay every communication to a riderless horse from now on—and whatever was wrong out there went away.

Danny didn't know for sure what had just flared through the ambient. But in the preoccupation of two overwhelmed parents he didn't know whether they'd heard it at all.

Next thing, papa said at supper that night, Jennie had to learn to mount without the manger wall—

"Just can't depend on those mangers being everywhere available," papa said, and Jennie, knowing she was being teased, swatted at her father's arm.

"You'll learn," papa said then. "Got to grow a bit first, though. Eat those potatoes."

"I want to go out to the den."

"It's dark out," mama said, and then—then there was a difference in mama's tone. "Well, —finish your potatoes first." Jennie couldn't <hear> mama. Rain was drowning everything out but him. But there was a difference all the same, and mama was going to let her do something alone she'd never been allowed to do.

Because she belonged where Rain was. It was a thought so wonderful she didn't linger at all complaining about the potatoes. She bolted them down as fast as she could, got up from table—said, "Excuse me," the way mama and papa were always scolding her to say. Tonight when she was grown up, she said it just because she *wanted* to, and tonight all the rules weren't walls around her, they were part of the familiar way things were and she hadn't any interest in being a kid and doing things the *wrong* way. She was Jennie Sabotay, Rain's rider, and the whole world was different.

She went and got her coat and her scarf, her hat and her gloves, she wrapped up and snugged down her cuffs *herself,* while her family and Dan sat at the table eating and trying not to watch her too obviously.

But there wouldn't be a thing in the world mama could find fault with in the way she dressed or acted, not a thing.

"I'll come back before I get chilled," she announced, because mama always said that, and tonight she was handling everything for herself.

She *hadn't* expected the relief she saw, like everybody at the table had let go a breath all at once, even when the ambient wasn't including them, just her and Rain and the other horses. She was puzzled.

But she had Rain <wanting her,> and it was a clear night. She went out the outside door, and shut it tight, and walked down the porch—mama was always saying not to run on the steps, she'd slip on the ice. So she got all the way down to the yard. But by that time Rain was outside the den, coming to meet her, and she hadn't another thought but Rain's thoughts, the way snow smelled and the way things looked—Rain had never really seen the stars, either, that *she* thought were wonderful, and Rain seemed a little confused where and what they were.

But mostly Rain wanted <Jennie> with him, and wanted <everyone else away.>

* * *

Callie was trying not to be disturbed about the situation. She was doing, Danny thought, a very fine job of holding it in, and he wasn't about to disturb what he perceived as a delicate balance.

"I'll go to bed," he said quietly, that being the only refuge he'd discovered where he could take his influence out of the family.

"No," Callie said. "You were trying to say something this afternoon. What?"

He honestly couldn't reconstruct where he'd been in his approach to Callie. Or what he'd said. "Just that—I hoped not to disrupt your lives. That I never meant to."

"She's gone," Callie said. "She's made her choice. There's nothing to do about it."

"Seems to me," Ridley said quietly, "she isn't *gone,* and the colt was on his way to making a choice. She's that age. So's the horse. Fisher, you've probably seen more pairings than either of us have. Seventeen and all."

Shamesey being the huge camp that it was, Ridley was right: you saw about everything in every combination of human and horse there'd ever been—some good, some you wondered about. "Good horse," Danny said ever so faintly. "That's just a real good young horse." He had another notion, realizing as he did tonight that neither Ridley nor Callie might ever have *seen* another pairing besides their own. "What I know—begging your pardon—if I could say—"

"What?" Callie snapped.

"It—sort of indicates to me that when Spook showed up . . . Rain might have gotten just a little more protective of her. I think it *would* have happened. But when an older horse came around looking for a rider, I think that pushed Rain into claiming *his* before he could risk losing her—and so he *had* a rider to help him fend this other horse off." The last thing he wanted was to lecture seniors regarding horses and *their* daughter. It was real dangerous territory to venture.

"Damn glad it's not the other horse," Ridley muttered.

"What in *hell* are we going to do?" Callie asked. "What are we going to do this spring?"

"Split up if we have to. You go with her. Or I do."

Meaning if—almost *when*—young Rain took out with wanderlust.

And it didn't call for a junior's opinion at all. But he had at least an alternative. And Callie had asked him to stay at the table.

"There's also me," he said, and waited a half a breath for an explosion. He didn't want to make the offer he made—he didn't want to tie Cloud down even to a village and even for the summer: he felt like a traitor in that regard. But he was at least partly responsible for the danger he'd brought, and he saw at least a small way to patch it. "I know you think I'm the devil, but if she goes out this spring, I'd stay here through the summer. Or I'd ride with her and you stay here. I've got a little brother. I *know* kids her age. I'd stay with her and see she got back here safe before winter."

He wasn't getting any reaction from them. He decided he'd said enough and maybe enough to offend them. Callie looked like a thundercloud. Ridley—he wasn't sure.

There was an ambient. But it was all <Jennie and Rain.>

"It's to think about," Callie said. And then added: "It's not you in question. It's that horse out there. It tried to get Jennie."

"It didn't," Ridley said. "It can't, now."

"It's still got to be stopped."

"I agree," Danny said. "It has to be."

They hadn't said what they'd do about Jennie this spring when horses started to wander or whether they even accounted his offer as serious or other than self-serving. But he didn't entirely expect they would say anything. It was an eventuality they didn't want to think about, and he wasn't the person Callie would want with her daughter, not at all.

He got up to refill the teapot.

The ambient stayed as it was, a contented kid, contented horse, both silly, both louder than anything on the mountain. That horse if it was out there had to know it had lost Jennie as a prospect.

Maybe it would be discouraged. But it had lost Rain as a rival, too. And that might well figure in the situation.

"There's something you can do now," Ridley said. "Which is asking a bit. But there's three riders at Mornay—that's the next village down the road—and they could spare one."

"You want me to ride to Mornay."

"If," Ridley said, "if we don't get that horse in the next couple of days, weather permitting. And supposing it comes back. We could go out with the hunters—escort you out to the first shelter between us and them and you make the trek over to Mornay and come back with help."

So Ridley *wasn't* just getting him to go winter over at the next village.

Counting that one of them had a pregnant mare, one was a stranger to the area and one of them was an eight-year-old just this week trying to figure out how to get onto her horse—getting help from another village was a real good notion.

"Sure," he said. "Sure, I'll do that."

"That's saying we have to," Ridley said. "Chances are—Rain's settling with Jennie may put an end to it. I hope so."

"Drink to that," Callie said, and got up and got the spirits bottle. She poured three glasses, gave one to Ridley, second to him—which she sipped beforehand. Third for herself.

Proof enough, Danny said to himself, and didn't hesitate to drink it when Ridley proposed, "To the Offspring and the horse."

"We did it," was Callie's second. "She's still alive and we are."

Jennie was staying out in the den and she might be out there the whole night. He didn't think Callie would get a wink of sleep. Maybe not Ridley. At the least they'd take turns.

And they talked about having gotten Jennie to a major turning in her life.

But he didn't think they expected it would be easy after this.

Nor that they wanted help waiting up for the kid. So he excused himself to his bed and lay there listening to an ambient as new and full of foolishness as could be.

Thinking of Cloud and himself. And beginnings of life and not endings for a change.

Darcy had made supper that evening and Brionne ate half a dish of beef pasta and a whole cookie and half of another for dessert.

But Brionne said very little—or what she said was so quiet that Darcy couldn't hear.

Once it sounded like, "I want to go home."

And another time, "Go away!"

But when Darcy started to leave Brionne said, "Where are you going?"

Darcy came back and sat down by the side of the bed. The girl had been dreaming awake, she thought. Not really sleeping, but not entirely aware, either. There was a strange feeling to the night—her own elation with the child's waking, or the unaccustomed feeling of life in this room, or just the knowledge that the days would change now. Everything had stopped at some time around Mark's death, and no day had brought anything different from the last. And now every day brought a possibility of things changing.

Now she went to bed at night thinking about tomorrow, and what she'd do, and what she'd try. She hadn't done that kind of planning in—a long time.

And tonight she lay abed thinking of Mark as she sometimes did, just thinking about him in the dark and the things she'd tell him—and wanting to tell him about all the things that had happened.

But there was so much, there was so very much she'd done that thinking about it became a job in itself, and made her sleepy.

Her edge-of-sleep thought seemed infected with cheerfulness. With recklessness and sheer anticipation that just wasn't like her.

She felt equal to anything. That in itself was unprecedented.

If the girl had come a year ago Mark wouldn't have died. Mark would have wanted to live if he'd seen this child, if he'd seen how much she was like Faye. But more, if Mark had *felt* the things she felt tonight, he'd never have wanted to die.

Right at the edge of sleep she pretended that Mark had seen her and that Mark was sleeping in the bed beside her. She knew better, of course, but she could think that for the night, the way she could tell herself that the empty room had a child again and that mistakes were all revised, and that she had a chance to do right all the things that had for a year been so wrong.

There was a tomorrow again. She'd run to the very edge of the money she had on account. She'd not collected fees for things she'd done on call, or at least not pursued any of the late ones—because she'd not cared.

But tomorrow she'd open the lower-floor shutters and open her office again, and she'd take patients. The miners always had complaints and aches and pains. Miners always had money on account.

And she'd buy Brionne such pretty things.

* * *

Things *felt* better. Maybe it was going to church. Maybe it was just getting another number of days between them and disaster and church days were markers.

But, sleeping in a proper cot alongside his brother in the warmest place in Evergreen village, with the banked coals making a comfortable glow and the stones lending warmth to a peaceful night, Carlo let go a sigh that seemed to stand for so much that had been piled up on him, so much debt, so much fear, so much anxiety.

Things were working out. Rick wasn't happy—least of all in the public scene this morning, with them being welcomed by the congregation and all. Ordinarily he'd have found it excruciating notice on himself, and had, for the duration, but it meant something. It meant something vitally important, to have the preacher's backing and to know that they *weren't* to blame for that horse that had scared hell out of the village.

Rider business. A horse *didn't* come within his responsibility. Wasn't fair for Danny to get tagged with it—but if the preacher didn't see blaming him and Randy for that horse, that left Rick Mackey as the only one with that notion. And precarious as his and Randy's situation was, he wasn't about to rush forward to claim the blame.

He just—just hoped to God it went away.

He didn't want to be listening to it when they shot it.

He had a fistful of pillow, doing violence to it without realizing it, and let it go, and let go another sigh, this time consciously, purposefully releasing all the pent-up worry.

He ought to take care of the rest of the pending business he had in town, pay off all the emotional debts and pin down the uncertainties.

Meaning going finally and finding out about their sister, what the doctor thought of her chances, what the outlook was, what the *debt* might be that she'd accumulated. He was responsible for her. He had to be. There was no one else.

Chapter

XV

"That's right, darling. Take another spoonful. There's sugar in it."

The girl swallowed down the cereal, and after three or four such spoonfuls, the girl heaved a little sigh and blinked and blinked again.

"You're in Evergreen, honey," Darcy said. She offered that information every time she thought the girl might have come close to hearing anything or truly absorbing the things she said—because there'd been that moment of lucidity—and then it had gone for the rest of the day. But she knew that if it had come once, it could come back—to the right lure, to the promise of safety and comfort. "You're in the village up the mountain. My name's Darcy. How are you doing?"

"I'm tired," the girl said unexpectedly and matter of factly. But Darcy didn't let herself show surprise at all.

"I imagine you are, honey. Do you want some more?"

"All right," the girl said, and ate the rest of the bowl before she shut her eyes and seemed to drift away.

Darcy was trembling as she set the spoon and the bowl down. She sat there by the girl's bedside telling herself she might really have won this one, and seeing in that wind-burned face, still lovely after the long trek up the mountain, and the hands all broken-nailed and cut, the evidences of a suffering and struggle her Faye had never known except in the few minutes of her death.

This child would never know privation in Evergreen, not while she was taking care of her. This child would grow up safe and have all the things a beautiful young girl should have, and she'd see to it.

She went downstairs and went on tidying up. She arranged things in Mark's office, and sterilized the instruments in boiling water, against the arrival of clients.

Then she went out on the snowy balcony of the second floor and opened the storm shutters. People about in the winter evening, the few who weren't using the tunnels in the light snow-fall, stopped in the street and looked up. No one spoke.

But two—two, while she watched, came from the street onto the walk, and stamped their boots on the porch and disappeared under the angle of the porch roof.

She heard a knocking at her door. Miners, she thought. Maybe clients.

It was bitter cold out on the balcony and she gladly went inside and down. She opened the door and set herself in the doorway in such a way that they couldn't just brush past her without explaining themselves, because some such clients were the sort that deserved sending right down to the pharmacist with an order for sugar pills or strong purgative.

"Ma'am," the tall one said. "Are you the doctor?"

"Yes."

"My name's Carlo Goss. This is my brother Randy. How's our sister doing?"

The girl's brothers. It came to her like a thunderstroke that *these* boys could take the girl away. It wasn't fair. They *couldn't.* Not now. They hadn't even asked how she was. They didn't care—

But in the same heartbeat and in deep confusion she had to amend that harsh judgment. They'd carried the girl to her with heroic effort. There were frost burns on their faces. How did they love her enough to do that—and not come to see her?

"She's doing pretty well," she said—hardly a breath having passed in those thoughts. Their arrival disturbed her for reasons she didn't even want to look at in herself. She didn't want to let them through the door to talk to them, much less admit them to the girl's room—but she couldn't say go away. They had rights. They could go to the marshal and complain, and Eli would have to come back and say, Darcy, you have to let them see her, and how would that look? And how would that feel?

"Come in," she said. She wondered whether she should ask them to take off their coats. She wondered whether she should offer tea. She wanted them *out* of the way, out of this house, but how fast could she push them and how much could she keep secret that wouldn't ultimately get back to them and color how they dealt with her?

Friendly. Friendly seemed the best approach. Court the boys. Make them comfortable so they *couldn't* turn on her.

"Would you like a cup of tea?" she asked. "Would you like to sit down?"

"To see our sister," Carlo said—and very businesslike, very much in possession of his rights over the situation. She was afraid.

"Come along upstairs," she said, then, constrained to cooperate.

"Nice house," the younger brother said as if he was estimating the value of the set-abouts.

"Thank you," she said, while her mind was racing over what they wanted and whether they meant to take Brionne and what she could do about it. She winced at bringing two such enemies into the heart of the house, into things that were hers and Mark's and Faye's, where they could see what she had and maybe calculate it wasn't as fine as where they'd come from and wasn't really a house they'd want their sister in. But she had no choice but take them up the stairs and into Faye's bedroom.

There they took off hats and gloves and loosened scarves. They brought deep cold with them. It clung to their clothing, on which snow didn't melt. They brought noise. They brought foolish fears into her heart—even to think of them taking her back. The brothers didn't know how to deal with her. They didn't understand how to take care of the girl—they'd failed. They stood above a sleeping sister—having failed.

And then—then—maybe a creak of the floorboards, or maybe just a sense the girl at times seemed to have—she opened her eyes and stared at them.

"Carlo?"

"Yeah," he said, and got down on one knee and took her hand. "Hi. How're you doing, Brinny?"

Dreadful nickname.

"All right," she said. Her hand rested listlessly in her brother's as he squeezed it.

"You slept all the way up," the younger brother said, and squatted down by the older. The girl lay on her prop of pillows and gazed into their faces.

"I don't remember." Her hand moved on the lace and yellow ribbons of the coverlet. "Isn't it a pretty room?"

"It's real pretty," the older boy said and squeezed her hand again. "—Listen, Brinny-boo, we're down by the gate. Got a job in the smith's setup here. We live there. We're fine. Randy and I are fine. You need anything?"

"Where's mama?"

"Mama and papa are gone, Brinny. So's aunt Libby. They're all dead. Nothing left of Tarmin but us."

The blue eyes clouded. She turned her face into the pillow and tore her hand from her brother's fingers.

"Brinny?"

"I want mama."

"Yeah. I know, I know." Carlo patted her shoulder as he got up from his knees and looked at Darcy. "I don't know what I can pay you right now, ma'am, but I will, as soon as I come by any money. As could happen."

"I'd like her to stay here. No charge. I have the room. I don't mind her using it."

"That's awfully kind of you."

"I'd be glad to take care of her." She became desperate, fearing she'd led herself into a dangerous dead end of reason, and having lost all her sense of what anyone truly wanted, she had nothing left to throw to the hunters but a tidbit of her privacy, to make them think they were friends and to make logical to them her position. "I had a girl about her age. She died. The house has been real empty. The girl needs someone all the time—a stable environment. She can't be moved to still one more strange place."

"If Brionne could live here, if you were willing to do that for her, we'd be grateful. We might be able to help out, do some fixing up and all. Next spring—next spring it looks like we'll be able to give you some kind of payment."

That didn't matter to her. Money didn't matter. Their separation from Brionne was the currency she wanted. It was wonderful news.

"I'm well set," she said, and walked out to the head of the stairs, luring them to follow as she kept talking. "I can take care of her. Of course you'll come and see her." By spring—by spring if they changed their minds and wanted their sister back, she'd argue the child was too delicate to travel with them and live in a ravaged village. It was a stupid idea for them to go back there, and by what she'd heard of Tarmin, though the buildings might be intact and all, they'd still have to get supplies there. By the time the boys were in any fashion set to want her back she'd have Brionne attached to *her,* that was what she'd do. So they'd never get her back. By that time Brionne wouldn't even think of going—to brothers she hadn't been tearfully glad to see.

"We'd really be grateful," Carlo Goss said; and the younger brother said, as they followed her down the stairs:

"Carlo and me get along all right. But it's pretty rough down at the forge."

"I'm sure you're right." She *knew* the smith, his surly brat. And his wife, as vicious and self-seeking a woman as ever she'd met—only woman in town who could have made Van Mackey worse than he was. "Your sister owes her life to you. It was a miracle you got up the Climb at all." She reached the front door and, since they had never taken their coats off and seemed in a hurry, gave them no grace at all of invitations to stay and talk. "You come back whenever you want. You'll know she's just down the street."

"Thank you, ma'am," the older boy said. "I'm grateful. We are. Really."

"Any time." She opened the door, waited just long enough to see the boys leave down the snowy steps.

Then she shut the door and latched it against the kind of drunken fools that sometimes mistook the private door for the office, and calmed herself enough for a sigh of relief.

The girl was hers. They hadn't, after all, come to make any other arrangements. They were no more than kids themselves, the younger boy young enough to need someone's care—but not hers. It didn't need to be her business. Nothing about them needed to be her business.

But in one thing she was puzzled—the impression she'd gotten that, after all they'd done to save her, they'd not been shattered by her condition—or cheered by her improvement. They'd just offered money—and left with nothing in evidence but relief.

Odd, she thought. That certainly wasn't the behavior of loving brothers. It just wasn't. And Brionne had shed no tears, none at all.

The kids *hadn't* come back down from the midway shelter when the weather cleared—which meant the two of them had a choice of going up what Tara called a hellish road, or going up a straight-up-the-mountain route that Tara swore she could make, and that Guil maintained, against her protestations, that *he* could make.

There *were,* Tara said, logging shelters and miners' cabins, and she knew with a local rider's knowledge where they were.

There was supposedly such a shelter ahead of them on their ascent, not of the road, but of the broad mountain face. It was a shelter, as Tara had imaged it, <clinging precariously to the mountainside, buried among the evergreens.>

But thus far Guil saw it only through the inner eye, in Tara's memory of a summer approach to the place, <miners wary of approach,> and not the sort she'd care to overnight among. The image was <gray rock, dark evergreen, small patches of snow among the trees.>

The reality was <evergreen branches drooping low into the snow blanket, rocks and ledges lurking hazardously under snow> and it was a good thing, Guil thought, that they had two experienced high-country horses feeling their way through the snow, *knowing* by the way trees grew and brush situated itself that there might be a ledge, knowing the soft, attractive snow was not at all reliable. It wasn't a rapid progress and, hazy as the snow-sifting branches had become to Guil's perception, he walked, or staggered, used Burn's tail to help him up the generally steep slopes.

It wasn't Burn's favorite way to make a climb, with a human pulling on a fairly important part of Burn's dignity, but Burn tolerated it, as Burn tolerated the baggage knocking about his ribs, <nasty thumpy things,> because otherwise his rider wasn't going to be able to follow Tara and Flicker up this damn slope—and that would have meant Burn, torn between <Guil> and <Flicker,> faced an unthinkably inconvenient choice.

Which would of course be <Guil,> but *damnably* dreadful to make.

<"Burn . . ." waiting.> Guil didn't talk out loud much at all—or hadn't, until the last few days. He didn't know when he'd last had someone to talk to—last time he'd ridden with Aby, he guessed; but it surprised him, now, the unaccustomed word coming out of his mouth, the way it surprised him that the snow was so gray and the world that was going around in such an unaccustomed way.

It was a very inconvenient place to fall. He had empty air at his back, rock under his feet, and feeling himself overbalanced, he grabbed a sapling evergreen, which bent, but which kept him on his feet and on the small ledge somewhere on a fairly steep slope. Even when the whole world went <gray> and an attempt to find footing failed; he only swung around with the tree in his embrace—facing he wasn't quite sure what direction, but it felt like sideways on the mountain.

"Guil? Guil, hang on!"

"Oh, I will," he said, and kept his arms full of tree, hoping that his sight would come back—he had Burn's view of <nightmare's rump> and <worried Tara standing on the crest,> but he didn't think that was directly in front of him. It seemed rather, like the rest of the mountain, somewhat to the side and behind him.

That persuaded him, along with the general inclination of the very flexible, smelly and prickly sapling, which stabbed right through his gloves and through a gap that had developed between his glove and his jacket cuff, that if he let go he'd fall—which would hurt his side and his headache far worse than hanging on was hurting him. So he clung.

Eventually he heard, through the gray that beset his vision, the scrabble of human feet and felt <worried Tara> much closer to him.

"Here." A hand closed on his arm. "I'll steady you."

"I'm not seeing."

"You can't *see?*"

"It's not bad. It'll come back."

"The hell it'll come back!"

"A little knock on the skull. A while back. I'm just dizzy."

"But you can't see."

"It'll go away."

"You're a damn *fool,* Guil!"

"Just wait here a minute."

"You should have told me you were having blackouts!"

"Just gray. It's fine." He blinked several times. He could see <Guil holding tree and Tara with Guil> quite plainly, looking down on the scene and slightly overlapped—his brain having temporarily lost the knack for sifting skewed images into one image. It made him dizzier, and for a moment he thought he was going to lose his breakfast into the bargain, which might make him let go of the tree.

Not a good idea.

And he supposed if it were just him and Burn, Burn would get back down here and give him something besides a tree to hold to; Burn had four feet, and he'd feel a lot better about that, than about Tara's trying to pry him loose.

"You can't hold me," he said.

"I want you to put your arm around my shoulder and I want you to put your right foot in the direction I go. All right?"

"You can't hold me."

"Shut up and let go! We're not that far from the shelter. *Trust* me, hear?"

He let go. He didn't grab her, fearful of dragging her off if he slipped, trusting if they slid, her instinct would save her; and he'd try for the tree. He could see a bit—at least a blur of white and gray that was snow and rock. He could see through Tara's eyes, clearer than that, once the human brain decided which view of things was compatible with where two human bodies were standing. Once he had that, he could climb, using her balance and her sight, up that slope to where two horses waited anxiously.

"Sit down?" she said.

"Yeah," he said, and found a rock and rested there until the blood got back to his brain or away from it or whatever unnatural condition was causing the gray-out.

Then he saw a log cabin in front of him.

"We're here," he said.

"Yeah," she said. "We're here. Mining camp. Halfway to the upper road."

He said, on a copper-tasting breath and with a pounding headache: "Told you I could do it."

* * *

Preacher John Quarles came to call at the clinic in the morning. John's mother had sent over a cake, which came welcome.

"Is it true?" John asked. "Has the little girl waked?"

"Yes," she said. She didn't want John to go and pray over her, but she didn't see any way out. She brought him upstairs, where the sunlight through white curtains, on white lace and yellow walls, made the girl so beautiful she liked just to look at her at this hour.

Brionne had actually been reading—one of Faye's books, that lay beside a white hand on the lace and satin coverlet. Brionne had nodded off, as she would almost every page.

"She's very weak yet," Darcy said in a hushed voice. "She asked for books. But she tires very quickly."

"An angel," John said, and launched into a quiet little prayer for "the Lord's own little miracle."

Brionne never stirred.

Darcy led her visitor downstairs again and, in the obligation to social courtesy, found herself *comfortable* with the visit—actually found herself in a buoyant mood as John sat and shared tea and cookies.

"Truthfully," John said, "it wasn't just the cake that brought me. I wanted to be sure you were aware—" John cleared his throat. "I trust there've been no visits from Simms."

"For what?" She reacted to every breath of wind that threatened the girl staying here. She'd come to hope—so much. And they *couldn't* change the arrangement. She didn't *want* to deal with lawyers.

God, did he suspect? Did he know it mattered that much?

"Knowing that child's welfare is precious to you," John said, "I think you should petition the court for guardianship—and have her rights protected."

"Against what?" Her nerves wouldn't take shocks. Not anymore. "Why?"

"This child has rights," John said, "to a lot of property. There was a village meeting about it. The Goss children are the heirs to the smith down in Tarmin. And a house. At least one house. Maybe two. It's been the talk in the village—"

"I don't get around the village much," Darcy said. "Socially. As you know."

"Well, in the Lord's wisdom, the boys and this dear child are the only living heirs—some say of the whole village, but the judge I think will rule that the village is salvage, except that the Goss family holds the blacksmith shop and the family house and maybe one or two other houses in the village."

"The boys came here talking about maybe coming into some money. *That* was what they meant."

"Seems they do stand to inherit quite an establishment. Now, the oldest boy seems quite a nice young man—but I just would be careful, Darcy. I think you should seek legal guardianship. In this child's interests. There are just too many who might seek it. If you understand."

Hell, she thought. *That* was why the elder boy had been so forward with his offers of money. She said with never a ruffle: "There's no way this poor girl can go down there. God knows the conditions down there. I hope you'll back me in that with the judge."

"I have no difficulty with that," John said. "The boys are good boys. But they have their interests in actually working the forge, in which I just do not imagine this fragile child has any skill. I do think they'll stand by her financially as the Lord blesses them—they seem good churchgoing boys, and they do seem right in their intentions, but the older boy in particular is at that age when some girl will take his fancy, and he'll start thinking of his own house. The brothers seem very close, and I think there's no worry for the younger boy, who I'm sure will apprentice to his brother, but I think to assure equity *for* this child there should be some provision for her, specifically, with some caring person, independent of means, to look out for her interests."

"I agree. Guardianship." Darcy found her hands trembling and tried to disguise the fact. John Quarles was an opinion that counted almost conclusively with the judge. John was also one to couch even his harshest judgments in very soft words, and John *seemed* to be saying that in his opinion the boys weren't that acutely concerned for their sister—in which conclusion her own observations thoroughly concurred. "Also," she said, "I do think—whatever my own reservations—it would be well if the child had exposure to church. You know I sent Faye. As traumatized as this child has been—I am thinking of taking her to services. And that tells you, John, how much I'm willing to commit to for this child."

"That in itself is a miracle, Darcy."

"Maybe—" She'd sell her *soul* for possession of the girl upstairs. And prepared to do it. "Maybe after all I've been through I'm willing to listen, myself. I at least think it's important to give this child every stable influence I can lay hands on. And this child needs a guide, John." She considered half a breath and threw all the chips on the table. "Maybe I need a change of heart, too."

That, God help her, led to a spate of praying right there and then, which she found incredibly ridiculous and embarrassing. But she bowed her head and said, feeling she would throw up, "Amen," when John was finished.

But it meant John would fight for her rights. John had himself a couple of challenging prospects. They were hard come by, in a village divided between the hard-drinking woods-dwellers and the villager youth who, after their usual pubescent foolishness, realized that their respectability and their standing depended on the church. Village youngsters fell, either as a matter of course or a matter of post-procreative contrition, into John's kindly hands. Those were no challenge. *She* was. Her attendance would set the village abuzz—and satisfy no few pious busybodies who'd included her in Sunday prayers for years.

Her Brionne. Her wayfarer from the storm—might be a wealthy young woman. A respectable, looked-up-to woman, churched, prayed-over, able to dictate her own way in the world and have anything she wanted.

That was what the boy had been talking about, this Tarmin business, and coming into some money. If he wanted to send money, if he wanted to pay Brionne her inheritance in cash, that was very good. She'd call Simms tomorrow and have a document drawn up, something to protect Brionne and assure her rights to her share.

She wrote out a prescription to the pharmacist for cough medicine which John and his mother both used.

"How soon do you think they *will* resettle Tarmin?" she asked.

"Oh, up and running by next fall. At least to get a substantial establishment there, and maybe some supplies up here. The marshal's organizing. The judge is drawing up documents. And the very clever heads are figuring how to deal with the lowland companies without getting into debt. There's a great deal of greed at work here, Darcy, an uncomfortable amount of worldly greed."

That, she believed truly shocked John. So many things did. It didn't mean John didn't understand them.

"I tell you," she said, "this child's been through enough. She deserves to stay up here and be very comfortable."

"Amen," John said. "Lord bless, and amen to that."

That afternoon, with the sun peeking through gray clouds and the office curtains back, and her porch sign saying *Open* for the first time in a year, Darcy had her first doors-open customer, when a miner came trailing in with a sliced arm he claimed to have gotten on a nail near the barracks and she knew damned well was a knife cut, likely gotten in the tavern last night, by the color and character of it, the sort of thing knife fighters often got defending themselves, and bad knife fighters at that.

Even before this last year she'd tended to send this sort of patient to the pharmacist for salve and bandages, since the man hadn't come in directly after the fight (he'd slept it off, she was sure, oblivious to the pain) and the cut was too old for the stitches it could have used. Probably it had been a clean knife. The likeliest contaminant was The Evergreen's steak sauce.

"I do appreciate this," the man was saying. Earnest was his name. Earnest Riggs. Miner, of the sort constantly trying to get a stake to hire and provision a couple of his fellows for some hole in the rocks out of which they did a little hunting, a little mining, a little of anything to keep going another season, for, of course, the big find, the vein he just knew was there. She didn't even ask if he was the down-the-mountain sort, or the up-the-mountain sort, which might have said whether he was panning or digging. She personally didn't care. He did have credit slips with the bank, which she asked for up front. But while she was getting the bandages, he was telling her what an upstanding citizen he was, and how his little company had a find—this was always preface to an appeal for funds, but he hadn't gotten to it yet.

She was aware of movement and a whiteness on the stairs a second before calamity—Brionne slipped, squealed in alarm and skidded a few steps.

Earnest leaped up and all but knocked her down getting from the office to the stairs to pick up Brionne who, both feet out from under her, was clinging to the rail. He was a big man with long hair and a grizzled, bushy beard, and Brionne was so, so slight in his huge arms, her white nightgown against his blue plaid shirt.

"You poor, pretty thing," Ernest said over and over, and hugged Brionne against his shaggy self. "Damn. Damn. —Are you all right, honey?"

"Let me see," Darcy said, anxious, and not alone for the almost fall. "Set her down. *Set her down!*"

"Poor little girl." The miner, Ernest, set Brionne down on the couch and Brionne sat and looked up at him with wide, dazed eyes.

And Earnest—

Earnest was clearly entranced. Nothing would do but that Earnest help Brionne up the stairs once Darcy had ascertained there were no injuries.

"She's perfectly fine," Darcy said, taking charge to prevent Earnest carrying the girl into the bedroom. "Downstairs. I'll be right down to take care of you."

"Now, don't you slight that poor little girl. This scrape's nothin'. You take care of that poor little lady first, and I'll wait downstairs. It don't hurt. I promise you, it don't hurt me none at all."

It didn't ease her mind. Earnest clearly had an interest in That Pretty Little Girl, as Earnest called her.

Himself being a big rough miner and of course not in any pain from a knife slice. Damn him.

Meanwhile, Brionne was just weak, was all she could detect. Brionne had gotten hungry and come downstairs, and that was easy enough to deal with.

Earnest, she feared, was another matter. Earnest had turned worshipful, and when she came downstairs to deal with Earnest, the deity in Earnest's universe was clearly upstairs, where Earnest directed soulful looks.

She was ever so relieved to get him out the door.

She was more than annoyed when Earnest came back an hour after she'd put him out the door, knocking at the streetside entry and presenting a box of cookies from the bakery, and a bouquet of paper flowers.

Ernest wanted to carry the cookies up to The Little Girl's room, but she wouldn't have that—no. She wouldn't let him in. But she took the bouquet and several cookies and a cup of tea upstairs and didn't tell Brionne exactly where they'd come from. Brionne was pleased with the flowers and ate two of the cookies.

But she'd no more than carried the tray downstairs again and begun to wash dishes than came a knock at the streetside door and—

Earnest.

"Now, look, Mr. Riggs," she began in exasperation, gripping the edge of the door and bracing a foot behind it.

"No, no, ma'am," Earnest said, and took off his hat, scarf and all, despite the bitter wind starting to veil the street in snow. "I know—I *know* I've bothered you three times today. But I been thinking."

She wasn't about to let him in. She was thinking about the marshal. "Well, I'm working, Mr. Riggs, I'm very busy, and if you don't mind—"

"Ma'am, I don't ask to come in. Just a minute of your time. I just was noticing how the porch rail is losin' paint—"

"You don't paint in the winter, Mr. Riggs."

"—and missin' some pieces. So's various things. You don't have anybody regular hired to fix those things—"

"The house will stand through the winter, Mr. Riggs. Then it may be time to think about it."

"By then ever'body ll be down to Tarmin, ma'am. And what I hear, what I hear, ma'am, that pretty little girl is from there. And she's due a lot of property if there was those lookin' out to protect her—"

"Not your business, Mr. Riggs."

"Well, them Mackeys have got her brothers, and those brothers is sellin' her out, ma'am. I don't know they know what they got into, but there's lawyers comin' and goin' out of Mackey's place—"

She had by no means meant to let Mr. Riggs in. He was just too persistent, and wanted something. He was a fearsome looking sort, with his wild hair and unkept beard, and dealing with miners was dangerous. Some would steal when your back was turned. Some would get ideas of different sort, and his infatuation with her or with, God help them, Brionne, in this place where miners very, very rarely found prospects among the local girls and even less rarely found women willing to go out into the privation of the camps, could easily get out of control.

But he had information she didn't have, that she suspected John Quarles didn't have, and if Simms or Hodges were taking money or promises regarding Tarmin property, forewarned was forearmed.

She opened the door. "Come in, Mr. Riggs." And stepped back, cautiously, all the while thinking of the gun in Mark's office.

But Ernest *was* probably harmless. He was very careful to wipe his feet and to dust the snow off.

"So what *about* the lawyers? Simms? Is it Simms?"

"A woman."

"That's Simms." Simms was the lawyer who *wasn't* related to Judge Hodges. The one she *wasn't* mad at for shenanigans with Mark's father's property and that damn brother of Mark's.

"Well, actually the *other* one was there, too," Earnest said. He was a careful man with his hat. He didn't roll it or crush it. His fingers kept dancing around the careful curves of it, smoothing the bushdevil tail that was its ornament. "I didn't get his name, either. But I heard say that's who it was. I kind of hang out at The Evergreen, ma'am, and that's right next door to the Mackeys. So's the barracks, for that matter. So, you know, winter settin' in and strangers come around, what they do, people watch. And gossip about."

"So what *is* the gossip?"

"How them brothers is dealing with the Mackeys for a stake to go down there come spring, and how they been hanging around with that rider lad that brought 'em in, and how there's just somethin' sharp goin' on, if you take my drift."

"Not entirely, Mr. Riggs. —Would you like a cup of tea?"

"I wouldn't want to put you out, ma'am."

"Oh, the water's generally hot. Come into the kitchen."

Sound from talk in the parlor could carry upstairs. And she wanted everything Earnest Riggs knew or suspected, but she wouldn't leave him alone near the office and the drugs, either.

So she led him into the kitchen, set him at the breakfast table, made two cups of strong tea and put out a piece of the cake John had brought over.

Earnest's eyes lit at that.

"So what sharp dealing is going on?" she asked Earnest when he had his mouth full of cake.

A sip of tea followed. "Well, ma'am, what they're sayin' is how the Mackeys is going to provide the backing for them boys, and how either they're going to trade 'em the shop and house up here, which ain't worth near what the one down in Tarmin is, for the shop and at least two big houses down there. Otherwise there's talk as how they got to employ Rick and pay 'em back near a hundred percent interest on anything they lent 'em. I ain't supposing there's been too much damage to the shop by the critters, but water comin' by snows and rains might not be too good, and a lot of doors was left standin' open, if you take my meaning."

"Entirely. In other words, it's going to take supplies of food, possibly of cash for metal—"

"Well, it's going to be worse than that, ma'am, I am greatly afraid."

"How?"

"Well, that the Mackeys *nor* them boys is going to hold out against the looters. That town's going to be a bloody mess. Law ain't goin' down there. Bunch of lawyers' papers—they ain't worth—Well, they ain't goin' to be worth a thing, ma'am. Miners, many of 'em, is fine folk. And some ain't. There's them that'd shoot you in the back for a nugget, let alone a house. And there ain't going to be any law down there. The marshal can't leave here. His deputies ain't fools. So—them as wants to *hold* the property that they got title to had better have guns and better be ready to use 'em. And I don't think the Mackeys have got the guts, if you want my opinion, ma'am. They're early in the game, but they're likely to end piss-poor or dead."

Darcy drew a long, slow breath. Sense told her she was hearing the truth from this man, a truth that didn't bode well for anybody holding rights down in Tarmin.

"So what's your proposition, Mr. Riggs? I take it you have a proposition."

"Well, yes, ma'am, I do. This little girl, her *havin'* rights and all, her brothers is dealing with the wrong folk in the Mackeys, and they're going to get sharped out of ever'thing they got due 'em. *Which* is fairly well goin' to take this little girl's property down with 'em, if you're relyin' on them two boys to protect her rights. Mackeys is going to get killed if they go down there. And so's them boys. But that little girl—she's such a pretty thing—"

"You said there's a *rider* backing the boys."

"Oh, yeah. And that's a powerful hand. Don't nothin' move cross-country without 'em. But once we get there, once there's walls, ma'am, us miner types, we know how to dig in, we know how to get by. First villager boy tries it, he's down something's gullet fast. But there ain't but your two riders, and they got a little girl to watch out for, besides they can't leave the village without riders. That's down to *one* rider, this Fisher boy, and some friends of his, supposedly, but that's still three riders and a lot of supplies to haul down—and how many places can this Fisher be at once? You got supplies to haul. You got Tarmin to sit guard on. Any convoy that moves ain't really safe without at least a rider to front and one to back. There's just a hell of a lot they ain't addin' up, ma'am. You got to have somebody to sit down there and defend a bunch of pukin' village boys who'd lose all their sense and rush right out into a lorrie-lie's arms, first night they heard the Wild talkin' to 'em, and you got to have somebody to ride with the truck convoys—granted they'll come with their own riders—but somebody's got to fix the damn phone lines, too. And that's another rider. Fisher can't be all those places. The convoy riders, they're another breed, and they got *their* hire. Before they can do anything like move supplies they got to get riders from the other villages, and then the word's out, and not a lot of people in those villages—*specially* the miners—is going to be damn happy there's a bunch from Evergreen who's gone down to Tarmin and squatted on the good property. Miner's laws goin' to rule this 'un when the dust flies, ma'am, and if somebody ain't looking out for that little girl's interests—she ain't going to get a penny."

"Then I can provide for her, Mr. Riggs. Sounds as if I'm going to have a lot of business."

Earnest leaned forward across the table. "Yes, ma'am. But that ain't the only danger. You got this little girl, same as them boys, walking around with nobody to watch 'em, and could happen—*could* happen, there'd be some snatch this pretty little thing on account of her being not only just damn pretty but also rich and having rights. And when the law *does* come down there in a couple of years, if you're alive and you got rights—the law's going to be for you and again' others in whatever dispute might be. You don't want to sign away what's due that pretty little girl."

"Yeah. I might, rather than see her involved in what you're talking about."

"No, now, ma'am, you can look out for that little lady's interest, you know, if you'd have somebody as can defend her claim down there."

Now it came to money. "Mr. Riggs, clearly you're expecting I'll give you a stake. And I don't have money for groceries. I've not been working the last year."

"You got this nice house. You got credit at the bank."

"Mr. Riggs, —if I *gave* you money and you went down there and got killed, I'd have a debt, the girl would be broke, and there'd be no recourse."

"Ma'am, we've thought of that. There's a number of us, five or six, that's willin' to go down there together to look out for ourselves, and the little girl's interest, well, you know men. It's a hell of a lot easier to keep guys headed the same direction, if they got a thing to do together. So while we're looking out for ourselves, we could look out for the little girl's property."

"Her *brothers'* property."

"Well, we could strike a deal with them for her third. Damn sure the Mackeys ain't going to pay anything to keep the property safe, and the boys are poorer than we are. We could hire *them,* howsoever."

"Let me have it clear. You're proposing to have me pay you money to shoot anybody who tries to claim the Goss property."

"No, ma'am. I'm proposing you buy us shells and flour and oil and such and we'll sit on the property and defend ourselves if someone's such a fool as to take on five of us. It's that little girl's legal title to the property that'd give us special status before the law, ma'am. And the property *around* it's what we'd claim for ourselves. Wouldn't lay no claim on the girl's property."

"That'd be a fair piece of the village you'd be sitting on."

"Yes, ma'am, it would."

"How much would you want?"

"Thousand. In advance. For supplies, ma'am. Not a penny more."

It wasn't so much as she'd feared. But it was a huge amount of cash.

"And what about the brothers?"

"Fairly well depends on them. How they like us for neighbors. Or we'd protect them, too, if they come up with an offer."

There were very sharp edges to this affair. And she *couldn't* trust that Riggs wouldn't strong-arm the Goss brothers once they were down in Tarmin with Riggs' crew all around them.

She was halfway surprised she didn't hear an offer to make sure The Little Girl inherited *all* the Goss property. But if she borrowed that trouble she lost all power to control the purse strings and thereby to control Riggs.

And there was a chance the Goss boys might—*might* try to prevent her gaining custody of Brionne. She wasn't a fool. She didn't give up her cards until she knew what they were worth.

And she didn't need to put a thousand in cash into Riggs' hands so he could drink it up by spring and ask for another.

"This spring," she said, "I'll have the cash for you."

"Begging your pardon, ma'am, but spring'll be a rush on supplies, prices are bound to go up. We'll need more if we wait till spring."

"Then I'll put it on account at the store and they'll reserve you supplies, but they won't deliver until I say so."

"Ma'am, you're one sharp woman."

"Yes, I am. You turn in your list to me. Can you write?"

"No, ma'am. But one of my guys can. We'll get a list."

"The other matter, Mr. Riggs, is—don't talk outside your group about my supporting you. If this becomes gossip around town, I'll know I can't trust you, and you won't get a sack of flour or a foot of rope."

"I do understand. And you don't have no doubts: I'm the one can get that little girl her rights. I can lay claim down there for her, fix up the place—what needs fixin'. I mean, if them houses was swarmed, it's going to be pretty messy inside. But I can do that. *Pretty* little girl."

"She's thirteen," Darcy said coldly, seeing exactly where that was going.

It set him back. Maybe. For about two seconds. "Well, that'd be about right, a few years on. Pretty little thing. Awful pretty. You got to watch out, them rough guys, you know."

"I'll tell you plain, Mr. Riggs, she'll never be any miner's wife. She might *hire* somebody. As I might. He might do all right for himself. If he was honest—he could be *very* well-set. Possibly go into business."

She had a big house, and all the equipment, and everything. But if Tarmin proved more viable, if Brionne's welfare somehow demanded better than the cold winters and isolation of Evergreen—there was, the thought came to her like a revelation—there was the Tarmin's doctor's establishment, better equipment, bigger population, once the village got going again. No drunken miners to treat. *Those* all came to Evergreen and Mornay.

Ernest might in fact be very useful to two women trying to get *their* share of what everyone else was scrambling to get.

And it was going to happen this spring. The treasure-seekers and the looters and ordinary citizens trying to stake claims to businesses and shops were going to be down that road like a nest of willy-wisps stirred with a stick.

"You know, Mr. Riggs, there was a doctor in Tarmin. Probably all the instruments are still there."

"Sure won't be, ma'am, if them loggers get there first."

"Yeah, well, how many properties do you think you can preserve unlooted? Would another thousand make sure *that* office was mine?" It was unreal to her to be asking a question of a practice she and Mark had never been able to dream of.

But it could be hers. Completely logical. No one *else* could use that office, that equipment. There was a doctor at Mornay. But he was old. She could *see* to it there were both options—and if it proved necessary to move to Tarmin, if it was necessary to do that to assure a good life, without the girl being subjected to winters up there, she would have a foot in either village. And assets which would be worth a great deal. She could *become* wealthy.

Wealth would protect herself and her baby girl, *her* daughter, against a world that was not and would never be the way John Quarles saw it. Wealth to buy the likes of Earnest Riggs, a small debt now to own a major part of Tarmin and a future for herself and her daughter.

"I'd think," Earnest Riggs said, "that's a lot to protect. I got to hire more men."

"Three thousand," she said, and got to her feet to give Earnest Riggs the cue she was through, on that point, and he could leave very soon upon her making it. "Free doctoring. My respectable reputation behind your claim on whatever property you fancy down there. You can *all* be well-to-do by next fall. That's all you'll see from me. You don't talk about it, don't let your hirees gossip drunk or sober."

"Yes, ma'am." Earnest got up, hat in hand. "Three thousand and we don't talk for nothing."

* * *

Tara did the woodcutting for the coming night. Guil had done the fire-building with the first small load Tara had provided him for the shelter's fireplace. He also did the cooking and the currying of snow out of nighthorse manes and tails, and he was damned tired of horses wanting in and horses wanting out of the cabin. Horses could stand out there in the next snowstorm if horses didn't make up their minds.

Thump. "Dammit, let me in!"

That wasn't Burn. Guil left the soup-pot simmering and got up and got the door, admitting a snowy Tara with a huge armful of wood; and, right behind her, head lowered, figuring to warm himself from the cold, but *not* quite sure whether he wanted in or out, came Burn.

"Are you coming?" he asked Flicker, who lurked coyly behind Burn's rump and who put forth a nose, but just at the threshold and while he was waiting with the door, Flicker kicked up her heels and gave the high-pitched squeal of a nighthorse wanting <male.>

Burn wanted out, then, and went right past him with a whip of a snow-caked tail that hit like a pelting of snowballs.

<*Snow* on Burn,> he sent in no uncertain force, and got back a completely distracted <*female,*> and <*sex.*>

There was snow in clumps all over the boards of the floor. And unless one wanted to walk barefoot over unexpected puddles in the evening, there was nothing to do but get the broom and sweep the lumps over to the fire where it might evaporate—melting streaks all the way across the dusty boards. These particular miners were sloppy campers, and they'd *not* cleaned up, they'd not stocked the cabin with wood against winter emergency—seeing themselves as their only concern—and they'd not left provisions, for the very good reason that it was a flimsy shelter and food inside would have invited predators to dig their way in and destroy the little furniture there was.

So it was a good idea they'd lugged supplies up the mountain.

Tara had dumped her firewood beside the fireplace. She'd been across the slope with Flicker and Burn for protection. The shelter had an axe, its one amenity besides the snow shovel and a single pot, and the axe instead of the hatchet they'd brought had meant larger firewood quicker. He'd been hearing the sound of the axe fairly steadily while he was arranging supper, and the pile she'd brought in was enough for the night.

"Quiet up there," she said as he picked out a couple of pieces to add to the cookfire. "Just real, real quiet. I sat out there a few moments, being nothing, trying to shape the mountain in my head. And the hole is back. I can't locate it—but *up*. Definitely somewhere *up*."

The thing they'd felt before, especially in the nights down in the lonely, lifeless woods at first stage—it came and it went above them. The thought of it showing up made him damn nervous in the afterthought of Tara having possibly taken out up this trail without him. There had continually felt to be places up above them on the mountain—not always the same places—where life didn't exist. And they still didn't know why.

Neither of them had ever seen a swarm on the scale that had happened at Tarmin. Maybe, they'd reasoned when they'd considered the question down at first-stage, creatures drawn into the events at Tarmin hadn't really ever gotten *out* of the swarm. Maybe groups were still spooking each other off at minor alarms, moving out of their territories in panic and not yet able to reestablish boundaries for themselves and settle down to a normal winter.

Their combined experience as riders just didn't cover what was going on up above them. One *heard* about rogues—rare as the condition was. But the folklore had never prepared them for the destructive force it had loosed, the lingering spookiness on the mountain even after the rogue was dead. They hadn't expected the mass movements of game that seemed to go one direction and then the other on the face of the mountain with no reason, with absolute vacancy at the heart of it. Weather had had *them* pinned down—but it hadn't been affecting the oddness up there.

A massive hole in the ambient, this moving darkness.

"You know, one thing that blank spot could be," Guil said, tucking a medium-sized piece of wood into the fire below the soup pot. "Big predator."

"Nothing ever like this that I ever heard," Tara said, hugging her arms across her, and added a moment later: "The *rogue* might have felt like this—in deep winter—if there weren't a lot of racket."

Meaning the natural noise in the ambient that all those lives had made in Tarmin village was gone now. Humans didn't send far without something to carry it—but an aggregation of living things even like a herd of cattle was noisy.

And in the silence on Rogers Peak they ought to have been able to hear very, very far across the mountain right now, not any specific creature, just—presence. Life. It was possible the villages were aware of that silence. It was possible they weren't. Too many people—like too much light—came with settlements. You couldn't see the fainter stars. You couldn't get a fair listen to this thing.

Kids, on their own, making their way perhaps as slowly as they were against hostile weather, could blunder right into it. It had worried him through the days that they were pinned down at first-stage. It worried him now that there was snow coming down with fair vigor out there. He didn't want to be wintered in here. He truly didn't.

Tara moved to have a look at the soup, and stripped the gloves off hands that just weren't used to the amount of wood-cutting she'd had to do lately, hands that, in the firelight, showed raw sores the gloves hadn't prevented.

He captured a hand and had a closer look.

"It's all right," Tara said, and freed it for a look under the lid of the soup-pot. Then added: "It's all right—just like your head."

Wicked woman. Halfway up the mountain looking for kids she maintained she didn't want to find about half of every day. She'd taken the risk, committed herself, given a damn; she was in danger of outright charity—figuring she could have stayed put and not budged from first-stage and not helped. She'd worked hard out there; holding and being held felt very good right now, in the absence of anything else to do, to make it clear he was very appreciative of the stack of firewood he hadn't had to cut. His head hurt. Her hands hurt. If they held a competition they could probably find other spots, but at least the couple of stitches she'd put in his side, front and back, some days ago, had held up during today's climb, and they were doing pretty well for a couple of fools.

Meanwhile the horses were cavorting around the rocks out there and one just hoped, as the ambient went scary with <near fall> from one of the two fools, that they didn't fall off a snow-buried cliff.

"Supper's ready," he said into her hair. "I made the whole mess of potatoes up. Figuring we can carry it."

"Temperature's just floating out there. It may go above freezing tonight. If it does—it's going to be just real nasty conditions. An early winter, but a slow one setting in. We could get real damn tired of potatoes."

"Beats bushdevil."

"By a bit," she agreed, and having found interest enough to be hungry, she served up the soup that was destined for supper and breakfast-to-come, and they settled down to one more night with the temperature still hovering. He'd cut up the whole supply of potatoes which the kids had left at first-stage and they'd carried it up with them: the perishables left there would have frozen soon, as they'd slightly frozen on the climb, in spite of the protection in which the stores had been buried. Tara had escorted a cart out with that load of perishables not too long before the disaster, supplies the road workers should have used fast, but, Tara had said grimly, certainly nobody down on first-stage level was going to need them—including two more of Tarmin's riders, friends of hers, besides the ones who'd died in Tarmin.

So at least they went to someone's use, and if they got bad weather they'd at least have potato soup for days before they ever had to resort to what might be very thin hunting on this face of the peak. But if they got their wish and the weather turned to deep cold and reliable freezing, their next night's supper, frozen, could pack up and go with them up the mountain, for an open-air camp or for very fast moving in their effort to get up to Evergreen. Then they could find out, in the best news they could expect, that the kids had made it alive and didn't need their help, or that the kids were stranded down at midway and *were* going to need help.

Better if the kids had been able to go this direction. But Tara couldn't have shown Danny Fisher this route: Tara wasn't totally sure of it herself. Experienced horses could deal with the trail they were using—but he'd hate to have sent Fisher and a young horse up the trail they'd taken. On second-hand landmarks they'd never have found the mining shack.

Their own horses of course wanted into the cabin, now that potato and ham soup had entered the ambient in a very vivid way. Tara did the getting up and let in two snow-caked horses.

And the instant two humans settled down again to their supper Burn leaned his head on his rider's shoulder in ambitious anticipation of tasty bits, namely all the ham and considerable amounts of the sauce. Flicker moved in on Tara in the same way, to look doleful and coy from the front.

They both could be quite hard-hearted until, dammit, they were through. *Then* they poured out a couple of bowls on the hearth-stones—quite a suitable platter for horses, and very unlike their dumping of snow and drip of melt onto the floor, there wasn't a smidge of soup left to mop.

Guil put a cover on the pot, determined to keep horse noses out of their several days' supply. And they sat, after the horses had cleaned the stones, watching patterns in the fire. Burn and Flicker settled down to mutual grooming and Tara—

Suddenly Tara thought of <cutting wood on the hillside, among the trees, lonely feeling, empty ambient.> She thought of <stopping, looking uphill, trees and white.>

She seized his hand, hard. "Think of something else. Now!"

<Still water.> It was the earliest childhood calm-down. <Sun sparkle on ripples. Stones beneath.>

<Fish,> she added.

The horses lifted their heads, hungrily and vividly interested in <fish,> though they were stuffed with hay and grain and had ham and potatoes to chase that.

Tara laughed.

Laughed and laughed, out of proportion to the image.

Guil knew where she was headed, the collapse after long and impossible strain. He sent her <fish on a spit> and Tara lay on the floor holding her stomach, the spasms were so intense. She'd sober up—and break out laughing again until laughter gave way to helpless sobs for breath.

Then came just hard breathing, and panic—panic that she'd stopped up since that night she'd spent <listening—listening to the Wild, hearing the slaughter at Tarmin and knowing her partners were dying—>

<White> hit the ambient, <white,> the way Flicker would send when Flicker wanted to hide. Guil tried to take hold of her: mistake. She shoved hard at him. It hurt his side.

That got through to her. It hadn't on other occasions. It brought her out of herself. "I'm *sorry,*" she said, and threw her arms around him while he was trying to get *his* breath back.

Panic in the ambient ebbed.

But <dark> was out there. The horses had forgotten all about fish, and lovemaking. They stood stock-still, heads lifted, nostrils straining for smells that were only in the ambient.

<Snow and cold. Evergreens.> And something—

Something that was <hunger> and <threat> and <bite.>

Guil didn't think about the pain. He was on his feet with his hands on Burn's neck. Tara had done the same with Flicker, wanting <snow. Quiet snow falling.>

Guil wanted the same from Burn. There was no cabin here. There was just <evergreens and snow.>

<Evergreens with branches laced and snow-blanketed. Deep, deep peace on this hillside.>

For a long time they stood like that, not letting the ambient go, not letting anything but those images into the night. There were no humans or horses here, there was no fire, there was no shelter, there was nothing but forest and snow.

When they let go, carefully and little at a time, the ambient was quiet. *It* wasn't there, either.

Darcy drifted, almost asleep when a terrible wail broke through the dark of the upstairs.

Then a sudden shriek, a thump and a second thump.

Darcy leapt up in a tangle of blankets, fought her legs free and ran for the balcony, thinking of the stairs and the chance of the girl turning toward them in the dark and unawares.

"Faye!" she cried, and intercepted the girl on the balcony, held her in her arms as she gasped for breath.

"Mama," the girl cried. "Mama, mama, mama, he shot my horse, *he shot my horse—"*

"Shot your horse— What are you talking about, honey?"

"They shot him, they shot him, and I *hate* him—I hate *her!"*

"Who?"

"I'll find them—*I'll find them! I'll make them sorry."*

"Hush, hush, child." Darcy hugged the trembling body against her own, shivering in the winter cold, and guided her back to the safety of her own room, holding her arm, talking to her gently. "I was afraid you'd fall. There's stairs to watch out for. You're on the second story. You mustn't get up and walk in the dark. Call me if you're want to get up in the dark."

"It was *my horse!"* the girl sobbed. "I want them *dead!"*

"Hush." Darcy set her frail charge down on the edge of her bed and sat down herself on the edge of the mattress, tucking the girl up in the quilt. "There's a love. You're safe. There's no one to hurt you here."

"I hate them! "

"Hush." Darcy combed the soft, tangled curls with her fingers. "Hush. You mustn't talk like that." She didn't know about horses. She didn't understand what the child was dreaming about, but it scared her, it was so unexpectedly off the map. "You were dreaming, honey. It was just a dream. You mustn't talk about horses. It makes the preacher worry. And we shouldn't worry the preacher, should we, honey?"

"I prayed to God for my horse! And he was *mine!"*

"Hush, hush, it's not a thing to say. You'll scare people. They won't understand it."

There was a shaky sob. "I want my mama."

"Yes, honey. I know, I know. But your mama's gone, honey. I'll take care of you." She stroked Brionne's hair and Brionne rested her head against her shoulder. Brionne's arms went around her.

"I'll find a horse," Brionne heaved a huge, shuddery sigh."One will come for me. I'll call it and it'll come."

Now that the panic was past, she was only halfway appalled: some children *did* fantasize about horses. Occasionally they listened to bushbabies or hung about near the rider camp trying to pick up images—a spate of curiosity at about age seven or eight, a spate of trying to pick up sexual images around adolescence. Shocked parents came with fair regularity asking what to do—and Brionne was old enough for the second phase. But it might equally well represent a bright and imaginative child's wish for independence, for a romantic event to transform her life from the settled routine she saw as her growing up.

Or even escape—from the very dreadful events down at Tarmin.

She'd done her own daydreaming, at such an age. She didn't believe in the preacher's God, never had, from *her* mother's knee, and her wish for escape had been from an apprenticeship rigorous and humorless. If a horse *had* ever called her in her youth she supposed she'd have gone out the gates without a qualm.

So she resolved to deal with the child's fantasies with far more humor and heartfelt understanding than her own mother had had for anyone.

To begin with she didn't call the girl a fool, or depraved.

"That's just all right, honey. Maybe you'll call a horse for me, too, and we'll ride all over the mountain."

"You're not scared of me?"

"Nothing scares me."

The girl's arms hugged her tight, tight a moment. "I love you."

She hadn't expected that. It was very difficult to get the unaccustomed words out of her throat, but she did.

"I love you, too, honey."

They sat like that a while. Darcy's feet went numb from cold. She didn't mind. Her arms were warm.

At last the girl heaved a vast sigh. "It's so *quiet* now. It's gone away."

"What's gone away?"

"The horse out there. Now I can't hear anything. It's scary, everything's so quiet. Can we light a lamp?"

"Sure. Sure, honey. You want to come with me? I'll light the lamp in your room."

There was a young horse in the rider camp. She didn't remember. She thought there was. She didn't know the status of it. She just hadn't hung about for gossip because she hadn't wanted the reciprocal questions into *her* business.

But if imagining horses and being scared of the dark were the only complaints the girl had after the climb up the mountain she'd done very well indeed.

A normal, natural little girl.

That was all.

Chapter

— XVI—

The curiosity in the tavern had died down. It was a weekday night, and a crowd even so—in Tarmin it had been only Saturday-night crowds of this size and noise level, but Tarmin hadn't had the winter influx of miners and loggers who had the credit to spend, no kitchen to cook in, and no families to restrain the consumption or the spending. There was music, a ring of tolerable guitar players among the miners in from one of the camps, who were leading a still suitable for youngers singalong interspersed with soulful ballads.

Most of all, native to Evergreen, there was good food: the miners had high standards, that was a famous and dependable fact; and the guy who ran The Evergreen in the winter months had to be a good cook or he wouldn't have lasted the week.

Carlo and Randy picked up dishes of the nightly buffet and went hunting for a table. The snowfall was getting thick outside, and when Carlo would have thought that families would have been home on such a night, the place was crowded not only with miners, but with Evergreen villagers, including Van Mackey *and* Mary

Hardesty, *and* Rick, plus a number of other village families and folk looking for society.

The end nearest the door was family territory, the left end nearest the fire was miner's territory, the right was loggers' district, the liquor was flowing from the bar that divided the room—except that there was between the town and both miners and loggers a no-man's-land of kids deeming themselves old enough to drink, both too old and not old enough to sit with their parents, not welcome either (Carlo understood the unspoken rules) in the outsiders' section where the almost entirely male village transients congregated for serious winter-break drinking.

Having a fourteen-year-old brother in tow, he'd generally taken a table near the bar, where the bartender and the cook maintained order, except there wasn't a table at the moment. Randy found a table instead on the border between the young folk and the miners and having his hands full of plate, bread, and pint of ale, he was willing to risk it and sit down—hoping that Danny might stray in, and looking only to see that they were visible from the door.

Then he saw they'd landed equally directly in sight of Rick Mackey, who was sitting at a table of young village folk. He didn't like that. Rick and a couple of the young lads had their heads together, looking their direction, and he liked that less.

Then another table came vacant near them, occupied very quickly by a cluster of the older village girls, who generally hung about in a group and talked under the music, and who, Carlo began to be uncomfortably aware, had *had* a table before they switched seats to put their heads together and talk behind their hands, with frequent looks in their direction.

Then one of the girls got up and swayed her way toward them—got part of the way before Rick Mackey was out of his seat, grabbing her arm to have a talk with her.

Carlo didn't like the look of that. Especially when the other girls got up from the table and surrounded the argument, shouting at Rick Mackey. The first girl jerked her arm free and, backed up now by her three female friends, *all* strolled over to his and Randy's table.

"Hello," came the inventive approach from the girl who'd started the march on their table. "You're Carlo Goss. I know about you from church. But I didn't come meet you. It was such a crowd."

She *was* pretty. You're Carlo Goss? as if Randy weren't even in the reckoning. "Yeah," Carlo said, and gestured with a move of his hand to Randy, across the table from him. "That's Randy. My brother."

"My name is Azlea Sumner. We own the pharmacy."

We, it was. That was fairly pretentious. He wouldn't have claimed to own the shop down in Tarmin. She was pretty, she was clearly leading the pack of available females in the village, and Rick had just lost his public bid to restrain the contact.

"Glad to meet you," he said, though he wasn't sure about it. "You probably know everything about us."

"Oh, I don't think so," she said, and dropped into the seat across the table and next to Randy, chin on hands. "What is there else we should know?"

A second girl sat down. A third dragged a chair over. Two more looked up chairs. Rick Mackey wasn't the only scowling face among the young men of Evergreen. Carlo could see that fact past the wall of eligible females, seemingly constituting *all* the eligible young women in Evergreen. It was promising to be a long, long winter: Randy looked to have figured out there was serious trouble, and cast him a silent appeal for quick thinking.

"I don't know," he said to her question. He wasn't interested in playing games. He wasn't interested in *her* games. If she wanted a roll in the blankets and it *didn't* entail the jealous observance of every unattached male in Evergreen, he'd still think twice about Azlea Sumner, whose introduction told him nothing but that her parents had money, and whose converse with him was all designed to get *him* to give *her* pieces of information.

Hell with that, he thought sourly. He wasn't that hard up.

"So what *happened* in Tarmin?" she asked, giving him the long stare at too close a range.

"A swarm came over the walls," he said, "and ate everybody but us. Just bones. You could see them in the snow. Just bare bones and little frozen pieces of flesh." He had another spoonful of stew. "Not a pretty sight."

He thought it might drive them all off. It brought grimaces and shivers. It didn't daunt Azlea Sumner.

"So you're heir to the smith's shop and houses and everything."

"Could say, yes."

"You must have been very brave."

"Lucky," he said shortly. "Very lucky. So tell me about Rick Mackey. He seems real interested in you."

"Oh, him."

"He's a jerk," Randy said helpfully.

"Contagious," Carlo said. "Nice to meet you. Who are your friends?"

Sumner didn't exactly plan to introduce her friends. That was clear. Azlea Sumner didn't like not to be the center of absolute attention.

Fine. He wasn't interested in playing, not if Sumner had been standing there stark naked. But he maintained small conversation with her and with her four friends, Cindy, Wilby, Lucia and Nilema. Nilema, last to drag a chair up, seemed by far the nicest of the lot.

But Randy was by now tired of being ignored, and very clearly didn't like being kicked under the table when he opened his mouth to say something. Carlo wanted to get Randy out of the tavern. Failing that, he'd like them away from the table.

Maybe his disinterest came through too obviously, though, because Sumner and her entourage just then spotted some new girl coming through the door of the tavern that Sumner didn't mind waving to and making a fuss over from a distance.

It was an escape: Azlea Sumner's, her friends', and theirs, though he feared they might steer the new arrival back to their table—in which case he was going to call an early end to supper and pocket a couple of sandwiches on the Mackeys' tab.

He was not quite relieved that Sumner and her entourage, having captured the new girl, retreated to the side of the room where Rick and five or six of the boys were standing, all sending foul looks in their direction and sharing some kind of joke.

"What was she after?" Randy asked. It wasn't a stupid fourteen-year-old question: Randy *knew* the obvious that she could be after. He was asking the serious question: What was she after?

"Finish your supper."

"Do you think she's pretty?"

"She's pretty and she thinks trouble is a lot of fun. Not our type. Thanks. We've seen real trouble. Eat your supper before something happens and we have to get out of here."

"We don't have to leave for *her.*"

"There are situations that could make it smart. Just *be* smart, little brother."

He downed the remnant of his supper, not without an eye to who came and went: *Rick* left, and he decided then he was going to stay longer. But Rick came back, probably from a piss, and the boys were still holding conversation at a table when, at his own pace, and in peace, he had the last spoonful and chased it with the glass of beer.

"Time we went home," he said then.

"Home," Randy said unhappily. "It isn't."

"Closest we have, kid. Take it as is." He got up. So did Randy. They left, past the adult area and out into the snowy evening—too short a walk to resort to the passages, though the evening was snowy and very cold.

Twilight had gone blued and strange. The sky was overcast. The evergreens that lined the street and stood outside the smith's shop were black in the dimming of the light, and the whole street was a row of odd, tall-roofed buildings and of snow-frosted evergreen.

They walked in via the side door.

And feet slipped. It was a sheet of ice they'd hit and they grabbed wildly at each other and at the door.

"Damn!" Carlo cried. There was water all over the floor, frozen, where it came near the colder spots near the walls and the doors.

"What happened?" Randy asked. "What did it?"

His mind was instead on the path the water had taken, over to the passageway door, and probably right down the steps, where it would make a hell of a slick spot for anyone coming to the house door via the passages.

But the source of it wasn't likely melt off the roof, and it *wasn't* likely an ordinary winter occurrence.

"Water tank may have frozen," he said, though that didn't seem likely either, in the warmth of the forge, and there weren't pipes to leak. "See if that's the problem."

He was thinking of that slick spot, himself, and Van and Mary coming home any minute. To forestall a noisy disaster and one with potentially serious effects, he picked up the sand bucket they kept to deal with fires from its place by the furnace. He scattered a little by the door they'd used, and went to the passage. He scattered the largest part of the sand there, and went back up into the forge proper.

"The tap was open," Randy said.

"Open?" he said, not too brightly, but he'd had a beer and a shift of direction. He heard the sound of footsteps coming back from, he could guess, the tavern, not long after he had, via the passages. And sure enough Rick came in, tried the flooring ostentatiously with his heel and yelled, "What in hell's going on? Where's the water coming from?"

"I think you damn well know," Carlo said.

"You're done, boy. This is your stupid fault. No question."

"We'll see."

"Big threat."

He found his temper coming up. And he wouldn't let it. "All right, all right, big joke."

"Beat him up!" Randy said. "You don't have to take that off him!"

"Little brother's got more guts than you have."

"Yeah," he said matter-of-factly.

About that time Van Mackey and his wife were coming back, and the cursing from the corridor was loud and clear. The sand hadn't prevented slippage altogether. He went to the door and said, "Watch those steps."

"What in hell happened here?" Van Mackey came stamping up through the doorway and looked at a forge floor glistening with standing water and ice. "The tank give way?"

"The kid left the tap askew," Rick said with a sneer.

"No," Carlo said. "No, sir, I don't think so."

"Like hell," Rick said, and his mother, in the doorway behind Van:

"Shut up."

"*Me* shut up! The damn brat flooded the place! It's pure luck nobody broke their—!"

"I want to talk to you," Van said.

"For *what? They* left the tap open."

"Liar!" Randy said, but Carlo didn't say a thing, thinking all in a flash that if Rick's ploy didn't work and Rick's papa beat hell out of him and Rick wanted to come back at him, Rick had better not come at Randy.

Because he knew now how to get Rick, every time. Rick was devious but not bright, and anything that went wrong around here was *not* going to be the fault of two boys Rick's father wanted on the good side of. Rick was about to get the shit beaten out of him and hadn't figured yet why that was.

Rick's papa ordered his son into the corridor, shut the door, and an argument started that could melt the ice out there. Van was shouting, the wife was shouting—Rick was shouting his innocence.

Then there was a lot of slamming of doors and shouting and screaming, the subject of which they couldn't hear but Carlo could guess.

Randy stared. Randy just stared.

"I guess he's getting it good," Randy said finally. There wasn't the triumph Randy might have showed. It sounded pretty bad in there.

Carlo understood that, in his own gut. Sounded like home. Their own household. The sounds were the same, the yelling was the same—only this time he was safe outside and just listening to it, and Randy was hearing it, and remembering.

The old cold fear was back. Not of Rick Mackey. Just—fear, the same fear he'd had when his father had used to corner him and Randy. They'd never done right. They'd learned a whole lot of lessons in the forge that had everything to do with avoiding blame and nothing to do with justice or *ever* satisfying their father.

He didn't want to hear it. He squeezed Randy's shoulder and thought he'd like to go back to the tavern and have another beer, and maybe not lie down to sleep with the upset in the stomach he was feeling right now.

But he couldn't. He had Randy to think of, and he had a damned fool girl trying to make a play for him for reasons his sixteen years told him weren't on the up-and-up. And, dammit, he hadn't seen Danny since he'd yelled at Danny and Danny had walked off.

He heard a door slam. He heard someone leave the house in a fit of temper and hoped to God whoever was bound out didn't skid on the ice. But whoever it was went out, and didn't break his neck, and he'd bet it was Rick or Van going to the tavern—where he consequently *didn't* want to be.

"Time to get to sleep," he said. "Get some rest."

"I'm not sleepy."

"Then we can pitch pennies, for who gets to *fill* the water tank."

"Rick'll have to fill it. Betcha."

"Might be. But if he doesn't, you do."

"Wait a minute," his little brother said. "Where's the deal that *you* do it?"

"You're learning," he said. "Not much, but you're learning."

"Hell," Randy said, and Carlo cuffed Randy's ear, not hard, but because he was the senior brother and somebody had to tell a fourteen-year-old not to cuss, not to drink, and not to be impressed with Azlea Sumner.

Fact was, he didn't feel like sleep, either. And he had some actual pennies, or at least change chits from the tavern, since, the barman said, the village was short on coin and tavern chits would buy you stuff anywhere in town.

Best use for them was pitch-penny.

And he played against his brother until they'd both calmed down and gotten sleepy; and finally they lost one of their pennies in the forge, and that was it. He told Randy give it up and go to sleep, and he sat down after he'd gotten Randy into his blanket and tucked into his own, with his back against the warm stones.

Van came in late. He knew it was Van. He heard the shouting break out again.

He really wanted a couple of beers. Tonight after a lapse of a number of nights he had the vision back again, the gunshot, the sound, the anger—

God, the anger. It was the Mackey house that conjured it for him, but it was there and it was real. It colored the space behind his eyes with red, and filled his ears with his mother's screaming.

He couldn't let their father hit him again. He couldn't let their father hit Randy.

You damn pig! was the last thing his father had ever said. The night had exploded—just—exploded. He didn't know when he'd picked up the gun. He didn't know why he had. He didn't know anything but his mother screaming—screaming at him a second time across the village crowd gathered in front of the marshal's office. Murderer, she'd called him.

He was, he knew that. He was eldest. He'd picked up the gun. Their father always kept it by the fireplace, and he'd grabbed it up, he must have—but he hadn't wanted to pull the trigger. His anger had.

Just like your father, their mother would say when he lost his temper as a child. Just like your father.

Meaning the first time he'd lost his temper as a man against a man—

He'd shot his father.

Danny offered reasons and said he wasn't a killer, that it was the rogue sending anger into the village—but he knew it was his fault; and he *didn't* want to fight Rick. He didn't want to fight anybody, ever again. Just do his job, that was all he wanted.

"You awake?" Randy asked out of the dark, while the fight went on the other side of the wall.

"Yeah."

"I don't like it here. *Why* can't we go to Danny?"

"Because we're not riders."

"I could *hear* the horses. I could hear it plain as plain the other night. I *liked* it."

"Yeah. Well, that's not for us."

"You say. *You* say. *You* don't know what I am. *You* don't run my life!"

"Yeah, well, kid, I'm just trying to get you to grown-up and then you can find a horse if you want one. But meanwhile *I* need you. *I* need you. Does that matter at all?"

"That's a cheat. You don't need me."

"Who the hell else am I doing this for? Who'd I haul up this damn mountain besides—besides our sister, who's not my reason." Luckily it was dark. Tears didn't show. "Kid, I'm tired. I'm really tired."

"You should have beat hell out of him."

"Well, I don't want to. And that's my business."

"I could catch that horse."

"You're a damn *fool.*" Of a sudden he had a terrible notion of Randy actually going out the gate, and he sat up on his cot, swung his feet off the side and grabbed hold of Randy's arm. "Don't you think about it! Don't you think about it, or damn you to hell, Randy Goss! Don't you double-cross me like that and get yourself killed—because that's what will happen!"

"I'm not going to," Randy said. "Let go. That hurts."

He'd held too hard. He bent over and hugged his brother. Ruffled his hair in the dark. "I love you," he said. He didn't know if he'd ever said it to anybody. He didn't know if anyone had ever said it to him. "You're a good kid."

"Not a kid," Randy complained.

"Not grown yet, either. I want to see you get there. All right?"

"Yeah," Randy said, embarrassed, Carlo was sure, and he got back on his own cot and pulled the covers over him.

Randy should have something good out of his life. Randy was smart. He was quick with people—like in church. Randy'd realized what he had to do, and he'd done it with a passion, and *made* people like him.

That was a gift. That was a real gift. He wished he had it.

Hell with this horse business, Randy was cut out for dealing with people and having a wife and kids he'd spoil rotten, if he just figured out that was the way families were supposed to work.

Because there *was* goodness in Randy. Randy was going through that stage of being too tough to think straight, but there was a good kid there, a good heart that deserved friends like he'd been lucky enough to have, guys that were dead down in Tarmin, names that just—didn't exist anymore.

He gave a long breath, realizing it was the first time he'd been able to think calmly about what had happened, having learned fast in all those days with Danny how to keep his mind off troubling subjects—and now really believing that nobody in the village could possibly hear his thoughts.

He hadn't realized until now he'd been scared of that. But he had been. Fear was a good teacher.

And when Danny had said he'd confessed to the riders all those things he'd not admitted out loud, he'd just blown up. Just blown up, in total startlement. Danny hadn't come back. He didn't know how Danny took it. Danny hadn't come back, and he and Randy went to church where Danny couldn't go. What had thrown them together was unraveling, and Danny probably thought—

—probably thought that it was a good thing, finally, to *be* in the rider camp, among people with whom he'd been able to tell the truth. And a good thing that he and Randy and Brionne were on this side of the wall, and that the world was back in order.

He'd no doubt that Danny would keep his promise in the spring and help him and Randy get where they needed to go. But by that time there'd be a decent, god-fearing distance between them, and he'd be—

Damn lonely.

But he'd get the shop back. He'd train Randy in the trade. The neighbors couldn't tell what they'd known. They were dead. There was no one—

A jolt hit his heart.

The jail record. Court records. All of that was intact down in Tarmin. Food and leather was gone. Paper—wouldn't be unless weather got to it.

All of those records. The court clerk had been writing that night, and that record was down there, in the judge's office.

He thought he might throw up.

Everything was ruined if that record was there. He had to get there. First. Somehow. Somebody had to, that he could trust—somebody like Danny, who could find those books and just get rid of them, or if he could go *with* Danny, who'd be under pressure from everybody in the village wanting to go down there, and the Mackeys and a whole lot of other people finding *him* the obstacle to their ambitions. Those records could give them everything they wanted.

He knew they'd written him down for murder. He didn't know, on account of Randy's age and his statement, whether they'd written him down the same. But they'd locked Randy up with him. Age hadn't deterred the law from that.

And the Mackeys—if they had that to use—they'd have no scruples.

All right, he said to himself. All right. There was time. There was all winter to figure it out. He could trust Danny. He could ask Danny for help. He could hope Danny wasn't angry at him.

The whole night had assumed a chancy, awful feeling. As if—as if the veneer of recent days had started to peel away a layer at a time—and tonight the undersurface was showing through.

He didn't hear the <blood on snow> sending now. He heard a single, faraway shot, but didn't think the shot had hit anything. It felt scary out there. Real scary.

He'd rather be afraid of the dark out there than think the thoughts he was left with tonight. He all but wished the horse *would* come back, and give him some other worry tonight, and give him some excuse to go to the rider camp with something other than what he could think of to say, like—

Danny, I know I was an ass. And there's a favor I have to ask you. A really big favor.

Like—get *me* to Tarmin. And *not* the rest of the village.

He felt—a falling, then. Tasted <blood> very strongly. He twitched, maybe the remnant of the shivers—maybe just the edge of a nightmare.

After that, there was just <dark> and <running through the trees, running and running> that was somehow less terrible than that short, sharp inhalation of blood that he could still smell—he'd never known blood had a smell. But after Tarmin he had a sense for it.

After Tarmin he dreamed of that smell—and didn't want to, tonight.

Didn't want to sleep at all. Just wanted to ride that feeling, <on and on, across the snow.>

Then he *did* see <blood on snow,> and he knew what had caught him in his dreams, and what carried him along, buffeted by evergreens and blinded by falling snow.

It remembered <blood,> too. And it carried him in a long, dizzy, heart-pounding flight along the snowbound road, back the way they'd come, he was sure of it.

It had a den there, where a slide had taken trees down. It had a shelter. That was where it was going—until it faded on him, and left him wandering that wilderness and then the dark of the forge, with his eyes wide open.

A sound rasped breathily in the night beside him. Randy was snoring.

Chapter XVII

The sun did come up.

There'd been no gunfire in the Mackey house. Rick showed up for work sullen and sulking, but cowed and not saying a word—so, charitably, Carlo didn't. The water still soaked the floor, but it wasn't standing in puddles, and it went away when they stoked up the furnace and the heat got up.

There was work to do. Winter was a time for large orders from the various logging companies and a time to make odds and ends of hardware and other items the miners called for, ranging from ordinary metalwork to things that would have been better welded—*if* they'd had the means. They were the manufactory for metal and wooden barrels, mining rockers and screens, water tanks and fuel storage. They made chain and hooks. They made latches and braces, tie rods and occasional machine parts for which they had a few special tools, but not the quality that Tarmin, which had an actual machine shop, could turn out. That was *another* business lying vacant down there, among other odds and ends about which Carlo didn't want to think, this morning.

Van even showed up to do actual work instead of leaving the shop to Rick's slovenly management this morning. Van even wanted to talk, and once they got down to business, it developed they each knew things the other didn't—there were tricks Van Mackey knew that their father hadn't. He could learn from this man, Carlo thought, unlikely as it seemed, and after the storm of the night before, things were relatively peaceful. Randy had something on his mind—that meant the bellows worked with unusual steadiness while Randy stared off into space.

But Randy was no more cheerful than he was. It was a grim look. He tried to keep his own face as pleasant as possible.

He *wished* he hadn't yelled at Danny. He had to go over there.

Maybe he could go over at quitting time and see him. With Randy in tow.

Which he didn't want. He didn't want Randy to know what the score was, and if he went into the camp, there were the horses to reckon with, and the likelihood they'd spill everything on their minds not only to Danny but to all the riders.

That wouldn't do.

He could send Randy over to Danny. Randy was scattershot, but he was a lot less likely to spill truly important things.

And what in hell was he going to *say* to Danny once he had him over here?

It didn't add up to too much more than asking Danny to double-cross the people he was living with and go solo with him.

That was a secret almost impossible for a rider to keep. *Any* secret was hard for a rider to keep. Danny had proved that to him. That was the whole point of the quarrel they'd had.

He couldn't hand Danny a secret of their running off together and expect him to keep it.

Which meant he couldn't tell Danny at all. That was what it boiled down to. He just couldn't talk to Danny until much closer to time to go down there. He had to hold onto the matter, keep calm, not—

Tongs slipped. He recovered them.

"That's all right," Van Mackey said.

"All right, hell!" Rick said. "Anything he does is 'all right'!"

"Shut up," Van said.

"I had it coming," Carlo said.

"And *you* shut up!" Rick yelled. "Damn you!"

"I said shut *up!*" Van yelled, and Rick stormed toward the door. "Sleep in the barracks tonight!" Van yelled after him. "Get a taste of it!"

Rick left the door open. Without a word Randy left his work and closed it.

Randy was scared of loud arguments.

So was he. His gut had knotted up.

"Don't be too hard on him," he said to Van. It was real hard to think of something good to say about Rick, but he felt obliged to try, for peace in the household. "I want to get along with him."

Randy shot him a look.

Which he ignored.

"Huh," was all Van Mackey said. In Carlo's less than charitable estimation, Van Mackey didn't even believe it was necessary to get along with his son.

Snow had been coming down since the middle of the night, and generally, was the impression Danny had from Ridley, that circumstance would stop a hunt: but not this hunt, for one reason, because the hunters had been pent in too long and the weather promised no better tomorrow, and secondly, because it was a hunt for a horse, a species that, along with several of the largest predators, *didn't* den up except in weather much worse than this.

So they went out: and that was what they were after—he, and Ridley, and four of the most experienced hunters in Evergreen, because *something* had been active last night; at least something they couldn't quite be sure of had been prowling about near the walls of the village, probably over on the opposite side from the camp, which meant certain houses in the village could hear very well and the camp couldn't.

But whatever it had been, it had had to climb a rocky terrace to achieve that vantage, and it had spooked the horses enough that Slip just wouldn't be worked with this morning until it was clear they were going <out> and <hunting.>

<Spook-horse> and <danger> was all Danny could get out of Cloud; and Cloud wasn't quite as eager as Slip to be out in the snow <hunting Spook-horse with men with cattle-tails.> Meaning that Cloud didn't like the hunters, and imaged them in ways his rider

had to amend in a constant battle of images, but Cloud never cared for his rider's reputation, no.

Personally, Danny was resolved in his mind that they *had* to do something about the horse, and he was very glad Ridley accepted him after difficulties with <bad horse girl> that he didn't want to argue out with Cloud in hearing of the other horses and least of all with the hunters in range.

Their going out on the hunt, though, necessarily left Callie alone in camp with Jennie, a pregnant mare, and a skittish two-year-old colt, in charge of guarding the village—and it justifiably made Ridley anxious the further they went from village walls.

They were casting far afield today. It made *him* anxious. He had his complete kit with him, pack and weapons and all.

And if at any point it looked on this snowy day as if the village was in some kind of difficulty regarding that horse that might require other riders' help, then he was fully prepared to use their trek out as the launch of a run toward Mornay. He was fully prepared to go on to the shelter tonight and reach Mornay tomorrow, to bring back reinforcement for the camp.

But from all they'd seen so far there was nothing either to indicate the horse was still about, or that any other game was. They'd sent the hunters up on the heights, but with the snow-fall they hadn't seen any tracks, and he personally knew that the horse, if that was what it had been, was damned canny.

He wasn't afraid, exactly, if he had to go on to Mornay alone. His real danger and Cloud's had been when he had horseless adolescents and Brionne Goss in his company. A horse and rider alone and armed, with nobody to protect but each other—that was a whole different story, the way Spook-horse wasn't that likely to go after four middle-aged men and two armed riders—if it had turned predatory and not simply lonely.

In that matter, Cloud wasn't worried at all. Cloud was <fierce horse.> Cloud could beat Spook-horse in a fight: Cloud would say so if Danny hinted otherwise.

And for days now Cloud had been thinking of <woods and snow> and wanting <Danny riding.>

So this morning as they set out, and while he'd shoved the rider camp gate shut with Ridley serene on Slip's back, his own silly fool of a horse had been cavorting through the drifts in a circle in front of the wall, careless of the fact a drift might mask a dip or a boulder.

Cloud fortunately led a charmed existence.

"Come back here!" he recalled yelling. In front of four stolid and senior hunters, "Dammit!"

Cloud didn't care if his rider looked the fool in front of the others. Cloud didn't care if the whole village turned out to watch.

But Cloud, giving up his notion of <cattle-tails on the hunters> as they trekked farther and farther down the road, grew pleased just with moving through the snowy weather this morning.

And with the wind carrying enough snow by noon to gray the trees, they still found nothing, seeing no game and hearing none, so the hunters, for whom this was the first chance to hunt since the storm, fell to grumbling and believed the horse in question was lairing down one of the logging trails down the face of the mountain.

"A lot of territory," Ridley said to that.

Ridley had no disposition to take off into what Ridley mapped in the ambient as a maze of trails and clearings. Be patient, Ridley said. We'll find it sooner or later.

But the hunters still grumbled. And while Ridley rode to the lead, and the sun was a bright spot in the white all around them, Danny joined him and found a chance to talk in some privacy.

"Just let me go on ahead," he said. "I'll go on to Mornay. I'll be fine."

"No proof now the horse is still here."

"No proof it isn't. Just let me go from here. I'll sleep at the shelter tonight and I'll be in Mornay noon tomorrow." He had a bad feeling about the silence, little experienced as he was up here. *Because* of that lack of experience he wanted to take every available precaution, and he still felt responsible. He trusted the map they'd given him as simple and direct as such a telling could be, and, always depending on the weather, believed he could be relatively sure of a fast trip. "I'll come back the same day. I'll bring a senior rider back and two of us will be safe on the road no matter what. Tomorrow night back in the shelter and we'll be here to help you noon after tomorrow."

Ridley shook his head. "No. No taking one of them out of their winter plans if we're not finding anything. Winter has yet to set in hard and fast, but it'll get bitter cold when it does. It has to get down the mountain to survive. It may have begun to think in that direction."

"Nothing says to me it's gone. And what are the hunters going to do?"

"See if we can bag something," Ridley said. There hadn't been a sign of game, not a track above the size of a flitter. "That's what would make these men feel better. Circle out ahead. See if that young horse of yours can scare something up."

"I'll try." Cloud had caught the notion of <them going ahead> and there was no holding him once he understood they were <going alone> for a space, however so small. Cloud gave a whip of his tail and broke into a jog to get good distance between them and the rest.

It wasn't long before Cloud, canny wretch, had scared up a wooly-spook, inoffensive creature, but fat, and worth a bit for hides. It ambled out, helpless, and Danny half wanted to tell it run, get away, escape.

The hunters shot it. They were happy. The less affluent of the village had meat and the hunters had a hide that would make a couple of good winter coats, not a bit of it idle luxury.

They took a while to skin and dress it. The blood drew vermin, several, two of which they bagged.

Bushdevil. He felt a lot better about that. Argumentative, chew your arm off, no saving graces.

They packed up, then.

He asked Ridley if he should come back or go on, and Ridley said to come back to Evergreen. That there was no evidence of anything but bad weather. Nothing of the horse they feared was out there.

Open air camp. Wasn't too bad. They'd gotten their deep cold last night, which had frozen beyond the chance of a melt turning the rocks slick or a fog soaking their blankets, and, Guil thought, he'd just rather move on, now that the weather had settled. Tara agreed. So they'd moved not toward a camp Tara wasn't sure of finding, but straight on toward Evergreen, as Tara had it set in her direction-sense. At least there were shelters around the town that they could reach tonight.

Tonight, in the bitter cold Tara had cut evergreen boughs for the horses and for themselves, and the horses were bedded down, and they were, on Flicker's side. Even amorous horses weren't going to stir in this cold, with the snow coming down as it was. There were limits to any reasonable desire to expose warm spots to the cold, and Guil was quite glad, with the considerable generation of heat the mare provided, just to be warm tonight.

They had rifles by them, sidearms, food and all in their nest in the snowstorm, and if anything came up on them they'd blow it to hell.

"Quiet out there tonight, too," Tara said. "I wish that meant anything."

"Yeah," he said. "Listening for what's not is pretty tricky."

"If it's a horse it's the damn spookiest one I ever met."

"Yeah," Guil said.

"Once in a great while in these woods," Tara said, "you get something really strange, being on the edge of the deep Wild. Have you ever been out there?"

She meant into the territory where settlements weren't. Where human settlements *were* was a pretty tiny patch, whether you reckoned it locally or against the world as wide as he'd seen from the high mountains.

"Been into it," he said, and painted her a <view from the side of MacFarlane Height, mountains as far as the eye could see.> He painted her <deep woods.> He painted her <far plains, rolling grass.>

She came back with <view from the high turns, mountains forever> and from somewhere he'd never been <deep forest.> He guessed it was on <Darwin.>

"Yeah," she said, warm against his side, drinking in all the things he thought were prettiest.

He'd never met a woman but his mother and Aby who'd been able to show him the vast deeper Wild in their minds. He'd never met any woman but them who wanted those sights, wanted to hold them steady, like holding something up to the sun to see it plain.

Border woman. He'd found her as a villager. But he knew now what she was—like himself, one who rode the edges of the world. Who was, except the question of those kids, as intrigued by the oddness out there as he was. It was something neither of them had seen. And they weren't spooked, either of them: neither were their horses, who had seen oddness in other places across the wide edge.

Respectful, oh, yes. But Burn wanted a closer look at it. If they were on a convoy job, he'd have said, No, fool. And this was almost that case: but the kids they were trying to match courses with and *this* thing were in the same direction.

So was Evergreen village.

Real, real quiet out there. No game. Nothing with any sense about it that wasn't also, like the other dedicated predators, lying very still tonight and measuring the threat against the threat they posed.

Exactly what they were doing.

Carlo was very glad when quitting time came, and gladder still that Van went off to wash up and didn't invite him to a beer in the house or in the tavern.

He wasn't glad at the prospect of Rick Mackey being in the tavern. But that was where they had to eat.

"You stick close to me," he said to Randy, and put a length of iron chain into his coat pocket.

"You going to fight him?" Randy asked hopefully, and he restrained himself from shaking the kid till his teeth rattled.

"No," he said quietly, and shepherded the kid out the door, down the street, up the steps and into The Evergreen.

"Hey, Carlo!" came the voice he didn't want to hear. "Come sit over here! Tell us about your sister!"

"That's Rick!" Randy said, with the disposition to go that direction; Carlo in a sudden panic grabbed Randy by the arm and went instead to the bar, where the bartender was maintaining a watch on the outburst. "Need a beer, a tea, and two suppers. Usual tab."

"I'll shut him up," the bartender said. "I don't recommend you go over there."

"No such intention."

"Beer and tea," the bartender said, and drew one off tap and poured the other from the pot. "If you beat hell out of him, do it in the street."

"See?" Randy said. "He thinks you should."

"I'll talk with you about it," Carlo said, picked a table far from Rick Mackey and set the beer and the tea down. "If you'll listen. I'm telling you—"

"I know what you'll say. Get along with everybody. He's going to do something."

"Fine. He'll be sorry if he does. Just you stay out of his way. All right?"

They went and picked up a good-smelling stew, and sat down.

He truly hoped for Danny to show up. He'd feel better if he could just talk with him, not on business, not about secrets, just to know that he could still count on him.

The noise in the other end of the room subsided. He guessed the bartender had made the point about starting fights. He thought he should be particularly careful going home tonight. He debated about another beer, and had it anyway, since the only trouble in his world was having another, and another.

Three was his limit, and he stuck to it, and shared a sip now and again with his brother. The bar didn't allow gambling in the establishment, but they provided cards for people who wanted to play for drink chips or toothpicks or whatever.

He sent Randy after cards and since Rick was the guy he was wanting to keep an eye on, he sipped beer and he and Randy played for toothpicks. The place grew empty of families.

Rick, also on the Mackey's tab, was still in the tavern when he and Randy left for the evening. Rick, having started earlier, was alone, passed out at the table, harmless or close to it, and as they went out onto the street, the snow was coming down thick and fast beyond the edge of the porch.

"Wait till *he* comes out," Randy suggested. "And bash him."

"Fair," he said. "You ever hear the word?"

"Fair, with *him?* He doesn't fight fair. Why should we?"

"Little brother, you want snow down your pants?"

"You wouldn't dare!" Randy swept a handful off the porch rail and started a snowball.

Carlo dived off the porch and ducked. And scooped up snow and had a big one ready when Randy threw at him.

Randy ran, stopped, and flung one that caught Carlo. His caught Randy. They stopped all strategy in the matter, stood and made snowballs and pelted each other until they were both powdered from head to foot and out of breath from laughing and swearing.

"I've got a handful of snow," Carlo said, and Randy, knowing its potential destination, ran for the forge, past the evergreen.

Carlo stalked him.

"No fair, no fair," Randy said, at bay beside the doors. "I haven't got the key."

"Oh, *now* fair counts!" Carlo bent, made a good snowball and stood up.

Randy's caught him fair in the face. His caught Randy on the side of the head.

Then they'd run out of snowballs and breath, and he gained sense enough to realize how late it was. The village was quiet. It was a deserted, lightless street, no light from the Mackeys' house, either.

"Everybody's gone to bed," he said. "Way late."

"Spooky," Randy said, and waited, bouncing a little with anxiety as Carlo opened the door with the key.

Randy went across the darkened forge and threw a log on the banked fire, huddled down by it and started brushing snow off as he undid his coat.

Carlo had a last bit from his pocket. And delivered it to the back of Randy's neck.

Squeal of indignation.

"No *fair!*"

"That's twice you've called fair. You give?"

"Bully," Randy said.

"Yeah." He figured the kid would learn a little finesse. At least in snow fights. "But that's enough. If we wake the Mackeys up, we'll be in the street. No kidding."

"Yeah, just you wait," Randy said.

He gave Randy a hug. With no snow involved. They hauled the cots they used out of the storage area.

He could hardly last long enough to hit the mattress.

Tired, tonight, real tired. His mind was quiet, finally. He thought he could sleep, now, and felt it coming on thicker by the minute.

Something had made a sound. Darcy levered herself out of bed, thinking she'd might have heard Brionne call out. She searched for her slippers and her robe without clearly thinking, in her concern for Brionne and those stairs.

"Are you all right?" she called out. "Honey, are you all right?"

"Mama?" the thin voice came to her, likewise alarmed.

Something crashed at the front door. Someone yelled.

Someone was trying to break in, rattling the door handle—she could hear it. She *knew* as if she could see it.

She ran to Faye's room, and the child was out of bed, on her way downstairs, crying out something, she couldn't tell what.

"Stay here!" Darcy cried. "Stay *here!*"

She ran to the stairs and took them clinging to the bannister, put out her hands in the dark and felt her way along the wall to Mark's office door—walked blind then to his desk, pulled open the topmost drawer and took out the gun—the gun that she never touched, never wanted to touch again; but it comforted her hands right now.

She listened. But the rattling and banging had stopped. She sat and listened in that stillness. The dark seemed alive it was so heavy and so dreadful.

The commotion had been on the public entrance porch. If it was drunken miners, the disturbance wouldn't necessarily cut her off from the passages—she could take Faye, she could go that way, and reach the marshal, or a neighbor—but it was too risky. It was quiet out there, maybe because they'd given up, maybe because the intruders were thinking of trying another way in. But she had strong doors, and if a whole crowd of miners had gotten to warring with the loggers or some such foolery, there might be riot in the passageway as well. There was a passageway entry off the street, not far from her door—as well as the direct access by the kitchen door. She was scared to try to go for help, and hoped that Constance and Emil, next door, might have heard. Emil was a big man. If Emil flung open the shutters and shouted in his deep voice to get the hell away—if there was anybody conniving in the shadows out there, they'd move.

"Mama?"

Faye was on the stairs, coming down in the dark.

Not knowing her way. Giving out a high, female voice that might only incite drunken fools. She kept her finger off the trigger for fear of tripping in the dark, and recrossed the cold floor to the office doorway.

"Here I am," she said in a calm, easy voice. "It's all right, honey. I'm right down a short hall. Just some drunks. Put your hand on the wall and just walk along it. I'm right here."

"I know." It was a quavery, scared voice. But closer. In the dark she could see the pallor of the nightgown as the girl inched her way toward her. She knew when the girl reached her, and reached out her hand and found chill fingers.

"Somebody wants in," Brionne said. "He wants in because *I'm* here. Do you hear it? It's scary."

"They're not going to get in," Darcy said firmly. "I have a gun, sweet. Don't grab it. Just stay close by me. If anybody breaks in, they'll be sorry."

Desperate hands clutched her. A frightened, shivering body pressed against her.

Silence followed. Then a dreadful sound above them, a sliding and scrabbling as if something had gone along the roof. The girl cried out, and Darcy's heart jumped.

Then she laughed. "It's snow, honey. It's just snow sliding off the roof. It's all right. Sometimes it does that, around the stove-pipe."

The girl wasn't so sure. But Darcy put an arm around her for reassurance.

"Tell you what. Let's go to the kitchen where it's warm. I'll make some tea and we'll have some of that cake. How's that?"

The girl didn't say anything, but she let herself be drawn along at Darcy's left side.

They reached the kitchen and Darcy carefully laid the gun down on the counter while she lit the oil lamp and got out the tea canister. The house stayed quiet. The child pulling back a chair at the kitchen table made a loud screech on the boards, and she stopped and looked apprehensively at the roof.

"I heard something," she said.

"I think you're imagining, honey. Go ahead. Sit down. I'll put on tea. Do you want a big piece or a little piece?"

"Either's fine." The girl's eyes were still toward the ceiling. "I hear it, don't you?"

"No, honey. I don't."

"It wanted in."

"Don't think about it." She dipped up water from the kitchen barrel and set the kettle on.

There was no more snow sliding. The house stayed quiet. The wind blew, and snow would be coming down. It was the buildup on the steep roof that had slid.

She was worried about the kitchen door, the one that led to the passages. She listened for footsteps out there, but everything was quiet. She thought still about going after the marshal and taking Faye with her.

Brionne—with her.

But they were all right here. It was quiet.

And there were five rounds in the gun. She knew. Mark had only needed one.

Chapter XVIII

There'd been something wrong in the night—they'd waked, at least Danny and Ridley had, armed and gone half-dressed out to the den, but they'd found nothing amiss. Ridley said he wasn't entirely sure it was Spook bothering them: small alarms during the winter weren't uncommon, and they'd taken their frozen selves back to the barracks and headed back to their beds.

The horses were still jumpy this morning, arguing that something had bothered them in a way that had put them in a lasting mood. Slip kicked at Rain, and Shimmer snapped. Danny took Cloud out into the yard to curry and comb him—and file a chipped center-hoof that Cloud had gotten from somewhere about the yard, possibly last night.

There were abundant horse-tracks in the snow of the yard, the overlain traces of the horses' paths to the walls and back, to the den and to the porch of the house last night, and a lot going back and forth over the passageways that made the only hill of vantage in the camp, a ridge in the snow, not much projecting above the ground, but a hump that made a nighthorse feel he'd reached high ground, silly creature.

And now he was combing manes and tails, and Callie, with a hammer and chisel, was doing some carpentry involving the den-side passageway door, which was new wood, and which had stuck last night when they'd been investigating the trouble.

Remarkable system, those passages. Ridley said when they built the village they'd blasted down a lot of gravel and rubble, and the builders had dug in with timber shelters buried in gravel where the wildlife couldn't get at them, and *that* was the start of the passages at this and other villages, except one that was totally passageways and no houses at all.

A lot of effort, Danny thought. They'd laid in dirt atop the rubble, probably hauled up from the lower slopes, and compost of evergreen needles, just anything the village could put down for the brief growing season, so he heard from Ridley, for gardens—for the greens and vegetables they couldn't afford trucked up. In summer, so Ridley said, all of Evergreen broke out in vegetable gardens and flowers.

No gardens on this side of the wall, however, where there were hungry horses to raid the plots.

Above this place on the mountain, with one exception around Mornay, was snow. Above here was uncompromising rock. It took a lot of effort just for humans to survive on what little soil clung here, and when a lad from the bustling crowds of Shamesey thought about it he marveled that humans not only survived, they built fairly fancy houses, and churches, and such, on the hard rock and thin soil of a mountain.

Pretty damn stubborn people, he said to himself, and took up a length of Cloud's tail to get a knot out.

Cloud of course switched the tail, being ticklish.

"Cut it out!"

A lot better if he could take Cloud outside the walls regularly and at whim. Village camp walls weren't as wide as Shamesey town's, and playing chase around a small yard just wasn't enough for Cloud. Ridley said they could go hunting whenever they liked, and often, once they could get the horse business settled—

But that wasn't amusement. And it wasn't settled. His personal guess that it wouldn't leave despite the turn in the weather seemed to have been right, and neither he nor Ridley was looking forward to that matter. He ought, he thought sometimes, to have gone on to Mornay—but what could he have told them? The suspicion of a suspicion of a horse no one could deal with? That two riders who ought to have been able to call it in had failed and now they were down to spooked hunters and short supply of game with a situation down the slope at Tarmin he didn't think maybe anybody had managed to tell Mornay or any other village up here.

Worrisome thought: maybe there were reasons Ridley didn't want Mornay involved, or people talking to Ridley didn't want Mornay involved. Certainly Ridley had been talking to the marshal from time to time, and they still had the horse on their hands, which, no matter the reasons that they weren't talking to the other village, he had some chance of dealing with. He could have dealt with it without harming it if it weren't for the Goss kids; and now he had Brionne Goss on his mind more often than he liked to have *any* thought of her near the surface.

He *wished* he'd been able to get his hands on the horse. That would be the best thing. But he wasn't sure it was possible—especially with the distraction and attraction the village posed; and with the Rain and Jennie business. Everything in the world had conspired to keep that horse a problem to them; and dammit, it wasn't fair, shooting at it.

But, mope about it as he would, he'd made *his* best and probably only good try at catching it that night he'd gone out on foot—and scared hell out of Cloud, who thought <cattle> about it at the moment and swatted him with the tail, which still had one good ice-lump in it.

"Cut it out! Dammit!"

Cloud backed into him. There was <bad horse> in Cloud's mind. There was—

<Ridley coming through the gate, on the surface route.>

Danny looked up. He hadn't seen Ridley when he'd come out to see to Cloud. He hadn't known Ridley had gone to the village, but it was a good guess in a small camp when he'd not immediately seen him at the horse den. He supposed that Ridley had gone over to confer with the hunters.

<Worry> hit the ambient. Callie left her door-adjusting and he followed Callie out into the yard.

"Is Jennie in the yard?" was Ridley's first question.

"Was," Callie said. Jennie had been out currying Rain till the horses got snappish. He'd mentioned it to Callie and Callie had sent young Jennie inside to play. "Horses are nervous this morning. Thought she'd be better off inside."

Ridley let go a breath. "Never had horse trouble before," Ridley said. "I've heard—it sets off people who aren't riders. And something happened last night. A miner's hanging around the doctor's place. Or he was."

<Brionne,> was Danny's first, leaden thought and it sailed through and around the ambient.

"Some disturbance there last night," Ridley said. "Somebody tried to open Darcy Schaffer's front door. And this morning when the doctor opened her door—there's blood all over it."

"God," Callie said.

"Knifing's what they think. Wasn't any sound of a gunshot. But the way the snow was falling—guess maybe there was a reason besides the stray that the horses were acting up. Maybe it wasn't even here last night."

He caught the scene from Ridley's mind, hazily, because Cloud didn't know buildings real well. But there was <blood around and on a door as if someone had flung it from a cup. Snow on the porch, like on the yard, covering yesterday's tracks.>

"Not impossible somebody was trying to get to the doctor to treat a stab wound, trying to get away from the guy who attacked him. And got hit again on the porch. They've been poking in all the snow drifts thinking somebody could have fallen there, but there's nothing. If we can get the gates open, I'm going to bring Slip around—"

"Into the village?" He'd never heard of such a thing.

"To see if he can find whoever it was."

It made good sense. But it wasn't something you'd ever do in Shamesey streets—bring a horse past the barriers, let alone into a murder scene. "You want some help?"

"No need of it. What there is to find, Slip will find. And they know Slip over there."

"Sure," he said. "Want some help to clear the gate?"

"That," Ridley agreed, "would be a good thing."

* * *

Earnest Riggs *wasn't* to be found. So the marshal said, holding the hat with the bushdevil tail in his hand—a hat Earnest Riggs had kept with great care, and now—now it, like everything about the porch, was spattered with blood; not that that appalled a doctor, but the memory of last night did. Darcy stood outside shivering in a light coat, while the marshal and his deputy stood officially at her front doorway and a snow-veiled crowd of neighbors, on whom the snow was gathering thicker by the moment, were standing and gaping and gossiping below her blood-spattered porch.

They were bringing one of the riders over—and the horse—to find the missing, or track the guilty, as the marshal or the judge sometimes requested. They'd shoveled the outer gates clear so the horse could get from the rider camp to the street—and she could see that distant figure coming through.

The crowd gave back in a hurry as the rider came at a brisk pace up the street. She wouldn't budge from the porch. It was her house, her office, her daughter upstairs in her bedroom. She'd spent a bad and a sleepless night, sitting up with the gun she passionately hated, and she wasn't giving ground to any threat—least of all one of their own riders, doing his distasteful job this time involving her porch, *her* property, which had seen all too much of notoriety in the last two years—the other two incidents with the law had had the sanctity at least of tragedy. This—this was an embarrassment in front of the neighbors.

Ridley Vincint was the rider's name, and the horse, by that fact, would be Slip. That was all she knew about riders—except that this man had been the escort supposedly watching over Faye, and she considered him directly to blame, and she *didn't* forgive him for that, or for speaking harshly to Faye, as others reported, on that day. She tried not to think about that as he rode close enough to let the horse sniff the air and sniff the blood around the porch rail. She watched it, thinking doggedly of *snow,* which was what she'd always been taught to do if she was around a horse or any creature of the world, just think of snow and it wouldn't be interested in her, and it wouldn't—horrible thought—spread her private thoughts and her private fears to the neighbors.

The door behind her opened. She knew who it was without turning around, but turn she did as, in her nightgown, Brionne came out, with a thunderously unhappy look. The child hadn't even shoes on her feet, for God's sake.

And suddenly the horse gave a snort and reared up, so the rider had to fight to stay on.

"Get the kid inside!" Ridley said harshly.

"Stop it!" Brionne cried. "I *won't*! You can't tell me what to do!"

The horse backed away, shaking its head, having just smelled something, evidently, about the porch. The crowd scattered from it in panic.

All but the marshal and Jeff Burani, who stood their ground, Jeff with his hand on his gun.

"It's *her*," Ridley said. "He doesn't like the girl. Get her out of here. Get her back inside!"

"Honey," Darcy said, in the grip of so much craziness she didn't know whether to protest or do what the rider said. The bare feet decided the matter. She flung an arm around Brionne to restrain her and had to hold tight to prevent her going to the rail.

"It's just like Tarmin!" Brionne cried. "You're just like the riders there! Go away! I hate you! I hate you *and* your horse! Get *away* from me!"

Darcy pulled her away and argued her back through the blood-spattered door into the house. For a moment—for a moment she thought she was having an asthmatic seizure or a heart attack. There was a tightness in her chest, and Brionne broke away from her toward the interior of the house, crying that she was going to get dressed and go back out there and talk to the rider if she wanted to, that she was embarrassed in front of the whole village.

"They're awful!" Brionne was crying. "I hate them! I hate them!"

Darcy didn't know what to do. She went back outside, trying to recover her breath and her wits in the cold air. Ridley and his horse were still there, in a large circle of spectators, a very large vacant circle, that had formed again near her porch.

"I can't get anything," Ridley was saying. "It's just dark. My horse is starting to get upset. The girl remembers Tarmin too clearly. I'll have to take him back to some distance. I'll see if I can pick up any trail on the perimeter."

"This is the craziest damn thing," marshal Peterson said; and about that time John Quarles arrived, and came up on the porch, blessing the place with holy water, a process Darcy would have skipped on most days, but right now it was her house that had been defiled, her doorway where yet one more life had ended, and holy water and John's willingness to face the devil both came welcome, with Ridley on his horse still in her sight, and Brionne inside swearing she was going to come out again, to what earthly good in this horrific business she had no idea.

But after riding all the way around the house, with much of the crowd both drifting after him and rapidly reforming their apprehensive circle when he came back, Ridley showed up again at the porch to talk to the marshal.

"I don't get any scent of anybody with blood about them. Just here on the porch. And I've got to get my horse out of here. This isn't good. I'd suggest you give the girl something to quiet her down. She's loud in the ambient. Dangerously loud. I can't hear anything."

"Meaning you can't *find* anything," Darcy said. "Don't tell me the problem's with the *girl,* Mr. Vincint, damn it, I won't hear it!"

It was certainly the closest she'd ever stood to a horse, and she was afraid—terribly afraid, all of a sudden. She didn't know whether it was a sending or what, but Ridley Vincint made his horse turn or it turned, or something pushed it back. It looked—if an animal could have such a look—crazed; and snapped at her, not to strike, because she was out of range, but to make clear its hostility.

"I'm going back to the camp," Ridley Vincint said, and the horse gave a furious whip of its tail and headed back down the street toward the outer gates, quickly graying out into the snowy distance of the street.

In the same moment the Goss boys were coming up the street ahead of a flood of miners and loggers from down by the barracks, and they passed each other, Ridley and the horse fading out, the newcomers growing brighter and more solid in the haze, until the Goss boys, arriving out of breath, forced their way through what by now looked like the whole village gathering to know what had happened.

God, she hated scenes. She'd had her fill, in Faye's death, and after that in Mark's. She hated to be the object of gossip, and she knew now she was the winter's topic for good and all, and maybe worse than that. She could only think in one term now—how it affected everything she hoped for, all she intended: her respectability to parent a daughter.

And the respectability of her dealings with Earnest Riggs.

The Goss brothers reached her porch and climbed the steps and that, too, was a scene bound to stick in neighbors' minds. The *Mackeys* were coming, too, with hateful Mary Hardesty marching in the lead, and there was no way to go inside and let them and the marshal talk out here in front of the whole village without her knowing what they were saying. She found herself trembling, fearing that the boys were intending publicly to fault her care of Brionne, fearing that someone, somehow, in investigating what might have become of Earnest Riggs, might uncover the financial dealings she'd had with him—God knew who he'd have talked to.

Someone had gotten wind of money—she was sure of the motive and daren't say anything to the marshal about it. If it got about that she was involved—

She didn't know what to say.

"What's happened?" the oldest boy wanted to know. "What's going on here?"

"Drunken fools," she said, that being the position she decided to take—total ignorance. But the marshal gave the long account.

"Earnest Riggs," Eli Peterson said. "The rider didn't find any trace of him. His bunk wasn't slept in. Found only his hat, lying sheltered on the porch."

"He was at the tavern last night," somebody yelled from the crowd below the porch.

"Ernie was *always* at the tavern," another voice yelled. "He's probably got in a fight and he's sleepin' one off!"

"Not with this," Peterson said. He scratched his chin and looked back at the snowy street. "I'm not finding him, the rider didn't find him. And there's a hell of a lot of blood. I'm taking a survey of everybody, searching all the sheds and such."

"Ask Carlo Goss!" somebody yelled. "He picked a fight with him yesterday. He threatened Riggs. Threatened to kill him! And he was up and about way late—I saw him!"

"That's a lie," the younger boy yelled back. "That's a *lie,* Rick Pig! He wasn't anywhere last night but with me. And you were passed out drunk!"

"Goss *said* he'd kill him!" That was assuredly Rick Mackey from near the fringes. "Riggs was talking loose about his sister and he said he'd kill Riggs. Now he's done it. *Naturally* his brother'd give him an alibi."

"Carlo Goss?" Peterson said, and all of a sudden the Goss boy just jumped off the porch and broke his way through the crowd and ran.

"Carlo!" the younger boy yelled after him.

But Carlo Goss was running breakneck down the street, disappearing into the snowfall.

"Get him!" Peterson yelled. "Bring him back here!" And *that* was a mistake. A number of miners took out running, chasing the boy, shouting encouragement to each other.

Then the younger brother ducked past people trying to stop him and ran after all of them, in the same moment Brionne, this time shod, came out onto the porch. Darcy put an arm around her as, in the distance, Carlo Goss failed her expectation he would go to the rider camp.

No, the boy was going farther than that, as she could see from her elevated vantage. The miners hadn't overtaken him. *Randy* Goss had taken that side street and gone off toward the rider camp. But Carlo, almost faded out in the snow, came to the village gates, and as she strained to see clearly what was going on, or whether Serge, who kept the gate, would catch him—he vanished altogether.

He'd opened the lesser gate and gone outside the walls—maybe to reach the rider camp across to *their* outside gate. Maybe he'd hoped to draw the miners away from his brother, and then go where they wouldn't—because from what she could see, nobody else passed that gate.

Gunfire echoed back. Someone had gotten up the steps and shot.

"Stop that," Peterson said to his deputy, and Burani walked down off the porch, went out into the street and fired his pistol into the air, at which Darcy's nerves jumped, and Brionne jumped, and the crowd got quiet.

Did they shoot him? she was wondering. Maybe it was suicide. Maybe Carlo Goss *had* had words with Riggs. Maybe Riggs had come to him trying to solicit more money, and the boy had gotten mad and killed him.

The marshal was shouting to Jeff Burani to go to the riders and get them to go out after the elder boy, and Burani lit out running on the course Randy Goss had taken.

Maybe Carlo *had* gone toward the rider camp's outside gate and some overzealous miner had shot him from the wall. Riders wouldn't necessarily turn him in—not until the marshal had made a case that it was village business and none of theirs.

She hugged Brionne against her side, in the blood-spattered venue of her porch, in the wreckage of the winter's peace. Brionne was what she kept. Brionne was hers.

"Sorry the girl had to see this," marshal Peterson said. "Honey, if your brother didn't do this, we'll find out. I just want to ask him some questions."

"He could do it," Brionne said bitterly. "He shot our father. He shot papa, Mama died. He was in *jail* down there. He deserved to be."

"Honey," Darcy began, hoping to stem the bitter flood, but Brionne wasn't finished.

"I was scared of him," Brionne cried. "He was hateful. He was always hateful. He never wanted me to have anything. And he shot papa, I know he did!"

The whole snow-blinded sky was screaming, a condition against which the gunshots were faint noise, and it didn't stop. Ridley couldn't get his bearings except by sight, and that was diminished to an insignificant sense in the noise and the fright that raged in Slip, in Shimmer and Rain and Cloud—Jennie was terrified and trying to protect Rain, and in the stubbornness and the skip-to-any-belief character of a youngster, might be the strongest of them. Jennie didn't equivocate—*Jennie* didn't care about anything but what Jennie wanted, and that was <them,> including all the horses.

But her father knew she was no match for that *thing* in the village, not in age, not in angry tenacity. Ridley kept by Slip's side, trying to keep *him* calm, and tried to be the stable center of their camp—but he'd compromised himself. He'd persisted against better sense, he'd tried with all he had in him to do the job his village asked him, even with that darting, unhealthy <presence> there, and he knew he hadn't made sense to the marshal or to the doctor when he'd suddenly known he couldn't make headway either against the search or the girl who so doggedly possessed that place. He'd had to get Slip and himself away from there.

There was <death> in that place, there was <blood> and <going

apart> and <wanting Slip, wanting *so much and so hard*> that Slip imaged it as <hunger and fangs and claws, here, there, here and apart> so quickly you couldn't track it, <goblin-cat in a darkness too deep to see, hungry and lonely and threatened and threatening.>

The rider camp gate had opened for them and now it was shut—Jennie and Callie and Dan had opened it for him, the horses all bunched and sending <us and ours> and <wanting him and Slip> so strongly that presence enfolded him, snatched him into harmony with one breath, one thought, <safe in herd> and <fighting outsiders.>

Now, slowly, they became <quiet falling snow> and <safe in den.>

But something <else> had come into reach, and it was <human> and <boy in snowstorm> first and foremost.

"Randy Goss," Dan Fisher/Cloud identified that presence, and they weren't afraid of it, skittish and angry mess that they all were. Dan was steady and Ridley held fast as Dan wanted <going to Randy in the yard.>

Ridley didn't want anything to do with the intruders in his village. He wanted <Callie and Jennie safe in den.> But he was sane, now, and he had a partner and a daughter with him that he wasn't going to let down. He separated Dan out of <us> and let him go, even while he walked to the door of the den and Slip and the rest of <his own> trailed him.

He wanted no part of the boy who came toward them—the girl's brother, it was. The young one. Who blurted out, spilling images right and left,

<"Carlo's run. Miners chasing him.> You got to help him!"

Dan didn't stop to question further. He wanted <Randy standing still with Ridley and Callie> and he ran alone for the gate, and into the village.

Ridley didn't know what they were supposed to do with a village boy. The boy was crying and trying not to show it. And Jennie was upset, and wanting <Rain> near her, where her hands could feel him.

Shimmer was <pregnant mare> and hanging back behind the others, both more and less afraid. Shimmer would kill if the kid made the wrong move, and on the instant of the realization how fragile Shimmer's truce with the situation was, Ridley moved, and

Callie moved, him to take the boy under his protection and Callie to hold Shimmer's temper under her calming hands.

"It's crazy," the boy gasped. "It's *crazy* out there. They want to kill him, and he didn't do it!"

"We'll prove it, then," Ridley said: the village called on them and the horses to untangle conflicting testimonies, sometimes outright scaring the guilty into confession—but they weren't usually as clear to the mind as this boy's impressions came, <Carlo and Randy in the tavern, Rick Mackey slumped at the table, blood on the porch, and the girl—the girl that Slip hated—>

<Jennie and Rain> came very loud just then. <Jennie and Rain> couldn't be still against the challenge that was pouring around them, and the boy just stared toward the rider-gate until Dan came running back, out of breath, with—

"He's gone *outside!*"

"You've got to go after him!" the boy cried. "Danny, you got to find him—he didn't *do* it! I was with him! They're lying!"

"You," Dan said, already running for the barracks, "stay in the camp."

Dan intended to go find the kid. Ridley had no doubt of that—at the same time that another certainty was running over his nerves, and <blood on snow> shivered through the ambient.

"That damn horse!" Callie cried.

Dan Fisher was headed to get his gun and his gear. It didn't take him long to run back again. Fisher was going after the horse and the boy—and he, dammit, had a camp and a village in his charge with a real problem outside his walls and a worse one in the middle of the village. He was staying behind, he had no question of it, same as if a chain bound him here.

While the ambient rang with loneliness and terror.

"Get the Goss kid on to Mornay if you reach halfway," he told Fisher, as Fisher swung up on Cloud's back, and the rest of them headed around end of the den to help open the gate. "In Mornay he's out of reach and out of trouble. Sort it out in the spring." They reached the gate and he flung the bar up. Callie and Randy and Jennie pushed it wide. "There's one shelter on your way—he'll surely know it, if he gets there! Hope to hell he doesn't go on the logging trails!"

"Yes, sir," Fisher said.

"Go fast! If you catch him before halfway come back and we'll organize a trek over. If it's a long run—good luck to you! Come back when you see a chance and bring us word how you are!" He gave a slap to Cloud's rump and Fisher was off.

That left him with one rider fewer. And one scared kid more.

Breath wouldn't come any longer. Legs wouldn't run anymore. Carlo sprawled downslope, plunged through snow and into snow until the mountainside finally gave him up again, just casually tumbled him out of a snowy embrace and into the snow-drifting air.

He lay on his back, facing the light—a light coming through the branches of evergreens, out in the deep woods, alone, with the snow coming down on his eyes, and himself with no inclination even to blink. He'd been lucky so far. Luck wouldn't last. Wild things didn't go on the move much while the snow was coming down. That was why he'd lived this long. He thought he was afraid. He was too numb, now, to know what he thought.

He couldn't let the accusations go the way they had the last time, with Randy swept up and jailed with him. Couldn't go to the rider camp gate. The mob would have piled up there and trapped Randy—God hope that he'd run there. He'd led them off from that, and then he'd seen the outside gate, and meant to go to the camp from the outside, and get Danny to help him.

But he'd forgotten that when he got there. With all the woods in front of him, he'd just run and run and run, free of all of them, drunk on it, not using his brain—

He wasn't hurt. He wasn't being chased anymore. He was back in the snow, in the woods out of which he'd come to Evergreen village, as if it closed a circle, somehow, and set things back at the point of change.

Foolish thought. Delirious thought. He was in dreadful danger, having run out here unarmed and alone—he'd done something self-destructive and stupid, and he didn't understand himself.

Except he was back on the road. When the day of the climb up here, despite the pain, proved the best day he'd lived, what could he say about himself? He knew the rest of the life ahead of him, shut in the forge, working with and for the Mackeys, wasn't alluring. The only time he'd ever felt free and doing something for himself was the association he'd had with Danny.

Now his future didn't even look to be going back to Tarmin, to live his life down there. It looked to be jail. Again. Locked up. With Rick Mackey to lie and swear he was guilty. Give Rick credit for brains. Not much. But enough to get everything he wanted.

Maybe that was why he'd gone crazy for a moment—until he went off a cliff. The fall and the landing was a sobering thing, that could persuade him he ought to go back and face the charges and try to prove he was innocent.

If he lived to get there. If—God—if Randy hadn't followed him.

If Randy had followed instructions for once in his life and gone to Danny—Danny would come after him. Danny was probably already out the rider-gate and looking for him, if he just made a little noise—in all this quiet.

Then something made a sound. A horse sound.

And his world—expanded.

<Cloud,> he thought with relief, and had that sense of *where* that told him <horse was behind him> as a sound came to him, of something moving. He lay still, asking himself wildly how he was going to explain things to Danny, how he was going to ask Danny to go with him, prematurely, in the winter, down to Tarmin, to get at those damned records—because he had a chance again.

<Horse-presence> came treading softly up to him, and it appeared to him incongruously upside down as he lay on his back. It—he—lowered its head and blew warm horse breath over his face—spooked up when he moved and turned and scrambled backward on his hands and knees.

<Blood-on-snow> was its name.

He saw <Carlo looking up at <horse looking down.>> It was inside out—or outside in.

<Blood-on-snow and Carlo.>

And if Danny was right it was a killer. Or could become so—on any provocation.

He got up very slowly, trying not to startle it. Danny had said, never startle Cloud, and he thought—maybe—if he just backed away very, very carefully and got to a tree—

The horse edged forward, leaned to smell over his gloved hands, got through his guard to smell his face, his snow-caked coat and trousers, his coat again and his face. The ambient was *there.* Spook-horse was <wary, excited.> Its friendliness could change in the instant it realized it wasn't his rider.

"Stupid horse," he said, trying to back away, knowing his thoughts were in themselves betraying him. He looked for a tree whose branches he could reach. And didn't see one. "Stupid horse." It was nuzzling his hands again, forcing its way closer. "What do you want?"

Then it dawned on him.

The horse following them up the mountain in the winter season. The horse persisting in harassing the village, even at risk of being shot. The horse—<wanting> and <searching> to the village walls at night—

It wanted its rider. It wanted *a* rider. *That* was what it wanted.

"Stupid horse." He kept backing, losing ground, cast a look back to make sure there wasn't another cliff, and it got its nose past his hands to blow breath in his ear. Which brought his head around and his chin into collision with its spooked head-toss as it backed off. He saw stars for a second, and found it coming forward again, pushing at his hands.

"Stupid horse, you've got the wrong one of us. It's my brother that wants you. Not me. I'm a blacksmith. I'm not a rider. Go away! Leave me alone!"

The black nose got past his protective hands, and nudged him full in the face, desperate for something, but Danny had told him the truth—he didn't hear everything in a horse's sending; and he didn't know what it was thinking—or expect it when of a sudden the damn horse licked him on the face, across the nose and bashed his lip when he flinched. He put out his hands in self-defense and it butted against them, rubbing its face on his gloved palms, with that odd sound and that feeling Danny had said was <happy.>

"Damn fool," he said to it, but to appease it he rubbed its cheek with his hands—otherwise it was going to rub its head on *him* and bash his face again. *That* led only to a harder push and a loss of balance. He went down backward in the snow and the horse nosed him in the face, or the hands, when he pushed at it, radiating <happy> and <looking down at Carlo in the snow.> He couldn't get up without its nose in the way. He got as far as his knees and had its head in his middle, butting him until he patted its neck and used it for a wall to lean on getting up.

<Happy horse. Delighted horse.>

"I'm not it, silly fool. I'm not."

But it wanted. It <wanted> and he'd been with Danny long enough to know that if a horse wanted to reach his rider, he'd go through or over anything remotely possible, and this horse wanted with that kind of intensity. It wasn't <blood-on-snow> in its mind any longer. It was something else—he didn't know what, but it wasn't <lost horse> any longer, either.

Neither was he <lost in the woods.> It had him, and he had it; and he couldn't be as scared as he'd been or as desperate as he'd been or as lonely as he'd been, while the creature he'd most feared was most interested in rubbing its face against him.

<Shape in the woods,> he kept seeing, but not a threatening shape, just a fast-moving shadow through the trees, horse here, horse there—the eye couldn't track it.

"Spook," he said to a back-turned ear, his arm at the moment encircling its neck from below. He was there instead of the person it most wanted, whoever that was. He was there because he'd happened into its path, was all, when Randy had wanted it, when maybe his sister had, in her untouchable dreams. It might get him back close to the village, might save him, but certainly he hadn't a right to it—

Which, he realized all of a sudden was his answer to every question of everything he'd ever had a chance for—he hadn't a right. He was the oldest. He had the responsibilities, he always had been the responsible one. He had to learn the craft. He had to stay and work. He had to go to Evergreen. He had to see to Brionne's life. To Randy's future. To the forge down in Tarmin. All those things. Only thing he'd ever done right, only thing good anybody ever said about him, was he was responsible, and what could he do now? He was a stand-in for his brother with this creature. It wasn't responsible to have notions of accepting it himself.

<Carlo and Spook> was the ambient right now. It was powerfully persuasive. It was so, so attractive to believe it could make a mistake like that, and that he might accept it and just not go back again to being responsible.

Couldn't. Randy wouldn't forgive him.

It could keep him safe, though, till he could deal with the charges and prove—whatever he could prove to the village.

It could—it could take him clear to Tarmin. It knew the way up and down the mountain. It could fight off predators. It could guide him, hunt for him, protect him—he didn't *need* anything he didn't have in his hands right now.

And the world around him had expanded so *wide,* and the smells had become so clear—he didn't know how much he'd lost when he'd left the ambient for the Mackeys' forge and the living he owed his brother.

If he stayed too long, he said to himself, if he let himself get used to it, he didn't know how he'd give it up.

"God, I don't know about horses. I don't know how to ride. You've really made a mistake, horse. I swear to you I'm not it."

Didn't make a difference. Spook was still there. Still wanting, exploring with a curious soft nose the gloved hands he put up to save his face from being licked raw. Hands failed. The horse butted him in the chest and wanted him to <ride.>

There weren't words. He felt presumptuous even to try what it wanted him to try. Danny if he were here would call him a fool.

But Danny wasn't here.

And he had no notion how to do the flashy move Danny could do, grabbing the mane and swinging up: he knew where that would land him. So he tried the way Danny would when things were chancy, and just bounced up to land belly-down across the horse's back and tried, with the horse beginning to move, to straighten himself around astride.

Too far. He made a frantic grab after a black and cloudy mane that like finest wool went almost to nothing in his hands—stayed on for maybe a hundred meters, breathless with what he'd done, was doing, could do. But when the course turned uphill he slid right off over Spook's rump.

To his surprise he landed on his feet, in a position to look uphill as the horse reached the top and looked down at him as if to say, God, I've picked a fool.

He slogged up the snowy incline, panting, and tried again—got on, and fell off more slowly, still clinging to two fistfuls of mane, when Spook picked up the pace.

Definitely there was a knack of balance he didn't have.

But he got on again.

He wanted to go back and find Danny. But Danny was <Danny with gun> and Spook didn't *want* to find Danny. He suddenly had that image. He couldn't just ride into Danny's sights—when Danny thought Spook was a danger to the village. He couldn't go back and get Spook killed for no reason.

He knew now as long as the village chased him, Randy had a chance to do what he'd told Randy to do if things got bad—go get Danny's help; with Randy staying in the rider camp, the marshal at least couldn't include a fourteen-year-old in a murder charge.

He had to talk to Danny. But on his terms. After he'd had time to think what to do, what he wanted, where he was and where he wanted to go.

Spook had hit a rhythm and broke into a run that didn't pitch him off. They'd reached a road—the road, *a* road, he didn't know—where there was easy moving and for a hundred meters or so he was *with* Spook, and no longer fighting for balance—it was just there. It was wonderful, wild, and *right* in a way he'd never found anything just *happen* for him.

Until the stop that almost pitched him over Spook's shoulder.

<Horse and rider.> *Danny* was there. On Cloud. With a <rifle halfway lifted for shooting horse.>

Spook saw it, too. Spook swung around and bolted and he didn't know how he stayed on, except the double handful of mane, both legs wrapped tight and his head ducked down because he swayed less that way.

"Carlo!" he heard Danny yell at him. "Carlo, it's all right, come back!"

Couldn't take the chance. Couldn't believe it. Couldn't.

<Run> was the only safety. It was what Spook knew. Or he did. He'd have trusted Danny. But Spook was afraid. And he thought now he should have been.

"Damn it!" Danny cried. "Carlo!"

But Carlo wasn't hearing him. Couldn't hear him, maybe. Or Spook-horse's state of mind was contagious.

Chase him, maybe. But push him on a mountain road with no-knowing-what ahead—no. <Going slower,> he wanted of Cloud, and tried sending into the ambient, <Danny and Carlo. Horses walking together.>

Cloud didn't think so. Cloud's mind conjured <bad horse> and <Spook following them.> Which wasn't the case, but that was where Spook had consistently been, long enough that it was part of Cloud's thinking.

Which he had to calm down. Cloud was of a mind to <fight> right now, and that wasn't what he wanted.

<Still water,> he thought, patting Cloud's neck as they walked along the well-defined track in the snow. "It's all right," he told Cloud. He didn't know how far Carlo might make the chase—but he was willing to go that far. He'd come out with his kit, his cold-weather gear and his guns. He was equipped. He'd taken longer than he wanted getting onto Carlo's trail.

He'd known when <Carlo and Spook> had hit the ambient that he'd been too late, and he'd only come up on them because they were so obsessed with each other, in that way of new pairings, that they wouldn't have heard a herd of horses coming.

He'd made his mistake when he'd hesitated—one way or the other, shoot fast or don't shoot. Spook *wasn't* a green horse from the mountains, playing tag with echoes of gunshots and sprays of dirt on the hillside, the way Cloud had done with the gate-guards down in Shamesey two years ago. Spook very well knew what guns were, and he'd had one rider shot to death.

Wasn't going to have a gun pointed at him, no. And he'd been asking himself down to the moment the pair turned up in front of him whether he was going to be obliged to shoot the horse to save Carlo.

The lingering question was, should he have, and whether he'd just stood back and let somebody he was supposed to protect go off on a horse that had last belonged to a crazy man.

Chapter XIX

It might have been a quick turnaround—out after the kid, and back again, with a live kid or a dead one, and then maybe a chance for negotiation with the village authorities, or an expedition to Mornay.

But neither had happened, and Ridley made a trip over to the villageside, through the little gate, this time, and without Slip, to talk to Eli Peterson.

"No luck so far," he said to Peterson when he met him on the street in front of the pharmacy.

"I feel bad about it," Peterson said. "I don't think the boy did it, fact is."

"Fact is, I wouldn't take the Mackeys' word for a sunrise I was watching."

"The girl, however," Peterson said, "the sister—"

"What?"

"Says the brother shot their parents, down in Tarmin. Says the boy was in jail."

Ridley drew a slow breath. "I've been aware of it."

"And didn't say?"

"Fisher told me all about it. Fisher thinks the boy's innocent."

"He's not a judge! Neither are you!"

"*I'm* asking you—let that matter lie. None of us were *in* Tarmin. None of us can imagine how it was. What I caught from the Fisher boy—you wouldn't want to see. Look at what happened this morning! I had a terrified boy running into the camp—"

"The words flew out of my mouth and the damn miners were after *somebody.* They didn't give a damn who. —How's the kid taking it?"

"I'm keeping him. At least till his brother gets back."

"You think he's coming back?"

"Eventually."

"Something *you* know?"

"Fisher's still gone. Fisher would come back if it was useless. The boy's with him. I'll be willing to bet. And the younger boy's been through too much as is." He hadn't told Peterson the central matter. He thought about it, decided finally on half a truth. The snow was still falling and passersby aboveground were all but nonexistent on this cold day—except a batch of kids sledding the snow-pile across the street on a piece of board. "That horse that's loose—can't tell for certain, but I think the older boy's contacted it. I don't know what to expect."

"You mean you think he's teamed up with it? As a rider?"

"It's possible. I don't say it's going to work. Or that he's going to survive it. He could fall off, break his neck—the horse could kill him."

"Do they *do* that?"

"Oh, I've heard of it happening. A horse that's just too spooked. A rider that's the wrong rider. Things like that. This isn't nice and controlled like Rain and Jennie. The kid could break his neck, the horse could go off a cliff—or the kid could come back here and then spook right along with the horse. I have to tell you this—don't take to account anything the sister says. She's not right. She's not innocent. I don't know how else to warn you. I had to get my horse out of there this morning. She spooked my horse."

"Scared Slip?" Peterson was clearly dubious.

"Marshal, if I'd kept Slip there to deal with her—she'd have spooked the *village* out the gates. Lorrie-lies and goblin-cats aren't as scary as what's in that girl's mind."

Peterson seemed to get the idea, then.

"She's not right," he repeated to Peterson. "She's been associated with the rogue down at Tarmin. She's dangerous."

"How—dangerous?"

Fisher had left him with a set of truths—and a situation. As camp-boss, he had a privilege to deal with things in camp. And he didn't pass blame—or legal matters—on to the village marshal. "Fact is—she was on the Tarmin rogue's back. And she's a lot safer with you than with us, is what I'm comfortable saying on the matter."

"That's not damn all you owe me to say, rider-boss!"

"Keep her away from the horses. This spring—we'll find a way to get her down to someplace safe. Anveney would be my advice. No horses in Anveney."

"Good lovin' God. What have you handed us? *What* am I dealing with?"

"Marshal, the situation arrived on us on the sudden, on a junior rider's best guess what to do. And with that horse out there, and what's gone on—I'd say Darcy Schaffer's got a real problem on her hands."

Peterson was mad. He couldn't blame him for that. Peterson walked off from him as far as the edge of the walk.

"What were my choices?" Ridley asked while Peterson stared off into the white.

"We could have put her with somebody else than Darcy Schaffer!"

"Yeah," Ridley said. "Counting that we've got to get that girl out of Evergreen—I'd say just about anybody else. But the girl could get better by spring."

"Better than what, rider-boss? Better than happened down in Tarmin?"

It was a question.

Serious question.

"I didn't have all the information at the start." *Being* rider-boss he didn't on principle want to pass the blame. But he wasn't going to have it attach to Callie, either. "Callie was doubtful. I was too inclined to go easy. I should have held Fisher to account. I didn't until I had clearer indication—and when I did get the truth it was a little damn late. I don't see he could have done better than he did, given the situation. That's what we've got for the winter."

"And this is the younger kid of the same family you've got in camp right now!"

"Scared. In love with the horses. Willing to learn—maybe. Maybe some horse will have him. I don't know. Maybe even Shimmer's foal. And if that horse has taken his brother it may solve our problems for the winter, if we can move him on, say, to Mornay and get that influence out of here. Or settled. A rider might calm that horse right down."

Peterson looked unhappy. But Peterson came back and met him close up. "Your guess. —No, dammit, your horse-guided opinion! You think the Goss boy is guilty or innocent of the business on Darcy's doorstep?"

"Better than a guess. My horse *knows* the Goss kid, at least from one meeting. Nothing on that porch led me to the Goss kid. Nothing whatsoever. *Everything* persuades me that the sister is a problem. He isn't. Neither is the younger boy or I wouldn't have him near the horses."

"There's talk that *Darcy* agreed to pay Riggs a lot of money."

"I'd sooner suspect miners and money for Riggs' disappearance. It makes a lot more sense. It *wasn't* the Goss boy."

"Riggs otherwise had no money." Peterson said. "And I'm inclined to think it's possible. Story is, Riggs was hiring men to claim property for the girl. Riggs had this notion of marrying her."

"She's a *kid.*"

"Yeah. And, your better-than-guess aside, there was reason for her brother to take offense. That much is true. —Then I ask myself—well, couldn't the Mackeys *want* to see the Goss boys charged and out of the picture? But that doesn't benefit them too much, while the girl's with Darcy. Unless they contracted to run the Tarmin shop for the girl. And between you and me and the rest of the village, Rick Mackey couldn't run that shop or *this* shop on his own, and if it came down to Mary Hardesty, she's a businesswoman but she's no decent smith, and without her, Van Mackey won't stay sober. Business is all she likes, work has to get done and the Goss boy, the older one, is the only likely one there is. So where's their motive?"

"On villageside and away from my business," Ridley said. "I don't try to figure what the Mackeys do. I'm sorry for Carlo Goss. I wish him well and far away. I've got my hands full with the younger kid. You've got the girl on your side of the wall and I'd say, soon as spring, we pack her on the first truck down with a strong dose of yellowflower and get her somewhere besides Tarmin."

"Darcy won't at all take to that."

"Then maybe Darcy can do something with her head. But she didn't do it on the porch this morning. I tell you, marshal, my horse and I were right out in the middle of that crowd. Same one that went for that boy. There was a reason things went the way they did."

"You're saying—what?"

"That the miners might have killed him. That *that* was why things went so bad so fast. Maybe it was why the boy ran for his life and went out those gates rather than stay in the village. He'd felt it once before this."

"At Tarmin, you mean?" Peterson was taking acute alarm. And Ridley didn't want that.

"The girl can't do any damage," Ridley said, "unless there's a horse near her."

"Or a bear or a cat or any damn thing—how in hell do we get her out of here down a road in company with a bunch of riders on horses we're not supposed to let her near?"

"Yellowflower. I'm serious. Asleep, she's fine. Dreams don't do much. In my observation. —Marshal, I had no choice, even if I'd known. Those kids would have died if I'd sent them on. At least two of them would have. And at Mornay it would have been the same risk if that girl was there, and maybe worse. Mornay's a smaller enclosure, more chance of sendings getting over the wall—if she were there. Play the hand close and we'll get her out of here come spring—and I'd advise we do it whether or not she improves. I'd say the village should buy out any share she's got in Tarmin, pay her and Darcy in goods, and get them both out of here."

"Our only doctor, dammit."

"Who hasn't been doing much the last year. And I'm sorry about Faye. I know Darcy blames me. But if Faye'd done what she was told, *Faye* wouldn't be dead. That's hard, and I'm sorry to say so, but that's the way it is. The kid left the secure area and went off on her own exactly the way the Goss boy's done—only the boy this morning had urgent reason and Faye was after her own pleasure. Besides her father was in attendance the same as I was and she slipped off from him, too. I'm not personally responsible for either one and in both cases I'm doing what I can—including sending a rider out there to deal with the Goss kid, including coming over here and personally warning you that the doctor's resentment toward me is reaching the girl, and that the girl *does* hear the horses and everything of like kind out in the Wild. If you believe one thing I say, believe this: the Goss girl has a real capability for setting off a mob or a village-wide panic of exactly the kind that opened Tarmin's gates and doors. If the doctor were likely to listen to me, I'd say keep that kid on yellowflower every time we have a problem near the walls. Which having *met* the doctor's mind directly this morning I don't think she will—"

"You're saying *Darcy* hears the horses?"

"I'm saying all of you did, marshal. Everybody in town."

"Not me."

"Some of you clearer than others. *You* were thinking about your job and you didn't panic. Some were looking for somebody to blame and they did. I'll assure you *Slip* didn't think of going after that boy. But upset, yes, my horse was upset. And a lot of people *being* upset did exactly what they'd naturally do if they were upset. The law stood firm and the boy ran and the miners chased him. —And the girl threw a tantrum. Am I right? At the far end and down by the gate I was farther than I usually am from the main street when I'm in camp. I'm flat guessing what she did and what you felt. But am I right?"

"Yeah. You are."

"I didn't have to hear it to make a guess. And what I did hear while I was there wasn't good."

"At that range?"

"You can pick up a few things. The world's never *quiet.* It's never really *quiet* while there's a horse anywhere about. And damn right that girl's noisy. I'm real serious. My notion is she doesn't listen worth a damn, but once she's in contact with the Wild she's real pushy with her images, real stubborn in what she sees. And it's not just my horse: it's *everything* all over the mountain, things so quiet you don't ordinarily hear them or if you do you don't know you're hearing them. She sends better than some and she doesn't listen. That may be more than you want to know about the horses, but that's the worst combination of talents you can own to go around them, and I don't want Slip near her."

"You had an obligation to tell us about the girl *before* we made certain decisions!"

"What would you have done different—besides not put that girl with Darcy?"

"That's about it."

"Then that's the one we've got to deal with, isn't it? If the Goss boy takes to that loose horse—it could be settled and we could have a peaceful winter, once that attraction is away from her. I told Fisher get him on to Mornay if he can catch him, and that's *still* the best thing to do."

"Do you hear him now?"

"I'm not near the horses."

Villagers never seemed to get that straight. Or cases like the Goss girl confused them. *He* just wished Darcy Schaffer's house was on the other side of the street because, knowing there was trouble in the village, Slip was a curious and a suspicious horse who might put out extra effort to know what That Girl was up to.

And *that* meant horses carrying the girl's troublesome images further than ordinary into the Wild. Get a panic started among the horses and they'd hear it in distant Anveney.

"Well, keep me posted," Peterson said.

"I will," he said, uneasy in knowing the man on the villageside who knew him best and who had the village version of his job didn't really to this day know what the abilities and the limits of the horses were. John Quarles was, ironically, his other best phone line to the village—but John just trusted the Lord and didn't try to understand things. You went and told Peterson when you wanted somebody on villageside to worry. You told John when you wanted somebody to nod sagely and assure you things would be all right.

Neither worked in this case.

So he had had nothing to do but go back to the camp, and to stay around the den where he could keep his finger on the pulse of the ambient, and that meant currying Slip, since his hands were idle, and trying to keep him calm. Callie and Jennie did the same, all of them hanging about the den where rumors could fly—or be sat upon, fast, before they spread to the village on the impulse of several nervous horses.

The younger Goss boy, Randy, hung about there, too, being very quiet.

And very unhappy.

"You think he's still alive?" Randy asked finally, coming up to him as he was brushing Slip's tail.

"Pretty sure so," he said. "Pretty sure he's with that horse."

"I hope he is," Randy said. And he heard from the kid right then <wanting that horse> and <wanting his brother> and knew that both choices came with real pain.

"A rider's pretty damn selfish," he said to Randy, "when it's him *and* his horse. If you can let that horse go, he'd never be yours. That's the truth, kid."

"If Danny finds Carlo he'll get him to Mornay."

"He'll get him there if he can. *You* stay here. No going back to the Mackeys."

"I've got to get the house down in Tarmin. That's *Carlo's* house."

"If Carlo's gone to be a rider, son, there's nobody but the Mackeys to go with you."

"But he *wants* to be a blacksmith."

"Not now. You hear it out there." Couldn't hear it now too distinctly: horse-sense said it had gone on in the general direction of Mornay, which was very good news. "You don't ever unchoose that. Lose one horse—you've got to find one and some horse has got to find you, or you're better off dead."

There was a long silence, Randy sitting on a rail by the manger, wiped his eyes. "He won't want *me* if he's got that horse."

"Not the same way, maybe. A horse happens along and a partner happens along both for reasons you don't exactly choose to happen, and sometimes who happens and why just doesn't make sense to you. Don't say won't. Don't say can't. Say—there's something waiting for you." It was what he'd said to himself before he met Callie. It was what he'd said to Jennie. And Jennie had proved that true, no question about it.

The boy looked up at him. "You think? You think maybe?"

"I think you better be ready if it comes. Can't say when. Neither could your brother. Just think good thoughts about him now and most of all think about him staying on that horse. It won't leave him. But it's bad country to get thrown. Worry about *that* if you want to worry about something."

"He'll show Rick Pig. He'll come back and he'll show him."

"If he comes back with that horse he'll take orders like any rider in this camp, kid. The way he'll take orders over at Mornay if Danny can get him there." He *liked* the boy. But you never let a kid think he was on equal footing when you might have to lay the law down and make it stick. "You get one thing straight: you don't do anything toward the village without consulting the camp-boss, including insulting the village folk. That's the first lesson you learn, or you better clear out and stay out of my sight, right down that road you took to get up here. Danny Fisher ran that line right close, and I know why he did it; and he knows he's on my tolerance. So you get it straight: if you stay in this camp, you do what you're told and you do it when you're told, and if you don't, Slip here will tell me."

"Yes, *sir*," Randy said.

"Good you learn that."

Chapter XX

The afternoon had gone to that strange daylight afternoons had in the woods, in the mountains, and the trail was going the same way it had—Cloud's burst of speed flagged in a high altitude gasping for breath. Out of condition, Cloud was. Born up here, maybe, but they were both a little soft, and settled to an unheroic amble through the woods, along the road to Mornay. He walked at times, rode at times. Cloud had carried him quite a lot to start with, and he didn't want to push Cloud to foolishness in his enthusiasm: it was possible to get a whole list of ailments from too much exertion at altitude and he'd heard them all from Ridley as well as Tara and Guil.

Miraculously, in Danny's opinion, there hadn't been any more Carlo-shaped holes in the snow, and the horse was traveling at a fair clip along the road, faster through the trees, which was generally a good idea, considering the habit of lorrie-lies and other such tree-dwellers that liked to fall on you from above. Cloud did much the same as he tracked Carlo and Spook.

He was resolved not to scare the horse twice. It hadn't been the brightest move he'd made, coming up on that horse ambivalent about shooting. Now he was sure he wouldn't. He tried, because Cloud could be a fairly loud horse when he wanted to be, to encourage Cloud to send out friendliness and goodwill to the ambient at large and an image of <Danny and Carlo riding side by side.> But no, Cloud wouldn't. <Danny and Carlo> was the best he could manage, and Cloud gave a shiver and a twitch, just thinking about <male horse.>

There were tracks of game—though sign was rare, and totally absent along one area of the road, well-shaded and sheltered from the snow-fall, where he would have thought small tracks might have persisted. Nothing but themselves was moving about—he didn't pick up the <rider on horse> view of things at ground level that the little spooks sent. But the snow had fallen thick and swirled in under the trees, while the little game, undisturbed by hunters, was in burrows. The silence was deep and wide across the mountain, a kind of breathless slumber, except for the track Spook laid down and the track he laid over it.

He thought that Carlo might be heading to Mornay on his own: Carlo might never have traveled in his life, but he was well familiar with the fact of the shelters. When in his first days with Cloud, and inexperienced as he was of the Wild, he'd taken out to the open, he'd had far better weather and no such shelters in reach.

<Shelter and warm mash,> he thought, <Danny and Cloud in the rider-shelter.>

Cloud shook his dark abundance of wooly mane and whipped his tail about.

<Fierce nighthorse male,> Cloud sent into the ambient, and Danny tried to think of <Danny and Carlo.> That didn't make him or Cloud more comfortable. But he didn't *want* to challenge the whole ambient the way Cloud was minded to do, and he wanted <riding.> When Cloud let him up he wanted <going faster,> just because it seemed to him—

He wasn't sure. He couldn't put a name or a label to it—and nighthorses weren't the only large hunters on the mountain. He'd long since put curves of the mountain face between him and Evergreen—a lot of them. And now, just since the last sharp curve, the nape of his neck prickled as they rode, which sometimes meant something watching—and sometimes didn't. Sometimes it was just a human's own imagination padding along behind him, never there when the rider looked back, and never close enough to leave tracks in the rider's sight.

Which was ridiculous. If anything had been behind them, Cloud's vision would have spotted it, Cloud's horse-sense would have located it, Cloud's knowledge of the Wild would have identified it with far more surety than a human could.

He just decided, in all that silence, not to call out to Carlo aloud as he'd sometimes done, and not to send so loudly as he'd been urging Cloud to do. He rode along through a shadow that deepened as they passed into woods. But past a little wooded spot and around a little curve, he found open road ahead.

And there—he was ever so glad to see—just past those last trees, a wall of logs. The Evergreen-to-Mornay shelter was ahead. He'd sworn to himself he wouldn't have to tell Ridley he'd missed this one in a snowstorm, and, thank God, despite the snow-fall, he hadn't.

The road went past it. But the trail he was following didn't go there. It veered off down a broad gap in the trees that led past the shelter, and just kept going.

Damn, he thought. A logging track, and Carlo had taken it, shying off from the cabin. He stopped Cloud, and stood looking down it. Snow-fall was thick enough the trail disappeared into white haze, along with the farther trees.

It might be stupid to follow. But *he* had gear and a gun, and Carlo didn't. *He* could stay on his horse, and he wouldn't bet on Carlo's chances if that trail led down to rough ground.

It was a question how hard to push Carlo, how hard to make him run. He didn't want to create a disaster. It might be smarter to hole up for the night, use the supplies in the cabin to make a good hot supper and hope Carlo could smell it on the wind.

But when he rode up to the shelter, in which the ambient gave him no feeling of occupancy—just a wooden structure half-buried in snow—he kept thinking that with the snow coming down the way it was and a half-crazed horse under him—

God, what chance did <Carlo> have but him?

Cloud turned without his willing it, with the notion of <Carlo,> too, and a <bad> feeling about the precinct that came on a gust of wind. <Lorrie-lie> was Cloud's thinking at the moment; and <high in treetops.> Or it was something very like. Cloud blew steam in an explosive clearing of his nostrils and shook his mane in disgust at what he was smelling. Cloud had a notion of <bad> and <movement on the mountain,> and <gap in the world> that boiled up to the top of the ambient in a scary way he'd never before felt from Cloud.

"All right," he said, patting Cloud on the shoulder, agreeing on the trail in front of them.

The overcast had gone very gray and dim above them. They might be fools to be going away from shelter.

But he hadn't gone too far at all before they crossed another such clearcut, and came on a bowl-shaped little nook where a big forested crag thrust out from the mountain, rock veiled in snow, bristling with evergreens. It was one of those unexpected vistas the mountain could give you, just unfolding from around a turn. A broad patch was clear of trees and brush, and the immaculate flatness of *ice* showed where the wind blew the snow clear.

A mountain pool, frozen over. Tall evergreens stood about its banks.

He knew where he was: the pond Mornay and Evergreen shared for excursions.

The pond where the doctor's daughter had drowned.

Unlucky place, he thought, scanning that scene from Cloud's moving back like a painting on a wall—loggers hadn't taken the trees here, only cut a trail through, about wide enough for the ox-teams that dragged the logs up to the roads: a pile of cut logs where a trail went off across the mountain awaited the teams that wouldn't come next spring. Surprised by early winter, he thought, as Cloud pace-pace-paced along the track that a single horse had left along the side of the pond.

Cloud felt skittish, looking left and right and moving faster than his rider thought prudent. A <smell> was in the ambient, something Cloud couldn't identify, and Danny was acquiring the same nervousness.

Another glance toward the pond showed a lump in a snow-hazed treetop.

<Lorrie-lie,> he thought. His knowledge of the predators of the Wild was all secondhand, but it could account for Cloud's faster pace.

Didn't pick up anything, though. Old nest, he thought. Old and abandoned. If—

Cloud shot forward so suddenly in <startlement> he almost went off. In the same moment he caught <Carlo and Spook below them> as the ambient did an uncanny ripple of <there> and <not-there> and nothing was the same as he'd seen it a moment ago.

Trick, he thought in a wash of panic. <Goblin-cat> could do that. He'd never heard lorrie-lies did.

Suddenly it didn't feel lonely out here. It felt—dangerous. It felt—occupied. Alive. And scary of a sudden. Very scary. <Carlo> might be an illusion some hunter got from his mind.

<Goblin-cat> had that talent, too.

He didn't quarrel with Cloud's sudden rush. Not now.

The way ahead was a white gash through the dark of trees, a path dropping lower on the mountain, steep and almost all an inexperienced rider could do to stay on—a logging cut, Carlo thought it was. He didn't know *why* the horse had shied from the cabin and taken him in this direction, but he was scared beyond clear thinking by the situation as well as the route they were taking. He kept feeling oppressive danger in the place, not on either hand, but above them—and that worried him more than it would have if Spook's fear had been of *all* the trees.

This had direction. And it didn't have to do with <rider following them,>not now. Spook remembered <Danny with gun,> but he didn't carry that image continually—and wouldn't stop, just *wouldn't* stop, though by now Spook was breathing hard and his jogging pace was jarring his rider's teeth loose as he wove back and forth down the centerline of a depression in that white gash the sides of which Carlo feared might conceal stumps or brush. The center might be a road—he didn't know. He had no sense of what Spook was doing or how Spook avoided obstacles under the snow—just—sometimes—Spook didn't avoid them until the last second, and threw him violently off balance.

Carlo didn't want to fall off and find himself on the ground with that feeling of <danger high in the trees> that was continually riding the edges of Spook's awareness. He knew very well he didn't have a rider's skills or a rider's knowledge of the dangers out here even on an ordinary day; and he didn't have a rider's sense of how to help his horse—he'd seen Danny take precautions and perform certain things with Cloud that he figured he ought to do for Spook if there was a problem.

But that would have to wait for shelter—if they could find one. He'd known a moment of hope when they'd seen the one—but Spook seemed to be rejecting any thought of it—maybe of all shelters, not knowing his rider didn't have the skill to make a camp.

Maybe Spook had feared that <Danny following them> could trap them there. He didn't know.

But all of a sudden he perceived <shadow in the treetops, blackness against the sky,> and Spook lurched downslope in a reckless run.

He stuck tighter if he clung lower, and he made himself as flat as he could on Spook's back—Spook wasn't a young horse, Danny had said so. Spook had been a ridden horse, a horse that could keep him safe only if he didn't fall off in front of whatever nameless terror was above him.

Something broke through the brush. *Sound* added itself to impressions piling up in the ambient of something horrific after them. <Goblin-cat,> he thought. He'd never seen one. But it might be. Or a <lorrie-lie.> They went in trees.

Then an impression of <horse> was back there. And <rider.>

He didn't know whether it was Danny. He couldn't turn to see without risking their collective balance as Spook took a sudden series of zigzags down the road, not all-out, now, but scarily fast for so many turns.

<Horse ahead> flashed to mind.

Or the ambient was changing on him. <Fear> was thick as the snow-fall that veiled the evergreens, as urgent on his heels as the <rider> image that chased him down through the woods.

Spook stumbled on something and his hindquarters dropped as he swung sideways, slid, clawed for balance and went down. He didn't know for a moment that Spook *had* fallen, but he was off to the side with his feet on the ground, and he hadn't anything left but a double-handed grip on Spook's mane as Spook gained his feet.

<Darkness in the trees> was coming. It was <there.> And *he* couldn't get up—Spook was trying to move, he couldn't get footing

to spring upward for Spook's back, and Spook wouldn't stand still as <darkness in the trees> bore down on them.

<Gunshot> rang out and <pain and anger> washed through him. He couldn't see anything but Spook's neck as Spook struggled to turn, dragging him around as Spook went on guard against <rider coming at them.>

His feet found a rock, then, beneath the snow, and Spook's sweating body walled him off from whatever was coming down on them. Spook wanted <running.> He jumped for Spook's back and Spook took off with him lying crosswise and barely aboard, struggling to right himself on the downhill.

<Danny> was in the ambient.

"Carlo!" he heard behind him. *"Carlo!"*

<Riders in front of him.> Spook tried to dodge opposite what he expected just as he almost righted himself, and Spook's back slid right under his leg as he went flying sideways again, still with a grip on Spook's mane, jerked along with Spook's sideways try at escape.

It ended with Spook down again against a snow-covered wall of brush, and him still clinging to Spook's mane, which he began to understand in his panic was impeding Spook's try at gaining his feet.

Two riders had come up the road on them, cutting off the downhill direction. He didn't know them, but <Danny and Cloud> were still behind him, and Spook was <afraid> of Danny, more afraid of <shadow in the trees> and terrified of <rider on the right. Gunfire echoing off mountain, rider sliding—blood on snow—>

He couldn't get back on. He was scared to let go, scared of losing Spook or leaving Spook a target; meanwhile Spook, stumbling on objects under the snow, kept backing up, hemmed in by snow-covered brush, by <rider behind> and <danger in trees.>

But suddenly he *knew* these riders, and knew he'd met them. He tried simultaneously to hang on to Spook's mane and still put himself between the riders and Spook, <terrified of riders shooting.>

<Water running over stones. Light through leaves.>

It was a rider's calm-sending. It was an urge to <quiet,> he knew that much, and desperately wanted to believe in it.

"Don't shoot," he said, finding his voice. "Don't shoot. He's not crazy. I'm not. I didn't kill anybody!"

"Just calm down."

It was Guil Stuart and Tara Chang. Tara was the rider Spook was afraid of. And Guil Stuart only slightly less so.

But <still water,> was insistent, washing over his vision, alternate with the white of real snow and those snow-obscured figures that had him pinned against the wall of brush.

"Carlo," came Danny's voice from behind him and uphill. "It's me. Calm down. It's all right. Quiet him down. Calm the horse down. Nobody's going to shoot."

He wanted things quiet. He wanted <Spook standing still,> so he dared let go, because he had Spook's mane twisted in both his hands and he thought it might be hurting Spook and compounding the problem. "Settle down," he said, scared to let go as Spook stood shivering. "It's all right." <Carlo and Danny> was in his head. He didn't know whether it was his idea or not. <Horrid black thing in snow> was in his head, too, and he didn't know how, but he thought it came from Danny, by the direction-sense that quivered along his nerves, like awareness of the faintest breeze.

"Carlo," Danny said, "I got it, I shot it. —Guil, I—don't know what the hell it is. Lorrie-lie, maybe."

"Back there?" Stuart asked, and he and Chang at least made a move or the intent of a move in that direction, which gave Spook a notion of <running,> but Carlo didn't want that now. He tried to calm Spook down, and fortunately or because the others realized Spook's inclination, they kept Burn and Flicker in the way on one side and Cloud on the other.

Carlo freed one hand and used it to pat Spook on the shoulder—heart pounding, took the risk of freeing the other, awkwardly patted Spook's resisting neck and secured of Spook at least a trembling quiet.

Then Spook turned his head, butted it against him, <Blood on snow. Spook and Carlo, Spook and Carlo> was the sending, until, his doing or Spook's or the others', he gained awareness of the other riders, other horses, distances, minds, intentions, <strong, not moving, quiet water running over brown stones.>

"I'm here," Danny said quietly, aloud and in the ambient. "I'm just behind you."

"I know," he said. "Danny, I didn't do it. I didn't kill anybody!"

"I can hear it. I believe you." There was a lot of <wanting> and a lot of <anxiousness> and a lot of <Stuart and Chang> in the air, with not quite an easy feeling to it—rather a skittish wariness that calm-sendings didn't stop.

"Devil meeting you here," Stuart said. "Did you kill it?"

He was talking to Danny, Carlo thought, and what hit the ambient wasn't comfortable—it was that <shadow> sending that upset Spook. It was <nest in tree beside the water.> It was <Danny and Cloud in the woods, following his trail, under shadow in the trees.>

"How did *you* get here?" Danny asked Guil, visualizing <road and ice,> and from Guil and Tara, Carlo guessed, came different images, <cabin in the woods, steep snowy climb through the forest.>

That and something he couldn't get, but didn't think he wanted to, either. For a moment there were images pouring every which way, <Evergreen village> and <Brionne in furs,> and <rider-shelter with the local riders,> all, he realized suddenly, provoking memories and images from him, <doctor's house, Brionne in bed, awake> and <Rick Mackey shouting at him in the street> and <him running, running for the gates> with what he knew now was a desperate <fear of jail> and <fear of the mob> and a sense of <safety in the Wild.>

He tried not to contribute to the confusion. Danny had gotten mad when he'd poured too much in on Cloud, in the days when they'd climbed the mountain. But he didn't think Danny was angry now. Danny and Cloud became <quiet cloud. Cloud on a sunny day.>

Then Danny left Cloud to come over to him, <wanting him to reach out his hand.> And he did reach. He kept one hand on Spook, and he felt <anxiety> as his gloved fingers met Danny's.

They stood like that a moment, with <fear> and <wanting> running through them like electricity through a wire. Carlo *felt* Danny's awareness and calm good sense go along his nerves. He *believed* Danny was different from anybody he'd ever met. And if he'd damned himself in the eyes of preachers, if riding a horse would do it when his other faults had missed, he made a conscious choice now to be where he was standing, in rider company, a killer with a horse riders called crazed and a would-be killer itself—but he wanted their company, he *wanted* their acceptance among them.

He didn't know why Danny radiated <wanting contact> and he didn't know how to understand the <flight> impulse in Spook until the second Spook tried to break away into the clear in complete panic; but he wouldn't *let* Spook run from help, not except <running over him,> and he wouldn't have it, wouldn't allow it, had himself in the way and his hands on Spook without even knowing which one of them had moved first. He just stood there <wanting quiet> and holding his whole weight against Spook's shoulder. <Carlo and Danny> was in the ambient and he had the presence of mind finally to join into it, <Carlo and Danny> as hard as he could think it. <Carlo and Danny and Spook and Cloud> while he pressed with all his strength against Spook's trembling shoulder.

"Kid's new?" Stuart's voice asked.

"Today," Danny said. "Hours. Just barely hours."

"Easy," Chang said, and with every word the ambient grew calmer. "Easy, kid. You're all right. You're doing damn fine. He's just on edge. It's not your fault. Calm. Calm down."

"Yes, ma'am," he said. His voice was shaking. "He's scared of you. Spook's especially scared of you."

The ambient sank further toward quiet. Tara Chang was quieting things, he thought, and the world unfolded further—wider and wider so that, with his hands on Spook's side, he was aware of Guil Stuart's physical pain, Chang's grief, Danny's anxiousness—aware of two horses, Burn and Spook, that had known each other in the past, and that were and weren't enemies; and two horses, Spook and Flicker, that had encountered each other at a point of death and change, far, far down the mountain.

Aware, then, of the mountain far and wide—and a breathless silence fallen around them.

Danny didn't know what he would have done without Stuart. He didn't think he could have quieted Spook *or* Carlo. Cloud was all right with Spook now that Spook had a rider and there wasn't a threat to his own. Burn was protective of Flicker, that was clear to him and to Cloud, but that was the way things had been, and Spook, with a junior and uncertain rider, was at the bottom of the status list, Cloud just behind the pair Burn and Flicker made.

That meant peace, and peace came as a shakiness of the knees and a thorough relief. Danny still didn't figure *why* Guil and Tara had come up the mountain when they'd said otherwise, but the first-stage shelter was among the images he'd gotten. He guessed that

Guil and Tara had ridden over to check on them and then—then they'd have found his warning about Spook.

And he was very glad they had.

"Where did you drop the thing?" Guil asked with a fleeting image of what had been <chasing them.> Tara had gotten down, but Guil hadn't, hurting too much, Danny had no need to ask. It had been a risky and probably a painful ride for Guil—straight up the mountain, by trails and logging roads, he guessed that by the images floating past him.

"Back in those trees," he said to Guil's question, and supplied the only image he had, <black shape, total surprise as it crashed down through the limbs.> "I don't know what it was, but it dropped at me and I shot."

Burn took his rider slowly and warily in that direction. He and Tara went along with Cloud and Flicker in close company, and Carlo and Spook followed uncertainly hindmost—scared, still flighty, and with Spook—he was almost certain the source was Spook—giving off images of <dark> and <vacant mountain> and <shadow in the treetops.>

But it found echoes.

So did <blood on snow.>

Which was all they found when they rode up on the area where the thing had fallen.

"I left it there." Lame excuse. Danny knew he should have put another bullet into it. But Carlo had already been running. He didn't know how he'd have caught Carlo if he'd taken to firing: he'd have scared Spook and Carlo could have broken his neck, a new rider, a tired, scared horse on that slope—

"Best *I* could have done," Guil said generously, and did slide down off Burn for a closer look. Light was getting dimmer and the snow was coming down thick and fast with little wind.

Such traces as remained, a large depression in the snow, would go away very quickly. The blood was mostly obscured already. But there wasn't, after all, that much of it.

"There's <a nest> over toward the pond," Danny said.

It found an echo. For a moment the whole mountainside vanished in a strong sending of <black shape> and <danger in woods> and <Spook-horse going to fight> that stirred memories from another source of <cabin, moving darkness on the mountain, fear and disturbance.>

It took a moment to get the ambient calmed down again.

"The horse hunted it," Guil said, with that economy of words Danny had found among borderers. "The horse came up here tagging you, and you went into walls. The tree-climber was here first. But this horse was hunting *it* to get its territory, until he got what he wanted. Then he was going right down the mountain, fastest way he could." It was true, too, that senior riders could sift a lot more out of a single image than juniors could do. And older horses both packed more information and traded it with more dispatch. There'd been just too much flying past him a moment ago for him to catch all of it—without resurrecting the fear that had gone with it. And he didn't want to do that.

Guil walked over where Carlo was and patted Spook on the neck. "Better have a look at his feet. Been running wild till today, was it?"

Carlo didn't seem to find it easy to talk to Guil. Not at all. "Yes," Danny said in Carlo's stead. "He was."

Guil walked around Spook, hand on Spook's back, looked at him, looked at his legs, just a fast pass around, while Carlo uneasily dodged around Spook's neck and stayed out of the way. "Needs some seeing-to," was Guil's pronouncement. "Had you staked out for his for a while, did he?"

"I—don't know. I guess. Yes, sir." Carlo wasn't doing well with words—not easy to talk when images were warring for your attention. And he was scared of Guil in a way Danny hadn't seen in him, down in the cabin near Tarmin.

"Damned well playing tag with the tree-sitter," Tara said, and <dark in trees> was in the ambient as Guil stared off into the woods and Tara walked up beside him.

"What are they saying?" Carlo asked quietly, his arm under Spook's neck, <skittish> as Spook.

"They think whatever I shot, whatever has the <nest by the pond,> is something—I don't know—some of it's hazy to *me.* But they think Spook and this thing have been fighting each other up here. Spook had *you* pegged for his. So he wasn't leaving. The thing in the nest, it wanted this whole ridge for its territory. And Spook was hellbent he was going to get you out of the village if he couldn't get that thing out of this territory."

"One argumentative horse," Guil said, paying attention when Danny thought he hadn't been. He walked back and laid a hand on

Carlo's shoulder. "Hell to manage. Got to warn you. He's used to a rider that picked fights."

Tara walked back over with a tuft of fur in her gloved fingers. Falling snow lit on it and stuck; horses laid their ears back as they smelled it, but there wasn't a thing from Burn or Flicker, just from Spook and, to Danny's surprise, Cloud, who laid his ears flat and did that <shadow in trees> sending but nothing clearer.

Took a second for the implication to get through. And then a very anxious feeling hit the stomach.

"Never met anything Burn didn't recognize the smell of," Guil said.

Neither Burn, who was far-traveled, nor Flicker nor Cloud recognized it, and Spook, who'd been playing tag with it for days along the road, didn't have a clear image of it.

"There's a lot of unknown territory," Tara said, "on this mountain's backside. And beyond here—there's just unexplored outback. With the rogue-sending taking Tarmin down, the whole mountain upset—that sending would have carried clear around the mountain flanks, clear to God knows where, so long as there were creatures to carry it. —Danny, you got anything better on it?"

He tried to image it. Wasn't sure he succeeded.

"I'm from Shamesey," he said by way of explaining his limitations. "From in town. I never even saw a lorrie-lie real clear. Just what Cloud knows."

"This is nothing anybody knows," Tara said. "It could be *like* a lorrie-lie, but it seems bigger. What would you say, seventy, eighty kilos?"

"I couldn't judge," Danny said. "I really couldn't judge."

"Sometimes in autumn, when things get restless, something does stray across the Divide. Never anything this big, that I've heard of."

"More than that," Guil said, staring off into the woods, and that <shadow in the trees> image was steadier and longer than Danny personally had held it. That was Guil and Burn, Danny thought, with real appreciation for seniors. <Cabin. Moving vacancy in the ambient.> "Predator. Strong one. Smart. Not enough blood. Didn't hit it solid enough."

"There's the villages up here," Tara said, and with the hair prickling on his arms Danny was entertaining the same thought. Cloud didn't like it, and he moved to the side to lay a hand on Cloud's neck.

"Shelter near here," Guil said.

"So's its nest," Danny said. "It could be its nest, at least—near the shelter."

"Bad business to leave anything wounded," Tara said. "Snow's already taking the trail, and it's likely gone up in the trees anyway. Check the nest is my recommendation."

"Sounds good to me," Guil said.

It sounded good to Danny, too. And there'd be cramped quarters for four riders and horses in the shelter, but there'd be safety, too.

They'd run a hard course, as Guil and Tara were at the end of a day's travel from somewhere below. Tara set out walking beside her horse, Guil did the same, Danny followed with Cloud, and Carlo trailed an uncertain last.

But feeling that uncertainty, Danny lagged back at Cloud's tail and put himself near Carlo.

"Sorry about the scare," he said. "Wasn't your fault we ran to hell and gone. I should have been more careful coming up on you."

"I'm all right," Carlo said. "But what about Randy?"

"Rider camp."

"He made it."

"He's fine, last I saw."

"Danny, I didn't kill that man."

"I know."

"*How?* Did they find who did it?"

"No. But I hear you clear. Horses carry it. Took me two years to learn to lie. And you're under camp rules, now. Village law can't take you without Ridley's say-so."

Carlo was vastly relieved at that."Randy either."

"Randy either. You stick with me. We'll think of something. Randy's safe. Ridley Vincint, he's camp-boss. He'll take care of him until we can arrange something ourselves. He'll be fine."

"I owe you. This is twice I owe you."

"That horse was doing pretty damn well keeping you in one piece."

"Nobody'll shoot him if I go back?"

"Not a chance. Nothing wrong with that horse—now. Besides,

I'm supposed to take you on to Mornay and get you out of trouble. On Ridley's orders."

"No question here," Carlo said. "If Randy's all right with him, I'll go."

"I think even Callie's going to stand by him. I think it's all right."

Guil and Burn had stopped. Tara gave Guil a hand up to Burn's back and Guil looked, in the dim light there was, fairly done in, head down, arm across his middle for a moment. <Pain> was evident, not bad, but there, and it was clear to Danny that Guil and Tara had pushed matters hard getting up here.

He wished there was something he could do to reciprocate. There wasn't, except if he could guide them to where they could settle the problem of the lorrie-lie or whatever it was. But they weren't fit for a chase: Burn wasn't going beyond a walking pace, Guil not favoring any jolting right now, he was well sure, and Burn having done more carrying of his rider than a nighthorse wanted to do on a steep road. There was little chance, Danny thought, that the creature was going to put itself in their sights tonight—and he personally hoped they just got to shelter. Guil didn't need any excitement that might set Burn to rapid moving—besides that, the daylight was going and the snow was still coming down.

Meanwhile they followed his and Carlo's backtrail to the wide road and followed the road beside the pond, within snow-obscured view of the <tree where he'd seen the nest>—and when they reached the vantage he'd had, the nest was plain to see, covered in snow, a lump in an otherwise symmetrical tree.

They left the road and came to the very foot of it. No tracks led to it, though it stood apart from other trees. Danny looked up, searching for life in the ambient all the same, remembering how it had shifted things on him—

A shot went off. Spook went straight up and Carlo grabbed for a double-handed and desperate hold. *Tara* had fired, discharged her rifle up into the nest.

Nothing resulted but echoes, a spatter of snow, a fall of shattered twigs.

Bones followed, one pair with blue and white plaid still clinging. The missing man in the village, Danny thought, might have worn a shirt like that.

But that would mean a *large* hunting range. And a beast that traveled far in its hunting. And didn't fear a village.

"Damn sure no leaf-eater," Guil said, scanning the other trees around about them.

But it wasn't in the nest. There was no blood, no sound, nothing to indicate Tara's upward shot had hit a living creature.

<Shelter> was Danny's thought. It found agreement from Carlo. But something else was going on with the ambient, horses and riders <listening,> transparent as the winds. Danny made himself very still and tried to slip Cloud into the effort, but Cloud was unnerved and broke it up.

"Sorry," Danny said.

"It's all right," Guil said.

"It's hard to get an image of." <Sending in the woods. Land rippling in his perception. Carlo—>

He tried not to spill beyond his intention to inform them. But Guil <wanted.>

"Rest of it," Guil said.

<Rippling sending. Carlo and Spook.>

"It blotted things out," Tara said. "Damned strong." Danny was <frustrated.> He didn't understand what it had done. And *he'd* experienced it.

"It can blot out another sending," Guil said. "Take another sending *out* of the ambient it passes on. A horse can do it."

"But a horse has to learn," Tara said. "This thing's got tricks. Complicated tricks. Like Guil says, it's smart, it's a predator, and I hope to hell there's just one of them. Last thing we need is a colony going."

Thoughts hitting the ambient were stirring real apprehension now from Spook. <Shadow against the stars. Anger. Ripples and shadows in the ambient. Shadows moving. Running. Blood—and hunting, down a wooded road.>

"Get ourselves settled in tonight," Tara said, and they left the place, through a snow-fall that stuck to eyelashes and piled up on clothing and horses' backs. Tracks were filling in, even the ones they'd made. But there was a trace where something large had crossed the snow, a depression too snowed-over to read much of it.

But the horses didn't like it, and there were unpleasant images, horses taking information from each other, Danny thought, fast and furious—*he* was learning, too, of a feud, horse and beast, that had gone on for days around Evergreen, out in the woods.

The seniors were learning from him and Carlo, the same fast, disjointed and sometimes exceedingly accurate way, about the village, the camp, the blacksmith shop—

<Brionne,> the image came, a command, a question, he thought from Tara; and it was Carlo's image that came back, <house with fine furniture, Brionne in bed, awake and talking to him—>

The ambient wasn't happy about that. Not at all.

"We'd better get over there," Tara said. "Soon as we can."

"The camp-boss told me to get Carlo on to Mornay," Danny said. "I'm not so sure."

"Not a good idea right now," Guil said.

"More riders at Mornay than Evergreen," Tara said. "Fewer further on."

Danny wished to himself he'd aimed better. They weren't good thoughts that were populating the ambient right now, <danger to the villages and to rider camps.> He'd had the chance to prevent it. *He* could have stopped and made sure of his target. If he'd known it wasn't a lorrie-lie. *If* he'd known what to do first and what second in Carlo's likelihood of rushing off a cliff or whatever other danger he could find out there.

"My fault," Carlo said, "isn't it?"

"The pair of us," Danny said honestly. "You don't rush around out here. You just don't hurry." He became excruciatingly conscious he was repeating Guil's advice to *him* last summer, and thought Guil might remember it, as he hadn't clearly remembered the green kid who'd asked him how to get good jobs.

The green kid who'd survived up here as far as he had, all on Guil's advice.

The green kid who didn't need a senior's advice to feel the hazard as they came up that logging road and passed beside the shelter.

"Don't like this," Carlo said to him quietly. "I really don't think Spook likes it."

"They know," Danny said, smelling something he'd never smelled, a scent heightened by the horse's sense of it as they came up along the logging road.

"It's gotten in," Tara said, as they passed by the blind wall. "Too big for the chimney."

"Seems so," Guil said.

They rounded the corner toward the door itself. The horses weren't advising them of any presence there. <Vacant shelter> was how it seemed. But the smell was there despite the snow, beyond human noses, maybe, to detect.

The shelter looked normal. The latch-string was out, which would pull the inner latch up and let a traveler inside.

"Guil," Tara said, "you get out of the way. —Danny, you open it."

He didn't object, though Cloud wasn't happy. It was just a case of taking no unnecessary chances, putting someone who could move fast in the right spot, and having Tara standing behind him with a rifle that packed a high-caliber punch—in case the beast had dug in under a wall and gained the place for a den, and in case it was capable of lying in wait. He stepped up to the door, wanting <Cloud beside him,> and pulled the latch-string and pulled the door open.

The place, he could see even in the gathering dusk, was a shambles.

"It's gotten in," he said. He had no trouble at all smelling the creature at this range. Bedding was all over the floor. He hoped that accounted for all the scraps and rags of cloth. "Shall I see if the supplies survived?"

"Got a match?" Guil asked him from the doorway.

He had. He went in as Tara took up a position to the inside of the doorway and Cloud came all the way in, smelling both <bad smell> and <dark in the trees> and on the defensive.

A fire ready to use, the ordinary and courteous condition in which one left a shelter's fireplace, had been scattered around the hearth. A tin of cooking oil had popped its metal stopper and spilled, and in the expediency of getting a fire going, he opened the flue, stuffed a few pieces of oil-soaked wood and an oil-soaked blanket in and touched a match to it.

It lit the room. The damage was thorough, flour thrown about the walls and ceiling—cots broken, absolute wreckage.

"Hell of a mess." That was from Tara. "This isn't vermin damage. They'd have gotten the oil and the flour. Vermin have never been in here."

Cloud sniffed a torn mattress and jerked his head up with a snort of disapproval. Guil and Carlo were both in the doorway against a backdrop of dusk near darkness.

"Vermin were supper for this thing," Guil said. "Search the edges. Look for an entry hole. And be careful."

Danny started looking along the edges of the fireplace. Tara made a faster circuit, kicking bedding aside, shoving the broken cots out of the way, making Cloud dodge her path. Flicker came in and helped <smelling for burrow> all around the edges of the cabin.

"No entryway," Tara said. "That thing came in the way *we* did and left the same way; the flue was still shut, and something that size wouldn't fit up there, anyway."

"Damn, damn, damn," Guil said. Carlo said nothing at all. And Danny was putting together a scene he didn't at all like.

"You think it just pulled the latch-string to get in?"

"Curiosity might have pulled that string," Tara said, and in the dying light of the blaze he'd made in the fireplace she ran a gloved hand over dents and scratches around the doorframe. There were others, Danny saw, by pulling the door back, on the inside of the door surface. "That door," Tara said, "took some abuse. Must have been shut, at some point—can't figure why else the dents inside. Maybe spooked it. Till it figured out to shove the latch up. By accident, maybe."

Bad news, Danny was thinking. Cabins were safe with latch-strings out. No creature on the planet knew how to pull the cord and simultaneously handle the door while the latch was up. Complicated operation. A ridden nighthorse knew somewhat *how* to do it, but didn't have the right equipment to make it work. Lorrie-lies had fingers, but didn't have the brain.

"Camp outside tonight," Tara said. "It's foul in there. Let the wind blow through it."

He didn't want to stay in the shelter with the stench, either. He shooed Cloud out to clean air and made a fast search for supplies, found a blanket, some cord, a metal drop-lid bin of the size to store grain, which should have resisted pilferage—though there was grain on the floor.

"Spring lock's been opened." He used a stick of the scattered firewood to pry the lid up and had his pistol in hand when he lifted it. There was grain inside that hadn't been spoiled: the drop lid had caught a lot of blows, but the bin, while the lock was open, seemed to have frustrated the creature both in its wood-reinforced weight and in its uninteresting, vegetable contents. He threw another couple of sticks on the fading fire to maintain enough light to see by and began to carry grain out on two battered metal plates that he found in the tangled bedding.

The horses in the main were fastidious enough to smell over the grain he put down on the snow, but Spook had far less hesitation to go nose-down: Spook's ribs were in evidence under his winter coat—he'd been eating small catches, Danny guessed, but nothing but berries and lichen, else, and precious little to keep his gut full. The other horses were in good shape and might skip a meal, but Spook was willing to shove higher-status horses for his share of the grain, and the other horses weren't driving him off for his manners, sensing a horse more desperate than challenging for status.

Meanwhile Carlo had brought firewood from the rick outside and, with Guil advising him, was doing the one necessary thing he could tolerably well manage. Tara began unpacking her kit—and they were in business as a camp, just that fast, with a fire about to get going, snow for melting, a blanket for Carlo and enough guns and horses to make sure the beast that had devastated the cabin was their quarry and not the other way around tonight.

"Shut the door when you've finished," Tara said. "No sense drawing visitors tonight, and we could need it tomorrow. When we leave, we'll put the pots in the drop bin and leave the door open wide. Fastest way I know to clean up the mess."

Courting vermin was the damnedest way he could think of to do housecleaning. But it made a certain sense, and *this* junior rider didn't want to have to scrub it down. He put Carlo to helping him cut evergreen boughs for beds for them and the horses—peculiar thing to be doing, using a perfectly intact rider-shelter for a windbreak, but with the green boughs underneath them, and with the blankets over them and their horses next to them, they'd do all right.

He assured Carlo so, catching anxiousness on Carlo's part. It was a lot of changes for a kid in one day. But he knew how that was.

And he knew, after he'd had a chance to sit down at supper with the senior riders and get their view of matters, that Spook had *had* no choice but the course he'd run—trying to get his rider down the mountain, down the only gap in what was otherwise a rocky face opposite Evergreen, once the truck route had iced and drifted shut.

Same way Guil and Tara had come up, by way of a series of logging cuts and a set of trails Tara knew—they'd come when they'd gotten his message about Spook, and realized they were in trouble. So he forgave Tara if there was anything at all to forgive. And he wasn't consulted, exactly, about their plan to hunt the beast he'd wounded, but he thoroughly agreed that they should try at first light to account for it here, and that if they couldn't, he and Guil should get immediately to Evergreen and advise Ridley of the danger.

"The other two of us will go on to Mornay," Tara said, "and advise them down the road to relay on the warning. We've got to find this thing."

The horses settled in a close ring about them, winter though it was, and although Burn and Flicker made a close-knit pair: it was safety at issue, and <horses watching the night> and <horses and riders keeping warm, snow falling, making white on nighthorse backs, white on blankets.>

Carlo didn't show a disposition to sleep immediately, but he didn't seem to track a great deal, either. Carlo leaned against Spook's shoulder and the ambient grew warm and strange with a new rider's amazement at the creature settled next to him, at the <woods around them> and the sense of <belonging to each other.>

"Harper never used to call that horse a name," Guil mused when the evening was winding down toward sleep. "Used to say it wasn't anybody's business. Damn-you-horse was the closest to a name I heard him use. Spook's a good name. Horse that can't be caught."

Carlo's hand was under Spook's mane. Spook was nosing his rider in the ribs.

They were in that lost-in-each-other stage that Danny had grown up thinking was a boy-girl folly. Then he'd learned what that horse and rider tie felt like—and he understood. Whatever Guil said was lost on Carlo right now. And Guil shook his head, knowing the same truth, beyond a doubt.

Quiet night, Ridley thought, listening to the silence about camp—silence in the woods, in the barracks, at the fireside. They'd risked going off-watch at the den and gone inside, enjoyed a quiet supper, and had no alarms. Jennie played by the fire, and Randy Goss, cheered by his promise, perhaps, that having no news out of the ambient was a sign Carlo *was* on horseback and traveling far and fast, got down on the floor and taught Jennie a game of squares and crosses with a piece of charcoal on the stones.

It was a new game for Jennie, who after a terrible day and a worried evening was laughing and giggling with the first human being even remotely near her age who'd sheltered in the rider camp.

It was good to hear. It made Callie laugh. Callie was on her way to accepting the boy, no matter his relatives: the plain truth was, Callie *liked* kids, and the plainer truth was, he himself was an easy mark for a youngster needing help.

When the games wore down and eyes grew heavy they put the Goss boy to bed in Fisher's room, figuring Dan wouldn't mind, and of the several rooms, it was clean, dusted, and they'd opened the door vents to let the heat in from the main room.

He put Jennie to bed, with Callie waiting in the doorway.

"Is Randy going to stay here?" Jennie wanted to know.

"Seems likely," Callie said. "He might. If he's good and minds what I say."

"I hope he is," Jennie said, and snuggled down into the pillows.

Ridley pulled the covers up and kissed his daughter good night. He and Callie went to bed, and he and Callie made love for the first time since Fisher had come to the barracks. The ambient was that quiet.

For the first time since Dan Fisher had arrived at their gate there was peace in the camp.

Chapter
— XXI —

Cloud twitched and brought his head up, an earthquake at Danny's back, and Danny came straight out of a dream of endless grass and open skies to see, in the dark of night, Tara Chang leaning toward the fire, adding another stick to the small blaze.

"Too quiet," Tara remarked to Guil, on whose face the firelight cast a slight light. "Yeah," Danny heard Guil say. Guil's eyes were half-open.

And having gotten maybe an hour or so of sleep, and considering they were dealing with a beast that could manipulate latches and camouflage itself in the ambient, Danny found himself wider awake.

"I'll stay on watch a while," he said to Tara.

"Trust the horses," Tara said. "They don't get surprised. No need to lose sleep."

"We don't know this thing." If he hadn't been waked on the sudden he wouldn't have argued with a senior rider, but Tara just frowned and looked off into the dark. Guil had shut his eyes, but he wasn't asleep: the ambient was too live with his thoughts: <Tara and Danny across the fire.>

"Understand," Tara said. "Sending you on. I'd no idea about the horse. Or anything wrong."

He couldn't come back with what he thought was Tara's real reason, <Guil lying sick>and <Tara wanting Guil.> He tried to keep his thoughts out of the ambient and had no luck at all. "I knew that," he said. "Figured it out, anyway. I shouldn't have moved from the shelter. Hell, I should have shoved Carlo there out the door and we'd have been fine."

"Except what's moved in on the mountain."

"Yes, ma'am. That's for sure."

Tara gave a short laugh. "I'm no villager."

"No—" Ma'am was his mother's manners. "No," he said, unadorned.

"Get some rest. We'll fix things tomorrow."

"Right," he said, having presumed as far as he wanted to on senior riders' patience, and he leaned back against Cloud's side.

Tara settled down against Flicker. Carlo was out cold, in the ambient just barely, in that very faint way you could pick up someone sound asleep, at very close range.

Carlo *and* Spook were out, Danny judged, Carlo exhausted from nights of worry, and Spook from nights of exhausting Carlo and the rest of Evergreen village.

Fighting a solitary war with whatever-it-was. Keeping it penned up here, near the lake, because it *wasn't* going to drive him off the mountain and away from the rider he'd gone through frozen hell and climbed a mountain to choose.

Stubborn horse. Very stubborn, canny horse.

So was the horse he was leaning against, the one keeping him warm in the icy cold air. He pillowed his head against Cloud and, patting a muscled shoulder, received a rumbling contentment-sound in return.

Jennie had a very scary kind of nightmare. There was a girl, a very angry girl, who *wanted* a horse to come to her. And she, Jennie, was in the camp on the other side of the wall when a sending came wanting Rain, but *she* wouldn't let this girl have Rain. Papa said—papa said you didn't own horses. Horses just were. You got along with horses.

She was in this girl's house and she told her that. She told her so very firmly, and told her she couldn't have Rain and she was sorry, but that was the way it was. And the girl was very angry and told her to get out.

So she flew back over the camp wall and told Rain he shouldn't listen to this girl.

But something listened. Something came close, and it might be a horse. But she didn't think so. And she flew back to that girl in the doctor's house and stood in the middle of the room and wanted to warn her this wasn't a good idea, and she shouldn't call out beyond the wall like that.

Then something waked her up and she was in her own bed and mama was in the doorway and so was papa.

"Jennie," mama said. "Jennie, —what's going on?"

"I don't know," she said, and papa said, "It's that damned *girl.* The horse must be back."

"Is Dan back?"

"No," mama said, and sat down on the side of her bed and set a hand on the other side of her. "You stay out of the ambient, Jennie. Something's going on out there."

"It's really real?"

"It's real. You don't go out there."

"But she wants Rain!"

"Rain won't go to her," papa said. "The ambient's just really loud tonight. The horses are upset. I'll go out and calm things down."

"Probably both of us should," mama said. And Randy had shown up in her bedroom doorway, dressed, but with his shirt half on. "You stay inside and see Jennie stays inside," mama told Randy.

"It's my sister," Randy said. He sounded scared. "It's my sister. I know what she sounds like."

Then the bell was ringing again. Jennie thought confusedly, Serge didn't tie the bell again. Then another bell was going. And another. The ambient went terribly <upset,> then, her mama and papa and Randy all scared at once.

"That's the breakthrough alarm," papa said, and she remembered papa and mama had always told her if she ever heard all the bells, the gate's big and little ones and the church tower and the fire bell all at once, then she should lock everything down tight and get the box of shells and set them on the table.

And never, never, never go out to the horses.

But *Rain* was out there.

Rain *needed* her.

"You stay *put!*" papa said in his harshest tone. "Randy, can you do anything with your sister?"

"I don't know."

"Yellowflower," mama said. And papa:

"Jennie, put your clothes on. Get dressed. Right now."

"Everybody's in my room!"

"We're going over to the village."

"What about the horses?" She *wasn't* leaving Rain. She'd never been so scared in her life.

Then half the bells that had been ringing so frantically stopped—leaving just the church bells and one other.

"Is it done?" she asked.

"No," papa said. "Get dressed!"

Burn got up all of a sudden—which left his sleeping rider scrambling awake, sore side and all, and reaching after his rifle and struggling, with it for a prop, toward his feet, as the rest of the horses surged to their feet and the ambient that had been very quiet suddenly got louder by reason of one young horse that was overwhelming it with question and fright. There was the sound of bells, was what it sounded like, echoing from somewhere distant. Or maybe it was coming through the ambient, which was <there,> and more lively about them than it had been. <Fear> was contagious.

"Danny, get him quiet," Guil said, catching his breath, and still leaning on the gun instead of relying on it for protection, because it seemed to him that the danger, like those bells, was very far off.

And it seemed to him that it came from the direction of Evergreen.

Evergreen—where Brionne Goss was resident.

Not a good thing. Not at all a good thing.

"That's Evergreen," Tara said. "What did the ride take you, Danny?"

"Half a day. Six hours at least. I stopped some." <Depressions in snow. Carlo falling off. Danny riding fast.>

Six hours' ride from here, if Danny's account was straight, and neither Danny nor Carlo had been lazing along when they'd covered that distance.

"We've got to move," Guil said, in the full knowledge there was no way he could last on that kind of ride. Bells in the night were a cry for help, from anyone in range. It seemed to him he *did* hear them with his own ears—and it was possible, given the folds of the mountain that made it that long a run for a horse.

It wasn't saying the beast used the roads. It was past midnight. Since dark—it had had time to move, and *it* might well have had a place it wanted to go.

The same place Spook, until tonight, had been discouraging it from going.

Half the bells that had been ringing were quiet now, a sudden, frightening kind of quiet, but the bells of the church and the mayoralty were still ringing. In want of other remedies Darcy Schaffer went about brewing tea. Brionne had come downstairs in the dark, distraught and unhappy, as small wonder the girl would be, with alarms in the night. It felt to be blowing up a storm—which didn't entirely account for the breakthrough alarm, but it could well be the cause of such an event—creatures getting desperate as they did before one of winter's truly deadly storms, and all it took was someone near the walls on the forest side not watching their cellars or some warehouse foundation eroding. Creatures didn't dig well in the rubble fill under the dirt, but now and again water made an incursion.

It was amazingly quiet, yet, but she supposed the barometer at the mayoralty might have dropped and advised the night guards. The air had that feeling about it, and with murder on her doorstep this morning and Brionne's brothers running, one to his death outside (or to a horse: that was the whisper in town) and the other to the rider camp to stay—small wonder Brionne had complained of bad dreams.

Occasion of her own uneasy rest—the Mackeys had come to call in the afternoon. They disavowed all knowledge of their son's accusations, and wanted to assure Brionne that they were still taking care of Randy.

"He's in the rider camp," Brionne had said in icy tones, with an aplomb which she had inwardly applauded. "The riders have him. You don't."

Even that rebuff hadn't set Mary Hardesty back. "But he'll have a place with us when they straighten this ridiculous mess out. Our son thinks now he was mistaken. He thinks it could have been another miner he saw quarreling with that Riggs person."

A wonder Rick Mackey hadn't come in for stitches after some fall down the stairs today. She'd put various stitches in him during his growing up, usually for falls on the Mackey stairs. So Mary Hardesty had always claimed, and she'd bet any amount that Rick and his father had gone at it.

She *hated* that woman.

And of course Brionne's coolness to their well-wishes didn't dissuade Van Mackey from offering to see that the Tarmin properties were taken care of and that the forge was working.

"You think Rick can do that?" she'd been cold-blooded enough to ask. Rick's lack of meaningful competence was well known even outside of Evergreen, by what she knew, but Mary Hardesty never flinched.

"Well, until we can hire help. In the girl's name, of course."

She'd gotten them out the door shortly after that, smiling all the while she was wondering whether the Mackeys had heard about Ernest Riggs' proposal to her and whether *that* had been the reason for Riggs' violent demise.

They never had found the body.

She poured the tea. She added spirits to her own. She set a cup in front of Brionne, who sat in Faye's nightgown and Faye's lace-collared robe. Brionne's golden curls were tousled from the pillow—Brionne had banged her shin and overset a chair in the dark in the lower hall, scaring the wits out of her.

But Brionne didn't ask about the goings-on, or the bell, probably because it was perfectly clear that there was an alarm, as there would have been in Tarmin, Darcy was sure. Brionne didn't seem to want to acknowledge the crisis, after embarrassing herself in the lower hall, and Darcy didn't mention her own apprehensions of a breakthrough and reasons the marshal and the village guards might be abroad tonight. It wasn't their business, after all. They had their latches tight, and her house was near the rider wall, not the outside, so there was no need to check the foundations for burrows from beyond the village confines. They'd done their part.

She sat down at the table with Brionne. "It feels like blowing up a storm, doesn't it?" she asked, to fill the silence. "It's been snowing all day."

"I don't care," Brionne said. And apropos of no remark of hers: "He had no right to go out there! He *hates* me."

He was very clearly the brother. And that was at least a clue to Brionne's state of mind. She didn't know whether it was the truth, what Brionne had said this morning about her elder brother shooting their father. But she had no reason to doubt it, either. "Honey," she said gently, "don't think about it. You're safe here. And you don't ever have to go with him. We'll go to the judge. We'll be sure he hasn't any rights over you."

Brionne wiped her eyes.

"I hate him."

"Don't hate people, honey. It's not good for you. —You know what we should do? We should both go to the store tomorrow. You're strong enough, aren't you? And we'll get you a new coat, and some yarn for sweaters if we can't find one we like. What color would you want?"

"I want a leather coat. Like riders have."

"What about for church?"

"A red one."

"And for Saturday nights? We used to have supper at the tavern on Saturdays. And everybody shows off their nice clothes. What would you like to wear?"

Brionne seemed to be thinking. She stared off into nowhere.

"He hears me," she said. "He hears me. I can still talk to him. He *won't* go with my brother."

"Brionne. Honey."

"He'll come for me. He will!"

Horses. Adolescent fancies. Children pressed to the limit by a violence within the family that had finally found a way to attract outside attention. There was nothing, on the surface, amiss with Carlo Goss. But there'd been something deadly wrong in that household. Maybe it was Carlo. Maybe it had been the parents. But Brionne sat talking about going off with horses when this morning she'd accused her brother of murder. There was a certain tendency toward denial in the Goss children, which she could plainly see. But knowing that, she could afford her dear Brionne a little extra understanding and bring the girl to love her.

The thing was to humor the swings from fact to fancy and provide the girl a clear baseline of reality.

There was a battered pack of cards in the kitchen cabinet—hours and hours of solitaire had worn them smooth-edged. But she took them out and began to deal them.

"Do you play cards, dear?"

Peterson said they couldn't open the gate, that they *daren't* open the outside gates and he wouldn't allow it: even relying on the lesser gate, the rider-gate swung too wide and they wouldn't risk a swarm such as happened at Tarmin.

So they had brought a logging saw, one logger on the village side of the camp wall and Ridley on his with the other grip, ripping through the substantial vertical post that, buried deep in ice and earth, barriering the camp and the village apart from each other, so that no horse could pass it. It had taken too damned long, first arguing with the marshal about going around to the gates and then getting the saw from the supply store, because nobody wanted to go about the street to open the store, but now that they had it, the teeth made fast progress. The log went down in short order and Ridley and the logger, a man named Jackson, grabbed it up and carried it through to the village side, where they tossed it to the side of the gate.

Slip followed through that gate no horse had ever been able to use, not from the village founding.

Callie and the Goss boy, Jennie and Rain and Shimmer came across, too, the horses in a rush as if they expected the gate to shut or the pole to reappear.

It was scary in this dark and strange business. Jennie was scared. Rain was scared. Ridley had no trouble admitting the same to his daughter and anyone else who might ask. With a breakthrough warning gone silent like that—with the unprecedented measure of taking down the barrier between camp and village to get the horses through without using the outside gates—even a child could understand that this had never happened before, and a rider child a lot faster than that.

"Shut that gate," Peterson said. "Bolt it good."

"We'd better take a look down at the main gate," Ridley said. To this hour they didn't know why the bell had stopped. The only encouragement was the lack of specific alarm from the horses, who carried an ambient void of native presence around the village. But Serge Lasierre had undoubtedly rung the alarm for some reason. And stopped—for some reason.

"I haven't wanted to scatter people out and about," Peterson said. "Could be Serge is locked in. Could be there's been a tunneling down there—we don't know what the hell."

"I want you and Jackson there both behind walls. Leave the streets entirely to us."

"We'll be in the office."

"Good. —Randy, I want you to go with the marshal right now. Get behind solid doors."

"I'd rather—" Randy began.

"*Go* with the marshal."

"Yes, sir," Randy said, having believed him about obeying the camp-boss and maybe having caught the warning in the ambient. Jennie, meanwhile, was a worry he couldn't dismiss: Jennie had the one horse that, if they could keep him from panic—and separating him from Jennie wouldn't help—was the loudest, strongest-sending horse of their three.

He swung up onto Slip's back and rode to one side of Jennie as Callie rode to the other, down the middle of the village street, through a snow-fall that hazed the few lights left in a tightly shuttered village.

"It's <scary,"> Jennie said. "Everybody's <hiding and scared.">

"Don't babble," Callie reminded her. "Talk when you *need* a word. The ambient's enough, miss."

Frightened people were awake everywhere. The shutters were latched. People behind those shutters had guns, every one of them, as much a hazard to them as to any swarm of vermin that might have gotten in. The Schaffer house wasn't in this end of the street, for which Ridley was entirely grateful. It was down where the marshal and Randy had taken refuge—and where he hoped there wasn't any native creature the Goss girl could pick up. It had seemed quiet down there, and it still seemed quiet at their backs.

But the warehouses and the granary that lay right along the rider camp gate and those running behind the houses and along the rider camp wall, and those behind the church and the public offices, were a warren they might have to go into. Those would be the target of a breakthrough and a swarm of vermin, if it once sensed food stored there as well as the living food within the houses. The grain-eaters weren't usually the vanguard of trouble; usually it was the meat-eaters that came through, and the others followed, but the grain-pests were equally as dangerous, partly because they were more numerous, and partly because some of them weren't averse to a varied diet.

They passed The Evergreen, which wasn't shuttered, and which cast lamplight through its glass-windowed doors. Patrons were inside, huddling in a <fear> and <challenge> that blazed as bright as the lamplight into the ambient. Jennie, who'd kept quiet after her mother's reprimand, asked meekly,

"They're not doing right, are they?"

"No," Ridley said. "Those are fools. We look out for people doing necessary jobs, first, like us and the marshal and Serge. Second, people taking care of themselves, like in those houses, locked down tight. *Fools* come last on our list, always."

They passed the blacksmith shop and the Mackeys' house, where God knew the state of affairs and he didn't care to.

Then the miner barracks, that was at least to outward appearances shuttered tight and proper.

After that came one warehouse set back from Serge's place and then the Santezes and the Lasierres, who were closest to the wall. Things felt all right there.

They came all the way to the gate, where he saw nothing—nothing but the tracks one might expect about the elevated stairway to the gate-guard's tower. Serge's tracks. Maybe another man's. They were just slightly rounded over by new snow. Serge had gone up there not a long time ago—maybe talked to some other man. Those tracks were trampled over. He'd need more light.

But Slip didn't like what he smelled here. Truly didn't like it. Neither did Rain and Shimmer.

"Serge?" he called out.

There was no answer. There was nothing in the ambient to advise him Serge was there—but Serge might be unconscious. Might just have slipped on the icy steps and hit his head. He *hoped* that was the case.

He slid down from Slip's back at the foot of the tower steps. He had had a shell in the rifle chamber all the way down the street, and he carried the gun carefully and had it ready as he climbed the steps as far as the first turn.

What—met him—wasn't a body. It might have been one before something ripped it to shreds and draped it on the rail.

He spun about and took the stairs at a skid. Slip was at the bottom of the steps and he didn't even think clearly about launching himself for Slip's back, he just landed there.

He didn't need to explain to Callie or Jennie. What he'd seen, they'd seen, and Jennie had never imagined the like. She was <scared> and Rain was <scared> with her.

<"Easy,"> he said. <"Easy.> Keep Rain calm."

"Was <that> <Serge?"> Faint voice. Tremulous voice.

"Most likely," Callie said firmly. "Look for tracks going away, Jennie-cub!"

"Is <*that*> them?"

In fact it was: Ridley got off again to take a close look at <long-footed tracks in snow> on the *other* side of the stairs, where something had—not vaulted the rail: the snow was still intact there—jumped from higher up, was what the intruder had done. He found the depression that indicated a jump clear from the next-to-last tier of the steps, <tracks rapidly filling with snow, tracks going away from the landing it had made and going toward the houses.> He let Slip smell the trail.

Slip snorted and brought his head up, dancing about nervously as Ridley swung up. Slip had smelled it twice, now, and still didn't have a clear image of it. Shimmer walked back around and smelled the stairs and the railing, and didn't have an image, either.

"Where did it go?" Jennie asked—justified question.

"Houses. It jumps and climbs." <Lorrie-lie,> was what he was thinking. There was a snow ridge across the tracks and he rode Slip through it—picked up the trail of footprints on the other side, both scent and tracks, until it reached the Lasierres' porch.

The Lasierres seemed <alive people, quiet inside the house.> He didn't want to disturb them or have them unbolting doors to the night—and possibly they'd caught the disturbance and warning from their horses out on the street and were staying close by their fireside.

They made a circuit of the house. He rode in front. Callie and Jennie rode at a little distance back so they could get a vantage for firing at anything <dropping down on them.>

The tracks that had disappeared at the porch didn't show up on any side. He considered the gap between the Lasierres' roof and the Santezes' roof, and it was wider than the gaps between most. But if whatever it was wasn't lurking up there—it had jumped it and headed further up the street.

Silent in the ambient.

Slip sucked in a breath and blew it out again. <Bad smell.> There was *that* to track it by, a muskiness Slip amplified for his senses.

Jennie was aching with <questions.> And <keeping quiet.>

"Horses don't know what it is," Callie said to her. "They've no clear image. We've never seen those tracks before, and they've never smelled it."

"Let's go back up the street," Ridley said. "Get away from the overhangs."

They did that, and rode up again past The Evergreen. "Fool-time," Ridley said. He slid down, his dismount bringing Slip to a halt, and with Callie and Jennie to watch the roof edges, he went up the steps to try the door.

Locked, at least. Light came brightly through the frosted glass. He could see patrons inside through the clear lines in the etching. He could hear the talking stop as he knocked.

"It's Ridley Vincint!" he called out to the occupants. "You don't have to open the door—just take your drinks and get away from the glass! Get into the back room and lock the doors! Don't come out! Something's inside the walls and it's traveling on the roofs! It's killed Serge Lasierre! We don't know what it is!"

A buzz of dismay broke out inside. They'd heard him. He didn't wait for anyone to acknowledge the warning and he didn't wait to argue or provide details. He went quickly down the steps and vaulted onto Slip's back.

Telling the marshal had to be the next step.

Then all of them had to patrol the street until they had daylight to help them find a target.

And they could only hope daylight didn't signal it to hole up somewhere in the village.

It was twenty-one and a stack of counters. Poker and twenty-one was what Darcy had played with Mark when they'd courted. She played twenty-one with Brionne between occasional moments that the storm-feeling grew terrible.

At such moments Brionne would rise from the table and pace the floor in an angry frenzy.

"Go *away!*" Brionne shouted now, and leapt to her feet, and looked up toward street level, which was well above the floor of the house's sunken kitchen. *"Go away!"* It was a scream, a shriek against which Darcy steeled her nerves, having determined that ignoring the behavior was the best course.

"Come back to the table, dear."

"They're hunting, is what they're doing! The horses are hunting. But it's too clever for them!"

"Dear—"

"I hope my brother *dies!"* Brionne cried. "You hear me? I hope he dies!"

"Dear—"

"Get away from me!"

Possibly hysterics had worked in a family that didn't have normal mechanisms for a young girl getting attention. Perhaps that had been the mother's tactic. Or perhaps shattering the other party's nerves had been the way to win acquiescence or attention in that family. She refused to react at all. "Pick up your hand, honey. This could go on a long time. Sit down and concentrate."

"My brother's out there. My little brother. I can *hear* him."

"If the horses have come over, I do imagine they've brought him, too. I don't need to hear the horses to understand that."

"I hear them! I hear everything they're thinking. They're thinking, Let's not let Brionne associate with us! We're too good for Brionne. *We're* too important! They hate me! They're too *stupid* to know I hear everything they're thinking! *Shut up, do you hear me?"*

Pans littered the kitchen. This time Brionne picked up an iron skillet, whirled it around and let fly.

It hit the bottom cupboards and dented the door.

"Your deal," Darcy said calmly. "Don't pay attention to disagreeable people, dear. That's the way to handle such things."

"Do *you* hear them?"

"No, dear, I'm sure I don't. I don't hear horses."

"I do. I hear them perfectly clearly. *You hear me, Randy? You're a brat! You're an unspeakable little brat!"*

"*Do* sit down. I'd rather play cards than listen to them. Hadn't you? They're not important people."

"They're hateful. "

"I know, dear, but it's just no good worrying about other people. No one else in town can hear them. Whatever they think. So just tell them they're hateful and sit down and let's play cards."

"I don't like cards."

"Well, what *would* you like to do?"

"I don't know."

"Why don't we go into the sitting room and I'll read to you."

"Because I don't want to!"

"You'd rather sit here and mope."

"Yes!"

"What would make you happy? —Would you like to go to the store tomorrow? I'll bet some of Faye's things would fit you. And then you and I can go to the store and buy anything you like."

Brionne drifted back to the table. "Anything?"

"The finest things in Evergreen. You and I will go to the tavern Saturday night and we'll get a table. That's where *everyone* comes. And we'll have the nicest clothes and all the young people will think you're the prettiest girl on the mountain."

Brionne sat down. "Do they have nice things in the store?"

"Oh, very nice. And if you don't see what you like, we'll go to the tailor and pick out patterns."

"I want a fringed jacket. Just like the riders."

"Well, I'm sure no village girl ever had a fringed jacket."

"I *want* one."

A social disaster, Darcy thought. A religious calamity. Or a fashion. "We can *have* one made. Of red suede. Would you like that?"

There were gunshots. She knew gunshots. She flinched in spite of herself, and dealt out cards, not asking a girl who didn't know her own mind whether or not she would play.

"Someone's shooting," Brionne said.

"I'm sure it's the riders after vermin. It's perfectly fine." She arranged her cards. "Oh, I think I can beat you with this."

Brionne picked up hers and began to arrange her own hand. Brionne's frown grew. Darcy wished she knew how to cheat at cards. Brionne was far happier when she was winning, and she wished she could arrange that a certain amount of the time.

Brionne simply could not add worth a damn.

Gunshots again. A lot of them. Brionne hadn't wanted to go to bed. She'd wanted to sleep on the couch in the front room, but Darcy didn't want that, thinking of the windows there.

And very quietly she went and got the gun from Mark's office, and put it in the pocket of her robe, and came back to find Brionne sleeping, or seeming to, with her head down on her folded arms.

At least the bells had stopped, one by one. She hoped it meant all clear.

There'd been nervous fingers on triggers toward the forest wall—that had proved nothing, after they'd ridden breakneck to the site: the Jorgensons, opening their front door and shouting at them there'd been something trying their downstairs back window, but whether they'd fired first in a set of three houses claiming disturbance, was impossible to say. No one was killed and, in Ridley's earnest hopes, the nervous trigger fingers had scared the intruder back over the wall.

But their initial search had turned up nothing, and they'd been all the way back up to the marshal's office and, leaving Randy with the marshal's wife, picked up the marshal, the deputy, and the hunters, all armed with shotguns and rifles, to go on a house-by-house patrol.

In Ridley's hopes, too, no one would mistake *them* for intruders as they made their slow pass down the street, knocking on doors and giving out verbal warnings building by building and house by house—at least Peterson and Burani did that duty, the hunters escorting them with rifles and watching the perimeters of the porches while the three of them stayed on horseback in the middle of the street and watched the roof edges. He was aware of <fear> in the houses. He knew the horses made themselves felt when they went near a building—and he was glad to have two of the town guards and the marshal's wife and daughter, all with guns, to keep watch in the upper end of the village, near the Schaffer house, where he *didn't* want to take the horses.

<Girl> kept entering the ambient. It kept Jennie spooked, though Jennie was doing amazingly well at holding herself calm and not talking. Rain, between Slip and Shimmer, was behaving with

more sense than he'd have believed, part of that to Jennie's credit, as he meant to tell her at some moment on the other side of this.

But the snow-fall was the creature's friend if it was still in the village. Now and again the horses caught a whisper of something in the ambient that made all three of them in direct contact with the horses entirely uneasy, it was impossible to see what might be more than three buildings away, and hard to focus up into falling snow to check the roofs.

"Papa," Jennie said once, in a very quiet voice—a kid asking for reassurance; but with good reason.

"Hush," Callie said. "We know. We—"

Shots went off down the street. A flurry of them. Glass broke. He wanted—and Slip was off, Shimmer and Rain close behind, leaving the marshal and the hunters and the others to hold the middle of the street in mid-village as he and his went down the street, Jennie clinging like a burr to Rain's mane and staying up with them all the way to the black clot of scared men grouped in front of The Evergreen.

Those men, some with guns, were screaming in panic at others still inside to get down as sounds of breakage resounded in the building. The shattered glass still in the doors showed dark spatter against the light, more dark spatter showed on the walls and a chaotic wreckage of overturned tables lay inside—<blood> was in the ambient, <blood and anger> and something else. Alive. Hurt.

And <predatory.>

"Stay <here!"> he said to Callie and Jennie, and rode Slip for the side of the building, the <back of the tavern> and the <warehouses.>

He saw what looked and felt like <man hurt and running across the alley,> and in that split second too long knew it *wasn't* a man as it swarmed up an evergreen in the back of the tavern and up to the roof in a cloud of dislodged snow.

He let off a shot, and knew from <Callie and Jennie in front of the tavern> that they were aware of him, and aware of danger, <Callie's gun aiming for the roof edge.> His own shot hadn't hit anything—the ambient held *nothing* of the thing he'd seen, and that was something he'd never had happen to him or to Slip.

He rode Slip breakneck back around the building, fearing that at any moment the thing might come <plunging down on top of him>

or onto <Callie and Jennie out front> where the ambient from the miners was awash with <alarm> and the air was confused with shouting voices.

He reached Callie and Jennie, and shouted for order among the miners who, the worse for drink and the scare of their lives, were all trying to report and debate what had happened. Hell, he *knew* what had happened—broken glass and <something large and black and deadly crashing right through the damn tavern,> was what had happened, with carnage left and right.

Laughing at them. *Eluding* them.

Slip wanted <fight.> So did Shimmer, now. Shimmer's peace had been challenged, the vicinity of her winter den disturbed.

But something else had flared into the ambient: <girl> and <wanting> and <anger.> Jennie was outraged, <fighting bad girl> for Rain, for the ambient and her own place in it. It was *Jennie* first and foremost that that sending challenged, not them. It was his daughter who flung that challenge back, and the threat of Brionne Goss calling out and welcoming that thing that had come into *his* village, the threat of Brionne Goss challenging *his* daughter for whatever was at issue between them diminished the miners and their bloody calamity to a distant concern in his world.

"Dammit," he said to the clatter of miners shouting appeals and drunken orders at him, "get <inside!">

<*Jennie and Rain*> was the defiance at that instant blazing out into the snowy dark, a challenge to all comers, flung out with all the force a young fool horse could throw into a sending. Rain wanted <fight for his rider.> Rain wanted <territory around his rider for *his territory*.> Rain's rider wanted <bad girl going *away!* from her village>and knew no sensible fear of the threat: <*Jennie and Rain*> were in possession of the street and the village that was their world, and nothing could come into it and take it from them.

"Stay with us!" he ordered Jennie, and fought Jennie and Rain for the lead as they bolted up the street. He was just barely able to cut Rain off short and prevent a charge right to the Schaffer house as they reached the marshal's position. "Hold him, dammit, or get down!"

He'd never sworn at Jennie. He'd told her from earliest time that the way to stop a horse that wouldn't otherwise stop was to slide off, and she didn't do that—she wanted <stopping> and somehow made it stick, clinging to Rain and holding on, because she wouldn't *let* him go across that street toward the <bad girl wanting him.>

Neither was Slip going to lose one of his own herd, young male or not: Slip was sending a strong <Slip to the fore,> boss horse, and Shimmer came in with <*mama*> fit to chill the spine of an intruder.

They'd stopped in the midst of the marshal's group, guns all around them, guns aimed toward roof edges—when all of a sudden <challenge> rushed right *under* them and up the street.

"God!" Peterson cried.

Callie said, "It's found the passages."

Chapter
—XXII—

Run and run and run down the dark of the road, carrying only the rifle and a dozen shells—Danny ran by Cloud's side as Tara ran by Flicker's, the two of them, alone in the dark, ran and ran until the horses had caught their wind in this high altitude. It was swing up and ride until the horses were tiring under their weight, then run, then walk a distance, at last resort rest a moment, humans and horses alike, heads down, trying to warm the air they breathed. A rider *knew* the state of his horse's body as a horse knew his rider's. He knew what they could possibly do. He discovered reserves in both of them. And Guil had told them, go, run and ride, get there as fast as they could, stripped down to the absolute minimum they had to have in the Wild if something stranded one of them: a knife and a burning-glass, matches, Tara and him with rifles, the very least they could survive on and the lightest weight they could carry and make speed.

Guil and Carlo were coming behind them with the rest of their belongings at the best rate they could, a man healing of a wound and a new rider whose chief use to them was outright strength—carrying three riders' ordinary gear.

It was up to *them* to get to the village with horses that might make the difference—to prevent another Tarmin.

The bells had gone silent an hour ago at least.

Slip reared, then lunged at invisible threat under his feet as the creature raced right under them, and the <anger> went flaring off toward the church.

At that place, by the light of lanterns hung on the village hall posts, two men stood on watch with shotguns.

But more volunteers were actually heading down into the passages, by the church front access, to try to get a shot at it point-blank. Hunters had volunteered for that harrowing post, village-siders accustomed to standing their ground in dicey situations, and Ridley entirely gave them their due: *he* didn't want to be in their position at this precise instant.

Jennie was with him and Slip, <scared for mama>; and Callie and Shimmer were down almost at the church along the course of the tunnel. "Now!" he heard from Callie, signaling presence right under Shimmer's feet, and *"Now!"* the shout came from the men on the porch, the signal for the hunters in the tunnel to open the door to the church access.

There was a muffled blast of shotgun fire below.

And for a moment the presence in the passages seemed to have split in four, behind them, ahead of them, under the church, under the row of houses—

Rain jumped sideways in startlement and Jennie was <down, with the wind knocked out of her, head hurt.> But Rain took up guard right over her, and Ridley, ignoring the temptation to look to his injured daughter, was trying to keep a view simultaneously of all the perimeter, no longer sure where it was and fearful of losing track of the thing.

Playing games with them, dammit. And he daren't leave his view of the edges to help Jennie, who was <picking herself up out of the snow, trying to get back on Rain,> which she couldn't manage without something to stand on. Without leaving his scanning of the perimeters, he slid off Slip's back, gave Jennie the boost she needed and delayed only a heartbeat to pat her arm.

"All right?"

"Yeah," she said. The lamplight showed tears smeared on one cheek. Jennie was <mad> as well as <scared,> and thinking about <girl in house> although she knew she wasn't supposed to and they'd kept her away from that house. Rain was frothing at the mouth he was so mad, <wanting fight,> wanting his teeth into anything he could identify as the <enemy.>

And <enemy> was there, here, all over the place, and Jennie and Rain alike were looking this way and that trying to find it.

"It lies," Ridley said with a sense of desperation. Their trap hadn't worked. They knew that by the simple fact that the thing hadn't been sending for a moment, having conscious control of whether it did or didn't: that was a larger brain at work, larger and cannier; he'd become increasingly sure *how* the creature imaged where it wasn't, catching pictures from minds around it and just throwing those moments back at the hearer—a little different from a horse, that tended to displace terrain sideways to your vision—this thing imaged a scene without itself in it. What they hunted was dangerously intelligent in that regard—if he understood what it was doing—replacing land-now with land-as-it-was. It could go silent at times, and rarely got so confused it began to locate itself. There and then not there—and he didn't know how long or with how much complexity coming at it in the ambient it could shut down like that. There were thirteen dead down at The Evergreen. There was Serge—dead. There was Earnest Riggs—dead; because he hadn't any doubt now that the same creature had gotten in *that* night, too, with its uncanny gift for stalking absolutely silently. Carlo Goss *had* been innocent, and there couldn't be any doubt of it, now, in anyone who'd seen both the Schaffer porch and the tavern a moment ago.

He wanted Jennie to come with him, and collected Callie to go up to the church and regroup, taking a course as far as possible across the broad uptown street from the Schaffer house, which all along they had avoided—the horses actively *hated* it, and Rain wanted to go over there and pick a fight, to harass Brionne Goss, out of reach mentally as well as physically. He'd never seen a horse that determined on giving a potential rider grief, and he was anxious all the time he had Jennie in any wise near that place, for fear she might not hold him.

He was relieved when Callie was by him again, the other side of their defense of Jennie and Rain; and the three of them went up toward the porch of the village hall, next to the church where the hunters, having failed to hit the beast, were coming up from the small enclosed access to the passages.

The ambient prickled then with <Randy Goss> coming outside the village hall in Peterson's wife's company, Randy and the wife and then the daughter all armed with shotguns, as the defense of the administrative buildings. Reverend Quarles came behind them, not so evidently a preacher in his snow-gear and carrying a rifle.

"Didn't work." Peterson said the obvious.

"It's tricking us," Ridley said. "It's diverting us in what it sends."

"Then move the horses back from us!" Peterson's wife said.

"That won't work," Callie said. "This thing sends. *This* thing sends. You don't need a horse near you to hear it—but it's going to lie to you most when it isn't sending at all. Hope it sends and we pass it to you, or you won't know where it is."

"That *girl* talks to it," Jennie said, completely out of turn, but Jennie was <upset> as hell. So was the horse. "She *wants* it. I hear her."

"It's the truth," Ridley said, and an uncomfortable silence followed—broken by another young voice.

"She rode the rogue, down in Tarmin."

"No," someone began to say, but Randy's voice overrode it.

"She's my *sister!* She killed the whole village—but she couldn't get the door open to get us!"

Shock followed. Deep, unsettling shock. And the *thing* seemed to ricochet around the street, here, here, here, with no settling point.

"Lord save us." That from the preacher. "The child's only thirteen."

"So I'm fourteen!" Randy cried indignantly. "She blames us! She wants Carlo *dead!*"

"It is the truth," Ridley said. "I think it *is* the truth, preacher, as true as I can tell."

There was, surprisingly, no panic about the matter, just a settling of a very uneasy regard toward that house with the large wraparound porch, with its shutters thrown, with, in the ambient—which he wasn't sure anyone but Callie understood—a ravening hunger for presence, a hunger for the ambient *it—she*—couldn't ever satisfy, because no sane horse would have her.

Dammit, he thought—it took a fourteen-year-old and an eight-year-old to understand the reasons behind what it did: it wasn't adult desires they were fighting. It wasn't a hunter after food or a beast after a lair. It was a thirteen-year-old kid supplying its ideas and playing damnable, bloody pranks down at the tavern and through the passages while it mapped the place, damned well *mapped* the village the girl had never seen with her own eyes.

That accounted for the occasionally true and occasionally skewed direction-sense: it was frolicking around, exploring the village and getting the upper hand over everyone trying to stop it.

Never ask how Earnest Riggs had crossed the girl's notice.

"Wait for daylight," the marshal said into the silence. "Just let it settle down. We've got about—what time is it?—it's got to be toward dawn."

"I can go look," his daughter offered.

"No!" Peterson said sharply. And more quietly, "No. Not a good idea." Peterson didn't want his family scattering out, and neither did Ridley.

"That thing is running us wherever it likes," Jeff Burani said. "We've got people down there at the bottom end of the street. Miners in barracks. Loggers in the hostel. The riders don't want to split up, but we can't be everywhere and we can't move fast enough. We can't protect just our houses and our families, the miners'll lynch us!"

All those things were true. But those things were only half their danger. The marshal was advising they wait for daylight—but Ridley didn't think it was going to hole up, if he had his guess. It might go right over the wall again and come back for more mischief tomorrow night.

Which might give them time to do something about Brionne Goss—but they *had* as close to agreement in present company as they were going to get on that issue, tonight: the key people *knew* now—and the panic he had feared if they knew the danger in Brionne Goss wasn't, thank God, happening. The event was with them, and this one select group of villagers were at least willing to use their heads and try to out-think the beast that had come in on them—

Which wasn't a horse, wasn't Carlo Goss, and wasn't a rogue cat. This *thing* was a better climber. It was smarter around structures, very fast—which might be human intelligence feeding images into it—but it also figured out the tunnels as a means to play a hideous game of hide-and-seek so that they hadn't gotten a clear shot at it. That was smart. And a rogue of whatever species didn't by all he knew *acquire* abilities, it just lost all sane braking on the abilities it had until it killed itself. So this thing wasn't a rogue. It wasn't any threat Rogers Peak had ever seen, and the only reasonable conclusion was that a stray from the outback, maybe attracted by the crisis in the ambient, had come into the area like a willy-wisp to the smell of blood.

"It's attracted to the girl in Darcy's house," he said. "It's concentrating its mischief up at this end. But never there—because it's being elusive and that would give it away. That's what I'm thinking. The girl's attracted it and the girl's guiding it, consciously or unconsciously. She's got to be silenced. Stopped. Put out cold."

"That's pretty hard-minded," John Quarles said. "That poor child, rider-boss, —"

"I don't say do her any lasting harm, but if we quiet Brionne Goss it *might* forget why it was here. At least it won't have a human mind steering it. Slip her something. Darcy's a doctor, for God's sake. She's got to have *something* in the office that won't hurt her. This thing's mapping the village for that girl. It's going all around the village, but not there. It *will*. And *then* what happens?"

"You can't even tell us what it is," the marshal's wife said.

"I can tell you it's not from this side of the mountains. I can tell you it's damn smart. I can tell you while we're arguing, it's picking up our intentions in the ambient and telling a thirteen-year-old girl what we're apt to do, and it's only begun to do its work on this mountain if we don't stop it here, Lucy. I'll *swear* that to you."

"I'll go put it to Darcy," John Quarles said. "She'll listen to me."

"Not alone," Ridley said. "Line of sight. Rifles lined up and us watching."

"I'm aware the beast is dangerous," the preacher said. "But if your theory is right, diminishing the threat to the girl *and* the beast might actually lessen the danger."

"I'll have that porch in my rifle sights. —Listen to me, preacher. I'm asking you, don't endanger anybody including that girl. Trust *my* good wishes and if you hear anything untoward on that porch, drop flat instantly and I'll shoot right over you. Don't confuse our aim. *Trust* us. All right?"

"I've every confidence," Quarles said, and handed his shotgun to the marshal. "But most of all, I'll trust in the Lord."

Quarles walked out through the falling snow, then.

Brave, Ridley gave him that, as he slid down from Slip's back and lifted his rifle—not the only one drawing a bead on that area.

"Stay still," Callie was saying to Jennie, and to all the people around them.

"She's just real mad," Jennie said quietly, her thoughts rising very softly to the top of the ambient. "She knows we're here. She knows Randy's here. She knows about the preacher coming to the door. She's not happy at all. She wants it to come and drive us away."

Jennie was sending too much, Ridley realized that too late. Jennie and Brionne were trading *far* too much, and what had been a quiet struggle between two kids was suddenly reaching after all of them. The rifle wanted to shake in his hands as he stared down the sight and widened his focus to the whole porch, any movement in the snow-obscured night.

Then he knew something else—a wider ambient than had existed. It had direction. Distance. Outside the wall.

Horses. On the road.

<Danny and Cloud,> it was. More than one rider. But that was definitely <Cloud.> And Jennie and Callie knew it from him.

<Danny> hit the ambient and shivered in the air, force added to their force.

He thought then of calling out to the preacher to come back. But he thought if a preacher could ever *be* in the ambient, John Quarles was there right now, and if ever they had the chance to reach Darcy, they had it now. Quarles knew something had changed just now, surely. He *had* to be aware of the arrival.

<Danger> flared through the nerves, and Danny still ran. Tara was beside him and he kept going, the way they'd challenged each other all along. The light was coming in the east, and they were on that last stretch of road that led them to a village under assault, a village where <blood> and <fear> had run riot and <desire> crazed the ambient.

They wanted, too. They wanted to be there, and around the next turning of the road, obscured in a thin veil of snow, Danny saw the village wall. He knew then they'd arrived and he pushed himself despite the ache in his side to keep running and not even to waste time getting up on Cloud. A jarred and frantic portion of the working brain said that in a crisis no one might be able to reach the gate to open it for them, and he might need to be on the ground to try to open it from outside. If the village had left the rope outside that made that possible.

He ran, he told the ambient <riders coming> as he stumbled down the last of the road. Cloud wanted <taking him up,> Cloud wanted <Shimmer and Slip and Rain, inside the wall, sensing danger. Horses listening to them as they came. Riders aware of them. Danger present—>

They reached the lesser gate through a trampled space that said that this gate at least had opened—but not in hours, Danny judged by the rounded edges of the prints. Horses were <inside the village,> at the other end of the street, no one was near the wall, and neither village gate had budged since yesterday.

Bad business. And the pull-cord *wasn't* out.

"Damn it!" Tara said, and with her knife through a gap in the timbers tried to raise the heavy bar inside. Danny lent his hands to the effort, both of them pushing and struggling until finally it *was* lifted as high as they could hold it, and it wouldn't clear the trip-latch.

They were *at* Evergreen, there was all hell broken loose inside as they listened to it, and nobody could let them in the gate.

He let off a rifle shot. It echoed off the mountain and into the ambient in a massive wash of <fear> and <hope> as everyone in Evergreen, deaf to the ambient or not, realized there was someone outside.

<Anger> came, too. Someone else—was fiercely <angry.>

They were shooting again, and Darcy flinched, though this shot was far away. "Listen to me," John Quarles was saying through the closed front door. "Darcy? Darcy, —just for safety, I want you to find a sedative. I want you to find a strong sedative and get the girl calm. I know you want to protect her. You have a sedative, don't you, Darcy?"

"Yes," she admitted. But she didn't want to do that. She didn't want to lose the girl's trust. Brionne was suspicious and afraid. Brionne suspected everyone out on the street, and John said terrible, incredible things, how something was prowling the village passages and it had killed people down at The Evergreen and it had killed Earnest Riggs.

She knew it was true, though. She knew the way she knew that people were outside and that they had designs on Brionne. It was as if pictures of everything were pouring in on her, John coming with the marshal, bringing her Faye's body. She'd heard gunshots going off and it conjured that single shot that had echoed through the house, that moment she had known it came from downstairs, from Mark's office. There were memories of blood, so much blood. Mark was a doctor. And he'd chosen that way, when there were easier ways in the locked cabinet. Mark had *wanted* violence in the leaving of his life. He'd been so quiet. And he'd chosen violence for *her* to deal with.

He—*dared*—leave her—that unspeakable sight to remember. It was his anger. It was his spite. It was his blame. It was Mark saying again as he'd shouted at her the day before he died, *Damn you, Darcy, shed a tear! Yell! Blame me out loud, don't just look at me like that!*

She wasn't sitting on the couch, with John talking about God's mercy, she wasn't rocking back and forth like a fool, and still not able to cry, and John talking inanely about what colors to use at Mark's funeral, as if anyone gave a damn. She was standing at the front door, and John was on the other side, begging her to drug the child senseless, when Brionne knew, she was sure Brionne knew people were betraying her. Pans were flying about the kitchen, crockery was breaking.

"I've got to go," Darcy said.

"Will you do it?" John shouted through the door.

"I don't know," she said. And then thought—if she did that—if she did that, John would be on her side. John was her arbiter of what the village thought. What John said was what they thought was good.

And if she quieted Brionne down, then everything would be quiet and John would help her.

So she went to the cabinet, and turned the key and shook powder into a prescription vial. Her hands were shaking, but she got it in, knowing fairly accurately the girl's weight. She thought she'd make another pot of tea and put it in that. She stopped the vial and tucked it in her waistband, under her sweater.

Then she went to the kitchen, where Brionne was having a tantrum. The crockery was all broken in pieces all over the floor. The teakettle was lying against the wall. Brionne was crying and had a metal plate in her hands.

"Honey. Put it down. It's all right. I told him go away."

"You're lying!" Brionne clanged the plate down against a chair, and bent it, and flung it away against the wall. "I hate you! I hate *all* of you! They're all talking about me! My *brother's* out there, and he's telling lies about me and everyone believes them!"

"I'm sure I don't believe them. I think it's all rather silly." The playing cards were all over the floor. She crossed the kitchen and picked up the teakettle. She wasn't sure there was a whole cup in the kitchen.

"My friend will come for me," Brionne said. "You just watch! He'll come."

"Not a horse?"

"I'll have a horse. I'll have a horse when I want one! And *everybody* will be sorry."

Darcy felt such an *anger* from the girl, from somewhere, so much *anger* and confusion . . .

Brionne headed down the three steps to the passageway door.

"No!" Darcy said sharply, expecting obedience, but Brionne didn't stop. Brionne flung up the bar, and Darcy crossed the kitchen in four fast strides, reached to stop Brionne and slam the door shut.

The door banged wide. A black shape was there, yellow-eyed, yellow-fanged. It reached a shaggy arm—an *arm!*—around Brionne, snatching her away, and the other arm swept with a force that flung Darcy back against the wall. It hit her again, and again. She was numb, and astonished—totally astonished—to see the blood spatter wide across the wall. Like Mark's, that day. . . .

Very much like that day.

Danny was trying to move Cloud into line with the gate to use Cloud for a ladder—but he <heard> people coming then, a <mass of people on the other side of the wall>that very soon he and Tara could hear aloud, swearing and encouraging each other.

"Open the gate!" Danny and Tara yelled, almost with one voice, and that reassured the people on the other side. Someone opened the gate, and Danny got through first, rifle in hand, the pain in his side grown acute, and his throat so raw he immediately went into a coughing fit. Cloud was behind him, and then Tara and Flicker, but the people in front of him, shadowed by the wall, were faceless to him, a mob, a mass—men from the barracks, villagers, he didn't know.

He did know <horses and riders and danger in the distance, something inside the walls,> and he didn't waste time trying to understand the shouts about <beasts> and <bears> and <men dead,> he just got control of his coughing enough to swing up to Cloud's back, feeling the wobble in himself and the wobble in Cloud's legs as he landed. He started moving through the crowd, aware of <Tara on Flicker behind him,> and it was a measure how frightened the crowd was that people bunched around two riders on horseback and pressed up close to the horses as a point of safety.

Cloud wasn't used to that kind of treatment. It was a question whether they were going to get through before or after Cloud bit somebody, but the instant there was an opening Cloud jumped forward, instinct-driven toward the <nighthorses ahead> of him, and Cloud's rider was along for the ride for an instant, Cloud knowing beyond any doubt there was <safety in the nighthorse herd.>

Flicker was close behind them as Cloud ran, and Flicker might not know the horses ahead, but they were a band Cloud knew: <Slip, Shimmer and Rain> was the presence at the mountain-end of the street. <Cloud and Flicker> flung the ambient wider and louder than Danny intended, but it was five horses now, with one mare in foal and a boss horse aggressive as hell toward whatever threatened their vicinity.

They came in where Ridley, Callie and Jennie were holding the area across from the doctor's house. Randy was there, with a couple of armed women Danny didn't know, with the marshal's deputy, some of the hunters, and a very shaken-looking preacher, whose total contribution to the ambient was a roiling chaos of <fear> and <relief> at them being there.

"Tara Chang," Danny said to Ridley and the rest, by way of introduction. "Guil Stuart and Carlo are coming, but they'll be longer. What's happened?"

He got more than he wanted. Cloud shied back from a rush of <beast with yellow eyes> and <Brionne Goss> and <blood.> Someone had died. He thought it was the doctor. He *thought* the worst of the sending came from young Jennie, in the way of loud juniors and young horses, but he wasn't sure, and rapidly there was more of it, <man running from the porch,> the echo of confirmation sounding in his head to be the preacher, and <beast-presence climbing in the house, flinging things, breaking things> was current and happening now—along with a presence he knew from brief encounters: Brionne Goss was the core of it, but it was <anger> and <confusion> and <looking for something> before it darted aside on <anger> again.

"Tarmin," Tara said beside him. "That's what it was like."

Like and unlike, Danny was thinking. The Tarmin rogue wasn't essentially a killer. It opened gates to those that were.

This thing—this confusion—had hands and walked upright, or it was Brionne herself.

"It's in the upstairs of the house," Ridley said, and how glad Ridley was to see the two of them was evident in the ambient. "It's strong. God, it's strong. We haven't dared get close to it."

"Five of us, now," Tara said. "Let's push it. Let's get it out of here and hunt it later."

Ridley was <scared,> and thought of <Jennie and Rain.> Danny understood the fear he had, bringing a kid's mind close to that thing. But *not* doing it guaranteed she'd be close for sure when the thing went further over the edge than it was.

"I don't think it's a rogue," Danny ventured to say. "Part of it's the same, but it's not crazy. I don't think it's crazy." A dreadful comparison occurred to him, and he unintentionally let it loose: <new rider with young horse, first ride, louder than anything near Shamesey; Jennie and Rain, louder than any horse in the camp. Brionne and the yellow-eyed predator.>

Tara, last person he'd have thought would agree, slid into that image with astonishing quickness and memories of <ruined shelter> and <nest. Bones with plaid cloth, near the lake.> "Smart like a horse," she said. "Damn sure."

"Paired with *that?*" Callie said in disgust.

"Nothing I want to see leave here," Tara said, and intended <shooting it,> no question, while Randy Goss hovered in the low edges of the ambient, <scared,> and <sad,> and <homesick for

Tarmin.> Danny knew that image of <Tarmin streets and the blacksmith shop and the house there,> the way Tara had to recognize it.

But Tara was trying to pull them together in <fighting the intruder,> which with Flicker's essential skittishness had its difficulties. So *he* wanted it, in support of Tara's effort, and Callie wanted it; then Jennie was there, fiercely so, and *that* spooked Ridley into a direct attack that wasn't native to him: Danny suddenly felt what Ridley and Slip could be when Jennie was threatened, and all of a sudden the marshal and the preacher and the rest were clearing back from them.

But Randy stayed. <Randy> was there with them, <wanting Brionne, remembering Tarmin,> recalling <that night locked in the jail with the swarm in the streets,> all of it with an overlay of <anger> and <grief.> Randy didn't want the <jail.> Randy wanted <Brionne at the breakfast table, Brionne playing checkers by firelight, Brionne throwing snowballs, younger Brionne in a red coat, running toward him through the snow.>

Glass shattered at that house. Wood broke. A throat uttered a sound not human. <Rage> came back at them. <Terror and anger.>

"It's going *up!*" Callie cried aloud. " It's <heading for the roof!> Get a sight on it!"

Danny didn't expect it to show on the street side of the building. But there, in the murky light that had been growing around them, he saw an upright darkness on the very crest of the roof, a darkness with something white hugged against it—with what a blink of snowflakes cleared into the sight of Brionne Goss in her nightgown standing on her own feet *with* the creature, balanced on the snowy rooftree of the doctor's house.

He didn't trust he could hit it and not spook it out of the sights of those with a chance. Tara, beside him, and Ridley, had rifles.

More than those two guns went off. A ragged volley made Cloud jump and him blink, and in the stench of gunpowder and the smell of snow around him afterward—there wasn't anything on that roof.

"Did we get it?" Ridley asked. Randy's shock was racketing through an ambient that was just them, now, nothing in, on, or beyond that house.

"Don't trust not hearing it," Danny said. "Not till we find it dead." He rode Cloud forward, and the rest of them were with him,

Randy attaching himself close to Cloud afoot, and Tara and Flicker going on his other side.

That silence persisted. The doctor's house stood adjacent to outbuildings, small sheds behind; but a warehouse roof came close, and he and Tara went down the alley it made, rejoining the others along the wall.

The post was absent from the rider-gate. Danny knew that from Ridley and Jennie and Callie. The post was still in the tunnel access, but that wouldn't have stopped a beast on two feet, either—if it had had the chance to get in there, but none of them believed it had.

The marshal and his group came now and joined them as, in the very early dawn and among the shadows that still were left, they looked for footprints.

They didn't find them until they went through the rider-gate. The tracks of one set of long humanlike feet and sometimes two, the second clearly human, went toward the den.

Shimmer was <outraged,> and Slip pulled the rest of them in, as a band of five horses went toward the den intent on <driving out intruders.>

But the tracks went around to the outside, to a rider-gate left standing open to the forest and the light coming through the trees.

Danny and Tara went out hunting straightway. But the trail, which showed blood now and again, went aside into the trees before it had gone a kilometer down the road, on a diagonal line down the mountain. The trail all along had been tending toward the south, toward the truck road, but now it left that. Cloud and Flicker were sure about it going into the trees, and downhill, after which, with the beast's tree-climbing ability, it was capable of going cross-country and above brush and rock that would stop a horse.

So they both thought it more prudent to go back to the village and in a day or so, with full kit and enough gear to survive what began to feel like chancy weather, set out to warn other villages. There was nothing they could do chasing it now; and a great deal they could do by warning the other settlements.

Besides, with the beast's talent for misdirection, and the possibility of a human mind helping it, they didn't want to leave things in disorder in the village behind them—in case it didn't find itself discouraged.

* * *

Guil and Carlo came in the early afternoon, with snow coming down heavily. Guil was decidedly hurting, Burn was exhausted, and Carlo had walked, so as not to overload Spook. Both of them had pushed things more than they ought.

They came in the village gates. In the middle of the street and in full view of the curious, Carlo slid down off Spook's back and held out his arms for his brother, who until that time had held himself reserved and quiet. Things weren't reserved or quiet for some time, then, in that quarter, among riders and villagers alike.

And introductions went quickly, rider-fashion, the ambient thick with self-protection and reserve for a moment, then warming up considerably. Yes, the Evergreen camp had known Guil's lost partner, they'd liked Aby Dale, they trusted her lifelong partner; and they knew that the last Tarmin rider hadn't survived by scanting duty, any more than Tara had done since her arrival at Evergreen.

They stayed villageside, all of them, including Guil and Carlo, with the horses, to survey the damage, to help the marshal sort out the dead and make sure the village felt safe. With the smell of blood on the wind it was certain in their minds and in the minds of very anxious villagers and winter residents that the wildlife *would* come back to the area, and relatively quickly if the beast hadn't hunted it to nonexistence: Guil said the ambient had formed at their backs on their ride along the road like water flowing into a gap, as if wild things knew that a horse's presence in this instance was an assurance of a worse predator moving out of the territory.

And in truth that night and the morning after there wasn't a sign of it coming back—hard to imagine a creature you had to recognize in terms of the silence that went around it. *Slink* was the name some villager came up with for it, and it might stick, who knew? It was certain at least that the High Wild produced some odd creatures, some strange, some deadly, and that humans who'd come to the world had yet to see most of them.

As Tara said, they just hoped this one stayed wherever it had gone. Weather came howling down, and that, the village hoped, finished that. In all senses.

Even the Goss brothers' mourning was short.

Chapter —XXIII—

Water dripped off the icicles that rimmed the barracks roof—which often happened on sunny days even in deep winter, but when it went on all day and, after a cold snap, started up again for several days running, then it was relatively certain the thaw had begun.

Likely there was already green in the fields around Shamesey. Danny began thinking of that, and thinking about going back again, maybe this year, maybe not, for a visit.

But with, as Guil put it, water beginning to run downhill again, the village was crazed with packing, the lure of mining and to some extent the solid pay of logging forgotten in a different kind of gold rush. The only way supplies were going to get downhill until trucks got up the mountain was in hand-carts, and while riders might help get fools down the mountain to Tarmin to stake claims, they weren't going to risk their necks or their horses' necks shepherding anybody who was overloaded.

So carts were being built and axles and wheels reinforced. Wood was at a premium. Van Mackey had had more work all winter than he wanted to get around to, and had to do it alone: Rick Mackey had been at The Evergreen that night, and Carlo never had gotten the chance to sort grievances out with him. There was a cave in the mountain that served to keep the dead, and Rick Mackey and twelve others were there, besides Serge Lasierre and Darcy Schaffer. Except Earnest Riggs, whose body they never had identified for certain.

The village was without a doctor, but the pharmacists, husband and wife, served as they'd begun to do during Darcy Schaffer's year of retirement, and their daughter, Azlea Sumner, had settled down to the notion *she* might apprentice to the doctor over in Mornay—the doctor there, in the second and third times the two villages had met for skating outings on the pond, had talked about resettling to Evergreen, as a far bigger establishment. The doctor had a son, and Azlea Sumner was very interested.

Van Mackey and Mary Hardesty had set their sights on hiring Randy Goss, Carlo having clearly left the trade, and the work and the potential prosperity piling up the way it was. But with carts wanting wheels and fittings and all of Tarmin and that shop lying down there unclaimed and apt to fall to the Mornay smith—Randy Goss had no interest these days in anything but Shimmer's imminent foal, which had begun to image, and which was (Ridley and Callie had begun to call it fate) another colt.

In all of it, Randy just played games with Jennie, and Tara taught them the elements of marksmanship, while Guil Stuart told all the junior riders and the potential junior the kinds of things they might need in the open country.

Juniors who had their wits about them (and they all had) paid strictest attention. Jennie, for as young as she was, had acquired a certain sober knowledge that night, and so had Rain. She knew about the dangers on the mountain, and Jennie was in no rush to go out the gate quite yet, even with spring in the air and the wild things coming out of burrows and birthings and silliness imminent.

Wild things coming out of burrows was the part that made them all nervous. And on a certain day Danny, out hunting with Carlo, was troubled to see Carlo and Spook just standing still and staring off down the road to the south, all with a very strange feeling in the ambient.

"Sometimes I wonder if she's dead," Carlo said, when Danny rode up beside him. "Sometimes I hope she is. Sometimes I wonder—if that thing's like Spook, if you could halfway talk to it—or if she could."

Danny personally didn't consider talking to it a good idea, inside the ambient or out loud. They still hadn't heard a thing from it since that night, none of the shelters between there and the south road had been opened that they could detect, when he and Tara and Carlo and Ridley had gone out to check them and to hunt the thing.

So his own opinion was that it *was* dead. He damned sure didn't want to find *that* breed coming across the mountain ridge, laying siege to village walls, and calling village kids out for company. Horses had become addicted to human minds. Horses had never been predators on humans—just curious, just vastly and immediately curious when ships came to the worlds and landed in the horses' range down near Shamesey. This thing was a far different matter. And he'd shoot one if he saw it, without a second thought about its intentions.

"I sure don't want to find another one," he said. "And the ambient's back, normal as can be."

"Yeah," Carlo said.

They were going down the mountain, too, as their plans were. Guil had confessed to all the seniors and to him and Carlo that there was gold in that truck that had gone off, and that a shipper down in Anveney wanted it back.

But meanwhile there wasn't any way to move it, and by that fact, in lieu of retrieving the truck cargo, he and Carlo had acquired a long-riding job, to go down and north to Anveney and to talk to a man named Cassivey, a shipper. They had to say to him that if he wanted his gold he had to get some trucks *and* some oxcarts arranged with supplies.

And then they were going to tell him that if he wanted a share in the property that was to be had at Tarmin, Randy and Carlo Goss had title to a deal of it they were willing to sell, and on which Carlo could provide a deed. The village lawyers and the judge had helped work those papers out, and in not many days more, by their intentions, they were going to head down the trail Guil and Tara had taken up the mountain.

Guil and Tara were going to have what they called an *interesting* job, getting band after band of overexcited and heavily armed miners with handcarts and overwrought anticipations down the grades of the truck road, as many as could tent-up around midway: that was the limiting factor on the size of the groups, and the lottery for position was set for the morning. Guil and Tara didn't need two more riders to house in that very small shelter.

It might, Danny thought, be a good time for them to set out for the lowlands, before that craziness got started.

Meanwhile Cloud and Spook were enjoying the open air and they hadn't shot a thing yet, nor really been inclined to. They called it hunting.

Mostly they didn't do the hunters' work for them. Being riders, they didn't carry cargo. And having the ambitions they did, to ride the borders, they only hunted for *their* needs, and carried the gear *they* needed, nobody else's.

The little light that filtered through the evergreen boughs and the deep blue shadows along the road said that camp soon was a good idea. The thought came to him that a warm fireside in a barracks this crowded with good friends was a scarce thing in the world, and that they should enjoy as much of it as they could before they rode apart for the year, maybe to come back again, maybe not. There were no certainties.